THE GOBLINS
ARE REVOLTING

BOOK 3

THE GOBLINS ARE REVOLTING

D. D. WEBB

ISBN: 978-1-0394-5786-7

Published in 2024 by Podium Publishing
www.podiumentertainment.com

Podium

THE GOBLINS
ARE REVOLTING

1

In Which the Dark Lord Steps in It

"What the hell is all this?"

"It was left outside the fortress first thing this morning," Minifrit explained, as always striking that off-center pose that accentuated her hips and pausing to blow theatrical streamers of smoke. "The sentries reported that members of the cat tribe placed all this on the road in front of the gates. Quickly, not responding to hails or challenges, and then ran back into the forest. Kasser has looked over everything."

She turned to Kasser expectantly, and he took over, straightening up from where he'd briefly knelt to pick up and examine some shells.

"It's all good stuff, Lord Seiji," he said, dropping the piece of akornin back into the basket it had come from. "Really good quality. The shells are in the biggest pieces they can be, right off the animal, and they're all properly cured, ready to be worked. We've got some that are suitable for making armor; the rest Harold can carve into basically whatever we need. Tools, nails, blades . . . And this akorshil, see? They didn't send much, but this stuff is rare. It's . . . well, it isn't all that *useful*, because of how soft it is, but shachshil like this is quite valuable. These khora only grow wild, never in plantations. Mostly used for decorative carving. Pretty expensive on the markets, which I assume the cats knew."

He was all but salivating at this haul. I watched Junko investigating the fascinating smells among the baskets and gave him a moment after he trailed off, looking back at the various shells, before clearing my throat.

"And . . . the rest?"

"Oh!" Kasser ducked his shoulders awkwardly, having been caught indulging his passion for shell-carving while on the clock. "Uh, yeah, the rest of it is also good quality. We've got some nice pelts—looks like elk, dhawun, and wolf. Even some pieces of nheichol leather, which is *nice* stuff." He bent to pick up what looked like the skin of an enormous snake, observed my nonplussed expression, and continued explaining. "Very flexible, airtight, and really tough for how thin it is. Good stuff, also pricey. Nheichols are hard to hunt on Dount; they live in lizardfolk territory. I suspect the cats traded for this. That one's full of blankets. Oh, and the baskets themselves are pretty solid. It's a decent haul, all around."

I bent to pick up one of the blankets, unfolding it. The cat tribe's weaving was almost . . . impressionistic, that was the word. They used a combination of quilting with curved pieces of fabric and embroidered patterns on top to create abstract, organic-looking designs with no straight lines or angles. The one I held up used patches and thread in different shades of light blue against dark gray background pieces.

"That's really beautiful," said Aster, sounding surprised.

"I bet it'd also be pricey on the market," I agreed.

"Yes and no," said Minifrit, exhaling a spicy-sweet cloud. "Some highborn collect and display tribal art. Lowborn who are caught with it risk being accused of consorting with beastfolk. The suggestion alone can suffice to have their property and possibly their freedom confiscated."

"One day," I complained. "I'd just like to go *one day* without learning a fresh reason Fflyr Dlemathlys sucks. Anyway, the important question is *why* did they feel the need to bring us a pile of gifts? You don't suppose it's all dusted with poison or something?"

"I would not expect to see any such aggression out of that tribe in the near future," Minifrit said dryly.

"It's tribute, boss," Biribo explained. "Remember? You told the cats this was now your land and they could live here at your sufferance. That girl we talked to made a point about how she didn't have any authority, but I'd interpret this as the message being conveyed back to the tribe and your terms accepted. So, like they used to demand tribute from the North Watch gang, now they're sending it to you."

"I didn't *ask* them for . . ." I dragged a hand down my face. "Crap. I specifically wanted to start mending fences, not kick them around further."

"Lord Seiji, I think it's worth considering what they *didn't* send us," Kasser said. "When Rocco was in charge and dealing with them, he mostly wanted stuff that could be bought in Fflyr markets, and mostly food. Nothing they sent us is edible. After the Inferno . . . I mean, their stores can't have been completely wiped out if they had all this stuff to give us, but they may be hard up for food. Especially with the winter coming on."

I drew in a deep, slow breath and blew it out all at once. "All right. Well, we already figured the tribes were going to be in bad shape after that. The plan was to reach out to them all and let the local cats come to us, but . . . I think I better pay them a visit first and straighten this out."

"If nothing else, they're closest," Aster agreed. "It'll be a handy trial run for when you have to deal with other tribes who don't yet know they should be afraid of you."

"Lord Seiji!" Madyn burst out of the fortress in a panic, already yelling and waving as she skittered into the courtyard, where we were gathered around the tribute baskets. "We need you! The kitchen! It's the goblins!"

"What the *fuck* now?" I growled, but was already in a dead run past her, rather than waiting for an answer. There was nothing she could explain that I wouldn't figure out when I got there, and given how unflappable Madyn was in general, whatever was going on was clearly too urgent to stand around chatting about it. Aster and Junko, of course, fell into step beside and just behind me, leaving the others to follow more discreetly.

In the mess hall I could already hear distant yelling from the kitchen. People were naturally gravitating in that direction; just as naturally, they cleared out of the way when the Dark Lord came tearing through, accompanied by his dog and bodyguard. Both had to fall behind me as I entered the narrow corridor to the kitchen, but seconds later we all emerged into a scene that I could only call barely restrained pandemonium.

Restrained only because violence was not currently occurring, though it clearly had and just as clearly was about to. Two goblins stood in front of the open door to the tunnel, both holding swords, but they were raising their hands above their heads in a peaceable gesture—somewhat spoiled by the fact that neither had put the swords *down*. Gannit loomed nearby, snarling and brandishing both a frying pan and cleaver in a clear display of her opinion of this intrusion into her kitchen. The only thing separating her from the goblins were three women pointing loaded crossbows at them, shouting muddled and contradictory orders to disarm, leave, and surrender.

"There he is!" exclaimed one of the intruders, waving eagerly at me—with the hand not holding a sword, fortunately for him. "Dark Lord Seiji! This is all a misunderstanding!"

I ignored him. Streaks and tracks of blood led from the tunnel entrance into the middle of the kitchen, where the bedraggled form of a goblin I recognized lay face down on the floor amid a spreading crimson pool.

"**Heal!**" I barked, pointing.

Nothing. Invalid target. Slowly, I lowered my hand and shifted my stare from the body of Maugro, the information broker, to the goblins still on their feet.

"Okay, it doesn't look great," said the speaker, grinning at me. He *grinned* at me. "Listen, everything's—"

Junko charged past my legs, barking viciously and snapping her jaws centimeters from the intruders. That made the impression even the armed women hadn't; I'd observed that goblins were terrified of Junko even when she was being friendly. Both yelped and scurried away to the corner, one dropping his sword in the process.

Bad move. You *never* run from an aggressive dog.

I whistled sharply as Junko started to lunge and she froze, then turned and obediently trotted back to stand next to my legs, still growling a warning but no longer about to go for the kill.

Then, before anyone else could speak, the half-ajar door was kicked wider, and Donon emerged from the tunnel. His face was stricken and streaked with tears, and in his arms was another little green body, dripping fresh blood on my floor.

"**Heal**," I tried, already suspecting . . .

"It's too late, Lord Seiji," Donon choked. He stood there as if lost, just cradling Mindzi's lifeless form as it failed to react to the spell. Her head lolled over his arm, vacant red eyes staring at the ceiling. "I . . . I tried to . . . Before I even got there . . ."

Madyn had followed the rest of us into the kitchen and now stepped up, gently taking Donon by one of his fully occupied arms and pulling him away. He let himself be led, seeming to lack volition of his own.

I drew in a deep, steadying breath and expelled it slowly. Well, how about that. Goblin blood smelled the same as human.

"Explain," I ordered.

Both goblins immediately started babbling over each other, gesticulating wildly. Then Junko let out a bark that echoed deafeningly from the bare kitchen walls, and they just as quickly fell silent, pressing themselves back against the corner.

"So we were minding our own business, doing the cleanup after breakfast," Gannit said into the ensuing lull, "and there was this horrible yelling and banging from the goblin door, there. Sounded like a fight, so I stopped Donon from opening it and yelled for backup. These three came in from the mess hall; seems they were the only ones in there who had weapons on 'em." She nodded at the women still covering the goblins with crossbows, one of whom nodded back. "As they were coming in, the door busted open and that guy there, Maugro, he comes stumbling in all beaten and cut to shreds, with *those* two fuckers in the middle goin' at him with those swords. Well, the crossbows scared 'em off doin' that quick enough. Maugro says something about saving Mindzi back in the tunnel, and fucking *Donon* goes runnin' in there like the suicidal goddamn numbnut he is."

The old woman paused, grimacing, then took a step over to Donon and placed a hand on his shoulder, giving him a gentle shake. He had just set Mindzi on the floor next to Maugro and didn't react, just staring vacantly at the ground. Poor guy, he was taking this a lot harder than I'd have expected. We all knew Donon had a thing for goblin ladies, but apparently he was nursing a serious crush on Mindzi in particular.

"Good man," Gannit said in a slightly rougher voice, then cleared her throat and turned back to me. "Anyway. Madyn went runnin' out to find you at some point during that, and we got this under control in here, and . . . well, you're caught up."

I looked at the bodies, at the living goblins, and then swept my stare around the kitchen, looking for a particular barrel in the corner which was conspicuously absent.

"Gannit, where is the healing slime that belongs in this kitchen?"

She grimaced again. "Loaned it to Khadret for morning practice. The sword drilling group needed an extra; they keep breaking each other's fingers or some shit. Anyway, we were just doing cleanup; if all three of us get hurt badly enough by *washing dishes* that we can't walk into the mess hall to use the slime in there, we don't deserve to live."

"And look what happened," I snapped. Gannit actually looked abashed, which was something I'd never expected to see. "Get your slime back and *keep* it in here. If anybody else needs a spare, they can come ask me. It's not like *my* supply is limited. This is the room where you work with knives, fire, and hot oil. The kitchen healing slime *stays in the kitchen*."

Gannit opened her mouth, shut it, then nodded once, avoiding my eyes. That was as close to an apology as I ever expected to get out of the old woman, and I didn't consider it worth pressing for more. She deserved to keep some pride, and I didn't care to open a discussion about our respective recent fuckups and how many people they'd gotten killed.

Instead, I paced forward, every step slow and controlled, until I stood between two of the armed women keeping our uninvited guests under control. My expression remained carefully neutral. I almost resented squandering the effort on these little fuckers in particular, but showtime was showtime. Besides, showtime was helping me keep control over the rising tide of rage, which I could feel pounding up the back of my throat.

I stared at each of them in turn, in total silence, for a slow count of four each. Then I put on a tiny little smile.

"This had better be *very* good."

The first goblin, the one who seemed to be the speaker between them, grinned and adjusted his lapels in a gesture that reminded me strikingly of Maugro, which definitely didn't work in his favor.

"Lord Seiji? First of all, sorry about the rough introduction. That was supposed to be a quick, discreet job; it was purely our fault that we lost control and it spilled into your kitchen. You have my personal apologies, and my promise to make it right. I represent the interests of the Goblin King, who you can rest assured wants *only* the most amicable relations with the new Dark Lord."

Goddammit, they knew. Well, if they'd killed Maugro and chased him all the way in here—in that order, somehow—it was undoubtedly for a reason, and it made sense that they knew at least some of what he knew. Why else would they go after an information broker?

There was a lot of other stuff in that handful of sentences I didn't like, apart from the goblin speaking. I could already tell he was the most annoying kind of person—socially adroit enough to be suave and charming, but not enough to realize when being suave and charming is the absolute last thing you should do. One minute in and this guy was already reminding me of every dipshit tourist in Akiba who condescendingly complimented my English.

"Make it right," I repeated, speaking slowly and enunciating. "So you can raise the dead? Impressive."

"C'mon, now," he said with a disarming grin, which very nearly earned him a kick in the throat. "I *know* you weren't on close, personal terms with

Maugro. Dude's habit of keepin' everybody at arm's length is ninety percent of the reason this ended the way it did for him. Don't get me wrong, playin' every end against the middle is solid practice in normal goblin society, but he shoulda known better than to try that with a Goblin King in charge. But don't worry, Lord Seiji! King Jadrak has nothing but respect for you and wants to be on the best of terms. We, ah, we weren't exactly s'posed to be initiating contact today, but I do know for a fact the Goblin King will wanna offer anything reasonable to smooth over this little kerfuffle here."

"*Little—*" Donon started to surge forward, but Aster blocked his way and Madyn grabbed him by both shoulders from behind. Neither were doing enough to physically restrain him, but he stopped, at least.

I probably should have asked him to excuse himself from what was now first diplomatic contact with a new rival power, but fuck it. He and Junko were projecting exactly the impression I wanted right now, and nothing Donon did would make this go any worse than the direction I was leaning toward sending it myself.

"So, there's a Goblin King?" I said, keeping my tone and expression mild. "First I've heard about it."

"There is *now*," replied the more talkative of the two goblins, while his silent companion kept a wary eye on Junko. "Things are changing in the tunnels, Lord Seiji. I dunno how much the goblins you've met have told you, but with power consolidated, a Goblin King is in a position to be a *real* asset to a new Dark Lord. Jadrak wants to meet you and talk terms as soon as possible."

"So I see," I replied with a pleasant smile, "considering he seems eager to kill off any possible rivals for my attention, including *in my fucking kitchen.*"

"Now, now, let's not exaggerate," he chided me, grinning and wagging a finger. The rising tide of rage bubbled ever hotter, and only my pure commitment to showmanship saved his life in that moment. "I already said this spilled outta control, and I was serious about offering reasonable restitution for your inconvenience. *But,* these events were initiated and brought to an *effective* conclusion on goblin turf and outside yours. Maugro barely had enough life left to stagger in here after he got the door open. Technically, all this was still goblin business by the time it got to you."

Technically.

He grinned up at me broadly, as if he had just settled the matter to everyone's satisfaction. The other one still didn't chime in, but put on a similar smile. Like they had scored some kind of *victory* with this.

White hot fury filled me with manic energy that demanded an outlet. I was either going to vibrate apart in my own boots, slaughter everyone in this room, or . . .

I matched his grin, and allowed a chuckle to escape me. Clearly taking that as encouragement, the goblins exchanged a glance between them and then chortled right along with me. Haha, look at us lads just having a giggle over a couple of corpses.

It never ended. They *kept doing this*. The five murdered Rats, the seizure of the Alley Cat, the raid on North Watch . . . Why did all these fuckers think they could push me around? How many forests did I need to burn down before all the assholes in this wretched little ruin of a planet learned *not to fuck with me*?

My pulse hammered in my throat so hard I wouldn't have been surprised if the vein was visible. Rage swirled in me, like fire and lightning, my whole body practically vibrating. The laughter rose in pitch and intensity. The goblins mirrored me, guffawing and slapping each other's shoulders with increasing enthusiasm as we all shared a good chuckle over this.

By that point, everyone else in the kitchen was staring at me with varying degrees of confusion and alarm, including Junko. I let it flow, for the moment, just riding the energy. Why it expressed itself through laughter, I couldn't have said, but hey, it seemed to fit the setting. I was the Dark Lord, after all, and isn't it an established *thing* for villains to laugh uncontrollably when something horrible, and not at all funny, has occurred?

The goblins continued to match me, and if their own laughter was an act I was pretty sure I saw the relief behind it. We all three brayed in mirth, partially doubling over and struggling for breath, all while I cackled through flashes of all the *fucking bullshit* I'd endured from people like this, who thought they could come to *my place* and push me.

Cat Alley, awash in blood. Gray's thugs chasing me across the Gutters and all the way into the river. Virya twisting me like a fidget toy just to prove she could.

Kastrin falling off the wall.

I snatched the crossbow from the woman next to me and shot the second goblin through the skull.

The weapon wrenched itself out of my hand, of course, one arm nearly whanging me on the temple. It was one of the bigger military models, designed for punching through armor; the recoil was enough of a bastard when you weren't stupid enough to fire it one-handed. I got off lightly, relatively speaking. The goblin hit the wall behind him with as much a splatter as a thump. As I'd observed when educating the cats on my philosophy of justice, at this range these things made almost as much of a mess as an actual gun.

All laughter in the room was cut off as if by a switch, the surviving goblin—the smarmy one who liked to talk—reacting with impressive speed and precision. Of course, his dash for the door wouldn't have worked; Junko would've grabbed him if nobody else did first. Needless to say, it did not get to that point.

Immolate.

Down he went in a shrieking fireball, causing Junko to abort her lunge at him; she had better sense than to charge headlong into a source of pure flame.

That made one of us.

My whole body still resonating with furious energy like a plucked guitar string, I stepped deliberately over to one kitchen counter, picked up one of Gannit's heavy oven mitts, and slipped it on. Everyone silently got out of my way; Aster opened her mouth to say something, but apparently thought better of it. The goblin still had a good burn going, probably just about to crest the bell curve into the stage where the healing magic would begin to overtake the fire, when I reached him again.

Bending down, I grabbed him by the neck with my mitt-covered hand. The heat was intense, nearly to the point of pain—these things were not designed for this—and hoisting someone half the size of an adult human with one hand was not easy, even after my months of exercise and training. Neither fact made a difference, the haze of adrenaline and sheer rage pushing me right through the heat on my skin and the strain in my muscles as I stood, hauling the burning goblin fully up into the air.

"You come into my home," I snarled, stalking over to the tunnel door. "You murder one of my allies, burst into my kitchen, and then you have the *absolute fucking gall* to plead innocence on a fucking *technicality?*"

I had never been in the goblin tunnel before; it was dark and unsurprisingly cramped, though the ceiling wasn't as low as I would have expected. I only had to hunch over slightly. Stepping inside, I threw the goblin to the ground, shadows flickering across the walls as they were cast and distorted by the flames emanating from his bouncing body.

He was definitely on the descent by that point. I discarded the oven mitt—which was still on fire—and cast a quick **Heal** against the burns I'd inflicted on my own hand doing that, then folded my arms and waited.

"I have a message for the Goblin King," I stated the instant the intruder was no longer actively on fire, not giving him even a second to recuperate.

"Yeah, of course," he wheezed, peering up at me through panicked red eyes and nodding vigorously. "I'll tell him whatever you want!"

"No, no. You *are* the message."

Summon Fire Slime, **Tame Beast**.

He was immediately howling again, trying to roll away and swat at the burning slime which I had just conjured right on his coat. The sole command with which I imbued it was to cling and resist attempts to dislodge it.

I stuck two more fire slimes to him for good measure, then strode back into the kitchen and slammed the tunnel door.

It wasn't silent, what with all the screaming from just behind that door barely muffled by the thin layer of akorshil planks separating us from it. But, under the combined shocked stares of those present, it *felt* like a silence.

"Kasser," I said.

"L-lord Seiji?" he replied hesitantly.

"I want this door barricaded as soon as you can get it done. Take whatever you need from the supplies; this is currently priority one. Someone find me Naz—ah, perfect timing."

The elf herself poked her head into the kitchen at that moment, no doubt drawn by all the noise. Her expression was confused and alarmed, as she had missed the action but could plainly see all the corpses and hear the ongoing screaming from just inside the tunnel.

"We've lost our convenient goblin contacts, and you're the only one I'm aware of who knows another entrance into the goblin tunnels. Maugro is gone, but some of his employees may have escaped. You mentioned meeting another guy who works for him, right? I need somebody to try to make contact. If not with them, then with someone in Sneppit's organization. Supposedly she's a pretty big deal down there."

"I . . . uh, *yes*, but that's way over by Flynswith, Lord Seiji. Near the eastern edge. It's an all-day ride from here at best speed, three times that on foot."

"Then you'd better move *quickly*. It's still safer and likelier than that pub in Gwyllthean. Bring along whoever and whatever you judge necessary and don't take risks. Avoid human contact, and if the only goblins you can find answer to the Goblin King, report back."

"Okay, this is on me," Biribo interrupted before she could answer. "My bad, everybody. I definitely should've explained a *lot* more about goblin society to you, boss. I mean, it's not like anybody else here would've known.

It's just . . . You tend to glaze over, y'know? If I just front-load you with details, most of 'em disappear by the next time we talk. I've learned to answer questions as they come up and try to brief you on the fly whenever anything seems like it's gonna be important soon. Not that I'm blaming you! This is a problem for all the Champions who get brought here. A whole world's worth of information is way too much to dump on anybody at one time; context and significance are really important for memory retention. But, uh, after this, I think we better start having regular tutoring sessions or something. You clearly need a more thorough grounding in Ephemeral politics, or we're gonna keep bouncing from one mess like this to another."

"Biribo," I said, gathering up every last flickering ember of patience within my being, "I can tell you're building up to something I'm not gonna like and trying to soften the blow. Which is appreciated, but I wish you'd just rip the bandage off and be done with it."

"Right," he said ruefully. "Well, uh, boss . . . A barricade isn't gonna cut it. You just committed us to a war of total annihilation with the Goblin King. This won't end until one or the other of you is dead and their whole organization destroyed."

So, that was how my day started.

2

In Which the Dark Lord Descends

That little vignette was basically the problem with human/goblin relations in miniature," Biribo lectured minutes later when I convened my lieutenants in the conference room. "Culturally, goblins live up to the Viryan emphasis on personal strength by cultivating their skills and wits. They're suspicious of any powerful authority and contemptuous of brute force. Contracts and agreements are a *big* deal in goblin culture; they like to have everything laid out in very precise terms. Understanding the nuances and working every angle is not only expected but morally laudable to them. They do not *have* a concept of 'the spirit of the law,' that's a human notion. To goblins, the letter *is* the spirit."

I scrunched up my face, trying to process this. "So when that asshole started going off about *technically* not having killed Maugro in my goddamn kitchen . . ."

"You're not alone, boss. Most humans would react poorly to that," Biribo agreed, bobbing up and down in midair over the center of the conference table. "But to *him*, he was in the right, both factually and ethically. And that is how any productive deals between humans and goblins usually end up, sooner or later—with both parties feeling the other cheated them and devolving into violence, which the goblins almost always decisively lose. So that feeds into the race relations as they exist now. Zero trust in either direction, humans regard goblins as pests whom it's justified to attack on sight if you see one anywhere they're not supposed to be, and goblins . . . Well, to goblins, a person who can't honor their deals has no right to own property or participate in society as an equal. So, as they see it, stealing from humans is like harvesting or hunting wild animals in the forest. It's dangerous, because they'll kill you for it if they can, but it's not *wrong* in any moral sense."

"Did any of you know any of this?" I asked of the rest of the table.

Amid the blank stares and shaken heads, only Minifrit spoke up. "Consorting too closely with goblins is one of the many things which is socially and potentially *legally* unacceptable in Fflyr society. There are those who do it, but they are the first to be grabbed whenever the Kingsguard needs to pin a crime on somebody."

Man, poor Donon.

"This is all interesting stuff," I said, directing my attention back to Biribo, "but what's it got to do with the Goblin King and killing my information broker in my kitchen?"

"Right! So the relationship between goblins and humans is mutual, but it is *not* equal. Humans are twice their size, and they occupy the surface, which provides a lot more resources, especially of the edible kind. So human populations grow faster and *bigger*, and individual humans are more likely to be well-fed and healthy, plus they have more sizable and sophisticated power structures. In basically every place where the two races coexist, humans hold the power and goblins are some degree of oppressed."

"Isn't the current Lord of Godspire a goblin?" Aster asked.

"Yeah, but Godspire is an anomaly in basically every way, politically speaking," said Nazralind. "It's best not to consider anything that happens there as representative of . . . well, anything else."

"Go on," I told Biribo with a nod.

"Constant persecution builds up pressure that eventually demands an outlet, and for goblins, a Goblin King or Queen is the form that takes. The rise of a Goblin King on Dount means that a quorum of the local goblins have reached a point where they're so fed up, they are willing to completely reverse their culture and outlook on life. Instead of living by wits and skill alone, suddenly the goal is *pure violence*. A Goblin King's first task is to bring rival powers to heel, because anybody down in those tunnels who's got any authority or privilege does *not* want a Goblin King on their watch. His goal is an uprising, to have goblins come boiling out of their holes to inflict vengeance on their oppressors. In a disorganized mess of a country like Fflyr Dlemathlys, they might even manage to take and hold some territory for a little while, but goblin uprisings *never* succeed in the long term, and even a fifth-rate military like the Kingsguard would be able to put them down once they mobilize properly. More likely, the King's Guild would send their best in to take out the King himself; that's what usually happens. Once he goes down . . . *very* occasionally another goblin can step up and keep the momentum going for a little while longer, but usually it all falls apart when the King falls. *Then* the human powers retaliate, with results that verge on genocide."

"I knew that was usually the result of goblin uprisings," said Nazralind, looking faintly queasy, "but you're suggesting all of them *know* how futile it is and do it anyway?"

"Not really," Biribo replied. "At least, not all of 'em. Goblin Kings or Queens always rise from a cult of personality and usually rally supporters with rhetoric about vengeance or freedom. It helps that goblins usually have an oral system of education and most of 'em are fairly ignorant of politics and history beyond the island they're on. The big movers and shakers, like Sneppit—and probably this Jadrak himself, if he was enough of a somebody to proclaim himself King and have people go along with it—know the uprising can't succeed. Undoubtedly, Maugro did too, which was why he had to die. That's what Jadrak'll be doing to anybody else down there who's got any influence and won't throw in with him."

"I think I follow you so far," I said. "Now get to the part about . . . how did you put it . . . A war of total annihilation?"

"Yeah, about that." Biribo swooped in the air, flicking his tongue out, and though his little triangular lizard face was as inscrutable as always, his delivery gave me the impression of a wince. "A Goblin King gets to call himself that by riding a wave of pure anger and violence. It's the most precarious kind of rule—he has whipped his people into a mob, and has to *keep* 'em whipped up while also keeping that energy directed properly. Specifically, at human rulers who treat goblins unfairly and oppress them with violence. *You* just made yourself the first point of contact between the new Goblin King and the surface people, and you did it by making a big display of everything they're reacting against. Big powerful human responds to something he doesn't like with spells and crossbows and zero dialog—I know you had your reasons, boss, but that was textbook human arrogance from a goblin's perspective. He *has* to fight you now. If he surrenders, or even tries to make a truce, his followers will turn on him. And in *his* position, that doesn't just mean a loss of power. They'll probably tear him literally limb from limb."

Everyone turned to stare at me, and it required all my poise to ignore them.

"So," I said slowly, "prospects for diplomacy are . . ."

"Up in flames?" Aster finished pointedly.

"It's worse than that," Biribo continued in a morose tone. "Boss, the absolute *last* thing a Goblin King wants is a fight with a Dark Lord. Your organization against his is probably something close to a draw at this point, but you, *personally*, represent a physical force that can rip through just about anything he can throw at you. On the contrary, I bet this Jadrak was *really* gambling everything on making an accord with you. Positioning himself as the lieutenant of a new Dark Lord is basically the *only* way for a Goblin King to succeed on anything like the long term. You were his one prospect for victory, and instead, he now has to fight you to the death."

I opened my mouth to speak, but for once, Biribo talked over me, zipping back and forth in agitation.

"Boss, I can't emphasize enough how badly you just ruined Jadrak's day. He is *dead* now. *You have killed him.* He's gotta pitch everything he has against a nascent Dark Lord, which is an absolute nightmare scenario for a nascent Goblin King. While it's not a *sure* thing—don't get overconfident—that matchup heavily favors you. If he somehow kills you, his organization will be so beaten up that the King's Guild will be able to walk in and wipe him out on a whim. He doesn't have the option to rest and rebuild his forces; they'll turn on him if he fails to keep up the forward momentum. The only question now for Jadrak is *when* he meets a bloody end. It's definitely going to be sooner than it would've been if you hadn't involved yourself. You're dealing with a dead man walking, who has to watch his doom coming at him, and knows all of it's your fault."

"So basically . . . he's gonna be *slightly* less reasonable than the usual run of people I have to kill."

"Well," Minifrit drawled, "I cannot help but feel there is a *lesson* in all this."

"Hey, how was I supposed to know any of this shit?" I demanded. "None of *you* did!"

"No one's saying reacting to what happened with anger wasn't understandable, or appropriate," Aster retorted, meeting my glare without flinching, "but you knew we were dealing with the first envoys from another organized power. Circumstances aside, what possible *good* did you think could come from shooting one and setting the other on fire?"

"In my experience," Nazralind added, "intimidating people into compliance is always the temptation for somebody in a position of power, and it can even work sometimes—well, a lot of the time, actually. But it has *major* potential to backfire. It's the only way the Clans seem to know how to subdue resistance, and it's also the reason resistance never entirely dies out, no matter how hard they squeeze."

"All *right*!" I exclaimed. "What's done is done, *now* we have to deal with it."

"What's the plan, then?" Minifrit prompted.

"I don't see what choice we have. We're going into the tunnels to put this Goblin King down before he can come at us. It sounds like this can all work in our favor if we play it right; the goblins' grievances sound really familiar to all of us who've been living under the Clans. So we take out . . . what was his name, Jadrak? Finish him off, take over his movement, add the goblins to our ranks, and we'll be in a much better position than when we started."

"Except it's *not* going to be that easy," Biribo said immediately. "Boss, don't forget what I said first—under normal circumstances, goblins are contemptuous of violence and brute force and won't trust anybody who relies on those. The Goblin King's minions are *not* going to pivot toward any human who proves his point about how violent humans are, and the *rest* of the movers and shakers down there will not fall in with anybody whose only claim to power is killing off other claimants. I agree that we *need* to take out Jadrak, because it's him or you, but the fact that we have to go in there and do that pretty much precludes getting the rest of the goblins on our side."

I inhaled slowly, mastering the temptation to claw at my face with both hands. Fuck me running, I'd really shat the bed this time.

"Okay," I said aloud after a momentary pause, in which everyone had better sense than to interrupt my ruminations. "New plan. We go in there, find and link up with Miss Sneppit's organization. She can give us the lay of the land and hopefully guide us toward straightening this out. We definitely need a local ally, and we've already worked with her people to mutual benefit."

"And if Sneppit won't deal with us? Or Jadrak's already killed her?" Kasser asked.

I bared my teeth. It was not a smile. "Plan B is to kill whoever and whatever we have to until we work our way up to the Goblin King. Kill *him*, fuck off outta there, seal off the tunnel, and write the goblins off as a loss. I would *prefer* to come out of this mess with allies and some benefit, but I will settle for ending the problem if that's all we can manage."

"The first issue I can see is that this will involve *going underground*." Aster was already grimacing in distaste as she spoke. "I've noticed you don't seem to have much problem with digging and such, but this is a *major* taboo for everyone on Ephemera who's not a goblin."

"The King's Guild regularly sends adventuring parties down there to 'recover stolen property' and generally keep the goblins suppressed," Minifrit retorted. "People *will* venture underground, when impelled."

"I don't want to create a morale problem," I said. "If we make this a volunteer only operation, do you think we'll get enough?"

"Yes," Minifrit said immediately. Aster was a second behind, but she nodded agreement.

"The general mood throughout the organization is defiance toward the old strictures and taboos," she clarified when Minifrit gestured graciously for her to take over. "That, and you have a lot of personal loyalty among our people, especially the Cat Alley girls. This prospect is going to freak out a lot of them, but I'm confident enough will come along willingly to put together a solid strike force. Considering we're going into goblin-sized tunnels, a smaller team is probably best, at least at first. Greater numbers won't mean much down there."

"Good," I said. "Then put out the call. Minifrit, assemble arms and supplies for everybody. I want to move within the hour; every minute we're not going on the offense is an opportunity for the Goblin King to gear up and strike first. Kasser, I want you to come with the first group."

"Me?" His eyebrows shot upward. "I, uh . . . That is, I'm not afraid to fight, Lord Seiji, but I thought I already had a job?"

"That's exactly why you're coming. Don't worry, I don't want you at the vanguard. In fact, you're valuable enough, you'll be the last one in, and don't poke your nose through until we've secured our foothold. The tunnel from our kitchen comes out in Maug—in what used to be Maugro's offices. We're going to move in, sweep out Jadrak's forces, and secure it, both because we need that foothold and because Maugro will have all kinds of files and information stored there. That's another reason I want to move quickly, before Jadrak's people have time to clean it all out. We're going in there blind, and information will be precious. Once we've taken it, I want you to see what we're working with and then get to work fortifying it. That office is something we *have* to keep; if we lose it to the Goblin King, he's got a corridor straight into the heart of North Watch. For the same reason," I added, turning back toward Aster and Minifrit's side of the table, "I want armed guards posted *in* the kitchen, as well as in the corridor to the mess hall. The kitchen's side door into the stairwell is to be sealed off as thoroughly as we can until further notice. In the worst-case scenario, the kitchen corridor is another useful choke point, and if we're forced to fall back from there, the mess hall itself has enough elevated surfaces to make a perfect killbox with our crossbows."

"Gannit's going to *love* this plan," Nazralind commented with a grin.

"Gannit will live with it," I snapped, "and obviously the kitchen staff will have to be evacuated anyway if the worst happens. All of these contingencies are because I'm not taking risks with North Watch's security. Let me be clear, losing our foothold in Maugro's place once we take it is *unacceptable*. I'm relaying all this because I will need to lead the team that moves deeper into the goblin tunnels to take out Jadrak, so the commanders staying behind need to know the plan. Make sure to pass it down the chain, Aster."

"I have people I trust to manage things," she agreed, nodding. "Since I *will* be coming with you, I'd like to recall Goose from the main road group; she's best suited for overall military command, I think."

"Agreed. We'll send one of Naz's riders to retrieve her. Who do you like to replace her position?"

"Khadret's competent, and I think putting her *there* rather than *here* will help break up that little clique of her friends. I haven't seen any actual trouble out of that group, to be clear, but you did say you preferred we not have people developing little factions within the ranks."

"Are you sure it's a good idea for you to go with Lord Seiji?" Nazralind asked. "That big honking sword of yours isn't gonna do you any favors in dark, cramped tunnels."

"Yeah, not looking forward to that." Aster grimaced. "But yes, I am going and that's final. Every time I let him run around unsupervised, he tries to get himself killed."

I hastily interjected before Nazralind's grinning face could begin spewing more back talk. "Then we've got a plan. Everybody get organized. We move in one hour."

My people really came through. Aster gathered up volunteers for the underground expedition from the many curious faces that had assembled as word of the kitchen attack spread through the fortress. Kasser distributed weapons and armor and Minifrit arranged other supplies, and all told, they were ready to roll out in less than half the time I'd allotted. Not even thirty minutes after the meeting broke up, I stood in the kitchen at the head of a strike force of twenty—not enough for a full invasion, but sufficient to seize and hold the offices at the other end of the tunnel and scout beyond.

After all the bullshit I'd experienced in Fflyr Dlemathlys, it was enough to bring a tear to a Dark Lord's eye. Just imagine it—*competence!*

If only I could be as certain of all of Aster's personnel choices.

It was almost all women, which was not a problem; these were, as predicted, Cat Alley girls, who'd been with me the longest and done the most training. It was just some of the individual choices that gave me pause. Adelly was here, which made sense; she had the Lightning Staff in her hands, ready to go. I was less sanguine about both Donon and Madyn being fully kitted out for war, and to judge by her scowl, Gannit shared my opinion. *Both* the assistant cooks? Donon was obviously hankering for some payback, which was fine, but I'd thought Madyn hated fighting. That was why she worked in the kitchen.

And, of course, there was Ydleth, who had probably been among the first to volunteer to accompany me anywhere. Ever since that embarrassing scene in the mess hall she'd been my biggest fan. Now she gave a huge smile when I entered the room, and I had to dip slightly into showtime to nod at her without grimacing. I was *not* awkward about her, uh . . . crotch situation. On the contrary, *that* was useful to me. I was building my whole case to the people of this world as the guy who would offer them a fair shake no matter who or what they were, in contrast to how they'd been treated under the current regime; the more obviously unusual types I had around, the better. She was such a *pain*, though. Shrill, pushy, argumentative . . . I felt guilty for disliking somebody who I was pretty sure would take an arrow for me, but Ydleth was just not much fun to be around. Oh well, at least she was pretty good in a fight.

I moved to the head of the group, near the tunnel door, and raised one hand. The general shuffling and chatter quieted down on command, everyone giving me their undivided attention.

"Thank you for agreeing to this," I said simply. "I know you've all heard what's up from Aster, so I won't bore you with a—"

"Speech!" Ydleth crowed, grinning.

I inhaled and exhaled once, slowly.

". . . speech. Because time is short, *and* because goblins apparently have very good hearing. Back when there were allies at the other end of this tunnel, we used to summon them just by yelling."

I did not look directly at Ydleth, so I had to enjoy the sight of her wilting in place peripherally, as everyone nearby turned to give her scathing stares.

"We know the Goblin King will be gearing up for an attack, and he probably expects the same from us, so the element of surprise is a lost cause.

Still, we will make our initial strike as quick and quiet as possible. I will take point, Aster right behind me. The rest of you know your formations."

I paused, looking quickly around to make eye contact with a few people before continuing.

"The only other point of major importance is that dethroning the Goblin King is our primary objective, not our only one. We are going down there to make allies from among his enemies, and that means being willing to welcome goblins into the fold. I've made my position on discrimination clear up 'til now, but I will repeat it for emphasis—there will be none of that in the Dark Crusade. If you've got a problem with goblins, you will keep your mouth shut about it. Reaching an accord with them is going to be an uphill trudge as it is. Anybody who makes it harder will be the recipient of my full displeasure."

A pause to let that sink in, and then I nodded once, smiling slightly.

"And that's it. I appreciate each of you for your willingness to come along. Ladies and Donon, let's kick some ass."

There was no cheering, because they could follow directions. Taking that as a good sign, I turned, opened the door, and stepped into the tunnel.

No sign of the goblin I'd left here covered in fire slimes; Gannit reported that the screaming had faded with distance and then stopped entirely. There was no body, either.

Right away I gave up on the idea of stealth. Everyone had to shuffle along behind me, single file and hunched over, and the echoes off the dirt and stone walls made this short walk feel as loud as a train ride. Yeah, they were gonna hear us coming.

Maugro's door at the other end was, I noted with surprise, not any sturdier than the one I'd had Kasser build. Well, for all that he'd had longer to put it in place, he probably wasn't expecting anyone to try to break in, given how the Fflyr felt about tunnels. Stepping up to the surface of pitted akorshil planks, I could hear quiet voices and shuffling sounds on the other side. They could definitely hear us, then.

I turned the latch, and it broke off in my hand. On closer inspection, the entire thing was knocked loose from the wall. Well, there *had* been a serious fight here just a few minutes prior. An experimental shove only moved it a few centimeters before it thumped against an obstruction. A second push rocked it a bit further. They'd had time to put up a barricade—though, from the feel of it, not a very sturdy one.

I took a step back, causing Aster to shuffle backward into the woman behind her, and raised my foot.

Hell, it's not like subtlety was ever my strong suit anyway.

The first kick splintered the akorshil and made the entire door buckle inward. Two more impacts and something gave way with an ugly *crunch*, causing the half-broken door to sag from one hinge, barely held up by whatever was trying to block it from the other side.

Planting my feet firmly on the ground again, I grinned savagely and raised both hands.

Windburst!

The backdraft from it roared up the tunnel behind me, of course, generating quite a few complaints and causing me to stumble backward. Still, most of the force succeeded in its job, sending the door and barricade flying into Maugro's offices in pieces. And with that, I took my first step into the domain of the goblins, in my own inimitable style—grinning, arms held wide, wild-haired from the Windburst and altogether carrying the *presence* of ten lesser men.

"OHAYO, MOTHERFUCKERS!"

So they all shot me.

3

In Which the Dark Lord Has an Idea. An Awful Idea. The Dark Lord Has a Wonderful, Awful Idea

I was honestly disappointed. A throwing knife landed in my upper arm and an arrow in the opposite shoulder—an arrow from a goblin-sized shortbow, which barely packed more power than one of our stingers. Another projectile I didn't see properly whizzed over my head to impact the stone wall. And . . . that was it. My artifact amulet, of course, protected me from lethal hits, but it wasn't taxed by the effort; compared to the volley of crossbow bolts that had pitched me into the river, this was nothing.

Sure enough, there were only three goblins in the cramped, disheveled office. No, four; one poked his head up from behind an overturned desk while I obviated the entire result of their pathetic attack. Being impaled twice provided enough of an adrenaline surge that I was able to use both arms despite their state. Probably not a good idea, under ordinary circumstances, but in my case it didn't matter. I ripped out the knife and arrow, threw them to the side, and burst alight with the pink power of **Heal**.

"Really? That's *it*?"

In response the archer nocked another arrow, so I nailed her with a Slimeshot. The office wasn't big; at that range it was way too much kinetic energy for a goblin-sized body to absorb, and she hit the opposite wall in a splatter of slime and blood.

That finished breaking the feeble defense, and the three remaining goblins scurried out through the door opposite the tunnel. I followed, not running but keeping pace quite easily given that my legs were as long as they were tall.

The tunnel came out in some kind of storeroom full of shelves and filing cabinets, which looked like it had been ransacked, even before my Windburst made it worse. I stepped out of that into the front part of the office, following the shrill calls for retreat, just in time to see a scrum at what was apparently the main entrance to the whole building—or cave, I guess?—as the three fleeing goblins, and two more who'd been out there, collided with each other in their haste to escape.

I could've decimated them in that moment with a few Slimeshots. I considered it.

But I let them go. Seemed unsporting to shoot people in the back. More importantly, my larger strategy down here hinged on convincing as many goblins as I could that I was a reasonable person and decent leader, not some bloodthirsty monster who would indiscriminately slaughter all before me. Besides, it wasn't like I lost anything by allowing them to report back to Jadrak. He had to know I was coming, and they hadn't seen anything but me and my imperviousness to their feeble attacks.

Let him chew on that.

"Seems underwhelming, though," I said aloud, pacing across the front of the office space to warily approach the exit. The door hung open, the sounds of fleeing goblins echoing through the pitch-black tunnel beyond. "Biribo, are you *sure* the Goblin King is preparing to throw down with us? That was a pretty pathetic defense against an incoming Dark Lord."

"He *has* to be, boss. But we don't know what kind of forces he's got or what else they're tied down doing; if he was just now killing the likes of Maugro, it stands to reason he's still got other opposition in the tunnels."

"Hm. We clear?"

"Nobody else in the tunnel outside, boss. There's one living goblin in the side chamber over there. Lying down on a cot; I think he's injured."

"Well, well. Let's see what we can find out, shall we? Aster, take two archers and cover the front door. Biribo, keep an eye out for incoming up the tunnel and warn her if we get visitors. Madyn, go back up to the kitchen and fetch Kasser. Everybody else, fan out and see what you can find among the papers in here. This was an information broker's office; there's gotta be something useful."

"Uh, Lord Seiji?" Donon had picked up a windblown piece of paper and now held it up. "All of this is written in Khazid."

Oh. Right.

"A lot of it's probably in ciphers on top of that," Biribo added.

"Of course," I sighed. "Madyn, while you're up there, tell Minifrit to ask around and see if anybody else can read Khazid."

"You got it, Lord Seiji!"

"Everybody else, see if you can find anything you *can* read and bring it to Nazralind. Naz, organize whatever they get and brief me when you can."

"On it."

I could read Khazid myself, obviously, but I needed to delegate this task to someone because I had to take point in the campaign against Jadrak, and moving fast would be central to success on that front.

The ceilings were surprisingly high in here, which meant we were able to stand mostly upright. Getting through a doorway required ducking. So I ducked into the side room, which was furnished less like an office and more like somebody's cozy living room, to find a folding cot, on which lay a heavily bandaged goblin, audibly struggling for breath.

He wasn't bandaged everywhere; apparently, they hadn't had enough clean cloth. The uncovered wounds had been slathered with some kind of salve, but under it I recognized some *nasty* burns. I also recognized his face.

The smarmy, talkative goblin who'd killed Maugro and then tried to charm me over his corpse now looked up at me in a clear blend of pain and terror. I didn't often get to see the horrible aftermath of the things I did to people quite this vividly. It made me feel . . . not great.

Showtime, then.

"And *look* who it is!" I said cheerfully, putting on a broad grin. "Not looking so hot anymore, are we? **Heal.**"

Pink light flashed, blinding in the dim and cramped space, and he arched his back, gasping loudly as he could suddenly fully expand his lungs again without the charred skin on his chest pulling itself apart.

I grabbed one of the overstuffed armchairs Maugro had kept here, which would've been throne-like for him but I doubted I could actually sit down in, at least not without looking absurd. Instead, I spun it around so the back faced the cot and straddled it, sinking down to perch on the armrests and leaning my crossed arms against the high back.

"I've recently been educated about some of the particulars of goblin culture," I said while the subject on the cot experimentally pawed at his skin as if disbelieving he had it all again. "It has been brought to my attention that you may feel you've been treated *unfairly*. I gotta say, man, that is *wild* to me. From where I'm sitting, getting burned to the brink of death and back, twice, is a perfectly reasonable and proportionate comeuppance for the bullshit you pulled."

"That sounds like human logic, yeah," he said, narrowing his eyes.

"Aw, what's with the 'tude, my man? I remember you being so *charming* a few minutes ago. What, a few little third-degree burns and you can't even fake a smile?"

He bared his sharklike teeth at me in what was definitely not a smile.

"Well, that's fine," I said easily. "We are not going to be friends, you and I, so no need to waste time faking it. To business, then! How come you only had a couple buddies in here? Seems unwise, what with a pissed-off Dark Lord right up the hall."

The teeth were exposed further as his upper lip curled into a sneer.

"No? What else shall we discuss, then? Oh, I know! What can you tell me about the Goblin King? Available forces, location, strategic weaknesses, things like that?"

"Go fuck yourself."

I grinned. "I know I should probably be annoyed, but hell, that's exactly what I'd say in your situation."

"Oh, we'll just *see* how long that lasts," said a strident voice from behind me. Mastering my expression, I twisted my head around to behold Ydleth and Ismreth having followed me into the little room. Aster had probably sent them because she had this *thing* about me needing to be guarded. I assumed it was Aster due to Ismreth's presence, as she tended to follow orders and think before acting, unlike Ydleth, who I could well believe had just gotten bored picking through goblin documents and wandered in here. Now, she sneered down at the recently injured goblin, folding her arms. "Little bastard has no *idea* how much pain he's in for."

The goblin barked a derisive laugh at her. "Oh, you think you've got something worse than burning alive? Cos *I* fucking don't. Shoulda held that in reserve, *Dark Lord*. You've blown your entire wad and I ain't impressed. Fuckin' *try it*, asshole."

"Ydleth," I said with every last iota of my immense store of patience, "be so good as to shut the *fuck* up. We do not torture people for information."

"We don't?" Ismreth sounded mildly surprised.

Okay, I had to acknowledge there was some justification for the subtle rebuke in her tone.

"Torture is for punishment or to gain compliance, not information," I heard myself say out loud, and holy fuck my entire career on Ephemera would land me in front of a tribunal in the Hague if anybody on Earth ever learned about it. "If you torture somebody for information, they'll just say whatever they think will make the pain stop. Not only is that not a good way to get useful intel, it's a *great* way to get led into a trap. Is Kasser down here yet?"

"I heard my name." Seconds later, the man himself poked his head through the door. "Lord Seiji?"

"Ah, perfect. Did you finish building the cells I asked for? How's that coming?"

"Done as of a week ago, Lord Seiji. I put that at a higher priority after the thing with the cats. Figured we might have a need soon. Well, for a given value of 'done.' I'm still doing tests, but so far our work has beaten everybody we've tried it on."

North Watch, being an old military fortress, did have a prison, but it wasn't usable; we were storing nonperishables in the half-collapsed space. Instead, I'd set Kasser to renovating some of the smaller rooms in a thick-walled section of the ground floor to hold prisoners. The nice thing about having an organization full of bandits was that we had *lots* of experienced people who could test how easy a place was to break out of.

"Good man. If it's held for a week, it'll do. I've got your first live target here. It won't be a problem if he's half-sized, I hope?"

"Shouldn't be." Kasser stepped the rest of the way in, giving the goblin a critical look. "It's a cell with a thick akorshil door, not bars."

"Good. All right, ladies, escort this gentleman back to the fortress and put him in the cell. These are the instructions I want you to convey to Miss Minifrit: no beating, torture, deprivation, or any other rough treatment. He's to have enough pillows and blankets to sleep comfortably, clothing as needed, adequate provisions for sanitation, and he gets the same food everyone else eats. He may have *one* book at a time."

"A . . . book?" Ydleth tilted her head, visibly mystified. "What the hell for?"

"What do you usually do with books?" Kasser asked her.

"The boredom of being locked up alone in a small room with nothing to do counts as that torture I said we won't be doing," I clarified. "Just one, though, because everybody else uses the library, too. He can request a replacement book once per day. Unless he destroys or damages them, in which case he loses that privilege. I want someone on duty outside the cells at all times and prisoners are to be checked on at irregular intervals not more than two hours apart. And Izzy?"

"My lord?"

"Inform Minifrit that this is to be the standard of prisoner treatment going forward, for anyone who ends up in the cells. If this one decides to spill any beans about Jadrak, she may consider granting him more comforts or privileges at her discretion."

"Very good, Lord Seiji." She folded down her hands.

"Why?" the goblin asked, squinting up at me suspiciously.

Why? Because in the same internet reading, which had schooled me on why torture was not an effective information-gathering tool, I'd learned what *was*—breaking a prisoner involved developing a rapport with them. Unfortunately, I had absolutely no idea how to do that. It hadn't been interesting enough to me to read up on, back when all of this had been purely theoretical; and let's face it, making friends has never been one of my strong suits. Plus, I definitely didn't have time to spend on it. For now, he'd just need to be stashed somewhere until this Goblin King business was wrapped up, but treating him with some basic decency was the only start I knew how to make.

Obviously, I couldn't explain any of that to *him*.

"Why?" I said aloud. Leaning closer to him, I smiled. Slowly, coldly, with eyes half-lidded. "It's simple. Because I'm *better* than you."

The sneer returned to his green face. "You *might've* had a point there, if you hadn't opened with all that torture."

Well, shit, he had me there. Not that I'd ever admit it.

"I said what I said," I replied sweetly, "*fully* aware of the context. Take him away, ladies. You may employ whatever force proves necessary, but permit him to walk with dignity so long as he complies."

"What're we gonna do with him after we finish off the Goblin King, then?" Ydleth asked.

Which was not her place to ask, and definitely not now, but I didn't call her down as it presented me with an opportunity to further make my point.

"We'll let him go, obviously. *This* fellow isn't my enemy, he just works for him. Once Jadrak is gone, he's just some guy. We're not in the business of hurting anybody who doesn't specifically need it, ladies. All right, you have your orders."

Belatedly, I realized that after I'd allowed the other goblins to escape, I might as well just let this one go *now*. Well, too late, I'd already made a big production of giving my orders. And some good might still come of it. Getting my minions and foes alike accustomed to the fact that Lord Seiji treated prisoners well was worth a head start. And who knows, he might eventually decide to cough up some intel.

"Yes, my lord." Ismreth, like most of Naz's noblewomen, preferred her shortbow to the crossbows the rest of the organization used, but she at least had added a stinger with sleep darts to her arsenal. It was this which she now leveled at the goblin, stepping aside to create a path for him to the door. "This way, if you please, good sir. Let us be civil about this."

The goblin frowned at her for a long few seconds, then back up at me. He was clearly thinking deeply about this. But in the end, he got up and walked on his own.

Nobody approached the offices from outside while we took stock, which was starting to seem ominous. According to Biribo, Maugro's place appeared to be on the outskirts of the goblins' underground town, so it made sense that people wouldn't just happen by. What made less sense was the lack of anyone responding to our attack, given that the goblins we'd driven away had had plenty of time to inform Jadrak of what had happened. Well, since I'd let them escape alive, if he didn't know of my presence before, he would soon.

Some of Maugro's documentation was written in Fflyr and uncoded; Nazralind didn't find anything immediately relevant to our interests, but he had a surprising amount of dirt on various Fflyr Clans. On the basis of that alone, I ordered all the paperwork in here to be gathered and carried up the tunnel for us to go over at our leisure, when there was more time. Maugro had had his stubby green fingers in a *lot* of pies, apparently.

In his offices, we didn't find much else of immediate interest, save another slain goblin who, being unarmed, had probably been one of Maugro's staff, and three distinctive greasy smears that were what happened when you doused a fire slime with water. So that was how the others had gotten the slimes off their buddy. The good news was none of the slimes themselves had survived, so Jadrak was not in possession of one of my secret weapons.

To my considerable chagrin, that hadn't even occurred to me until we found their remains. I'd been lucky this time, but I needed to tighten up my game. More slipups like that were going to cost me.

"The good news is this place could not be more defensible," Kasser reported, thumping one fist against the wall. "Solid rock all around, and only one exit into the tunnels. The original door's sturdy and seems intact; they must've taken Maugro by surprise. I can fortify it and put together a *proper* barricade, not like that ramshackle mess the gobs half-assed. Nothing will hold forever, Lord Seiji, but it won't take much time or effort at all to make this place stand up to any assault for a good long time."

"Music to my ears," I praised. "Don't forget, though, fighting goblins isn't going to be like fighting Fflyr. These guys are the source of those fancy munitions we've been using, and you can damn well bet they didn't sell us everything they have, or even the best stuff. We'll be dealing with gas attacks, explosives, chemical fires . . ."

"Mmm." He narrowed his eyes in thought, rubbing his chin. "Good point. Okay, I should be able to build a barrier across the door that's both airtight and fireproof. The only downside is that won't be a door we can open or close at will; once all that stuff is in place, the thing is not going to open again until it's destroyed, and then we'll have to start from scratch to reseal it."

"That's acceptable."

"I'd like to put some barricades in the tunnels outside," said Aster, "with archers behind them. In both directions."

"Why?" Kasser scowled at her in annoyance. "I just said this door is the most defensible point."

"Yes, but I don't like risking everything on a single point of failure. If we light up the tunnels, put up barriers, and have people with crossbows to discourage attacks, that will at least slow anybody coming at us enough to retreat in here and fortify. Plus, rather than sealing *our* people behind a barrier, it gives us control over the entrance and the freedom to come and go until the Goblin King sends a big enough force that we have to shell up. That's gonna be important, since Lord Seiji and our strongest hitters have to go *out* there and take the fight to them."

"Hmm, okay, I follow you," he said a little grudgingly. "Well, that's simple enough. We can turn over some tables and desks, set 'em out there in a staggered pattern. Yeah, that'll buy time in case of an attack and might be able to repel a weak one. Okay, you're right, Aster. Good news is you won't need any craftsmen to do that, we can just cart out tables and desks and turn 'em over."

"While we're thinking along those lines," I said, "I do want us to hold this office if at all possible, but it's the tunnel to North Watch that *cannot* fall. Can you do something to improve that?"

"Oh yeah, easily," Kasser answered with more enthusiasm. "It's long, narrow, and sloping down here from the fortress, that's just *begging* to be booby-trapped. One person with armor could hold that against an army, but we can just, y'know, roll junk down there and ruin anybody trying to take it from below. Gimme some fire slimes and barrels of asauthec in the kitchen, and I can stand in the kitchen door and massacre anybody trying it."

"Good. Fortify the door up there, too, but that's a last priority. I want this place locked down as tight as it can be first."

"Will do, Lord Seiji."

"As soon as you and Kasser are satisfied with the defenses," I said to Aster, "we're moving out. I want a small group of hard-hitters, like you said."

She nodded. "The biggest problem is going to be light. Goblins can see in the dark, Lord Seiji, so there won't be lights out there. We're not as bad off as most human forces would be; between your spells, light slimes, and Nazralind, we can provide our own light for basically no cost or effort. But it does mean that in order for us to be able to *do* anything, we're gonna have to let them see us coming long before we can see them."

"Hang on," I protested, "there were lights in here already. Why would the goblins have that if they didn't need them?"

"Cos this is an office full of paperwork, boss," Biribo explained. "Goblins' dark vision is a magical ability. They can perfectly see shapes in any level of light including absolutely none, but to see *colors* they need about the same amount of light as humans. That means if they wanna read, they need lamps."

"Huh," I mused. "I didn't know goblins were magical."

"Oh yeah, that's pretty normal. Most sapient races have magical abilities, it's just humans and beastfolk who don't. Goblins get their dark vision and super strength."

"Hang on, *what* super strength?" Donon demanded. "Goblins aren't any stronger than a human."

"Uh, yeah." Biribo zipped in front of him, sticking his tongue out. "A goblin is about as strong as a human, at half the size. You need me to walk you through the arithmetic on that?"

"Oh," Donon mumbled, crestfallen, then rallied. "But don't forget the super hearing!"

"I was talking about *magical* abilities, Donon. Goblins don't have magical hearing; they hear better than humans because they got those big ears. Even *elves* hear better than humans, though not by much."

"I have no idea what he's talking about," Nazralind said haughtily as several people turned speculative glances on her. "Please, by all means, go on gossiping about me just outside what you assume is my earshot."

"Goblins . . . are magic."

Something in my voice made everyone stop what they were doing and turn to look at me. I wasn't sure exactly what image I was putting off at that moment, being fully preoccupied with my own suddenly swirling thoughts. I wasn't even sure, yet, where this burst of insight was going. *Something* had clicked together, forming connections I was following inwardly.

"They're . . . magical creatures," I repeated, staring at nothing. "Magical abilities. Dark vision and double strength. Which . . . can be shared . . . with Spirit Bond."

"I thought that spell only worked on monsters?" Nazralind said hesitantly.

Aster's eyes widened as she realized what I just had. "But a *compound* spell with Spirit Bond's effects and something else's triggering conditions . . ."

"What the hell is a compound spell?" somebody asked.

I ignored them, preoccupied as I was chasing this sudden epiphany down the next branching pathway.

"Biribo."

"Boss?"

"What monster races on Dount possess inherent magic? And what abilities do they have?"

"Well, uh, *monster* is a subjective term that comes down to politics, boss, but as far as races with magical abilities? Elves—both kinds. Light elves can make light at will, dark elves have magical stealth. Goblins have dark vision and enhanced strength, like we were just discussing. Harpies have magically enhanced vision, and they can adjust the acuity at will, and also have magically reduced body weight, which is the only reason a humanoid creature is able to fly under its own power. They can also reproduce with genetic material from other species. Naga have a pretty amazing package. They can regulate their body temperature to an incredible extent; you can freeze one solid or set them on fire and the damage is superficial. They're also able to withstand immense amounts of atmospheric pressure and can see and hear clearly through any medium through which light and sound are able to pass. Also, they can breathe water, which is kinda the key to the whole pattern—those are abilities designed to give them humanlike function deep underwater, but it has the knock-on effect of making them way overpowered in most other circumstances. There are other races, but that's it for the ones you'll find on Dount."

"Naga are tough bitches," Aster agreed. "In the King's Guild, newbies are told to leave them the hell alone; that's a fight for a powerful Blessed. Luckily, there aren't many of them, and the ones on Dount have always minded their own business. So long as people stay out of their territory."

I had it now. I needed more details, but I could see the shape of it. The sheer weight of the revelation was making me vibrate in my artifact boots.

"Biribo." Only the full strength of my performative ability kept my voice steady.

"Boss?" He, by contrast, sounded both wary and avidly eager. I was never sure how much Biribo truly knew, but right at that moment I got the distinct impression he'd been waiting for me to realize what I just had.

"Of the magical races extant on Dount, how many of them are . . . matriarchal?"

"Is that even a real word?" Ydleth stage-whispered from somewhere in the near distance.

Biribo actually did an excited little pirouette in midair before he started expositing.

"From most to least? Harpies can't really be considered a matriarchy because they're not any kind of archy. They are strictly solitary and extremely unfriendly with everyone, including each other. On Dount, the only place they live is up on the nearby mountain, and the fact that there's more than one in the area means they're pretty much always fighting. Harpies are an entirely female species; they have that magical reproductive strategy, like I mentioned. When a harpy wants to mate, she'll usually just grab a male from whatever race is unfortunate enough to be nearby. And usually eats him afterward."

"Damn. Is it bad that I kinda like them?"

"*Yes*, Ydleth, that's pretty fucking bad," Adelly said in exasperation.

Biribo ignored the byplay, just watching my face while he carried on his explanation. "Naga are sort of matriarchal by default. They're the *least* humanoid of the ostensibly humanoid races, and have a very different core biology from most. Naga are incredibly sexually dimorphic, to the point you probably wouldn't guess the males and females were the same species if you didn't happen to know better. Male naga are . . . well, it's questionable whether they're even sapient. They don't really communicate and aren't good for much beyond grunt labor. About as smart as a dog. So it's only the female naga who have anything that can be called a society."

"Huh," Aster grunted. "I was told naga were like harpies. No males at all."

"The local dark elves are ethnic Savins," Biribo continued, "which means, unless a *lot* has changed in Shylverrael in the last century and a half, they are an explicit legal matriarchy. Think . . . basically the same gender politics as the Fflyr, except in reverse."

"Okay, I *definitely* like them," said Ydleth. "Is that *okay*, Adelly? Am I *allowed* to like the dark elves?"

"Considering we'll probably end up allied with them, that's probably for the best."

"And goblins," Biribo said with relish, coming to the end of his recitation, "are strictly meritocratic. The local goblin culture doesn't really have defined gender roles in the sense you think of them. Whichever goblin is smart and skilled enough to outperform their competition gets to be in charge, until another one muscles them out. Goblin leadership is therefore a pretty even split, but they have zero compunction about taking orders from a woman as long as she proves herself worth obeying. Same rules as for men."

He paused, did a little loop the loop in the air, and flicked his tongue out eagerly.

"So, boss, yes. Every magical race found on Dount, with the exception of the Fflyr light elves, is either necessarily or at least *potentially* matriarchal."

And there it was.

The worst part, I realized, was that it wasn't even my idea. The plan that burst into being behind my eyes would chart my course for the remainder of my conquest of Ephemera, well beyond the borders of Dount and Dlemathlys, but it wasn't something I had created. Merely something I'd come across, following the trail that had been left for me.

She'd put me here, on this particular island. With this particular bonus ability . . . and that very particular set of beginning spells. All of it had been set up from the beginning, just waiting for me to connect the dots. Now I knew exactly what kind of show Virya wanted to see.

I burst into hysterical laughter, because it was that or scream, weep, and claw my own eyes out.

"Lord Seiji?" Aster exclaimed in alarm.

I staggered weakly to one side until I reached a wall and slumped against it. Howling with despairing mirth, I pounded one fist impotently against the stone.

"He's doing it again," somebody muttered.

"No escape," I wheezed. "There is no getting away from it! Every time I think . . . But no. Here on Planet JRPG, under the Weeb Goddesses, there is just no escape from *otaku bullshit*!"

I raised my head to see that everybody looked disturbed now. That caused me some regret; I didn't want to dishearten my people and I *knew* this wasn't the image I should be projecting right now, but it was like I could feel my consciousness being unraveled from the inside by the revelation I had just experienced, and I had to vent *somehow*. It was this or kill myself.

"WITNESS ME!" I roared, surging upright and throwing my arms wide, causing everyone to shy a step back from me. "For I have beheld a glorious vision of our future—our wonderful, terrible, *stupid* future. And it is a future built upon the shoulders of *monster girls*!"

4

In Which the Dark Lord
Finds His Sparkle

My people worked fast, but even so, the effort of locking down the offices gave me sufficient time to compose myself.

Kasser and Harold brought in their full crew and rigged up the door with a solid bar to hold it shut, and a barricade that could be pushed against it at need. All of it was supported by alchemical glue, ironically bought from the goblins, which Kasser assured me would hold up to stress, as well as any spikes hammered into the stone walls, and it was a lot easier and faster to apply. Meanwhile, others upended a series of desks, tables, and crates in both directions along the tunnel outside. Crossbow-wielding women took up positions behind them, and light slimes in bottles were set up ahead to illuminate the approaches. This was all but guaranteeing some of those slimes would fall into goblin hands, but oh well. Better that than risk my people getting ambushed in the dark. Besides, by the end of this the goblins would either be working under me or too reduced to be a threat.

By the time all that was done, Maugro's offices had been cleared of paperwork and everything else we thought was worth carrying out. Including the dead goblins, whom I had been instructed would be laid to rest respectfully, friend and foe alike. Hopefully Fflyr funerary customs wouldn't be offensive to their spirits. More importantly, when I returned to the newly fortified underground office after saying goodbye to Junko and the kids, fully armed and ready to roll out, I was once again composed. And Aster was just finishing up explaining things to the girls when I rejoined them.

"So, hang on," Norrie was saying as I entered, "this spell only works on pretty women?"

"It works based on attraction, and it depends on the caster," Aster replied in a patient tone, which told me this wasn't the first time she'd explained this. "For Lord Seiji, yes, that means pretty women."

"Well, hell, it's not like I'm interested in magical theory. Lord Seiji's obviously what matters here." Norrie turned a speculative look on me that suddenly made me feel very much like a fancy pastry in a glass case. So did several of the others.

"You see my problem, then," I said smoothly, ignoring the hungry looks. "Instead of any qualities that are actually *useful*, like competence or intelligence or loyalty, this requires me to recruit talent, first and foremost, based on how hot someone is. *That* is going to cause problems."

"Recruit who, though? Why?" Kellin asked, subtly repositioning herself to push out her chest and causing me to quickly avert my eyes, because the last thing I needed right now was a flashback. "We're right here, Lord Seiji."

"Weren't you listening to that talk about monster girls and matriarchy?" Nazralind cut in.

"If by 'talk' you mean 'unhinged ranting,'" Aster muttered, but quietly enough that I'm not sure anybody else heard.

"If I understand the plan, it's actually kind of brilliant," Naz continued. "Lord Seiji can build a core group of lieutenants from every Viryan race sharing a Spirit Bond—which means they'll each have *all* the magic abilities of *every* race, as well as all three Blessings. Each, uh . . . 'monster girl' would end up being an absolute powerhouse. More important, they can be installed as leaders of every faction, where their strength would make it easy for them to rule a Viryan culture *and* keep them firmly loyal to Lord Seiji, since he'd be the source of all their power. One move to achieve multiple military and political goals. It's . . . elegant." She gave me a look that was both impressed and a little more surprised than I thought was fair. "But, of course, that means it's the monster people who matter for these purposes. Lord Seiji doesn't gain anything by casting this spell on humans."

"He gains followers who have multiple Blessings *and* monsterfolk powers," Norrie protested. "And all that's needed is that the target be sexy, right? Come on, Lord Seiji, you've got an army of whores here! Why is this only coming up *now?*"

"Knock it off," Ydleth said curtly. "It's Lord Seiji's business *and* his decision. None of us are entitled to special magic powers just for showing up with a nice pair of tits."

"Come off it, Ydleth, just because—"

"*Stop* putting pressure on him," Ydleth snapped. "This whole business is hard enough on Lord Seiji because of his, you know, problem. He doesn't need you making it worse!"

That actually shut everybody up for a moment; the girls who'd been eyeing me like a side of meat seconds ago suddenly looked abashed. I repressed the urge to sigh. Yeah, of course they'd noticed; these were women who'd been trained on the job to be attuned to signs of male attraction. My . . . *sessions* with Minifrit were helping, actually. The flashes were less severe and less frequent, but they were not gone, and spending an hour a couple nights a week in repeated foreplay that never managed to lead anywhere before being interrupted by waking sleep paralysis episodes was absolutely exhausting.

"This isn't as straightforward or simple as that, either." Aster stepped in before I could think of something to say. "It's only sharing two Blessings, functionally. The Blessing of Wisdom doesn't work if you don't have a familiar, and I guess Biribo's powers don't extend to me. Also, you know how you've never seen *me* casting spells? That's because I can't use Lord Seiji's spells. I would have to get scrolls of my own—which is not happening, because *he* needs every scroll we can find. Even artifacts bottleneck the utility of Blessings; it's not like they grow in pods. There's no point in Blessing everybody in the army if we can't equip them to get any use out of it."

"Those restrictions do seem . . . annoyingly arbitrary," Ismreth mused.

"We're treading virgin ground here, ladies," said Biribo. "Far as I'm aware, the spell Enjoin has never *existed* before; we're having to figure out how it works as we go. Since it's cobbled together from pieces of other spells that were never meant to work that way, we gotta expect there are gonna be issues getting practical value out of it."

"Which is another thing," Aster added. "We *don't* know how it works— what it can do or what the *dangers* are. Can it share negative magical effects as well as positive ones? That's the biggest risk I can think of, and it's enough of a risk if Lord Seiji only Enjoins the core leadership. What if he applies it to as many of us as possible? Then we end up fighting a sorcerer who can cast . . . oh, I dunno, say the Curse of Eternal Sleep? If they can lay eyes on just *one* of our foot soldiers, they can neutralize Lord Seiji, the entire upper command structure, and half the army."

The silence which followed was far more oppressive, and I had to hold back a wince. Holy fuck, I hadn't even *thought* of that. See, this was why I followed Aster's lead and didn't contradict her, even when I didn't know what she was doing. Her careful, methodical approach to everything was a vital counterpoint to my bombastic, free wheeling style.

Biribo buzzed over to my shoulder where he could murmur right in my ear. "Boss, we got a lone goblin coming up the tunnel from the west. I'm ninety percent sure it's Gizmit. She's making a stealthy approach."

Oho. "Keep me posted," I whispered just as quietly. Gizmit was unlikely to be hostile, and in fact was exactly the point of contact with Sneppit I wanted; her stepping right into my path was going to save us a *lot* of effort. Also, I was interested in seeing how close she could get, to gauge both her capabilities and those of my sentries.

"And there's still the original drawback I mentioned," I said aloud, now that everyone was staring inquisitively at me. "Your former profession is one of the few in which people are actually more qualified if they're prettier."

"Hell, not even that one," Madyn said cheerfully. "Greatest whore I ever knew had to be Lorit, from the Cat—you remember her, right, girls? Bitch could drain the *soul* out of a man, I swear. They'd stagger out of her room barely able to walk and grinning like dust huffers. And *she* was bowlegged, had no rack to speak of, and a nose longer than Adelly's."

"Oh, fuck you, Madyn. I got more repeat customers than you ever did!"

"Exactly my point," Madyn said solemnly, stepping out of range of Adelly's arm.

"So," I said patiently, "in addition to killing the Goblin King and trying to reach a diplomatic arrangement with whatever organization is left over *after* him, I need to find some . . . and I feel slimy just *saying* this . . . cute goblin girls. That's right, our third and stupidest objective is to identify me some fuckable goblins in the hope that there's one among them with leadership potential who I can install as a Goblin Queen when we're done here." It would be ideal, I decided, if the legendary Miss Sneppit was pretty enough to work with, but knowing as little as I did, I wanted to keep my options open.

"I can help with that!" Donon chimed in, practically vibrating with eagerness.

"You have your assignment," Aster said, causing him to visibly deflate.

"The twists and turns of life sure are surprising," Ismreth commented.

"Get used to it; it's gonna get weirder," Biribo advised. "Dark Crusades never go according to plan."

Of course they didn't. That wouldn't be nearly as entertaining for the Goddesses.

"So, uh," Ydleth spoke up. "If this Enjoin spell is mostly untested . . . and it's only been used on Aster so far . . . and you're only finding out which parts do and don't work based on trial and error . . . Not to be a wet blanket, but how do you even know it'll be able to transfer monster-people powers to everybody in the Spirit Bond?"

Another silence fell. Aster frowned, considering, and the others exchanged uncertain glances.

"Well," Twigs said suddenly into the quiet, "we have right here someone from a race with magical abilities, who's already part of the organization's leadership, and is *definitely* pretty enough to qualify."

Everyone's eyes turned to fix on Nazralind. Her eyes widened under the scrutiny, and she ducked her head, giving me an uncharacteristically shy look.

"Oh, I, uh . . . I mean, it's a little *awkward*, don't you think? It's one thing to . . . That is, I think it might be, um, uncomfortable if Lord Seiji and I . . ."

Oh, for fuck's sake.

Nazralind trailed off as I stepped over to her. I folded my arms, putting on a show of appraising her like one would a prize horse.

"Hmmm . . . Yes, yes, good breeding. Graceful lines, clearly a healthy specimen. Indeed, quite. You shall bear me many fine sons."

By the time I finished, Ydleth was laughing so hard she seemed in danger of self-harm and Nazralind had a look on her face like she'd bitten into something extremely sour and slightly haunted.

"Naz, stop being weird," I ordered, dropping the act and scowling at her. "You *know* you're beautiful. Everybody knows it; we've all got eyes. That doesn't mean any of us was planning to *do* anything about it!"

"Dunno, *I* wouldn't kick her out of bed," Adelly commented, causing Ydleth to laugh even harder.

I ignored them. "Honestly, woman, you're like the little sister I had to meet to really appreciate being an only child. This is already awkward enough for everybody, *especially me*, without you making it worse!"

If I was being honest, had I met Nazralind when *not* suffering debilitating flashbacks at the thought of anything sexual, I probably would have tried to sleep with her. She was beautiful in an unearthly way that you really only see on 2D characters and people who've had way too much plastic surgery. But the situation was what it was, and when I thought about it now, the relationship we'd developed was just . . . not like that. It was Aster all over again, except with a bit more of a discernible reason this time.

At the very least, I had managed to defuse the discomfort of the situation. Or at last replaced Nazralind's unease with annoyance.

"You—that's so—argh!" For a second I thought she was going to slap me. "You are *such* a—I haven't felt this simultaneously flattered and insulted since the *last* time we had a weird conversation! How do you do that? How does he *keep doing that?*" she demanded, rounding on Aster.

"Well, see, there's your problem," Aster said reasonably. "You keep having conversations with him."

"Definitely Gizmit," Biribo murmured in my ear. "She's *right* up against the barricades, boss."

And no outcry from my sentries. Well, that was Gizmit, one, Dark Crusade, zero. Maybe I could poach her from Sneppit somehow? Or convince her to train my people?

"Anyway," I said in a milder tone, "with *that* out of the way . . . What do you say, Naz? Want to try the great experiment?"

"I think you mean *be* the great experiment," she muttered, but despite her pique of a moment ago, I could see the keen interest on her face. Nazralind might have been even worse at hiding her feelings than I was. "So, to be clear . . . This would give me all three of your Blessings?"

"Technically, but functionally only two."

"Right, no familiar, I got it. And I wouldn't get your spells. So, for now, that's just the Blessing of Might."

"*Just,* she says," Ismreth murmured.

"And," I said, nodding, "if it works as I'm hoping, Aster and I will both gain the elven ability to create light."

I had to admit, part of me hoped we wouldn't. That would let me off the hook for this whole stupid fucking idea. I was all but certain, though, that it would work exactly as predicted. All the events leading up to this were just too perfect for Virya not to have set it up on purpose so she could watch me have wacky harem shenanigans.

Fucking weeb.

"And this is effectively permanent," Nazralind said, her cheeks darkening. "Because the, ah, termination condition is . . ."

"Yeah, we won't be doing that," I agreed. "No offense, but—"

"You know what, I can do without hearing it again."

"You get used to it," said Aster.

"All right." Nazralind nodded, visibly steeling herself. "Let's give it a try, Lord Seiji."

I'd only used this spell once and barely remembered the sensation, but it came back immediately. I guess the recall mechanism for my spell library was designed to be maximally user-friendly; at least something on this damn planet was. In that moment of concentration, the globe of shifting symbols formed around me, the source code of magic momentarily revealed to my mind as I sought it out and activated it.

Enjoin.

Golden rings of light flared for just a second in Nazralind's black eyes, and then the spell passed and she blinked twice.

"Was that . . . it?" The elf took a step back and peered quizzically at her own hands, as if expecting some outward change. "I don't feel any differ—oh!"

"You can see it, huh," I said, grinning, as she looked rapidly between me, Aster, and Adelly, her eyes fixing on the various artifacts we were all wearing. My amulet was hidden by my clothes, but the ring, my boots, the Rapier of Mastery, and my invisibility dagger all had that subtle effect about them, a lighter aura visible only to those Blessed with Might. As did Aster's greatsword and the collar of the chain mail tunic peeking out from under her coat, and the Lightning Staff Adelly carried . . .

I unclipped the dagger's sheath from its belt and held it out to Nazralind. "Give it a try."

Wide-eyed, she accepted it in both hands, hesitated for a moment, and then pulled, drawing the blade out of its scabbard. Immediately the enchantment activated and Nazralind vanished into invisibility.

Adelly let out an appreciative whistle, echoed a second later by a delighted voice from thin air in front of me. "Oh, *hell* yes!"

"I'm glad you're having fun," Twigs said with an indulgent smile, "but that's not what we're supposed to be testing."

"Ah yes," I agreed. "So, how's this work, exactly?"

"That, uh . . . I have no idea how to explain it." Nazralind flickered back into view as she slid the dagger back into its sheath. "It's like . . . how do you lift your arms? Elves learn to do this about the same time we learn to walk. It's just . . . there. You know?"

"Hm." I accepted the dagger back from her. Aster frowned pensively, staring at nothing and apparently concentrating inwardly. Clipping the artifact weapon back onto my belt, I took a step backward from both of them, held up one hand in front of myself, and focused.

Light blazed from my skin, a shifting orange-tinged corona that looked quite distinct from Nazralind's golden glow. Ydleth let out a cheer, echoed by whistles and applause from the other girls present.

"It figures," Aster said in disgust. "Obviously anything involving making a spectacle of yourself would come as naturally as breathing to you. Well, the point is proved, anyway."

"Not exactly," Nazralind said, frowning now. "The whole point was to see if it propagates across the Spirit Bond and affects you, too, Aster. If it doesn't . . . Well, I guess the plan's not scrapped; gaining more powers would still benefit Lord Seiji. It just won't be as powerful a tool as we'd hoped."

"I don't . . . know what I'm supposed to be doing," Aster said in frustration. "I don't know what this should *feel* like. You're right, it's like moving your arm—if I suddenly got a third arm I bet I wouldn't know how to flex it, either."

"Mine looks different from yours," I commented, twisting my hand and watching the way the light shifted.

"Yeah, every elf's is distinct," she said.

"It's interesting that it works that way, though," added Biribo. "Obviously you're not using Nazralind's exact glow, boss. It's more like . . . accessing it *through* her gives you the base power, and you then make your own expression of it. That's consistent with how they can't use the spells you've added to your Blessing of Magic. That's worth keeping in mind for later; dark elf stealth is even more variable in how it manifests."

"Oh!" Aster actually jumped in surprise when she suddenly lit up. The corona surrounding her was pure white, and actually seemed brighter than Nazralind's. A grin of pure delight illuminated her whole face in a way that seemed reflective of the more literal light around her, as another round of cheers echoed in the cramped office.

"Congratulations!" Nazralind crowed. "You are now a living affront to the Goddess! A lowborn using the divine gift of the elves. The Convocation is gonna want your head on a pike as soon as they learn about this."

"Thanks for that," Aster commented sourly, though her grin barely diminished. "Oh well, working for the Dark Lord probably sealed that bargain already."

"Yeah, and aren't we killing all those assholes, anyway?" Ydleth added.

"We'll kill who we need to, but let's not go crazy with it," I said firmly, letting my brand-new glow drop. It really was completely intuitive once I got the knack for it, and basically effortless. "All right, ladies, power down and let's move out. Not that all this wasn't important, but we came down here on a mission, and fuck only knows what Jadrak's doing while we chitchat."

"Yes, right," said Aster, and I think I only registered the subtle reluctance on her face as she dropped her own aura because I knew her pretty well. "All right! Everybody, you've got your gear, and you know your assignments. Defenders, take your posts. Expedition group, form up on Lord Seiji. We're heading out."

Aster had divvied up assignments while the crew got this place shipshape and I'd gone back for a last check in North Watch, so the roster would be news to me, too. I had to duck to get through Maugro's front door, my second right on my heels, muttering in annoyance as the greatsword strapped to her back caught on the small doorframe twice before she finally crouched down and shuffled through. Amusing as that was, I controlled myself. We were now outside in the tunnel, and it was time to go to work.

Behind Aster came Adelly and Nazralind, solid picks for our backup. Beyond them she had apparently selected only two more team members, whose emergence made me momentarily hesitate. It was Madyn and Ydleth who followed us out.

Really? The cook and the . . . pest?

Then again, after she'd stood up for me in there, maybe I should go a little easier on Ydleth. She was the last one through; I gave her shoulder a squeeze as she emerged, earning a surprised and grateful smile that made me feel even more guilty. Then I turned to inspect our surroundings.

There were six crusaders already out here, three facing each direction with crossbows at the ready behind the improvised barricades Kasser's people had put up. Light slimes in jars had been set in alternating patterns up the tunnel in both directions, illuminating the walls. To my surprise, these weren't rough tunnels; the walls had long ago been cut smooth, and painted over with . . . I guess I could call it graffiti, since it was slathered everywhere in what was apparently a public space, but the art was *good*. Well, interesting, at least; I'm no judge of visual art. As many different styles as there'd apparently been artists working on it, a riot of clashing colors and distinctive visions overlapped each other and stretched into the distance as the tunnel curved away. And apparently, most of it wasn't even visible most of the time, since there were no light fixtures out here.

It was a stark reminder that I did not understand goblins or their culture. Among other things, I needed to correct that as quickly as possible.

"Left, behind the outermost barricade," Biribo whispered in my ear.

At the same time, Aster asked louder, "All right, which way? Should we flip a coin?"

"I have a better idea," I said. "Let's ask a local guide. Well, Gizmit?"

There was only a moment's silence before the goblin suddenly popped into view, hopping up onto the barricade.

"*Fuck*," exclaimed the nearest woman on watch, reflexively raising her crossbow before I gently pushed it aside. "I didn't even—how did you *do* that?! We were watching this tunnel the whole time!"

"Not very well," Gizmit remarked placidly. "No offense. You're decent, for bandits, but there's not really anyone on Dount with what I'd consider *proper* military training. For starters, when you're on watch, you should keep your eyes pointed *outward*, no matter how interesting a conversation your boss is having in the room behind you. Good morning, Lord Seiji. And this must be the familiar." Her eyes fixed on Biribo, expression not changing. "Nice to finally meet."

And that was a timely reminder that this goblin in particular had outsmarted me more than once already. The most likely reason for her to have lurked out here—with those big ears, which I'd recently been reminded were not just for show—was to listen to our interaction inside.

Also pertaining to that discussion, I now found myself noticing that Gizmit was pretty cute. Not so much that it was the first thing one tended to notice about her; on the contrary, she looked kind of hardcore, with her heavy boots and obvious armor panels sewn onto her vest and trousers, and a stylish trench coat fitted over all. But she was also, I observed, decently pretty, with her black hair in a neat pixie cut and pointed little features. Maybe I was just getting used to goblins, but I found the green skin and big ears exotic rather than unattractive. To borrow Adelly's words, I wouldn't kick her out of bed—but I was only able to think about this at all because I didn't feel a strong urge to be in bed with her in the first place. *That* would've just set me to spasming and seeing things.

A Goblin Queen candidate? Maybe. Gizmit was smart, skilled, and discreet, but her loyalties lay elsewhere. At least as far as I knew . . . for now.

"I don't mind admitting I'm relieved to see you," I said out loud. "I was expecting to have to bumble around in the dark until we found a friendly face. It was good of Miss Sneppit to think of me; I see she still doesn't miss a trick."

"Miss Sneppit isn't aware of your presence and has more urgent things to think about," Gizmit replied. "All of Kzidnak is going to hell right now, Lord

Seiji; she sent me out here to find and extract valuable personnel who . . . *unwisely* attempted to secure some of Miss Sneppit's assets that are coming under attack by the Goblin King's forces. You being here changes matters, though. If you're amenable, I think we can help each other."

"So Sneppit *is* against Jadrak?"

"She doesn't really see it as a choice," the so-called maid said evenly. "A Goblin King represents nothing but death and disaster. Either she and all of us die opposing him, or die under him when he launches a futile attack on the Fflyr. This way, we have a chance to hold out long enough for him to weaken and his organization to consume itself. Sneppit's the last player in Kzidnak big enough to even try. At least, that was the reasoning before. *Your* presence, as I said, changes things."

"Yeah, I have that effect," I said lightly. "Let's go rescue your personnel and, what was it, *assets* then, shall we? I assume you can brief me on the situation as we walk."

"We actually have a grace period right now," Gizmit said, nodding and hopping down from the barricade. She strode through our little fortification, leading us out the other side and up the tunnel, talking briskly as we left my meager defenses behind. "Jadrak's only just openly declared himself and has not consolidated control. A lot of those fighting in his name are disorganized bands just randomly attacking anybody they perceive as an enemy—which is anybody who failed to enthusiastically pledge themselves to the Goblin King. I think it was one of those that took out Maugro, probably hoping to earn Jadrak's favor."

"Well, *that* backfired."

"Indeed," she said dryly. "The point being, Jadrak's actual, organized forces that answer to him directly are *maybe* half of the available manpower willing to serve him. And right *now* they are currently occupied elsewhere. Hopefully they'll stay that way long enough for us to achieve our objective and withdraw to Sneppit's position."

"Occupied doing what?"

"You aren't the only incursion into the tunnels today," she said with a grimace. "The other Fflyr team that just invaded blundered *right* into Jadrak's main force, with chaotic results. They're vastly outnumbered, but a King's Guild raiding party *heavily* outclasses their opposition. When I got a glimpse of the action it was too close to call. Depending on where the fighting spreads, we might see them soon."

"And isn't *that* just the most interesting timing," I muttered.

Gizmit nodded. "I don't believe in coincidence, especially since this particular group has been sniffing around goblin business on Dount for months now and managing to do nothing but get led on various wild goose chases. Everybody's been having a grand old time screwing with them; Maugro's guy Maizo actually dumped them in a pit trap, I hear. But once the shit really hit the wall, I would not be surprised if somebody had the bright idea to *actually* lead them in here and hope they'd take out Jadrak."

I stopped midstep. "Wait a second. A King's Guild party that's been looking into goblin activity?"

"I'm afraid so." Gizmit sighed.

"You have *got* to be kidding me." I clapped a hand over my eyes. "Of all the fucking things I *don't* need right now."

"I'm very sorry if these events inconvenience you, Lord Seiji," Gizmit said in perfect outward serenity.

"Uh, what's the problem, exactly?" Nazralind asked. "Isn't this *good* news? I know we're not exactly buddies with the King's Guild, but if they're putting pressure on Jadrak, that makes our job a lot easier."

"In one sense, yes," I said. "In other ways . . . This just became a *lot* more complicated. They may share our enmity with Jadrak, but they are *not* going to appreciate our plan to help the *rest* of the goblins. Brace yourselves, ladies, something tells me we're about to have our first big clash with the Hero."

5

In Which the Dark Lord Helps

According to Gizmit, North Watch was a lot closer to the center of goblin society on Dount than to Gwyllthean, but we still had a bit of a walk ahead of us. Fortunately her shorter legs didn't slow us; Gizmit kept up at a constant jog without apparent effort, even though I set a pace that was brisk even by human standards. All of us knew there was no time to dally. We passed branching tunnels and several more doorways into goblin dwellings or offices, all shut down tight. Biribo reported some empty and others with goblins huddling inside, having barricaded their doors with whatever furniture they had.

I *knew* goblins weren't actually like the little green monsters from video games, but this was still a sobering reminder. They weren't waiting to spring out from around every corner, but just trying to survive. These were people, that was all, coping the way any people would if they woke up one morning to find their city ripping itself apart in a civil war and then being invaded.

I wondered how Yoshi was dealing with that reality. What he thought about it, and if he'd even noticed.

"We're in Kzidnak now," Gizmit said when I asked how far it would be. "We don't have defensive walls like a human town, obviously, but anywhere the tunnel floor is smooth and paved and you find art on the walls, that's part of the city. This is still the outskirts, of course. I'd like to avoid getting too close to Fallencourt too soon, and that's the part that *you* would recognize as a town. It'll depend on what's going on in these tunnels. We have to go there ultimately, but we need to gather some intel first."

Indeed, even though none of it was in our vicinity yet, we could tell there was bad business going down in goblin town today. Broken items, including furniture and tools lay occasionally along the tunnel floor—freshly broken stuff that didn't have the look of trash that had been here for a long time.

Worse, we could hear it. Raised voices, both angry and fearful, echoed from the distance, along with crashes and other indistinct noises. The way they were distorted and muffled by the acoustics made the sounds somehow more unnerving than if they'd been close enough to be dangerous.

"Don't worry, boss, I'll tell ya if anybody's coming close enough that you need to know," Biribo promised after the third time I paused at a distant scream and half drew my sword.

"Sound travels a long way in these tunnels, and bounces unpredictably," Gizmit said noncommittally. "Even for us it's hard to tell where it's coming from, or what it originally was. You get used to it."

"Not that I don't enjoy charging blindly into chaos," said Aster, "but where exactly are we going, and to do what? And what do we expect to find there?"

Gizmit glanced back at her, then nodded once as if to herself and began talking in her usual clipped tone, her breath clearly not troubled by the pace we set.

"My mission is to extract Miss Sneppit's . . . hairstylist from the Fallencourt tram terminal, where she ran off to without authorization to try to rescue the security team, who're supposed to secure it against the mob."

"We're rescuing Zui?" I asked, then stopped walking. "Hang on. *Tram terminal*? You have *trams*?"

"What's a tram?" Nazralind asked.

"It's . . . Look, I'd have to explain a lot of background technology for it to make any sense, you'll see when we get there. What I wanna know is why goblins have them! And by why I mean *how*."

"Trams are how we get around quickly down here," Gizmit said. "They're like carts on rails that go very fast. See, that wasn't hard to explain, Lord Seiji. As for how . . . that's what we do. Miss Sneppit does whatever business needs doing in whatever's available and seems profitable—hence our relationship with *you*—but originally and primarily we're an engineering company. She built and owns the trams, and the company is organized around running them."

Huh.

"The hairstylist tried to rescue a security team in the middle of an uprising?" Nazralind blinked quizzically. "Isn't that a little . . . backward?"

"Yeah, well, that's Zui for you," Gizmit said resignedly.

"Ydleth, keep up," Aster ordered.

I glanced back to see Ydleth having paused several meters behind us, staring raptly at a piece of the wall art in the last edges of Nazralind's glow.

"Sorry," she said, reluctantly tearing herself away and trotting up to join us. "It's just so *cool*!"

The particular piece that had caught her eye was a great example of how the various goblins who'd painted these tunnels had tried to complement rather than compete with each other, despite their clashing styles. A very pastoral landscape that looked like the khora forest of Dount viewed from high up was rendered in an impressionistic style, creating a very gentle and peaceful feeling. Someone had scrawled abstract art using bold colors and mostly jagged lines across the bottom of it and on both sides, but deliberately arranged their work to frame the landscape rather than obscure it. Across the top, high enough that a goblin would have to have stood on something to paint there, beautiful word art had been added, which reminded me of those illuminated manuscripts European monks used to make, the Khazid text gloriously embellished and given intricate shading that made it seem about to pop off the tunnel wall.

I decided not to tell Ydleth that the script was a poem, an ode to the poet's adoration of big human butts and his plea to Virya that he would forgive her for all the suffering of life if he got to fuck one before he died. Not because I thought it would ruin the art for her; on the contrary, Ydleth would find that hilarious, and she had a very loud, very shrill laugh. That would be an awfully silly reason to bring Jadrak's minions down on our heads.

"It is cool," I agreed, setting off again. "Hopefully when this is all settled, we'll be on good terms with the goblins and can come admire it at will. Right now we need to focus, though. Gizmit, what's the plan?"

She had given me a thoughtful look at my mention of hopes for future peace, but answered briskly as always. "The geography and architecture of Fallencourt is complicated—you'll see what I mean when we get there. I want to approach it as discreetly as possible and get a view of what's happening there before we move directly to the terminal. Obviously, we are not going to get through this without fighting *somebody*, but I'd prefer to keep things as peaceful as possible."

"Okay, makes sense. You know your way around down here. Biribo, help her find us the quietest, most unoccupied route to wherever she wants to go."

"You got it, boss," he said, buzzing down to hover next to Gizmit. "Left at the next juncture, right? Looks like the tunnels start branching a lot after that. If we take the leftmost corridor that slopes upward, we'll encounter the least traffic."

"You," she said, giving him an appraising look, "are *handy*."

"You're damn right, sister."

I did not expect it to be that simple, because nothing ever is, but somehow things went right for a change. As we progressed through the tunnels, the doorways and actual architecture built into the walls increased in frequency, and there were even lights in the form of luminous fungi cultivated on little ledges. Biribo reported many of the chambers we passed were occupied, but everyone was staying firmly behind their closed doors today. The noise gradually increased as we drew closer to Fallencourt; though its echoes were still too confusing for me to pinpoint any source, it was clear we were approaching the largest concentration of whatever was happening. Gizmit kept us going at a brisk yet cautious pace, frequently diverting down side corridors as Biribo gave warning of groups of goblins ahead, twice even backtracking to evade them.

We couldn't avoid them forever, but we were in unspoken agreement that the longer we put off being discovered and avoided violence, the better.

Then, quite suddenly, a corner we rounded opened up; directly ahead, the tunnel walls to the right disappeared, the light increased dramatically, and I could tell that past this last goblin house, what had been a tunnel suddenly became a ledge.

"Stay back and stay low," Gizmit ordered, then glanced back—and up— at us with a frown. "Well, as low as you can."

We crept to up to the corner and peeked out, me leaning directly over her, and I got my first view of Fallencourt.

Spreading out before my eyes was an absolutely colossal cavern, which was basically an upside-down ravine. The canyon walls extended until they opened up fully to what looked like a kilometer or two in the distance, and exposed this underground city to open sky. What was disorienting to me was that the floor was the ceiling; the canyon walls arched overhead to form a roof adorned with stalactites ranging from the titanic to too tiny to be distinguishable from here, but there was a terrifying lack of any bottom. The open floor just went down, down, until the sloping rock walls of the unthinkably enormous pillar of stone that was the island of Dount met the abyss. Below that, there was only the distant, swirling mists of Ephemera's core, lit by flashes of pink and red luminescence from some unknowable source deep within the fog.

The goblin city had been built here, into every surface. Terraces lined the walls, covered in doors and stone architecture. Many side canyons branched off from the main space, all of them so built up and carved down that they looked more like multilevel streets than natural tunnels from here. Bridges arched between ledges, ramps connected them—and to my horrified fascination, I saw that the bigger stalactites had windows and balconies, apparently having been hollowed out from within.

Though my first reaction was vertigo at the sheer scale of this, I realized it had a lot to do with the fact that it opened onto a seemingly eternal drop into nothing, a sight for which my life on Earth had not prepared me. The buildings and all the goblins present helped contextualize it, and I realized on my second look that Fallencourt was overall not nearly as big as Gwyllthean. Well, the part I could see, at least. Undoubtedly, most of it was buried within the surrounding rock.

And Fallencourt was having a very bad day. There were fires in multiple places, a number of more fragile structures smashed, and unmoving goblins scattered amid the wreckage. That it wasn't teeming with activity was probably just due to the overall smaller population and the fact that everyone who could escape from the center of the chaos already had, but what activity we saw was not encouraging. On two ledges there were massive multigoblin brawls with deadly weapons employed, and dozens of smaller duels and scuffles here and there. I saw three separate goblins giving speeches to gathered crowds, one of which transformed into another battle even as we watched when a rival faction descended on them. Shouts, screams, and crashes echoed deafeningly from the stone walls.

"The acoustics in here are absolutely amazing," I murmured.

"Thinking of giving a speech?" Gizmit asked.

"That's not a bad idea, when things calm down. I was thinking of music, though. Here's a question, Gizmit. It occurs to me that we've had no trouble walking upright down these tunnels, aside from having to duck through one doorway, and a lot of the doors we've seen are big enough that I wouldn't need to. There seems to be more of that here. If Fflyr won't come underground, and goblins are on bad terms with them, why is everything built to human scale?"

Her head was swiveling rapidly, expression intent as she studied the city and the pockets of movement, and for a few seconds I thought she was just ignoring me. She eventually answered, though, without ceasing her focused study of the chaos.

"Everything isn't human-sized, just a lot of the older stuff. Dount is an insignificant backwater *now*, but it has a very long history. Real funny joke the Goddesses played, dumping you and Shinonome off *here* of all places. You'll get it once you start learning some of the history the Fflyr have tried to forget. That's our destination over there."

She pointed at one large nook off to our right, a not-quite-tunnel, which was walled off in the front of a subterranean building with a surprisingly elaborate facade, complete with carved columns and tile mosaics between them. In front of it stood a wide, flat ledge, surrounded on two sides by cave walls and looking out at the great canyon of Fallencourt itself. The building's doors and windows appeared to have been barricaded from the inside, to judge by the trouble the mob of angry goblins in the plaza were having getting in.

"That doesn't look good. Let's move—"

"In a second, but look over there." Gizmit pointed at another side tunnel, a large one and the site of the biggest whirl of activity, which wasn't our target. "That's where trouble's going to come from. That tunnel narrows to a main path that leads to the general area where your boy and his party were last spotted."

"Uh, wasn't Jadrak's main army down that way, too?"

"Exactly, and whatever the Hero has been doing, it looks like the army— to use the term *very* loosely—isn't far from Fallencourt now. See all those armbands and scarves and whatnot? Goblins ostentatiously wearing green are Jadrak's partisans; that's the closest he's got to a uniform right now. Look, lots of injured coming out of there, others putting up improvised barricades nearby. And their overall numbers, way too small to be the main force."

"What're you getting at?"

She looked up at me seriously. "Even with numbers, they're no match for Blessed adventurers; goblins just don't have the armor or weaponry to compete. What the difference in numbers *can* do is force them to go where we want. Standard tactic for dealing with really persistent invaders is to herd them somewhere with a drop into the core and push 'em off. Good odds we're going to see a large group of angry Jadrak supporters push a small group of angry adventurers into Fallencourt and try to finish them here."

"I have the *worst* fucking timing," I muttered. Or, a suspicious voice whispered in the back of my mind, the *best* fucking timing from the perspective of certain string-pulling Goddesses who'd probably love nothing more than to smash me and Yoshi together in the middle of all this chaos. Were they able to manipulate events to such a fine degree? "All right, if we get to Zui, is the tram usable?"

"She took one to get here, but Zui's no engineer. If she crashed it, we've got a very long walk through hostile territory to get back to Sneppit."

"God fucking dammit. Okay, do you know a route closer to the tram station that's less exposed?"

"This way." She turned and darted back up the tunnel. I followed, the rest of my people trotting along with us. "Thanks for the help this far, Biribo, but from here speed matters most, and stealth will be a lost cause anyway when we get there. If we meet goblins decked out in green, attack on sight. Anybody else will flee from six armed tallfolk."

Aster moved up to join me at the front, pulling the greatsword off her back and holding it at her side, facing forward—about the only orientation at which she *could* carry it down here. Nazralind had been right about that thing—it was not the ideal weapon for cramped tunnels. Once we got out into the plaza she'd have room to swing it, but Aster's swing height would just be a mass haircut for that mob. Adelly would probably be more effective with the Lightning Staff . . . except Adelly wasn't wearing artifact armor and would drop like a sack of onions if we got pelted by projectiles. Should I have them switch weapons?

I decided it'd be best if everybody used what they were most familiar with. No matter what we did, this was not going to be pretty.

At least our luck held a few minutes longer; the only goblins we encountered were not of the enemy variety, and just as Gizmit predicted ran from the sight of us in screaming panic. Well, our presence here was no longer discreet, but that was about to not matter.

We got amazingly close to the plaza without having to take one of the exposed exterior paths around Fallencourt. In fact, Gizmit picked a lock and took us through an occupied structure; the scuffling of feet and slamming of doors was the only sign of the inhabitants retreating farther in as we passed through, paying them no mind. Through three rooms and down a hall, she brought us to another door which, we discovered when Gizmit opened it a crack to peek out, emerged directly into the plaza. The doorway was shielded in a small alcove, and the goblins out there were fully occupied, trying to get into the tram station, so they didn't notice the tiny movement immediately.

They'd improvised a battering ram and were hammering on the station's doors; those were apparently barricaded from the inside, but the akorshil planks themselves were badly splintered and about to give way. Zui was out of time, which meant so were we.

And it got worse.

"Boss," Biribo reported, "that goblin leading them, the one in the cloak? He's Blessed with Magic. Not very powerful, but I'd say he's got at least a couple spells."

"Shit," I whispered. "Okay. Aster, do you trust me?"

"You asking that question at a time like this makes me think I shouldn't," she hissed back.

"Just listen. *When* this goes badly, you come out there and back me up. Gizmit, try to get into the station and help Zui once that mob is distracted. Adelly, you're on door guard in case they come at this position; make good use of that staff. Naz, Ydleth, and Madyn, shoot from the doorway as best you can without getting in each other's way. Prioritize keeping them out of the station; Aster and I can take care of ourselves."

"Uh, Lord Seiji, you're beginning to sound alarmingly like you're planning to go out there alone," Nazralind said nervously.

"You always were a smart girl."

"Are you *insane?*" Aster screeched very quietly, a feat which I respected a great deal because I'm always impressed by good vocal control.

"No." I grinned at her, just to see her seethe, and pushed the door open just enough to slip through. "I'm the fucking Dark Lord."

"The second you step out there, you're gonna get bombarded," Gizmit warned.

"Did you not hear me?" I grabbed the handle of my dagger. "I said, *I'm the fucking Dark Lord.*"

Then I drew it from its sheath, vanished from sight, and stepped out into the plaza.

Man, being invisible is neat. I got all the way across the open space to stand at the rear fringes of the crowd without anyone so much as suspecting my presence. There were between fifteen and twenty of them; even up close I couldn't get a more accurate count because they kept teeming around, hammering and prying at the barricaded windows. The din of voices was deafening at this range, though easily sorted into three basic categories—the battering ram crew were chanting in unison to help coordinate their blows on the door, a lot of the rest were generally hollering and bellowing like hooligans, and the Blessed goblin Biribo had indicated was shouting slogans and clearly directing the group.

This one wore green—a stretch of ragged fabric that he'd improvised as a cloak. He was also a lead-from-the-rear type, standing behind the rest of the goblins under his control and encouraging their efforts with the broad gestures and hoarse yelling of someone who was really enjoying his role as rabble-rouser but clearly wasn't very practiced at it.

"That's it—we're almost there! Liberation! VENGEANCE! Soon we'll have the traitors by their ears! All who oppose the Goblin King will burn! Freedom for goblinkind! First Sneppit, then the Fflyr! Keep going, sisters and brothers! *We shall have retribution*!"

That was it, no rhythm or plan to it at all. Poor guy didn't even know how to project his voice—it was noticeably scratchy, no doubt from being overused all morning. Well, Lord Seiji was here to give him a crash course in crowd control.

Stepping up right behind the goblin in charge so that I loomed ominously over him, I drew a deep breath that expanded my lungs to their fullest, slammed the dagger back into its sheath, and projected powerfully from the diaphragm.

"**Ara, ara,** *ara*."

Fuck it, I gotta be me.

I certainly got their attention, between the *very* nice acoustics of this little cul-de-sac and my own very impressive vocal instrument. Goblins scattered, the battering ram was dropped, and the leader's voice broke with an embarrassing squeak as he scurried away from me, only turning around when he could retreat no further, thanks to the press of his followers.

Despite Gizmit's prediction, I was not immediately pelted with projectiles, I suspected only because everybody was too astonished by my arrival. What can I say, I know how to make an entrance.

"And why does goblin turn upon goblin?" I boomed, spreading my arms wide in a gesture of benediction. "In that station are your brothers and sisters—fellow children of Virya, who only disagree with the *means* by which you shall achieve your retribution. They know as well as you who the true enemy is. If you only knew how many allies there are, just waiting to join you—on the surface of Dount and beyond, only waiting to be rallied against those who oppress us *all*."

"I don't know who the *fuck* you are, but you made the mistake of your life coming down here, tallboy," declared the goblin in charge, regaining some of his poise and pointing at me.

It was a passably dramatic point; I could've done better, but I gave the kid credit for amateur effort.

"I," I declared in a ringing voice which overrode him, "am the one who can deliver what the Goblin King can only promise. I can lay waste to your enemies and bring you freedom where he will only lead you to a pointless death. I am Omura Seiji, the Champion of Virya." I grinned wolfishly. "And *you* are going to make me prove it, aren't you?"

They still weren't attacking me, too confused and thrown off their game to know what to do. *Damn*, I'm good.

"Bullshit," the leader scoffed.

"You want to be free of the Fflyr?" I retorted. "To repay blood with blood? Then it starts here, by laying down your arms and not turning your strength against your fellow goblins. You want victory over your oppressors? Then *kneel before the Dark Lord.*"

"Well, you may just be a crazy guy, but you're as good a place to start as any," he scoffed, raising a hand again. It wasn't pointing this time, but held his palm out. Casting posture. "**Fire Lance!**"

I indulged in a smirk while his melted away. Yeah, I felt for the guy. This target-blocking ring of Lady Gray's was some *real* bullshit the first time you found yourself on the wrong end of it. God, I loved it.

"Perhaps you didn't enunciate properly," I said. "Try again. Maybe if you say it louder this time?"

"**Fire Lance!**" the goblin sorcerer shouted, backing up and shoving his followers away in the process, his red eyes growing increasingly wide as his magic failed him again. "**FIRE LANCE!**"

I waited until he gave up in complete panic before speaking again, pitching my voice lower but projecting just as loudly.

"So be it. Those of you who survive, remember, I tried to do this the civil way."

Showtime.

Immolate.

6

In Which the Dark Lord Makes the Call

Unfortunately for this particular gang of Goblin King adherents, their leader had backed up so far into the crowd that he was pressed on three sides. Consequently, when the flames of Immolation took him, a good half a dozen got seared. Instantly, what remained of their attack group dissolved into panic, with goblins bolting in all directions and those nearest the exploding sorcerer howling nearly as loudly as he now was, rolling on the stone floor to put out the flames, which had spread to their clothes.

"**Heal**," I said, for once voicing my spells aloud because I wanted it to be clear what I was doing. "**Heal, Heal, Heal, Heal, Heal**. Anybody else get—ah, there you go. **Heal**. Despite what you may think," I intoned, still projecting at maximum strength and pitching my voice low so it wasn't competing directly with the burning Blessed's shrill howling, "I did not come here to slaughter goblins just trying to get by in the world, but to redirect your focus. As I have said, our real enemy—"

"He killed Fazfer!" somebody rudely shrieked in the middle of my speech.

"Fazfer, is it?" I gave the still-blazing goblin an appraising look; he was now in the fetal stage, the screaming petering out as his lungs and vocal cords were all charcoal. "Relax, he's fine. Or will be, in a minute. As for—"

"Who the *fuck* is Fazufero?" someone else yelled, brandishing a polearm at me, which appeared to be a kitchen knife lashed to a length of metal pipe. "Stop him before he casts that again!"

These little shits were seriously testing my patience.

"Do you *want* to be next?" I asked. "You would already be on fire if that was my intention. *Fazfer* will be fine momentarily; he's just learning what happens to those who are stupid enough to attack the Dark Lord. Jadrak is going to learn the same lesson before this is all over. None of the rest of you need to, unless—"

"DEATH TO THE BUTTS!" screamed the pipe-knife guy, charging at me and swinging it.

Excuse me, what? I was so startled by his inscrutable battle cry I almost let him stab me. I was forced to retreat a step to gain room to whip out my rapier, but once I did that settled the matter. What was a polearm to a goblin wasn't any longer than a human-scale rapier blade, and I was twice his height, giving me the advantage in leverage. I caught the improvised weapon against mine, deftly locked it between the blade and crossbar, and wrenched it out of his grasp.

The disarmed goblin looked amusingly nonplussed by this development, staring down at his suddenly empty hands, but I didn't have time to properly appreciate that before three knives, a hatchet, and a dented metal plate were all hurled at me, the latter in frisbee orientation. And then I made a discovery.

As Biribo had explained it, the Mastery enchantment gave its wielder not only the greatest possible skill with the style of weapon it was applied to, but augmenting them with all the necessary physical strength and agility to get the most out of that skill. With the Rapier of Mastery in my hand, I was essentially a peerless rapier swordsman—and it turned out that among the things a master fencer can do is parry objects flying at his face.

In the span of three seconds, I deftly swatted five projectiles out of the air and had to dive deeper into *showtime* to avoid grinning in sheer satisfaction. Oh, this was *handy*. You don't tend to think of a rapier as having much defensive use, and it wouldn't do anything against arrows—human reflexes do have their physical limits—but from now on, I was going to have it drawn and ready *before* going into a situation in which I expected to have stuff chucked at me. Sure, the amulet protected me from instakills and Heal did the rest, but that approach was painful and also resulted in my clothes being full of holes and bloodstains.

Plus, this looked cool as hell. Even the attacking goblins retreated from me after this display of prowess.

"There, you see?" I pointed the tip of my sword at . . . what was it, Fazfer? The flames were in the process of diminishing, and he was whimpering piteously, but burned skin was regenerating even as we all watched. "Reconsider your approach here, friends. The only thing you can hope to achieve is to press me hard enough that I run out of nonlethal ways to stop you. Don't you think enough goblins have died already?"

Fazfer finally flickered out. He was gasping, whimpering, and his singed clothes emitted wisps of smoke, but he was very clearly alive and whole. The rest were finally quiet and still, at least relatively; the ongoing noise that echoed through Fallencourt now came from behind.

"And *that* is why you don't fuck with the Dark Lord," I informed them. "Your dear King Jadrak? *He* fucked with the Dark Lord, and will learn the price of it. His sole achievement as Goblin King was to attack the *one* person on this island he should not have pissed off. Jadrak's fate is determined. The rest of you?"

Two beats for dramatic weight, and . . .

"That's up to you," I said finally, lowering my voice in both volume and pitch. Then put on a small, cold smile. "Are we going to be friends? Or *are you in my way?*"

The goblins considered their options for a moment.

"*Run for it!*" somebody squealed from several rows back, and apparently that was enough to generate a consensus. In a single mad scramble, the whole pack broke up and skittered off around me to my left. Because, I observed as I turned to watch them go, Aster was approaching from the other direction, artifact greatsword braced across her shoulder and her coat unbuttoned to show off her chain mail.

"This is *not* over, tallboy," Fazfer hissed. Abandoned by his followers and still smoking, he staggered upright and pointed at me. Again, dramatically, but not enough to be impressive. Guy just didn't have the knack. "You may be able to beat *one* little group, but when—"

"Oh hush. You no longer matter here." **Windburst.**

Being flung clear across the plaza and into the wall dazed him for a moment, but when he again stumbled to his feet, his next action was to limp off as fast as his jarred little legs could manage, chasing after his own erstwhile lackeys.

"Okay, so it's pretty loud in here but I'm *positive* I heard that guy yell 'death to the butts,'" said Aster. "What the hell was *that* about?"

"It's a slang term," Gizmit explained, striding past us toward the boarded-up terminal. "What part of you humans do you think is most immediately visible from a goblin's perspective?"

We both blinked at her, for the first time taking proper note of exactly where her eyeline was relative to us.

"Well, then," I said. "I guess I should just be glad they don't call us crotches."

"That one refers to humans who go after goblins sexually," Gizmit called back, already at the door and trying to peek through one of the big cracks. "Zui! You alive in there?"

"And that is why I had Donon stay behind at the tunnel," Aster muttered. "Girls! Form up, we're clear out here. You know, Lord Seiji, I do believe that was the first time you've tried to talk someone down and I didn't end up having to rescue you."

"Shut up, Aster."

The terminal door was opening, with much clattering and grunting from within as somebody dismantled whatever had been barring it shut. Deprived of that support, the abused planks began to give out, and the whole thing partially collapsed to reveal a familiar goblin standing behind it.

"I was gonna ask what the hell you're doing down here, but I guess this sort of explains itself," said Zui, staring past Gizmit at me. "The question now is—OY!"

Gizmit casually slapped her upside the head, causing Zui to back away, protectively clutching her scalp, though not with the complaint I would have expected.

"Not the *hair*, you thug! What's wrong with you?"

"Button it," Gizmit ordered. "Your green ass is gonna be smeared on wyddh when Sneppit's done with you. Of all the over-the-top bullshit, Zui, *this* is your crowning achievement in creating unnecessary work for everybody else!"

"*Lives* were at stake!" Zui shot back, getting right into her face.

Gizmit met her furious stare, profoundly unimpressed, then leaned to one side to look past her into the station. "Speaking of, did you manage to lose anybody?"

"All present and accounted for, Giz," replied a male voice, followed a moment later by another goblin in akornin armor, cradling a weapon, which I had to examine for a second to realize it was a large slingshot. It took me a moment to get down to that, because the shell plates of his armor were dyed a vivid, eye-searing *pink*. "It was looking like a close thing for a minute there, but we're all solid, thanks to Zui and Rhoka."

"You mean, thanks to *me* and the Dark Lord," Gizmit retorted, turning back to Zui. "You hear that? It took the intervention of a *Dark Lord* to fix your mess this time, you—"

"That was surprisingly well-handled," Zui said to me, striding out right past her. She planted her fists on her hips and gave me a contemplative look, having to lean back slightly in the process. "Not what I expected from you, but showing mercy was a smart touch."

"I meant what I said," I replied with a cheerful grin. "I'm down here to finish the shit Jadrak started with me, not to massacre goblins. Oh, and you're welcome, Zui."

"Should've killed the sorcerer, though," Gizmit commented. "Jadrak does not need Blessed working for him; every one of those left alive is gonna bite us on the ass later. Still, good call; mercy is politically and strategically useful right now. All right, *since* you were good enough to bring a tram with you, Zui, we've got our exit. Let's get that barricade rebuilt and fortified so Dap's squad can hold it—"

Zui rounded on her in a fury. "If you think I'm gonna just *leave* them here after—"

"I think you're gonna do as you're *told*, because this time the alternative is doing as you're told while knocked out and stuffed in a sack!"

"Holy shit, Madyn, that goblin's got even bigger bodice bouncers than *you*," Ydleth commented none too quietly, suddenly making me grateful the goblins were too busy arguing to pay attention to this. "Life's just not fair, is it?"

"Hey, I'm happy with my girls; we've been together a long time. Besides, long as we manage not to get killed, I'm coming out ahead just by *seeing* this shit. Finally, I've got a more exciting anecdote than my friend Maelind's donkey story!"

"We don't need to hear that one, Madyn," I interjected. Madyn was an inveterate storyteller, and she had *lots* of anecdotes about this Maelind, who had been her mentor in the oldest profession.

"Oh, don't worry, Lord Seiji, she didn't fuck the donkey."

"Well, that's a relief, but what I *said* was—"

"No, it was two dwarves on a donkey's back."

I decided I would rather get in the middle of the screeching goblin argument, and left a grinning Aster to whip my followers back into line.

"Can you two flirt on your own time, please?" I very courteously requested, immediately cutting off the shouting match and making myself the target of their mutual ire. "I'm anxious to finally meet the great Miss Sneppit, and not just because *we are standing in a war zone right now*. What do you need to get this tram moving?"

"The tram's fine," Zui huffed. "The question concerns who is getting on it, which is *all of us*."

The pink-armored goblin cleared his throat. "If I may? Pleasure t'meet-cha, Lord Seiji. I'm Dap; me an' my team were told to keep this station secured while the trams're shut down due to the, y'know . . . all this bullshit." He gestured vaguely at the chaos of the surrounding city with the hand not holding his slingshot. "Like I tried to tell Miss Zui an' the Arbiter, it's nice of 'em to think of us an' all, but we got contracts with Miss Sneppit. Standing in the way of danger is the whole job. If we was to cut an' run, we'd never work again."

While speaking he had gestured at another approaching goblin who must be the Arbiter, the sight of whom caused me to nearly do a double take. This one was in a trench coat, not unlike Gizmit's, though hers was brown and more visibly battered, and had a broadbrim hat to match. So broadbrim, in fact, that I couldn't see her face at all given the way I towered over her. Between the very fancy-sounding title of Arbiter and the fact that she had bands of purple cloth around both upper arms, I took this to be a figure of some kind of cultural and/or political importance.

Also, probably military, considering her weapon. The Arbiter was carrying what I could only call a mechanical polearm, a tapering metal shaft in multiple segments, which looked like it could be made to collapse or fold in on itself, with heavier sections at both ends that appeared to house some kind of machinery. One had grooves and little levers on it, the other a wide slot on the top from which emerged a tapering blade the length of my shin. Unlike the mostly improvised weapons of the rioting goblins I'd seen so far, this thing looked polished and precision-engineered.

"Arbiter, huh," I said by way of greeting. "What's your story?"

The brown-clad goblin casually rested her polearm against one shoulder and neither responded nor lifted her head enough that I could see her eyes, though I did not miss the way she adjusted her posture to keep my own weapon in view.

"That's just Rhoka," Gizmit said dismissively, "the only person who's gonna be in more trouble than Zui over this. Ignore her."

"Boss, we got incoming," Biribo reported. "Correction, incoming *fast*. They're not headed for this position exactly, but there's a major kerfuffle on its way out of the side tunnels, uncomfortably close. Situation in the city's gonna get hotter in a few seconds."

Everybody shifted position around us with commendable efficiency, starting to move before he finished speaking and creating a defensive line faster than I could respond. Dap's security team, a total of eight goblins in matching pink armor—which I was struggling not to find hilarious—were armed with those slingshots that had interesting designs which fastened onto their forearms and could be fired one-handed. They also had riot shields—metal ones—and placed themselves in an arc in front of the group, with Aster and Arbiter Rhoka holding the ends. Nazralind nocked an arrow to her shortbow, and Ydleth and Madyn raised crossbows, positioning themselves behind the security goblins and leaving me at the rear with Adelly, Zui, and Gizmit.

"I can't see anything," Zui complained, then dodged as Gizmit aimed a desultory kick at her shin.

Then, one level down from us and barely a block away, Yoshi and his team came charging out of a side tunnel.

They didn't seem to be doing too badly, at a glance. Out of breath, sure, but I observed no visible major injuries; all of them were at least somewhat splattered with blood, but there was no telling whose, and they were definitely moving more adroitly than people who'd lost a lot of vital fluids. The priestess girl, Pashilyn, was in robes, and Amell, the alchemist, in sturdy work clothes, but the rest had on armor. Yoshi, I saw, was in chain mail and leather that was either mundane or one of those extremely low-power artifacts, which were all he could probably make at this point, but the shield and arming sword he carried had the telltale glow of significant artifacts.

Also, wow, he'd lost weight. He was stocky, yeah, but nowhere near the pile of pudge I remembered from just a few months ago. Life on Ephemera would do that to a growing boy.

"**Firecracker**!" Pashilyn shouted, turning and throwing out a palm back toward the tunnel from which they'd come. "**Firecracker**! **Firecracker**!" Each cast produced a ball of sparks which didn't look *too* impressive, but hit the ground and bounced forward several times before erupting in a burst of flames that scattered the goblins who were pursuing them.

Damn, I wanted *that* spell. Not much on its own, but imagine what I could combine it with . . .

"That is *not* where you said they'd be coming out, Gizmit," I complained. "You made us wait while you made a whole big deal about how Jadrak's army had them pinned down that *other* tunnel, way the fuck over there."

"And Jadrak's people are still congregated down there," Gizmit said, peering around from behind Aster to examine the battlefield. "Hmph. Those clever bastards evaded the pincer and flanked them. When did they suddenly get competent?"

"It doesn't surprise me that adventurers are more skilled at violence than investigation," Zui said in a voice full of tension. "We need to leave. Now. *Everyone.*"

"Zui, hon, I love ya, but we got a job to do," said Dap from the shield wall without turning to face her.

They weren't going to move until this was settled, were they . . . "Why's this important?" I asked aloud. "What's the worst-case scenario if Jadrak's forces take the tram station?"

"Is that a serious question?" Gizmit demanded. "They have access to the whole tram network, including a straight line back to Sneppit's HQ."

"That's bullshit and you know it," Zui snapped. "There's a thousand ways to get into those tunnels, and if we take the tram and *leave*, they can't do anything but walk there, which'll take twenty times as long! Also, half those tunnels run over impassable drops that can't even be traversed without a tram."

"The station itself is still an important asset," said Dap, eyes still forward. "It's defensible, it's got stores of parts and fuel and tools to service the trams, *and* it's a perfect staging area to launch an operation into Fallencourt from the tunnels. If Jadrak's people take it, they can fuck up the tracks and make it impossible to bring a tram *back* here. That's worth defending."

"It's not as important as your *lives!*" Zui shouted, and this time I could hear the frustration and anguish cracking beneath her anger.

"I'd hate to find out whether that's true on paper," Dap commented with a grin. "But it's Miss Sneppit who tallies up those numbers, not us. We got a contract, and we got our orders. We're security, Zui; all of us are covered by risk of life and limb clauses, *and* you know Miss Sneppit pays out life insurance when the worst happens on duty."

"Retreat while we argue, please," Gizmit requested, already stepping backward toward the terminal doors. The rest of the group began shuffling along with her.

"Uh, I realize those guys are technically our enemies," said Nazralind, still watching Yoshi and company performing a fighting retreat along the level below us, "but they seem kind of . . . screwed. Should we do something about that?"

We were far from the only parties to have noticed their dramatic entrance. The main group of Jadrak's army had come boiling out of the tunnel Gizmit had indicated earlier, and were heading right toward the heroes. As armies went, it wasn't impressive—ramshackle weapons, little to no armor, no sign of any Blessed, and definitely no organization or leadership. No wonder the adventurers had outmaneuvered them; this was just a mob with a nominally shared ideology. But it was a mob hundreds strong.

"The enemy of my enemy," Aster commented quietly.

"Also, they're *right* between us and those angry goblins," added Adelly. "If they go down, we're next."

"Not if we *leave*," Gizmit exclaimed in exasperation. "They will be fine—they're all Blessed, they brought their own alchemist so they're all buffed up on potions, and one of them is the *Hero*. Let them buy us time; at least they'll be *useful* for once in their lives."

I suspected I wasn't the only one who could see at a glance that that wasn't true. The adventurers had been fighting in tunnels, where five people could easily fend off hundreds, especially if the five had a massive edge in firepower. Right before our eyes, they were floundering as they came under a hail of projectiles from higher ledges and bridges, and found they didn't even have enough bodies to make a defensive formation in the wider space they now occupied. The army was closing on them fast . . .

"Think we should let them into the terminal?" Dap asked, sounding dubious about his own idea. "Us, defensible structure, *and* a Hero party? We could actually hold it."

"They won't work with you," said Gizmit. "Two of them are Fflyr nobility, and the rest are King's Guild. Goblins are vermin to them."

"You!" I looked over at Zui's sudden movement, finding her pointing up at me. "*You're* the Dark Lord! You can order the team to retreat with us!"

"I, uh . . ."

"Lord Seiji does *not* have authority over Miss Sneppit's personnel," Gizmit shot back with a hard edge to her tone. "You of all people should respect that, Zui."

"This contract you have," Arbiter Rhoka said suddenly, and I whipped around to stare at her in surprise. I still couldn't see her face, but her voice was *young*. Goblins had higher-pitched voices in general, but from the sound of it, I was pretty sure she was a teenager. "It has a standard acts of the Goddesses clause?"

"Uh, yeah?" Dap replied, nonplussed. "That's boilerplate."

Rhoka's wide hat shifted as she nodded once. "The orders of a Dark Lord are an unusually literal case, but Champions of Virya or Sanora *are* living acts of the Goddesses, by definition. It's an old precedent, obviously; there's been no opportunity for it to come up in arbitration in centuries. But it stands."

"*Really.*" Dap finally took his eyes off the fighting for just a moment to look at me.

So did everyone else.

"Lord Seiji," Gizmit grated, "Zui's soft heart is an asset in its way, but this is an example of why *Sneppit* is in charge instead of her. Sometimes you have to make sacrifices to achieve goals."

"This is *not a strategic sacrifice!*" Zui retorted, directing herself to me instead of Gizmit. "Holding the station is impossible with eight people and not worth the cost of their lives!"

"Sneppit knows more about the situation than you, and gave her orders."

"She doesn't know what it's *like* out here! Who could have imagined that mob?"

Of all the fucking bullshit, at a time like *this* they had to shove an impossible moral dilemma into my lap! How the fuck was *I* supposed to know what was strategic or ethical here? If I was actually competent at running an army, I'd have conquered at least Gwyllthean by now! Couldn't these people just do their own fighting and call for me when they needed a dramatic spectacle or a big show of force?

"I . . . I don't . . ."

"Whatever we're going to do, we need to do *now,*" Aster interjected loudly. "Look, there they go."

The front ranks of Jadrak's goblins hit the Hero's party, and that whole situation went right straight to shit.

"**Force Bolt!**" Yoshi's voice shouted desperately, dispatching a blast of pure kinetic energy into the leading cluster of attackers and dispersing them, and then sweeping aside a much wider swath with his next. "**Force Wave!**" More spells I wanted. Pashilyn hurled more Firecrackers into the throng, then shouted a spell called Light Barrier which, true to the name, created a glowing wall of translucent golden light across the path in front of them, blocking off the attack. From behind the front line, Amell hurled a bottle of something— some kind of fancy magical Molotov cocktail, to judge by the explosion that resulted when it hit the ground and devastated the oncoming forces.

Fuck me, they were actually doing it.

For about three seconds. The goblins just didn't stop coming, and Pashilyn half collapsed as her Light Barrier shattered under the sheer press of bodies.

The three physical fighters rallied valiantly. Yoshi's sword and shield made for a solid defensive posture, and the two flanking him had reach—Flaethwyn with her Rapier of Mastery, with the same enchantment as mine, so I knew how potent it was—and Raffan jabbing with his artifact spear. The three of them simply could not hold that much territory, though, no matter their reach. In seconds they were being surrounded—

No, I saw; not surrounded, but flanked. The goblins pressed forward against the left wall of houses and storefronts, pushing the heroes toward the opposite side of that ledge, and I remembered Gizmit coldly explaining how goblins got rid of persistent interlopers.

There was no lower level beneath that ledge, just a drop of thousands of kilometers toward Ephemera's core.

These were enemies. They were buying us time. I should just leave them. Yoshi was a dumb kid who didn't deserve this, but . . . he'd chosen to be here. I remembered how *eager* he'd been, when Sanora appeared before us.

This was none of my business. It *wasn't my fault.*

The spearman stumbled, shoved out of formation by two goblins who'd ducked inside his weapon's reach. He was pushed against the rail—a barrier chest-high on a goblin, and little more than a tripping hazard for a human.

"*RAFFAN!*" Yoshi's cracked scream of pure agony was a spear through me as the first of his friends tumbled into the abyss.

Fuck it.

I vaulted over the heads of Sneppit's security team, rapier in hand, and dashed headlong toward the edge, then along it, veering to the side just as I came abreast of the Hero's desperate last stand. Cursing my own fucking stupidity and desperately hoping somebody decided to come back me up, I leaped off and into the middle of the Goblin King's army.

7

In Which the Dark Lord Cleans Up

A *proper* isekai'd Dark Lord would probably be some kind of military history otaku, someone who could take a bunch of bandits and use his armchair knowledge of medieval warfare to turn them into a real, effective army. Actually, from the tidbits I'd picked up, I think that might've been Yomiko's backstory. It was not mine. I haven't even read *Art of War* in its entirety; it's awfully dry. I don't know any military history because history bores me to the point of coma. Too many droning teachers and context-less lists of dates and names coming up through the school system left me rebellious at even the *thought* of studying history. What I liked were the stories—the interesting ones, the ones where it's most dubious that they even happened at all, because very little that's actually interesting ever does.

Musashi and his oar, Scipio sailing to Africa, Kongming playing his guqin atop the walls. Ironic twists and dramatic reversals, the stuff real wars are *not* made of. Real war is brief episodes of traumatic brutality to enliven what is otherwise the only thing more tedious than sitting in history class.

Later, when I was justifying my current insane bullshit to myself, I would inevitably think of Chamberlain's Charge, my favorite anecdote from the American Civil War. Colonel Chamberlain had been assigned the defense of a hilltop upon which hinged the entire flank of the Union army; he *could not* relinquish it, or the battle would be lost. Hard-pressed by the Confederates, his troops were whittled down to a skeleton crew, and eventually, entirely ran out of ammunition. They were about to be overrun.

He could not retreat, and could not hold his ground. So Chamberlain did the only other thing possible. He attacked. Outnumbered and practically disarmed, his few remaining men charged bayonets-first into gunfire.

And they *won*, capturing the Confederate forces in front of them who, like Sima Yi retreating from Zhuge Liang, surrendered because they smelled a nonexistent trap. Because surely no military commander could possibly be doing something as pants-on-head stupid as what Chamberlain was doing; there had to be a hidden danger.

I learned that day that in the heat of the moment, Colonel Chamberlain didn't think himself as clever as I and generations of historians retelling that story gave him credit for. He was just desperate, terrified shitless, and cursing himself for the stupidity of doing what was right instead of anything that made a goddamn lick of sense. Or, who knows, maybe he was thinking something completely different; the man had been dead for over a century by the time of Seiji's Charge. Maybe when I got to hell I'd ask him.

Should be any minute now.

I didn't so much hit the ground as land on top of a bunch of people, which, of course, wasn't optimal. Trying to surprise crowd-surf on a hostile mob is one of those suicidally stupid things that I only got away with thanks to bullshit cheat magic, in this case my Surestep Boots, which it turned out ensured me perfect footing on *any* surface, including the heads and shoulders of a bunch of goblins who immediately wanted me dead.

I'd run past Yoshi and company before jumping; they were now off to my right, busy being overrun by the crowd underneath me. In the second and a half it took me to position myself properly, I was bludgeoned three times and stabbed once, but then I got the angle right and cast **Windburst**.

Downward at a steep angle and toward the gap. Being close to the ground but suspended off it, this was enough to send me airborne again, but I had taken the precious seconds to get the angle right, so instead of flinging myself into space, I was instead hurtled backward to slam against the wall of the ledge off which I'd just jumped.

That hurt.

Obviously, I instantly cast **Heal** on myself and was ready to rock by the time my boots hit the ground.

More importantly, the Windburst had just made a complete wreck of the part of the mob that was trying to push the Hero party off the ledge, flinging quite a few of them into space, to judge by the rapidly fading screams. I cast it again, then again, and again, chaining Windbursts and forcibly creating a space around myself—*between* the main body of Jadrak's army and Yoshi's team. They were still partially encircled, but Yoshi and Flaethwyn were now making short work of the goblins in front of them with their swords, and

Pashilyn had put another Light Barrier up to prevent the flankers from continuing to push them toward the edge. That left a smaller group of around ten goblins who, seconds ago, had been the leading edge of the charge suddenly isolated between a wall, the Hero's party, and a surprise Dark Lord.

They did what most would do in that scenario and attacked with renewed frenzy. That barrier began flickering immediately as it was hammered with weapons; Pashilyn looked like she was about to lose consciousness.

"**Heal, Heal, Heal, Heal!**" Casting out loud to ensure everybody knew what was happening, I brought Yoshi and company back up to fighting shape. He and Flaethwyn had both taken hits and needed it; Amell looked fine and I suspected Heal wouldn't do much for whatever kind of magical fatigue Pashilyn was suffering, but it was worth a shot considering how little time and effort it cost me. "Crush that group before they can rally! I've got the front!"

After bellowing my instructions, I turned to face the oncoming crowd of goblins without waiting to see whether they obeyed. Barely in time, too; goblins might be as strong as humans magically, but they still only *weighed* half as much, and that sequence of Windbursts had tossed them like a salad. But there were still hundreds more, and the nature of a mob is that its inertia is not blunted that easily. I barely had time to cast again before the swarm was on me.

This was even worse than the slaughter in Cat Alley. Goblins in CGI are all mercifully copy-pasted from one base model. *These* were just . . . townsfolk. I could see their faces, see the horribly relatable fury and terror of people desperately protecting their home from an invader—in this case, me. I could see the way they dressed, how they wore similar styles to the Fflyr, each outfit probably stitched from castoff human scraps but made with care and individualized in a way that made sense, given the art I'd seen in these tunnels. It was howling, raging chaos, and I blessedly didn't have time to focus on any particular face, but even amid that I could tell.

Just people.

Windburst, Windburst, Windburst, Windburst!

I desperately bought space, but now I was trying to fight the full inertia of a charging mob channeled along one narrow ledge, one spell at a time. It wasn't working. I had to rapidly give ground and in seconds found myself alongside Flaethwyn as they retreated. At least they seemed to have managed to do something about the goblins who'd flanked them, or so I earnestly hoped; otherwise, I was about to get shanked in the back.

Apparently so, as this brought me even with Yoshi, and having done whatever they did to the other enemies, he was now able to direct his focus forward again. Having me out of the way opened up his options.

"Force Wave! Force Wave!"

That was an even more effective crowd-clearer than my Windburst. The two of us hammered the oncoming front line with spells, blunting the charge until goblins actually began to pile up on top of each other in front of us. We all three wielded swords when they got too close; I could tell that Yoshi only sort of knew what he was doing with his arming sword and shield combo, but with Rapiers of Mastery, Flaethwyn and I were like surgeons, precisely dispatching any goblin unlucky enough to stumble too far forward.

It wasn't enough.

Even when Pashilyn began throwing Firecrackers from behind, we were still being pushed back, and the most control we could exercise over our course was to prevent them, barely, from shoving us over the edge again. There was a ramp up to the next level where the tram station was, but it was angled the other way, and maneuvering to get up it with a mob forcing us every step was going to be a nightmare.

"That's the one!" a voice screeched above the din, and lo and behold, there was my old buddy Fazfer, about twenty meters deep in the crowd and apparently being hoisted aloft on the shoulders of his fellows. And, once again, pointing at me. **"Fire Lance!"**

Nothing happened, obviously. Guy just didn't learn. I'd have Slimeshotted him, but I couldn't spare the attention from the barrage of Windbursts. They were all that kept us from being overrun.

Unfortunately, he *did* learn.

"Fire Lance!" The next yell sent a shrieking spear of fire directly at Yoshi. He brought his shield up, but it looked like—

"Light Barrier!"

The barrier got up in time, but it was weaker than the others. Exhaustion was taking its toll on Pashilyn. The glowing wall shattered on impact, weakening but not stopping the spell. At least Yoshi caught it against his shield, but the force sent him stumbling backward.

Fazfer's crow of triumph was cut off by an arrow taking him right in the mouth.

The onslaught was beginning to slow, and I finally saw why as they rushed past us overhead; along the ledge I'd jumped down from, an entire row of ranged attackers were in place, hammering the mob from above. All eight of Sneppit's security crew were deploying those slingshots of theirs, which fired plum-sized balls of iron covered in spikes and made a *nasty* mess of whoever they hit at that range. Adding to that was Ydleth and Madyn's crossbow fire and Nazralind methodically picking off high-value targets as she identified them, including the sorcerer.

Then a blur charged between Flaethwyn and me from behind, coat flaring to reveal the flash of her artifact chain mail.

Aster brought that huge greatsword up and then down as soon as she was past us, dropping to one knee to skid along the ground toward the goblins and whipping the entire thing in a vast horizontal swipe at what would be just under waist height on a human. The length of that weapon meant her full-armed slash carved an arc nearly the entire width of the ledge, and she did it with the full force of her own forward charge backing up the sword's weight.

Blood fountained and heads flew as the entire front three ranks of the goblin charge were guillotined right in front of us.

That finally did it. An angry mob these goblins might be, but they were no soldiers, just folks whipped into a frenzy. They'd been hammered back by constant spellfire, peppered by sniping from above, and suddenly there was a new element that simply took them down like so much wheat before the scythe.

Aster adjusted her stance, preparing to flow into another mass-slaughtering swipe, but she paused as the attacking mob finally broke in front of us. They stumbled, slipping on blood and tripping over corpses; it wasn't an even retreat as the crowd took time to fully reverse its direction, but we were finally able to *stop*.

Even the archers above ceased once it was clear the attack had broken. We stood our ground, weapons up and gasping for breath, but we no longer had to defend ourselves as we watched our erstwhile attackers turn and flee.

That was how the battle ended; no sudden signal, just a sequence of reversals that took their momentum and eventually turned it backward. Trailing to a halt atop a pile of corpses and leaving us catching our breath, half-crazed with adrenaline and no longer having anything to stab.

I was looking at utter devastation. Bodies, *pieces* of bodies, and everywhere the stench. Not just of blood. That was something stories don't tell you about battlefields—the omnipresent stink of shit. Corpses don't have bowel control, and it wouldn't matter if they did when they died from the application of edged weapons to their internal organs. This entire ledge was splattered in blood and worse, like it'd been hosed down.

A few hours ago, this had been a street. People just living and working here. Probably at least some of the people now strewn across it in pieces.

So much for making peace with the goblins. Nobody was going to hear any good intentions out of me after *this*. Why had I even done this? Yoshi and his idiot friends weren't my problem or my responsibility. They were part of the very mechanism I was fighting to break, a political machine that sent him down here to keep these goblins oppressed and frightened in their own homes. And what credit did I even deserve for this "victory"? I was no Chamberlain, certainly no Kongming. Nobody would ever praise the tactical genius of Dark Lord Seiji. I'd only gotten away with this because a bored, demented Goddess turned me into a walking weapon.

So pointless. All of it.

Maybe it was the adrenaline ebbing away, but suddenly I was aware of sounds I hadn't been conscious of a second ago. Groans, weeping . . . And now that I looked, I could see movement among the bodies.

"Be careful," Aster urged as I stepped forward, hand upraised. I didn't acknowledge her, just focusing on the first goblin I could see who was still alive. He looked middle-aged, his spiky black hair beginning to be peppered with gray. Lying half on his side and staring glassy-eyed at the ceiling, gasping desperately in short wet gurgles. The neat hole of a rapier stab wound was just below his collarbone; the thrust had missed his heart, but his lungs were filling with blood.

"Heal."

I stepped carefully through the carnage, viscera squelching around my fancy artifact boots with every step. There were more dead than dying, and only a couple here and there trying to crawl away who seemed like they might have made it on their own. I cast **Heal** and moved on, not waiting to see their reactions.

This wasn't like the mad dash through Cat Alley in the aftermath of the battle there; I couldn't just cast it on everybody I saw. Of this I was harshly reminded when I Healed a goblin who had lost an arm to the greatsword swipe; the spell stopped him from bleeding out, but his arm was still gone. I did not look him in the eyes, just looked at another softly weeping goblin who was just a trailing mess of wet organs from below her ribs. I looked, and turned away, leaving her to die. I could Heal that, and condemn her to a much slower, more painful death as one third of a person missing a lot of vital bodily functions. I wouldn't be that cruel even if I'd hated her.

The triage got much easier once I was past the residue of Aster's great finishing move; nobody else had been hit by anything powerful enough to separate them from their vitals that way. I paused at one twitching man whose skull was half caved in and brains leaking onto the floor behind him, the spiked iron ball still embedded there, and then moved on without condemning him to life as a vegetable. The spell would fix what was still in the remains of his head—I'd seen it do so—but he'd lost way too much. Better to spend seconds that way than years.

Aster stayed at my side, stone-faced but eyes gleaming with unshed moisture, while I did what I could. It didn't take long; scarcely a minute later I was meters away from the other humans, looking around for more targets.

"See anybody else?" I asked quietly. Aster just shook her head.

"Why?"

I turned back to look at the young woman I had just Healed after pulling a crossbow quarrel out of her chest. She had one hand over the spot, glaring up at me with her reddish-purple eyes squinting in suspicious confusion.

So were the other . . . fourteen goblins I had Healed. Just fourteen that I could save. Well, most of them; a few were quietly sobbing over fallen friends. The rest were staring at me, clearly unsure what I might do next. Nobody had tried to flee yet, nor attacked.

I turned back to the speaker, the only one who had been brave enough to address me.

"I am the Dark Lord." I spoke without passion, with barely any inflection, just projecting enough that I could be sure they'd all hear me. "And I didn't come here to slaughter goblins. Listen to me very carefully. *I will kill whoever I need to.* But I don't *want* to kill anyone, and I will not harm anyone who doesn't make it necessary. Your king decided to attack me and mine, and for that, the punishment is death. The Goblin King will *die*, and so will anyone who gets between us. You had better decide whether that includes you."

With that statement, I turned and walked back to the others, paying the fallen goblins no further attention. Probably would've served me right if one of them shot me in the back with something, but nobody tried.

"Stop him!" Zui's voice suddenly shouted, and I lifted my head from watching the ground so I didn't slip in blood to see Yoshi charging for the edge, where there was nothing but an endless fall into the core.

Flaethwyn was closest and moved to block his way, helpfully shouting "Are you crazy?!" Yoshi roughly shoved her aside, and she staggered backward, looking utterly flabbergasted that he would dare.

I was *not* closest but moved into a run, slipping briefly on the blood before I caught my balance and managed to intercept him. The rest of his party, despite being nearer, were no help; Amell was a weeping mess on the ground, and Pashilyn swayed on her feet, looking confused and half-catatonic. Aster continued to follow me but did not get in the way as I managed to grab Yoshi's arm and stop him from lunging at the too-short barrier.

"Let go!" he insisted, trying to shrug me off. "Raffan could still be—"

"There's nothing to grab, kid," Gizmit said helpfully from somewhere behind us. "It's pure drop."

"You don't know that! I have to try, he could have . . ."

"Yoshi." The new voice was high-pitched and quiet, and I was confused for a moment until Yoshi's little familiar buzzed into view in front of us, a cute pixie-like creature with butterfly wings and, currently, a sad expression. "There's . . . Nobody is clinging nearby. It's a sheer drop; everyone who fell is . . . gone. I'm so sorry."

"But . . ." I could see on his face that nobody was getting through. His eyes were wide and constantly turning toward the gap, refusing to focus on any of us. "I can't just— You don't abandon your friends! If I could just—"

"YOSHI!" I seized him by the collar with both hands and jerked him back and forth until he focused on me. "*You. Are going. To lose people*! There's not a *thing* you can do about that. This whole world is built on bloodshed and foolishness; there's something horrible behind every shadow. It will happen behind your back where you never had a chance to help, and right in front of you while you *still* can't do a damn thing to stop it. And when the shit's still going down and there's work still to do, it *doesn't fucking matter*. Do your crying later when you're alone. As long as people are counting on you, you don't *get* to be weak. You are not *allowed* to break in front of your people. So long as they need you, you *keep. Moving. Forward*."

I ran out of things to say. Yoshi was staring at me—gaping, in fact. Amid the distant sounds of yelling and violence still echoing through the cavern, I could hear much closer the soft buzz of two sets of wings, our respective familiars hovering nearby and saying nothing.

Belatedly, I realized I had slumped forward while shaking Yoshi until I was half leaning on him, using my grip on his coat to prop myself up. I straightened, released him, and stepped back.

Everybody was staring at us.

After a second, Yoshi drew in a breath, closed his eyes, let it out, and nodded once. Then opened them again, and just like that, he was back with us.

"Right. Thanks, Omura."

I just nodded back, turning to sweep a look around our environs. Because obviously I should scan for threats, *not* because I suddenly felt awkward about anything.

"Don't touch me!" someone suddenly shrieked, and I swiveled to see Amell staggering away from Zui, who'd just approached her. "Get away, monster!"

The goblin's expression closed down, and she dropped her outstretched hand. Behind her, Gizmit rolled her eyes.

I sympathized with them. Honestly, I was surprised Zui had been trying to help Amell up, or show her any consideration at all. What would be the point?

Aster was looking at me, and I had a sudden memory that suggested maybe Zui understood more about life than I did.

Whenever you can, be kind.

"They're just people, Amell," I said. "Monsters, maybe, but no more than anybody else. You could see carnage like this in any country on this world with no goblins involved. People *are* monsters, and goblins are just people. This is *their* home; they belong here, not us. What would you do if someone invaded your home like this?"

The alchemist drew in a shuddering breath. Her face was a mess; streaked with snot and tears and lightly splattered with blood just for emphasis. Her eyes cut to me, then back to Zui, then over at the gory battlefield behind us, and she took another shuffling step backward.

"I don't seem to be helping here," I muttered. "Yoshi, could . . ."

"Yeah. Amell's a good person, Omura, it's just . . . It has been a lot." He stepped past me, lowering his voice and saying something quiet to Amell as he approached her.

Spotting movement, I shifted again to see the surviving goblins I'd just Healed trickling away. While I watched them, the girl who'd been the last caught my gaze and held it. She reached up, pulled off her green armband, then turned and walked away, dropping it in the blood.

Well. That was . . . something, I guess.

"Hey, Lord Seiji," called Madyn from the ledge above. "I think you should see this. Catch!"

She was holding up a long, thin object; I stepped over to stand underneath and she dropped it into my waiting hands. It was an arrow. Specifically, a beautiful spiraling missile that gleamed like platinum but was light as aluminum, currently half-covered in blood. I'd seen its like once before.

"Are you *fucking* kidding me," I growled. "Seriously? Of all the bullshit I do *not* fucking need."

"I can't believe you just *dropped* an arrow on him," Nazralind was exclaiming up above, interrupted midrant by Aster.

"Madyn! Where did you get that?"

"It was in a goblin who fell off the next ledge above us," Madyn called down to her. "Had a green scarf and a slingshot. Not a fancy one like our friends here, but she had several of those scary metal death balls with the spikes. I think she was gonna shoot at either us or you guys down below, but somebody sniped her first."

"Seems we have another ally down here," Aster said quietly to me.

"*This* idiot has already gotten enough of our people killed," I hissed back. "There are allies we don't need, Aster."

"Do you really want to talk about whose fuckups have gotten how many people killed?" she retorted, still keeping her voice low. "*I* don't. None of us would come out of that looking good. Here and now . . . Don't you think it's weird none of us got shot in the middle of that fight, despite being surrounded on all sides by ledges and overhangs and bridges and windows? This whole place is a sniper's paradise and it's full of hostiles. *Somebody* took them out before they could take any of *us* out. I'm inclined to start forgiving our shady dark elf friend, based on today alone."

"She ain't wrong, boss," Biribo commented. "The dark elf will be more desperate than ever to win points with you, after their efforts with the cat tribe backfired. You should think about *letting* them help. If they get to feeling confident enough to come out and talk to us, you can hopefully start giving them orders and not have to deal with their . . . improvising."

They had a point, much to my annoyance. Considering the repercussions of this elf's antics, I was not in a rush to forgive. But . . . my advisors were right. She or he had quite likely just saved at least a few more of my people from snipers.

I sighed in annoyance, then nodded grudgingly and stepped forward out of the blood and mess, leaving red tracks behind me as I rejoined the others, where they'd regrouped up ahead.

"We need to get the hell out of here," I stated, raising my voice to address everyone present. "We've secured an exit, and a route to rendezvous with somebody who can provide information, resources, and a defensible position. From there, we can figure out a way to take out the Goblin King and put an end to all this insanity. You coming with, Yoshi?"

"Come with *you*?" scoffed Flaethwyn, who notably had not been addressed. "You, and a bunch of these scurrying little . . . Just how stupid do you think we are?"

I could spend the rest of the day answering that question and showing my work. I could draw them charts, and compose a musical mnemonic to aid in retention. Right at the moment, though, taking Flaethwyn down a well-deserved peg was an extremely low priority.

"He just saved us, Flaethwyn," Pashilyn snapped. "*Again.*"

I gave her a wary look. On our previous encounter, I had pegged Lady Pashilyn as the most composed member of the group. Right now, though, she looked like a woman on the ragged edge of cracking. Understandably, considering . . . everything. Flaethwyn was too taken aback by the rebuke to keep flapping her yap, which was all we needed for now.

"Well, it's not as if I can force you," I said. "If you *want* to stay here fighting random goblins and getting picked off one by one while Jadrak is off doing who knows what evil bullshit, that's your prerogative. We're withdrawing to plan his end. Come along if you're coming."

I turned and walked toward the ramp that led back up to the tram station, my own people falling into step with me or trotting along the ledge above.

"Come on," Yoshi said curtly from behind me, and one at a time, four sets of feet started moving after us.

It was a start.

8

In Which the Dark Lord Gets Taken for a Ride

All the awkward silence of walking away from an emotionally draining experience with unfriendly strangers, plus the tension and fear of a loud city in the grip of multiple simultaneous riots, mostly involving people who would kill us if they thought they could. Yeah, the short walk back to the tram station had it all.

Aster stepped closer to me, leaned her head in, and spoke in a voice low enough that probably only the goblins and familiars could overhear.

"You remember when I told you to be kind whenever you could?"

I managed not to flinch. "What of it?"

"You are *really* bad at it."

I abruptly stopped and began turning on her with a scowl, but Aster smiled and took my arm, gently urging me back into motion.

"But," she continued just as softly, "you have never stopped trying. I just wanted you to know I see it. And it makes all the difference. Please keep it up."

Well. Less angering, but somehow not any less awkward. I deflected, because what the hell else is a guy supposed to do in that situation?

"You know, this isn't getting you any closer to my bed."

"Please." She dropped my arm. "Bitch, I could have you if I wanted you. And by the way, stop opening discussions by setting people on fire. I'm just a lowborn girl from a farm, but even *I* know that's not how diplomacy works."

Despite everything, I found a reason to grin. After the last few minutes, it was a relief.

We had just crested the ramp, rejoining the goblins and my people on the upper level, when Flaethwyn suddenly gasped.

"Who are *you*?"

I glanced back and found that she had finally noticed Nazralind, and seemed absolutely dumbfounded.

"Who, me?" Naz said lightly. "Just Conzart out picking hedge berries."

"Ah. Well . . ." Flaethwyn let out an uncomfortable little titter, which was still a happier sound than I'd have thought her capable of making. "I guess we're all Quaelisco's jailers down here, anyway. I just hope not to end up holding the wooden key."

"Once the pure moon rises, everybody's a smidge hunter," Nazralind agreed in a tone that managed to be both solemn and noncommittal.

"Y'know what I really appreciate about Naz and the girls?" Adelly mumbled, coming up on my other side. "They usually don't do *that* in front of other people." Aster and I nodded in agreement.

Dap pulled ahead of the group and darted into the tram station before us with three of his armored security goblins, leaving four accompanying us outside. Glancing back, I noted with amusement that he'd quietly stationed them in a loose box around the Hero's party, well out of arm's reach. The targets of this formation seemed not to have noticed; Flaethwyn was stubbornly ignoring the goblins, and the other three looked like they were barely holding it together.

"Still clear!" Dap called, poking his head out.

"Were you worried?" I asked.

"Not specifically, Lord Seiji, but it's a chaotic situation and this structure was absent our control for several minutes. Always gotta check in a case like that."

"Fair enough; I can see you know your work."

The pink-armored goblin beamed with pride, and I found myself wondering about Miss Sneppit's management style. Her people seemed extremely competent, but . . . Dap was hungry for approval, and Zui—who was clearly close to Sneppit herself—felt the need to disobey her orders over this.

It was worth thinking about.

The tram station was clearly not one of the older structures Gizmit had mentioned; its facade was Western neoclassical to me. I could tell because the door was goblin-sized; we all had to duck, and in some cases crouch, to get in. That door was actually more of a tunnel, revealing that the outer wall was probably thick enough to have withstood any siege had they managed to hold the doorway itself. Dap and company helpfully pushed the remnants of their makeshift barricade out of the way as they entered, so us tallfolk didn't have to struggle too much to get through, aside from hunching over.

Inside it was both alien and bizarrely familiar. Once you have seen a train station, you've kind of seen them all; they're all unique in their own way, but there is a limit to how much variation can be introduced without messing up the thing's essential functions. Tracks, platform, ticket office, vendor stalls, benches. Yep, this was a train station. Despite being abandoned and filled with evidence of recent fighting, even at half-scale, carved out of the living rock and with its interior structures all made of exposed metal, and the walls covered in those DIY murals the goblins loved . . . train station.

I wasn't the only one who noticed.

"They have trains," Yoshi said in a numb tone from just behind me. "They have a *monorail.*"

Impressive as this feat of engineering was, given the solidly medieval civilization that existed just above them, I found I wasn't anxious to climb onto the goblin tram, and not just because it was built for people half my size. It was indeed a monorail—the tram cars hanging from a single track affixed to the ceiling of the tunnel, which extended off in both directions from the station—but below that . . .

They were just hanging cages, basically. There was a front car with what looked like folded wings affixed; it took me a moment to recognize them as collapsible sails, which also added context as to why it was so damn windy in here. I guess the titanic drop to the core would produce updrafts which, properly harnessed, were a more efficient source of propulsion than anything fuel-burning. Clever as that was, the two passenger cars behind it were just square boxes with metal plates for ceiling and floor, and nothing but open-sided metal bars for walls, aside from a smaller plate along the front. The entire thing swayed gently from its track as gusts swished through the station, as if eager to get underway.

"Well, Zui," said Gizmit, "you got it here without wrecking it, so I assume you know what all the levers do."

"I know the basics, but Zekki's actually trained as an engineer," Zui replied, pointing at one of the armored security goblins. "It'll be a much smoother trip than Rhoka and I had if she takes over."

"Damn! You are?" asked another of the squad, lightly punching Zekki's shoulder. "I didn't know that. What're you doing slinging shots with us then, huh?"

"Hey, you gotta diversify your skill set if you wanna be competitive in the job market!" Zekki replied with a particularly sharklike grin. "Good things come to those who *hustle*. I aim to be management while you mooks are all aging in your armor."

"Nothin' wrong with being content where you are," another of her comrades objected. "I *love* this job. I get to stand around all day and occasionally hit people. Fuckin' bliss, man."

"You've worked in retail, haven't you?" I asked him, earning multiple grins and a couple of laughs from the goblins.

Zui cleared her throat loudly. "Right, so anyway, this means the squad is getting *on the tram*, everybody clear?"

"Yeah, that matter's still left unsettled, isn't it?" said Dap, turning to me.

Oh right, that. Great.

I glanced back, past the milling humans who were staring around the tram station in varying degrees of bemusement, at the door to the chaos gripping Fallencourt outside.

"I'm inclined to take Zui's side on this, after the shit we just went through," I admitted. "I know I really should not begin my personal acquaintance with Miss Sneppit by countermanding her orders, but I am extremely tired of watching goblins die, let alone being responsible for it."

"Make peace with it," Gizmit said curtly. "There's going to be a *lot* more of that before Jadrak's dealt with, one way or another."

"Smoke and rubble, Gizmit, that is *not* something to get blasé about!" Zui exclaimed.

"Excuse me," said Yoshi, stepping forward to join the discussion with a confused frown, "but what's the problem here?"

"Dap and his squad were sent here under orders to secure and hold this station against the Goblin King's followers," I explained. "Contracts and honoring your word are a big deal in goblin culture, so they're reluctant to evac with us."

"What?" His frown deepened and grew more incredulous. "That's crazy, you've seen what it's like out there. Eight of you can't possibly—you'll get killed! Just get on the train."

And suddenly, like an explosion behind my eyes, insight burst upon me. Yoshi had just handed me not only a resolution to the immediate problem, but a possible way for me to escape the rock and hard place I'd climbed between just by coming down here.

"Better do as he says," I solemnly advised Dap before anyone else could speak. "You wouldn't want to make the Hero angry."

"Wait, what? No, no, I didn't mean—*ow!*"

Yoshi stepped away, scowling at me in reproach and rubbing the ankle I'd just kicked against his other leg.

"Uh . . . hm." Dap looked at him, then at me, and back at him, and finally tilted his head in a funny little half shrug. "Welp, guess it's hard to argue with that. Acts of the Goddesses and all. All right, team, we're bugging out. Zekki, take the engineering car. Everybody else, load up before we get more uninvited guests."

"Good thing Zui brought a second car," said Gizmit, already heading for the rear one.

"Yeah, I was expecting to have to evacuate some extra people," Zui agreed. "Exactly *who* turned out to be a surprise, but . . . here we are."

I noticed Rhoka staring at me, having finally tilted her head back enough that I could see her face. Wow, yeah, she was young. Barely older than Yoshi, at a guess.

"Hmm," the Arbiter grunted, then turned to follow Gizmit.

I had a strange premonition that this one was going to end up being a pain in my ass.

"Pack the butts into the front car," Zekki called, sticking her head out of the engineering compartment, which she'd just clambered into. "You wanna front-load the weight; helps stabilize the ride."

"What does she mean, the *butts?*" Flaethwyn demanded.

As entertaining as it would have been to watch Nazralind explain that to her, I suddenly had another thought that demanded my attention. The tunnel behind us was still clear, and we'd been away from it long enough for, say, an invisible person to slip through and join us. The insides of those tram cars were going to be a different matter, though, once everybody was loaded in. Already we were having to compromise, with Madyn and Ydleth joining the goblins in the rear car.

Part of me reveled in the idea of forcibly ditching my invisible stalker; serve them right for setting the cats on us like that. That was the vindictive part that tended to just get me in trouble, though, and I tried to give more weight to the rational side of my brain, which recognized that Biribo and Aster's advice had merit, and also that the dark elf had probably just saved some of our lives out there.

"Hey, Zui," I said, zeroing in on the only goblin who hadn't yet climbed aboard. "Is it safe to ride on top of the tram?"

"What?" She frowned incredulously up at me. "I mean . . . The brakes put off a lot of sparks; that's why they've got solid ceilings. There *is* a shielded seat up at the very front of the engineering post that's used for engineers to service the track. It's goblin-sized, though."

"Bit of a squeeze for a human or elf, then."

"Don't ride on top of the tram, Lord Seiji," she said, exasperated. "There's room. Being a little snug for *one* tram ride won't kill you."

"Hah!" I headed for the front car, being the last to climb aboard. "Remind me to tell you about Japanese trains sometime."

It *was* a little snug, especially since there wasn't room for us tallfolk to stand up and we had to fold our legs a bit creatively to fit everybody. Also, to my surprise, I was not the last one in; Zui joined us in the front car instead of riding with the other goblins. She gave me one challenging look and I decided not to comment. The one thing I understood about Zui was that I was still a long way off from understanding Zui.

Up front, the winglike sails extended with a mechanical creak and clatter of gears turning, and immediately the entire train shuddered. Amell squealed and grabbed Yoshi; most of us clutched the bars for dear life, and we started moving forward.

The tram accelerated pretty quickly—not as fast as a powered mechanical train, of course, but I was impressed by how well it did with the level of technology on display. Also, it was much quieter than I would have expected. The constant but not overpowering whir from above us made me really curious about the mechanism up there, as I was pretty sure metal wheels on a metal track would make a lot more noise than that. For the most part, though, the noise was predominated by wind. It was certainly not *quiet*, at least not compared to the modern trains I was used to, but we could speak and be heard so long as we spoke loudly enough.

At first, nobody seemed to want to. We had all been through a traumatic experience, some of those present had just lost a friend, and everybody was doing their best to hang on. Even aside from the constant wind, these cars swayed quite a bit more than I was comfortable with.

"Sorry!" Yoshi said for the fifth time in a row, as going around a curve jostled him against Aster yet again.

"You know, you don't have to keep apologizing," she said with clear amusement. "It's okay; I am very much aware of the situation we're in."

"Uh, sorr—I mean, um." He ducked his head. "Right. Thanks. Habit, I guess." Yoshi looked up at me and managed a weak smile. "It's hard to adapt completely to a new culture. We're Japanese; we apologize. It's what we do."

"*Really.*" Very slowly, like a menacing owl, she swiveled her head around to affix me with what I think might've been the most intense Aster Look yet. "I have *specifically* not noticed that."

"What a surprise, the Dark Lord doesn't have any manners," Flaethwyn muttered, just barely loud enough for us to hear, which was how I knew we were meant to. Beside her, Pashilyn heaved an inaudible sigh and closed her eyes, but did not comment.

"Hey, give me a break; I'm American on my mother's side," I said. "In my people's culture, excessive apologizing is how they identify Canadian spies."

"You're a hafu?" Yoshi blurted in surprise. "You don't look—um! I mean, that is . . . uh. S-sorry."

I let him twist in the awkwardness for a few seconds, not least because explaining my personal business was high on my very long list of "fuck no" activities. *But,* the urge to fill this particular emotionally exhausted silence was strong. Everybody could use a distraction, and I felt Yoshi in particular needed something to think about other than the day he was having. Besides, my own plans—both short-term and long—involved reaching an accord with him, so maybe we could bond over Earth stuff. Since we had absolutely nothing else in common.

"My grandparents emigrated from Kyoto to California," I explained after a pause. "I've never gotten a straight answer on why they wanted to flee the economic miracle for a country that was getting its ass kicked by it at the time, so I suspect it was some family drama. In any case, they worked hard, got a little lucky, and made the right friends; they were able to get a good deal on some land and started planting trees. Oranges at first, then almonds and avocados—cash crops. These days they're pretty loaded. They were also pretty big into assimilating, so my mom grew up speaking only English and . . . I dunno, skateboarding? Whatever teenagers did in the nineties."

"Tamagotchis," Yoshi said, nodding sagely.

"Uh . . . right, well, whatever. Point was, they raised her as fully American as they could. Which was unwise and *kind* of futile, given the way racial politics work in that country, but that's a whole other can of worms. In any case, Mom didn't really know much about Japanese culture until she met my dad at uni."

"She came to Japan to study?" he asked.

I shook my head. "Other way around. Which is another thing I don't get. Dad's from one of those old-school, super traditional families, and nobody's ever clued me in on why he even wanted to study abroad, but . . . there they were at UCLA. Apparently, it was a real whirlwind thing, whole star-crossed lovers kinda deal. Anyway, yadda, yadda, yadda. I was born in San Diego, and then we moved back to Yokohama."

Everyone was staring raptly at me, despite the fact that for most of them I was spouting a bunch of nonsense words. Even Pashilyn had lifted out of her funk somewhat to watch my face closely.

"So. I am fully Japanese by blood. Legally, I have dual citizenship. Culturally . . ."

Everyone was still staring raptly at me. Suddenly, I wondered why the hell I'd kept talking so long about what was none of their damn business. I had *definitely* come to a subject I wasn't about to even try explaining.

". . . that's complicated."

The wind gushed through the loaded silence for a few more seconds until Yoshi repaid the favor by rescuing me.

"That's interesting, I didn't know you could actually get dual citizenship in Japan."

"*Get* it, no. I don't think either government grants it for any reason. But if you qualify for birthright citizenship somewhere else, they're also not going to insist you renounce it; that'd just be a lot of paperwork and diplomatic tension for no good purpose."

"Ah, gotta be born into it. I get you." He nodded. "Must be pretty cool."

Yeah, it was a fucking nonstop party.

"Well!" Flaethwyn tossed her head, making her golden hair flutter dramatically in the wind, and I was impressed that she did it at the perfect angle to avoid having it smack her in the face. That *had* to have been something she'd practiced. "*I* know a bit about being a stranger in a hostile land. We have been on this miserable island for *months*, and I've endured no end of harassment from the local authorities over some absurd grudge they have against my family."

"Yes, and I'm sure you've done absolutely nothing to provoke any of that," I said solemnly.

"It goes without saying," Flaethwyn agreed, causing all three of her own party to turn incredulous stares on her, and Aster to roll her eyes. "But there is just no *reasoning* with those people! Clan Aelthwyn are the most notoriously degenerate clods in all of Fflyr Dlemathlys, and everyone knows it. I'm sure *you* must have had your share of poor experiences with the Aelthwyns," she added to Nazralind, "considering you are . . . well, here. Thalissima in the courts of the Yadon, as it were."

"You're not wrong there," Naz agreed. "Right bunch of bastards, they are."

"Honestly, something is just *wrong* with those people," Flaethwyn nattered on, clearly encouraged. "It's just bad blood, you know. Like the seven stepdaughters of Madnat. Even among elves, there are simply some families who have something rotten in them that goes right to their brains. All the way from birth, you just can't do anything with them! I wish the king would step in. When the black lion is prowling the hedgerows, one must call upon Cadmin's spear, not the branch and broom of the forlorn priestess."

"Nice imagery," Naz said in a bland tone.

"Oh! Forgive me, all this hullabaloo has made me forget my manners. I am Highlady Flaethwyn of Clan Adellaird."

She tried to perform a heirat I hadn't seen before, accidentally smacked Amell on the forehead, then abortively tucked her hands back into herself.

Naz smiled at her.

"Aelthwyn Nazralind. Pleased t'meetcha."

I hadn't realized it was possible for a silence to be *deliciously* awkward, but damn if I didn't enjoy that one. Even Yoshi cringed. I felt an odd rhythmic twitching against my side that didn't match the swaying of the tram, and looked down to find Zui clutching a hand over her mouth and bouncing in place with silent laughter. And then had to instantly avert my eyes and shuffle as far as I could the other way, because she was *really* bouncing. Across from me, Nazralind winked with the eye that was out of Flaethwyn's view.

Nobody else got a chance to break the silence, though, as that was the point at which Zekki folded in the wings and hit the brakes. The squealing of metal from above us put an end to any further conversation, and I learned Zui had not been kidding about those sparks. The metal shields on top caught them, and I also observed that the ones on the front of the car were for more than blocking the wind—the entire tunnel lit up on both sides as the tram's brakes sprayed sparks the rest of the way to Sneppit's home base.

I had to wonder if getting into this rickety contraption had been a serious mistake. Almost unbidden, the weight of Heal formed in the forefront of my mind, ready to be deployed.

It worked, though; Zekki had even gotten the timing right. The tram progressively decelerated, and the scream of metal gradually diminished as we lost speed and finally eased to a stop at another tram station. It wasn't exactly a smooth stop, reminding me that Zekki may have been trained as an engineer, but it wasn't her main job. There was a lot of jerking the last fifty meters or so, as she had to keep pumping the brakes and then releasing them to make sure we came to a halt in the right spot. If *she* was having this much trouble, Zui and Rhoka must've had a really rough ride the other way.

Also a much longer one, it occurred to me. We'd gone straight to this station without halting, and the wind-powered trams could probably only go in one direction. Had they taken this thing on a complete circuit around the island to get to Fallencourt?

Whatever the case, we had arrived. This station looked smaller, with a relatively narrow platform and a broad flight of stairs, the entire width of it leading up to a landing, effectively a second platform about even with the top of the tram. There were also ledges overlooking the tracks, which was relevant as those were now occupied with goblins in pink armor carrying shields and aiming slingshots at us.

In fact, there were a *lot* of armored goblins. Well, maybe not a lot, exactly, but more of them than there were of us. And unlike the mob we'd just fought, these had matching armor, stood in formations, and were carrying weapons that had clearly been made to be weapons.

"Easy," I said as Yoshi gripped the handle of his sword. "These *should* be friends. Let Zui do the talking."

"*Friends*," Flaethwyn scoffed to herself, but we all ignored her. Zui stood and pushed the door open, turning to nod at me.

"It'll be fine. Just gimme a minute to reassure everybody before you hop out. I'm sure I don't need to tell you folks are *skittish* today."

"Yeah, I hear it's been rough," I said gravely. "Apparently somebody stole a tram!"

She stared at me for a moment, then sighed and hopped down.

Fortunately, the tension outside was already easing. Gizmit had gotten out immediately, followed by Dap and Zekki, and the rest of his armored squad were emerging. We tall types were still the focus of a lot of attention through the bars, but the welcoming party had already lowered their weapons at the sight of familiar faces, and someone I assumed must be an officer had stepped forward to quietly confer with our goblin escorts.

"Biribo?" I murmured.

"Lots of goblins, no Blessed," he replied. "I don't sense any sign of an ambush or anything like that among all the activity beyond. Looks like what it is, a reasonable security precaution."

"*I* would have said something immediately had we been walking into a trap," Yoshi's little pixie said haughtily.

Zui turned and beckoned to us, and I took the opportunity to be the first to crawl out of the car. My legs were more than a little stiff after being scrunched in there, but I managed not to embarrass myself.

"*Well, well,*" boomed a feminine voice from the top of the stairs, instantly earning my respect because this was a woman who knew how to *project*, "I'm sure there's a *fantastic* explanation for all this."

And that was how I finally met the great Miss Sneppit.

Which meant, of course, *showtime.*

9

In Which the Dark Lord Shakes on It

My experiences in Cat Alley, and points since, made me feel incredibly sleazy for it, but my more recent epiphany about Enjoin's potential made it the first thing I noticed—Miss Sneppit was hot.

Not in the effortless way of, say, Nazralind, who had never shown any indication that she knew how to operate a hairbrush. On the contrary, Sneppit was more meticulously and aggressively made up than even Minifrit, and her sense of style was splashy enough to practically fill the room. In fact, she suddenly made me think about that gyaru Yoshi and I had rescued in Akihabara Station.

Sneppit had a clear color scheme—pink, white, and gold. I couldn't tell whether her skin was a paler shade of green than any other goblin I'd met, or whether she was slathered with some kind of foundation, but she definitely had on vivid pink lipstick and ice-white eyeshadow. Her hair was bleached stark white and then dyed pink along the elaborate curls which hung behind her ears, accented by occasional golden highlights. Even her irises were pink, which I could tell because she had her pink-lensed, gold-framed glasses perched down on the tip of her nose, the better to glare at us over them.

She was actually dressed in very much the same style I was, in an outfit of the type favored by Fflyr noblemen—long coat with matching boots over a ruffled shirt and loose pants in a contrasting color, complete with a high turned-down collar and oversized cuffs. While I wore red on black, hers was—you guessed it—hot pink over white. We both had golden embellishments, though. In fact, her outfit was a lot *more* embellished.

I had a sudden distracting insight—rich goblins did that because rich humans did that, and rich humans did it to mimic the style of artifact armor and weapons—which the Goddesses had specifically and deliberately designed to look like high-end RPG equipment. No wonder everybody with money on this damn planet looked like an anime character—they were literally trying to. God, I hated Ephemera.

"Listen, Snep," Zui said, taking a first step up the stairs toward her irate boss.

"Don't you *Snep* me, you insubordinate, top-heavy little drain fungus," Sneppit barked down at her. "I'll deal with *you* in a minute. Right now I'm seeing a lot of other things on my tram platform that *clearly* don't belong here. Oh hey. Rizz!" She turned her head to shout over her shoulder. "Looks like she lived."

Another goblin ambled up to the top of the stairs, this one an older version of Rhoka. Well, the face was different, they probably weren't even related, but this spry middle-aged goblin was obviously part of the same social role. Her brown longcoat and wide-brimmed hat were identical in style, though considerably more battered and patched; instead of armbands, she wore a purple scarf affixed at the front with a steel pin. The mechanical polearm slung over her shoulder was identical to Rhoka's.

The elder stared grimly down at the Arbiter for a second before speaking. "Day's young."

Ooh, someone was in *trouble*.

Sneppit, meanwhile, was rapidly canvassing the assemblage of humans, elves, and her own employees milling around in front of the parked tram, her expression none too happy. She met my eyes for a moment before moving on to inventory the rest of the crowd.

"Well, let's start with the least insane part. Dap, you'd better have an excellent reason for being here and not at your post."

"That's my fault!" To my surprise, Yoshi stepped forward, then bowed, causing a stir among the onlooking goblins. "There was no way eight soldiers could have held that station against what the Goblin King was throwing at them. It was going to be lost anyway. *I* made them get on the tram. They would have died for no reason, otherwise."

Sneppit's eyes narrowed and she shoved her pink shades up to glare through the lenses. "So. Lord Seiji, I presume."

Ydleth brayed a shrill laugh and Flaethwyn made a strangled noise. I just blinked.

"Uh . . . sorry, no. I'm Shinonome Yoshi." He hesitated, then visibly steeled himself before managing to make the proclamation. "I'm the Hero."

Immediately, every armored goblin on the stairs and ledges aimed a slingshot at him and drew it back.

"These guards are under a contract with the standard acts of the Goddesses clause—"

Rhoka's attempted intercession was cut short by a sharp rebuke from Rizz, who it turned out could *also* project properly.

"*You* are not empowered to negotiate, or even render, contract advice when not under my supervision, *Arbiter*."

"Well, she isn't wrong, though," Sneppit said in a more even tone, staring down her nose at the eight abashed-looking goblins in armor who were clustered behind Dap. "Hm. Acts of the Goddesses. Never imagined I'd have to deal with a *literal* one, but the precedent on that's inarguable, isn't it? Fine. If the situation was that bad anyway, I'd rather not lose people over it. You *wipe that smirk off your face*, boy," she added at Yoshi, taking an aggressive step forward so that one foot was half off the top stair.

"I—I wasn't smirking—"

"And the rest of you idiots, lower those weapons!" Sneppit barked, causing the rest of her security detail to stop threatening Yoshi. "You think this situation isn't ugly enough without a Hero rampage on my own tram platform? That's better. And as for *you*." She pointed accusingly at Yoshi, who gulped. "That was a real nice gesture, saving the lives of eight goblins. Tell me, how many goblins did you *kill* on your way to get to them?"

He abruptly went pale and started to reflexively hunch his shoulders. "I didn't want—the situation was—"

"Oh sure, they were your enemies," Sneppit continued ruthlessly. "Mine too, for that matter. Did *you* know that, Hero? Were you aware that there *were* different factions in Kzidnak? Did you at any point pause to consider that some of the goblins you cut down on your way here weren't Goblin King partisans, but maybe just civilians trying to protect their homes?"

"I—look, that wasn't . . . I mean, we'd been *told* . . . Um, the thing is . . ."

It was at that moment I realized I'd just been standing here watching while everyone *except* me put on their own showtime. Sneppit had effortlessly dominated the room and reduced the Hero to mortified stammering with nothing but her own force of personality.

And she was a cutie.

Yep, no two ways about it—I was looking at Goblin Queen material here. If, of course, I could get her interested enough in working with me, and she didn't turn out to be another narcissistic monster like Jadrak. Which meant now it was *my* turn.

"Well, this is fun!" I said brightly, causing everyone's attention to swivel to me. "We should get out more often. I *never* get to meet anybody this interesting. Miss Sneppit, it's a delight to finally meet you in person. *I* am Lord Seiji." I swept a far more impressive bow than Yoshi's, not that he'd made it much of a challenge. "And I'd like to ask you for a favor."

"*Oh?*" Sneppit's eyebrows shot upward as she turned to focus on me fully. "And what might the great and terrible Dark Lord need from little old me?"

"For now? Just a moment of your time." In theatrical terms, this was tricky; Sneppit and Yoshi had embodied two poles on the axis of assertiveness, which meant that in order to stand out here, I had to take a completely different approach. Usually I just filled the air with bombast, but competing with the lady of the house was a bad idea. Instead, I opted to create a specific impression—calm, charming, reasonable. It's *hard* to do that without coming off like a sleazy salesman who wants something. "I realize you're already having a hell of a day, and that was before we dumped this trainload of weirdos on your doorstep, so I'm sorry to press. *But*, if you'll indulge me with a word in private before coming to any decisions here, I think you'll find it worth your time."

Sneppit regarded me thoughtfully from her high perch atop the stairs, and somehow I knew she'd instantly decided what to do. This dramatic pause was pure pageantry, a moment in which all her subordinates could see her symbolic position over the Dark Lord. I couldn't begrudge it, and not just because I, too, appreciate a good piece of showtime. She depended on maintaining her authority over these people, and given that I was hoping to use the resources and connections of her company, it didn't serve my interests to undermine her.

"Well," she said at last, "I can't really turn up my nose at a reasonable request like that. Sure, Lord Seiji, there's an office room nearby where we can talk for . . . not long, I hope?"

"Shouldn't be but a couple of minutes," I assured her with a smile. "I appreciate you meeting me halfway."

An armored goblin leaned over to whisper in Sneppit's ear, then jerked back as she made a swatting motion at him. Gizmit took that opportunity to begin climbing the stairs, adding her own opinion.

"Perhaps I should come along, Snep. I'm familiar with the Dark Lord, so—"

"He specifically said 'in private,'" Sneppit interrupted. "I know you two are just concerned with security, but use your damn heads. This is the *Dark Lord*. If he decides to murderize me, just what the hell do you think you'd do about it, anyway? I'll always make time for a man who can kill everybody in the room but still asks politely when he wants something. Basso, keep this station under control, but *don't* antagonize the butts if they don't start it. I'll be back in five."

"Keep the peace as best you can," I instructed Aster. "Punch Ydleth or Flaethwyn if they need it; the rest of this lot have manners. Won't be long."

"How *dare*— Hey!" To judge by her compounding outrage, I gathered that Flaethwyn wasn't used to people walking away from her midrebuke. Which, of course, was half the satisfaction of doing it. The other half was being away from her.

"He's not wrong, though," Ydleth said reasonably, which I knew was not going to calm the elf down, but for the next five minutes that was Aster's problem.

I bounded up the stairs six at a time, which made the security goblins visibly twitchy, but they all had the sense not to point weapons at me. Fortunately, these steps were wide enough to accommodate a human foot, though they were each half the height of human-sized stairs, and I wasn't about to mince my way up them one by one. Sneppit greeted me at the top with a nod, which I returned, and I was impressed anew that even towering over her, I didn't overwhelm the force of her presence.

Miss Sneppit curtly evicted two goblins doing paperwork in a small side room; I had to duck to get through the door, but inside the ceiling was high enough to stand up in, if only just. Which was good, because sitting in any of the goblin-sized furniture would have made me look ridiculous. The height disparity was probably why Sneppit hopped up to perch atop the desk rather than take any of the chairs.

"Hey, pretty nice," Biribo commented, buzzing around the chamber in a circle as soon as the door was closed. "Thick stone walls, no listening holes, heavy door. They take their privacy seriously around here."

"Glad you approve," said the mistress of the house, her tone less wry than she could have gotten away with. "So! What can I do for you, Lord Seiji?"

"I'll come right to the point," I said, getting an approving nod. "I'd like to ask you to extend some tolerance and hospitality to the Hero."

She raised her eyebrows. "Well. I expected to be surprised by whatever you had to say and even so, *that* one was a shocker. Wouldn't the Dark Lord want to jump on an opportunity to kill the Hero while you've got him at a disadvantage? That'd make the whole world your berry basket, as I understand it."

"I'm afraid your understanding is . . . incomplete," I replied. "The great game of the Goddesses doesn't end until the Dark Lord dies. If a Hero gets killed, Sanora gets to summon another one."

"Wish *that* surprised me," Sneppit muttered. "Everything everywhere is rigged in their favor."

"Killing a well-established Hero can buy a Dark Lord a *lot* of room to maneuver and strengthen their position," Biribo said, taking up the explanation, "but this early in the game? It's almost not even worth the effort. The next Hero wouldn't even be that far behind Lord Seiji."

"And more importantly," I added, "odds are good the next guy wouldn't be nearly as agreeable."

"Agreeable?"

"That's the issue, you see. Where Yoshi and I come from, there are no goblins—just stories about them, which don't resemble the reality very much at all. He's grown up thinking of goblins as greasy, predatory, barely sentient little monsters only good for fledgling adventurers to train themselves by killing."

Sneppit curled her lip contemptuously. "Sounds pretty much like the King's Guild's official line."

"Exactly." I leaned forward, watching her eyes and seeing that I still had her full attention. "So he started with those prejudices, came *here*, and immediately got them reinforced . . . And now he comes face-to-face with the reality. Goblins are just people like anybody else, in many ways more sophisticated than the Fflyr. What he's gotten roped into isn't a fun fantasy adventure; it's stomping through people's homes to murder them and steal their stuff. That is why I want him to see goblins at their *best*. Here's the thing, Sneppit— Yoshi is a good kid. Kindhearted and wants to help people, the whole classic hero archetype. When he figures out his allies have lied to him—including Sanora herself—and used him as part of a system of political exploitation, he is not going to take it well. What *I* want is to give the kid a life lesson in just what depravity he's participating in, and then send him back up top *knowing better*. Imagine how much we could get done if the Hero is too busy crusading against corruption among his own side to bother us."

"Hmm." She looked skeptical, but I could tell I still had her interest and pressed my advantage before it waned.

"But those are future concerns, and also *my* problem. You'll be wanting to hear what's in this for you, especially in the more immediate sense."

"Wow," Sneppit commented dryly. "Congratulations, that officially makes you the most considerate human I've ever dealt with."

"That's . . . really sad," I acknowledged. "But maybe not surprising. The reason I'm confident we can come to an understanding here is because you and I have basically the same priorities about this current crisis. To begin with, Jadrak has to die."

"I am actually somewhat surprised to hear you say that," she said. "Jadrak finding out there's a Dark Lord right upstairs is probably one of the things that emboldened him to openly proclaim himself. He was *definitely* wanting to reach an accord with you, Lord Seiji. I was more than half expecting you to be here to dictate terms of my surrender."

"I—really?" I blinked, processing that. "Ahh . . . If the trams haven't been running all day, I guess you haven't had the opportunity to get fresh intel from Jadrak's camp."

"I find myself curious what's got the two of you at each other's throats, though," she said pointedly.

I winced. "Ah well . . . The embarrassing truth is it started as a cultural misunderstanding. But neither of us can afford to back down from it, so here we are."

"That a fact," Sneppit said flatly. "Let me guess, his emissary said something you didn't like and you blasted him."

"Hey, give me a *little* credit," I protested. "I don't blast people for hurting my feelings. Murdering my allies on my doorstep, though, that's a reliable way to set me off. Considering our amicable *and* mutually profitable relationship thus far, I'd think you would find that reassuring."

"Very slightly." She folded her arms, giving me a look over the gold rims of her shades. Surely those things were just for style? You wouldn't use pink glass for vision correction . . . "Dealing with violent and volatile people is not *reassuring*, even when they're nominally on my side. And what's hanging in the forefront of my mind right *now* is that if Jadrak is committed to fight the Dark Lord to the death, he's a cornered animal and therefore ten times as dangerous."

"He was always a cornered animal. Even if all of Kzidnak was behind him, he has no chance against the Fflyr. Isn't that *why* you were against him in the first place?"

I couldn't really *blame* her for trying to improve her bargaining position at my expense, but that didn't mean I was gonna let her get away with it. Sneppit tilted her head momentarily to one side in a gesture of acknowledgment, and I continued.

"But as I was saying, we're in the same position and have the same needs here, Sneppit. We both need Jadrak to not exist anymore. All of goblin society needs that right now."

"We can agree on that." She nodded.

"*But*, and feel free to correct me if I'm mistaking any nuances of goblin culture, it's my understanding that you guys are generally not impressed by violence or shows of force. Killing the Goblin King, even if it's obviously necessary, is not going to be a good look. And Kzidnak right now is full of people convinced it is the *opposite* of necessary."

"I could maybe get away with it." She grimaced. "You're not completely wrong, though. That wouldn't help my social prospects down here."

"And I bet that goes double for *me*. Big swaggering human comes down here and destroys the goblin leadership with swords and spells—that's playing right into the stereotype that keeps you folks up at night in fear. I would *really like* to come out of this with good relationships established with Fallencourt, and the need to eliminate Jadrak all but conclusively rules that out."

Sneppit's eyes narrowed to slits. Then a slow smile began to tug at her painted lips, and I knew I had her.

"*But*," she said softly, "what if it was a Hero who killed the Goblin King?"

"That's what Heroes do, after all," I said in my most reasonable tone. "They kill people and wreck stuff. Nobody would be surprised. But I have an even better idea than that. What if we were to *supervise* this Hero while he worked? Minimize the collateral damage, protect people as much as we can. I'm betting that in the aftermath of Jadrak's fall, those of us who used our wiles rather than our fists to make sure the Hero *only* did what he came for and then fucked off would be seen in a much better light by the rest of goblinkind."

"Mm-hmm." It was amazing how much this woman could communicate through subtle shifts of her posture. Suddenly we were no longer two potentially hostile strangers feeling each other out, but friends colluding at some other sucker's expense. And she did all that with a smirk, the angle of her shoulders, the position of her head. Oh yeah, this lady was dangerous. "And then, of course, with a Dark Lord rising and no Goblin

King . . . Well, historically, goblins have formed the logistical backbone of most Dark Crusades. Isn't that right, familiar?"

"I've already told him about that, don't worry," Biribo assured her.

Sneppit winked up at me. "Well, there ya go. Seems like you'd need experienced help getting all of Kzidnak organized into something that'll best serve your needs."

"See?" I said cheerfully. "I told you we'd be on the same page."

"Well, speaking of pages, I can whip up a contract quick as you—"

"Whoa." I held up both hands. "You're cute and all, but no contracts on the first date."

Sneppit softened her rebuke by leaning flirtatiously toward me, and fortunately, nothing going on here was lewd enough to trigger a flashback; I was accustomed to far more explicitly sexual posturing from the crew back at North Watch. "You get a lot of leeway for being an outsider, Lord Seiji, but just for reference, that's a *big* gaffe in goblin culture. Refusing to sign a contract is tantamount to admitting you're planning to screw the other party over."

"That's just the thing, isn't it? I'm *not* that familiar with goblin culture. I could really use an experienced hand to guide me around down here, show me the ropes, and help me avoid fucking up too badly. But precisely because I don't grasp all the nuances, I'm extremely hesitant to commit my signature to anything. That's how I avoid getting into situations where I have to either break my word or do something I really can't afford to. Where *I* come from, it's trying to wheedle people into signing unnecessary contracts that's taken as a sign you're up to no good."

"Well, we wouldn't want to have another cultural misunderstanding," she said, "given how your last one went."

"You would have to work *really* hard to piss me off enough to even approach that scenario," I assured her. "The truth is, Sneppit, us coming to a long-term arrangement is definitely going to involve some serious, long-term compromises on both sides. Let's get to know each other a bit and feel out the possibilities before committing to anything."

"I see what you're saying," she replied, leaning back and giving me a more considering look. "Do understand what you're asking, though. Goblins very strongly prefer to have everything laid out in explicit terms. Ambiguity is dangerous."

"Especially with humans?"

"Hey, you said it, not me." She grinned. "For which I'm glad; that woulda been awkward."

"I do understand, and I appreciate your indulgence. If it puts your mind at ease, when it comes to finding another goblin who can be my lieutenant in the Dark Crusade *after* we deal with Jadrak . . . Well, at this moment, you've got no competition, Sneppit, and a major head start on any others who might pop up."

"I'd throw any goblin the fuck outta my office for talking to me like that," she informed me, then smiled again. It was a knowing, mischievous, and more than slightly flirtatious smile. "*But*, it is what it is. These aren't exactly normal times. All right, Lord Seiji, you've got . . ." Sneppit started to hold out a hand, then paused. "Ah, sorry. Force of habit. *Not* a deal, but . . . ?"

Gently, I took her hand and gave it a squeeze, noticing for the first time that goblin digits were slightly out of proportion to their height. Sneppit's hand was warm and not much smaller than a human woman's, not at all the childlike limb I'd expect of someone her size.

"Friends?" I suggested.

"Friends." She grinned and squeezed my fingers, then her expression sobered as she withdrew her hand. "I had mixed feelings, y'know. You've been a solid business contact, Lord Seiji, but also the living embodiment of exactly the kinda violent tendencies that make me want to shy away. It honestly is an immense reassurance that your plan down here is to play the angles and maneuver a positive outcome, rather than just hit your problems with maximum force until they die."

"Oh, there'll be a lot of hitting," I admitted, "and unfortunately more dying . . . but you're not wrong. I *really* would like to get through life with altogether less bloodshed than I've had to so far. Maybe you can help give me some pointers."

"Maybe I can, at that!"

My new friend, old business partner, and possible future Goblin Queen hopped down from the desk and opened the office door with no more ado, whereupon we were immediately blasted by the shrill clamor of a screaming argument from outside.

". . . that didn't take long," Sneppit commented.

"Flaethwyn and Ydleth," I sighed. "I probably should have separated them."

"You were expecting this outcome?"

"Not particularly."

"You are . . . *surprised* by it?"

"Not particularly."

She smirked up at me. "Ain't it wonderful, being in charge?"

"Not fucking particularly."

Sneppit laughed and lightly patted me on the hip before preceding me out of the office. I followed her feeling cautiously optimistic, despite the open question of just how much trouble I'd gotten myself into this time.

10

In Which the Dark Lord
Keeps the Peace

This must've started as soon as I walked away from them; by this point they weren't even arguing, just screaming insults. I got the gist as we strode back to the top of the stairs, moderating my customary pace so as not to overwhelm Sneppit's short legs. Just because Gizmit the spy—"maid" my ass—could keep up with me at a jog didn't mean the expensively dressed businesswoman could, or would appreciate being made to.

Ydleth was on a tear about how evil and generally insufferable highborn were, but she was nearly incoherent with rage, which wasn't helping her case. Being extremely right does nothing for you if you can't express yourself clearly. Flaethwyn had evidently sussed out her secret, which surprised me; Ydleth was tall but very fine-boned, and her mannerisms were more feminine than a lot of the Cat Alley girls. When she wasn't braying like a donkey, anyway. Surprising me further, Flaethwyn wasn't dwelling on that, aside from cruelly bringing it up every three or four sentences; she seemed to just be having a fit at the fact that a lowborn dared talk to her in such a manner. I couldn't decide whether this was to her credit or not.

I was inclined to lean toward "not."

"Wow, that's not even a debate," Sneppit commented as we drew close enough to see down the steps at the unfolding spectacle. "Just a couple of idiots screaming past each other."

"Sorry about this." I sighed. "I'll fix it."

"We can spare each other a few minutes to organize. An alliance like this is gonna require some groundwork; we need to set up a meeting first off to get everybody on the same page and plan our next move, and just getting my people to sit down at a table with the Hero will take some . . . persuasion. You'll probably have this straightened out before I do."

"Best of luck."

"Same."

She stepped to the side and was immediately met by Gizmit and the armored goblin who I'd taken to be either Sneppit's personal bodyguard or the head of her security division. I began making my way down to the platform, taking in the scene as I descended.

Ydleth and Flaethwyn were less than a meter apart, and I got the distinct impression the only reason they weren't nose-to-nose was the presence of Adelly and Pashilyn holding each of them back. It was actually sort of funny; I caught those two sharing a look of commiseration as the star performers shrieked themselves hoarse. Aster, to my annoyance, stood off to one side with her arms folded, watching and doing nothing. Zui was next to her in almost exactly the same pose.

Madyn was already making friends with a squad of the goblin guards; from her gestures I gathered she was telling one of her notorious tall tales, to their clear interest. I couldn't really blame them for deciding to ignore the incipient catfight. Yoshi and Amell both dithered about on the platform behind Flaethwyn, clearly wanting to intervene but too awkward to know how. Well, Yoshi was. Amell was probably just afraid of drawing the attention of an angry highborn.

"These are the two I *specifically* told you to punch," I growled at Aster as I arrived next to her.

"If they needed it, you said," she replied softly, her low voice no doubt inaudible a meter away thanks to all the nearby noise. "This is actually going very well."

Zui tilted her head to give Aster a long, speculative look. I just stared in disbelief. The two shrieking harpies were barely even coherent at this point.

"—not be criticized by a common whore—"

"—too inbred to even notice, the lot of you—"

"—never become anything better than a pack animal—"

"—the real face of evil in this fucking country—"

"—no one would even notice if your entire—"

"—should be lined up and axed like the—"

"Or was," Aster added. "I think this has run its course. Naz, if you would?"

Nazralind nodded graciously at her, then raised her head and deafened us all.

"Heeee yiyiyi! Hepep hatarak!"

Man, those traditional Fflyr gwynnek calls were something else. I'd always been impressed by how precisely they could direct their trained birds, but now I was in awe of just how *fucking loud* that was up close and indoors.

Total silence descended, even the two erstwhile combatants turning to stare in wide-eyed shock at Nazralind, who took advantage of the sudden quiet to speak at a more appropriate volume, in possibly the most cultured tones I'd ever heard from her.

"Congratulations, Highlady Flaethwyn. After today, you will be able to claim that you were once in a large room entirely full of goblins, every one of whom exhibited a more refined public bearing than yourself."

I'd noticed, of course, that elves, and the highborn most closely descended from them, had a prismatic quality to their skin—not that they sparkled or anything, but they had an oddly glossy texture and under direct sunlight showed subtle undertones of blue and gold that you wouldn't see on somebody pigmented solely by melanin. Magical genetic engineering by the Goddesses, I figured, or some adaptation to Ephemera's weird atmosphere. Now, Flaethwyn showed us that when an elf went completely pale and entirely stopped moving, they actually looked carved from marble.

Pashilyn, clutching Flaethwyn's arm, shot Nazralind the most irritated look I'd seen on the usually composed priestess, but the rest of the audience loved it. The delighted hooting, catcalls, and wolf whistles from the surrounding goblins pretty well ruled out any further argument.

"Holy shit, Naz," Adelly exclaimed, "you can't just *murder* somebody like that. You're supposed to provoke them until you get an excuse to claim self-defense. We have a *procedure*."

I couldn't hear Zui's sigh as the rest of the goblins were still carrying on, but her shoulders shifted heavily as she stepped forward. Flaethwyn was letting Pashilyn tug her back toward her group, and Ydleth seemed to be on the verge of lunging after the retreating elf when Zui stepped in front of me.

"C'mere, girl," the goblin said imperiously.

Ydleth stared down at her, scowling. "What?"

"Down here." Zui beckoned, then pointed at the ground with the same hand.

Putting on the particularly mulish look I recognized as the harbinger of malicious compliance, Ydleth bared her teeth and dropped to one knee, thrusting her face out as if daring the goblin to do her worst.

Judging by her expression, she was even more surprised than I when Zui stepped forward and wrapped her arms around her neck, squeezing her close. Ydleth lifted both her hands, then let them hover awkwardly, clearly uncertain what she should be doing with them. Even though I wasn't the one getting hugged, I could kind of relate. *Man*, it was hard to get a read on Zui. Every other thing out of her was either some new depth of saintlike compassion or being a prickly pain in everyone's ass.

Aster gently tugged me back out of immediate earshot of what had moments ago been the battleground, murmuring as we withdrew.

"So, you and I are, conservatively, eighty percent of the offensive force of the whole group we brought underground. Naz and Adelly are all the backup we'd need for a simple hunt-and-kill mission, and they might be overkill. I selected the other two because of the other mission you outlined. Madyn and Ydleth are our secret weapon for getting in good with the goblins."

I turned my most incredulous stare on her.

"Madyn has some of the best people skills in the organization, and that's among a group of former prostitutes," Aster continued quietly. "She has no hostility in her soul, and between having a funny story for every possible situation and always wanting to hear *more* funny stories, she can spark up and carry on a conversation with anyone. Look at her over there, already making friends."

Indeed, Madyn had now drawn a crowd of five laughing goblins, who were probably supposed to be on duty, telling them about a favorite client of hers whose kink was dropping trou, bending over the bedpost, and having her sing hymns to his butt. It wasn't the first time I'd heard this one, though I remained impressed that somebody in a preinternet society could be so imaginative.

"Okay, I see the point there, but . . ." I cut my eyes back toward Ydleth. "*Really?*"

During the intervening seconds, Zui had somehow broken down Ydleth's coarse exterior entirely. She'd withdrawn the hug but was now gently holding the woman's face in both green hands and appeared to be speaking softly to her, heedless of the tears dripping on her fingers. Ydleth was already reduced to hiccups. I always feel awkward seeing someone cry, but at least the silly wench was *quiet* for once.

"You mostly deal with Ydleth in the aftermath of her causing trouble," Aster said with a faint smile, "which is partly your own fault for avoiding her so much. Yeah, she's loud and brash and not great with rules. Does that sound like any other large group of small people we're currently trying to court?"

She looked pointedly around at the goblins, more of whom were drifting toward Madyn's storytime.

"Look at the kind of art they make, and where they put it. This is not a culture that wants a place for everything and everything in its place. Yes, she has a large personality and is prone to getting in arguments, but she is also really good at making up afterward. Did you know that she and Sicellit are practically besties now?"

I had not known that, and it made me blink in confusion. Last time I'd seen the two of them in proximity it had nearly ended in bloodshed. Wasn't that just a few weeks ago?

"Plus," Aster continued, "remember what Biribo said about goblins not having gendered social roles?"

"Well, I mean, they *mostly* don't, aside from some imitation of Fflyr customs that comes with being a subordinate society," Biribo said. "But for the same reason, they also don't have people like Ydleth. You can't really go against your culture's gender roles if those aren't a thing."

"Right, fine," Aster said a little impatiently, "but do you think the goblins will find it weird that she calls herself a woman?"

"Not really," I admitted. "If anything, they'll think it's weird that she's defensive about it."

"Exactly. It's already working, Lord Seiji. You only came in on the tail end of that, but you missed a *truly* amazing rant. It was almost as spectacular as one of yours. She tore Flaethwyn an entire new one about how cruel and rotten the elves and highborn in general are. Right in front of an audience of goblins, who now have ample food for thought about how goblins and lowborn have basically the same problems and should maybe be natural allies. That worked even better than I could have hoped; I wasn't counting on Flaethwyn making herself such a perfect target. Honestly, what is that woman's problem? Even for a highborn, she goes out of her way to be an insufferable bitch."

"Hm," I grunted, considering. Now I was kind of upset that I'd missed it. I'm something of a connoisseur of rants, if I do say so myself.

"This is *working*," Aster insisted, leaning closer to me and lowering her voice further. "I'm thinking, while the rest of us go off to take care of the Goblin King, we leave these two here. Have them help Miss Sneppit with whatever she needs as a show of good faith, and just let them work. They will earn us friendship and goodwill from the goblins; I guarantee it. Madyn is everybody's friend, and Ydleth is basically a really tall goblin herself."

"Okay," I said, a bit grudgingly. "I still have reservations, but I can see how this is already starting to get results. And it wouldn't have gotten this far if I didn't trust your judgment, Aster."

"All right!"

Everyone turned to look up at the loud voice. Sneppit had finished whatever backroom discussion she'd gone off to have, and now stood again at the head of the stairs, hands on her hips and looking down her nose at the assemblage below.

"So we've got here a Hero and an assemblage of King's Guild adventurers," she declared. "You all know what that represents—murder, looting, and general pointless destruction."

An angry murmur rose from the onlookers, and Yoshi's group pulled closer together, making a protective formation around Amell, who I gathered wasn't much use in a fight.

"More than that general fact," Sneppit continued, "most of you know *this* group as the posse of hapless goons who've been stumbling around Dount for months now, looking for a way to stomp down here into our homes and kick heads in for no better reason than the King's Guild thinks we goblins *might* be up to something."

"Now, see here—"

"*Wait*," Pashilyn interjected, cutting off Flaethwyn's shrill complaint.

Yoshi was staring intently up at Sneppit; I could see his hand quivering near the hilt of his sword, but he didn't draw or even grasp it yet. His pixie familiar had descended right next to his ear and seemed to be speaking quietly to him.

For my part, I felt a surge of unease at the direction Sneppit was taking. This was *not* what we'd discussed. Was she double-crossing me already? Couldn't I just *once* meet some new people and not immediately have to kill them all? Surely that wasn't too much to ask.

"*But*," Sneppit said after letting the tension build for a perfectly timed few beats, "Lord Seiji has just made a compelling case to me about desperate times and desperate measures, *and* has vouched for this guy Yoshi's good character."

Yoshi shot me a look of pure surprise.

"We all know Heroes and Dark Lords are brought here by the Goddesses from another world," Sneppit continued. "I admit, I've never bothered to sit down and think about all that that implies. Why would I? None of us expected to ever see either within our lifetimes, let alone both in one place. But upon having it laid out for me by someone else who's not even from Ephemera, I find I can understand how a person could land in Fflyr Dlemathlys, knowing nothing about goblins and hearing only the kind of bullshit the King's Guild tells, and *think* he was doing the right thing by participating in a raid on our home. Besides which, when it comes down to it? Jadrak, the would-be Goblin King, *is* the enemy of us all. Me, you, and also the Fflyr, if he manages to actually launch his attack on Gwyllthean like he wants to. So, not to downplay all the fucked-up stuff the King's Guild represents . . . I am tentatively willing to believe there is room for a dialog here."

"Are you serio—*ow!*" I couldn't see which of them had elbowed Flaethwyn, but it didn't really matter as long as it got done.

Now I could see what Sneppit had done, and I continued to be impressed. Just get up in front of a bunch of people and tell them something they don't like hearing, and you'll immediately lose them. *But,* if you start by pandering to their preconceptions, you can create a rapport and then more carefully bring them around to the position you actually want. It seemed to be working, too; none of the goblins looked particularly excited by this turn of events, but the green faces around me looked, at worst, thoughtful. Anybody who was feeling mutinous was keeping it to themselves, which would suffice for Sneppit's and my purposes.

Man, it was nice to meet somebody else who knew how to put on a good showtime and wasn't using it *against* me for once. I was starting to get excited at the prospect of what this goblin and I could accomplish together.

"So what do you say, Hero?" she demanded, raising her chin. "Think you can be a reasonable person and restrain your violent impulses long enough to work with us, and put a stop to this Goblin King nonsense?"

Yoshi's throat moved as he swallowed, but with his entire little harem— what was left of it—watching him in silence, his expression remained resolute. Almost stereotypically so; I wouldn't doubt he learned that exact configuration of facial features from watching anime. It wouldn't shock me if he'd practiced it in front of a mirror.

"It's—" His voice cracked and he blushed, swallowing again, but nobody so much as snickered. Glancing around, I was reminded by the wary expressions of the goblins that to them, a Hero was a monster out of legend. "It's obvious to me now that there's a lot going on here I don't understand. You were right, uh . . . Um, I'm sorry, I don't quite know how to address you? Politely, I mean."

"We're not big on formal titles," she said, folding her arms. "I'm Sneppit, and I'm the boss around here."

"Sneppit." He nodded deeply, one of those gestures that verged on a bow. "Hajimemashite. What I meant to say was, you were right that we came in here not knowing the details or the politics. And . . ." He winced, but steeled himself and continued. "It's increasingly clear to me you were also right about us, well, blundering around. We were invited into these tunnels by a goblin called Kalso who was desperate to escape the Goblin King. She said he was planning to invade the surface, and . . ." Yoshi paused, swallowing again. "We were attacked immediately, as soon as we came underground. Kalso was . . . was killed in the first ambush, and nobody else was willing to stop and talk with us until we met Omura-san and his friends, with your guards. I know you don't owe us anything, but I would be grateful if you'd explain the situation so we don't make any more mistakes or get anyone else unnecessarily hurt. We'll be in your care."

Stepping forward away from his group, he bowed to her again. All around the room, heads shifted as goblins turned to see how she would respond.

To my surprise, Sneppit smiled.

"*Suneppito*. Well, that's a new one." She glanced at me, then back at Yoshi. "Y'know, you guys have a crazy accent."

Yoshi blushed again and I deliberately kept my expression calm and faintly amused. It was fine; I understood what she was doing—using humor to humanize us and soothe the general mood in the room. Successfully, to judge by the chuckles she got. Everything was okay, and I was *not* pissed about this disrespect. Goddammit, I'd been living on Dount and saying Fflyr names for months now; my pronunciation was *not* that bad!

"The short version is that Goblin Kings are just something that happens every once in a while, and *wouldn't* if you topsiders didn't act like such shitheads all the time," Sneppit continued, the levity fading swiftly from her expression. "You ever pause to consider what it's *like* for a thinking, feeling being who's every bit as much a *person* as anyone else, to be treated like some kind of . . . infestation? We get pushed out, attacked on sight, stolen from, and murdered without consequence, starved and denied and generally kicked around like it's this country's national pastime. That *pisses people off*, Hero. You can only treat a group of people that way for so long before the anger and resentment builds up and there's an explosion of violence. All it takes is for some goblin with more charisma than sense to come along when that pressure is at its peak, and boom. Goblin King. That doesn't mean *all* of us are stupid enough to want this!"

She made a broad, annoyed gesture with both arms, and then began descending the stairs toward us while she spoke.

"Attacking the Fflyr is a *wildly* idiotic exercise in gratuitously messy mass suicide. Humans are twice our size, they heavily outnumber us, and they mostly have better weapons and armor and a *lot* more Blessed per capita. Only an absolute moron would do something like this, and despite what I'm sure the King's Guild has told you, *we are not morons*. This is only happening because a quorum of goblins have been abused for so long that they're too angry to think straight. Even among the Goblin King's followers, not all of them are in *that* camp; there'll be quite a lot just going along with it because everyone around them is whipped up into a rabid frenzy and they don't dare try to go against the flow. Mobs *kill* anybody they can single out as a target. It doesn't even take a good reason."

"Yeah," he said quietly, dropping his gaze. "Yeah, we . . . we saw that."

"So, yes, you'd better believe the Goblin King has opposition down here. The absolute *fuck* I'm gonna kill myself to *momentarily inconvenience* the Clans, or let that happen to the people I'm responsible for. And that makes me and mine a higher priority target than *you*, Hero. Jadrak needs all of us either obeying him or dead before he can afford to carry out his asshat plan. That means, whether or not any of us like it, you and I and Lord Seiji are currently on the same side."

"How *did* you end up on this side, Lord Seiji?" Pashilyn asked suddenly. "Historically, Goblin Kings have been among the most valuable early supporters of Dark Lords."

"Well, I can't speak for Ephemeral history, but *can* attest that Jadrak is a piece of shit and Imma kill him," I declared. "I was minding my own business, peacefully trading and socializing with a few goblins who were willing to talk to me, and that asshole sent his goons to kill them off, right on my very doorstep, apparently because he didn't want any competition for my attention. So, yes, the Goblin King really did want to throw in with the Dark Lord. Unfortunately for *him*, I do not *like* it when people murder my friends. It makes me . . ."

I inhaled deeply, and let the breath out through my teeth, flexing my fingers at my sides.

". . . *irrational.*"

"So . . . this happens . . . often?" Yoshi asked hesitantly. "Hasn't anybody ever tried to make a permanent peace?"

"It's a cycle, Yoshi," I explained. "Goblins live and die by the contract; they like making deals, they normally dislike violence, and keeping your word is *hugely* important in goblin culture. To them, a person who cheats or takes things by force isn't worth dealing with or treating with any respect, and taking their stuff is fair game. So humans cheat and rob and attack goblins because they're bigger and stronger and can get away with it, and goblins steal from humans because . . . why wouldn't they? Fair's fair. Then humans attack goblins because they're thieving little pests, and around and around it goes. Both constantly justify the other's bad opinion. It's a vicious cycle, and those only get broken when one party decides to stop, insistently do the *right* thing instead of the immediately obvious thing, and then *keeps* doing that long enough for the cycle to peter out and the other party to get on board. That is prohibitively hard to get any large group of people to do, under any circumstances. And here? Neither has any incentive. Fflyr society is set up to benefit a very small group of people at the expense of everyone else. Goblins and lowborn alike are all scrabbling to survive. To make permanent peace, you're asking them to take on a very big risk for very uncertain gain. It's not happening."

By the time I finished, goblins all over the room were nodding along with me, which of course was the point. I *could* have let Sneppit explain that, but it served my own agenda to be seen as someone who understood and cared about the plight of the common goblin, maybe the only human who did.

She glanced at me, her expression revealing nothing, but I knew she'd caught on to what I was doing.

"The only other thing that breaks a cycle," I said after giving them all a moment to think, "is if someone *else* breaks it. Some outside force more powerful than all the other forces involved."

Yoshi nodded slowly, his expression pensive. My own people had arrayed themselves behind me by that point so I couldn't see their faces; Flaethwyn looked so generally disgruntled and Amell so generally perturbed, I couldn't be sure how much they were even paying attention. But Sneppit gave me a look, a faint smile, and an even fainter nod. At the top of the stairs, I saw Rizz and Rhoka in their big hats and coats, both staring fixedly at me with unreadable faces.

And Pashilyn shifted her head to stare right at me, her expression flat and intent. A noblewoman and a priestess of the Convocation, she understood exactly what a Dark Crusade was and where I was going with this.

I looked right into her eyes and smiled.

She just tilted her head slightly, considering me.

Yup, this one was going to be trouble.

"All right," Yoshi said, drawing in a steadying breath and letting it out swiftly. He had his resolute Hero face on again, clearly oblivious to these undercurrents. "Then let's defeat the Goblin King. Together."

Wow, that was almost too easy.

That was how I knew it was inevitably going to get . . . complicated.

11

In Which the Dark Lord Gets the Bad News

Things moved quickly after that. Once Sneppit started giving orders, goblins scurried off in every direction, and we found ourselves swept along with the tide. Just minutes after the confrontation on the tram platform, Yoshi and I were being seated at a low—for us, everything here was goblin-sized—table in an obvious conference room, with Sneppit, Rizz, and several others I hadn't met yet.

"Sorry about the furniture, boys," said Sneppit, as the two of us seated ourselves on the floor, since fitting into goblin chairs wasn't really in the cards. "Nobody involved in building this place ever expected to be entertaining talls. We need to keep this meeting as efficient as possible anyway, so hopefully you won't be down there long."

"Oh, this is fine, we're perfectly comfortable," Yoshi said hastily, then gave me an awkward grin. "Actually it's sorta nostalgic, y'know?"

"Sitting on the floor is common where we're from," I explained in response to Sneppit's raised eyebrows. "In fact, this works way better than what I was trying to do. I had a goblin-sized chair built to human height for my conference room but it was always sort of awkward. Yeah, a low table, goblins in their own chairs and humans on the ground—this works much better. I should implement this myself."

"Well, glad to help, I guess."

"People might not like that," said Yoshi. "Fflyr aren't Japanese, Omura-san. The legs cramp up if you're not used to it."

"Well, they don't have to *kneel*."

"Plannin' to have a lot of goblins at your conference table, are ya?" Rizz drawled.

"Of course. If I'm going to be dealing with goblins, they should have a voice."

The conference room door swung open and Zui bustled in, kicking it shut behind herself without slowing. Sneppit shot her a grimace by way of greeting, and barked, "Well?"

I hadn't seen what, if any, comeuppance had been dispensed for Zui's unauthorized mission of mercy, but there was clearly some tension there still. Not that you'd know it from Zui's brisk response as she strode across the room to position herself at a little freestanding desk behind and to one side of Sneppit, who sat at the head of the long table.

"I set the butts up in the third level receiving bays, Snep. You know the one; the two warehouse spaces are connected enough they can mingle if they want, but have those dividers so we can separate the villain and Hero parties and hopefully *not* have any more screaming matches. Plus, each has got an attached office so the Hero and Dark Lord can have a private sleeping space. Both for prestige, and because they both brought all-female entourages and something tells me otherworlder humans aren't gonna be any less weird than the Fflyr about mixed-gender sleeping arrangements."

"As I recall," said Sneppit, "those bays were out of use because they were full of storage."

"Yeah, but that works out in our favor. What was being stored was spare lengths of track and fittings. I went ahead and authorized having those moved to the active bays on the first level, since it's a good bet Jadrak's assholes are gonna wreck whatever sections of track they can get to and we'll need to do major repairs as soon as he's gone."

"Ugh, that motherfucker," Sneppit growled. "He would, too. That's gonna mean a lot of cargo needs to get shifted before we can get our guests settled in."

"That's actually underway, and going much faster than usual," Zui reported. "The butts all chipped in to help carry, without even being asked. Even that horrible elf; she was the last to start working, and I think only out of embarrassment at being the only holdout, but even so. They're not any stronger than our own people but that height gives 'em great leverage. At the rate they were movin' when I left, the space will be cleared before the engineers cobble together something for 'em to sleep on."

"We're good with blankets on the floor," I offered.

"I'm guessing you don't see a lot of stone floors," Sneppit said dryly. "Even akorthist blocks have more give. Besides, you don't think we've got human-sized blankets just sitting around, do you?"

"Which elf is the horrible one?" Yoshi asked with a somewhat sickly attempt at a grin.

Everyone turned to stare at him. After a moment, he sighed and lowered his head to stare glumly at the tabletop.

". . . yeah, I know."

"Right," Sneppit said more briskly. "We're all here, then. For a quick round of intros, I'm Sneppit and this is my place; I think all of you know that. This is Zui," she added, jerking a thumb over her shoulder at the so-called hairstylist, who was now scribbling rapidly in a ledger. "She helps me stay organized and will be taking minutes. And *this* is Judge Rizz, who's just . . . here. As usual."

Each of the four union reps greeted me with a cheerful word while I sat there growing more and more confused.

"Wait, hang on. Sorry if this is a derailment, but . . . Why do you have four different labor unions within just one company?"

I immediately knew I had transgressed. One of those awkward pauses ensued, the ones that follow somebody ignorantly flouting a social rule so commonplace it shouldn't need explanation. The kind full of cringing glances and suddenly stiff postures as the whole room froze up from sheer discomfort. Everybody was embarrassed on my behalf and I was immediately annoyed by it.

"Well, he knows what a labor union *is*," Rizz finally said, "which is more'n I expected from a surface dweller. To answer your question, the function of a union is to distribute power laterally among workers to counter the top-down power of the company and its boss. Just having one is barely better than not having any; that just creates a new power structure within the old one, just as prone to corruption and the reps and admins getting a big head. If you want fairness, you gotta have *competition*."

"I . . . huh." I blinked rapidly, trying to follow that. "I guess I can see the logic in it, intellectually. In real world terms I gotta wonder how you people ever get anything done."

"The answer is we only sometimes do," Sneppit muttered. "Look, you don't need to worry about them, Lord Seiji, the unions don't matter for any purposes under discussion. They're only here because their contracts entitle them to have a representative present at all top-level company business. That is *not a complaint*," she added balefully as Zazoe opened her mouth. "I am *explaining* what I'm sure is an unfamiliar concept to people who aren't accustomed to workers having any say in anything."

"We understand," Yoshi said hastily. "Japan is very different from Fflyr Dlemathlys."

"Oh right, you're a high schooler," I muttered. "*Someone's* never hunted for a job in Tokyo."

"If introductions are done, let me get my biases out of the way," said Rizz, causing Sneppit to roll her eyes so hard she actually slumped backward in her chair, letting her head loll over the backrest. Rizz ignored this, just speaking evenly to the room at large. "I have adjudicated disputes involving Sneppit and/or her company on nine occasions, finding in her favor six times and three times against. I also purchased my bladestaff and that of my apprentice, Rhoka, from her engineers, paying what I believe to have been fair value with no discount. And presently, with the active danger in Kzidnak, my husbands are among the refugees taking advantage of Sneppit's offer to shelter civilians from the fighting."

"H-husbands?" Yoshi stuttered. "Plural? You mean . . ."

"You really wanna stop proceedings and discuss my love life, kid?" Rizz asked him pointedly.

He flushed bright pink and stammered for another second before finding a topic onto which to deflect. "So, uh, biases? I'm not sure I understand . . . Are you, um, officiating here?"

"No, she is not!" Sneppit exclaimed in exasperation. "Look, Judges are . . . Well, we don't have what you'd recognize as priests, and Kzidnak doesn't have any organized governing body. Or police. Judges are the interpreters of Virya's example as goblins understand it. They arbitrate disputes, and end up taking care of most of those other functions I mentioned."

"We keep things *competitive*," Rizz said, nodding.

"*Rizz* is only *here*," Sneppit continued, shooting her a disgruntled look, "because telling a Judge they can't attend a meeting just makes 'em think you're up to something relevant to their mandate, and I got enough bullshit to deal with today without Rizz and a bunch of her heavily armed friends rifling through my lingerie drawer. Judges are big on fairness and impartiality, so they start anything by airing out whatever relevant biases they might have. Just think of it like a religious practice. In this particular case it *does not matter*."

Behind her, Zui was shaking with silent laughter as she continued to record all this in shorthand.

I could sympathize both with Sneppit's obvious frustration and Zui's amusement at it. So far this "urgent strategy meeting" had been a farce of wasted time and waffling explanations. But more to the point, I suddenly felt I'd gained my first major insight into goblin culture, and one which accounted for something that had been increasingly bothering me since we first came underground.

I'd already known the goblins had better alchemy than the Fflyr; down here I'd seen that their engineering was *significantly* ahead. Between that and their artistic skills, it was really starting to look like Kzidnak was a notably more advanced civilization than Dlemathlys, to the point I found myself wondering how they were the underclass, even with the disparity in population. Now, I understood it—capabilities don't mean much if you can't organize and deploy them effectively. What had just been described to me was a kind of capitalist anarchy with—somehow—disproportionately powerful organized labor, overseen only by . . . cowboy Jedi inquisitors? It was like they'd taken all the worst parts from several mutually incompatible political systems and mashed them together into some shambling Frankensteinian corpse of a governance that couldn't possibly work.

No wonder even the hilariously inept Clans were kicking them around.

And also, just think what I could accomplish if I got all these goblins organized and pointed in the right direction . . .

"If we're all about done faffing around," Sneppit continued after a couple of seconds in which there were no further interruptions, "let's talk about what we're actually here to talk about: Jadrak."

"We're pretty in the dark regarding him," I admitted, glancing over at Yoshi, who nodded agreement. "I didn't know much more about the basic political situation than you explained a few minutes ago, Sneppit. Jadrak is whipping the normally passive populace of Kzidnak into a destructive mob, and only some of them are willingly going along with it, but it's enough to scare a lot of others into compliance or kill them if they won't. Obviously, what we need is to get rid of Jadrak, but that leaves a *lot* of room for detail. Yoshi and I have both been following a strategy of flailing around in the dark and would both be utterly boned already without your help. And by the way, in case I forgot to say it, thanks."

"You are welcome," she said with a wry, little smile. "Yeah, that's the long and the short of it. Until you showed up, my chosen strategy was to shell down and try to wait him out. I've been shoring up defenses and giving shelter to refugees in the hope that when he got around to attacking me I could fend him off. Ultimately, I wouldn't even have to *win*, just . . . not lose. A Goblin King requires momentum; if he got stalled out, unable to take out one of his rivals, he'd lose a lot of his followers. Most would abandon him, and some might even try to remove him themselves. That was always a gamble, though. In terms of assets and personnel, I don't have anything Jadrak doesn't, and he's got several advantages *I* don't, and that's before we consider the bigger numbers he can deploy. In tunnels, defensive fighting is usually stronger than offensive, and I've been preparing for this ever since the first rumblings started—well before either of you landed on Dount, as I understand it—but I was not excited about the odds."

"So offense is still the best bet," Yoshi murmured. "It's good of you to give shelter to those fleeing the fighting."

"Don't talk like it's some grand compassionate gesture," Sneppit grunted, grimacing. "A moral choice is one you make when the alternative would better serve your interests. In this case? More people in my complex means more warm bodies to man the barricades. Under other circumstances I'd quickly run out of food and medicine for this kinda crowd, but like I said, I have been preparing for this. Lord Seiji already knows I've been storing alchemicals away, and we've got decent stockpiles of food. Since Jadrak can't afford to besiege us, we only have to survive long enough to push back a few major attacks. Hopefully."

"Tell us about Jadrak," I said. "What exactly *are* we dealing with here?"

"Jadrak runs, well, I guess *ran*—I doubt he's still in business as such—a mining company. Biggest in Kzidnak; he's been the go-to guy for ore on all of Dount. We have limited dealings with the Fflyr, obviously, but I know he's supplied surface contacts with metal. Most of his business was here in Kzidnak, though. Obviously we weren't in direct competition, and I've been an indirect customer of his for years."

"Indirect customer?" I asked.

Sneppit grinned. "Raw ore is only so much use to me. *Refining* it requires proprietary asauthec blends that my alchemist hasn't cracked yet. I have some smelting capability, but quality workable metal has been the domain of another, somewhat smaller business that quickly got absorbed once Jadrak declared himself Goblin King. There's a trick to getting asauthec forges to burn hot enough and long enough to produce quality alloys. Zircko was the big name in refining, and he's been in Jadrak's pocket forever, because their businesses were too interconnected and Jadrak came out on top in their power struggle *years* ago. Zircko was either the first willing to join up, or his ass is dead and his assets confiscated by now."

"So Jadrak has basically bottomless access to raw metal *and* the ability to refine as much as he needs," I mused. "Hmm . . . What else?"

"The *good* news with regard to that is that Zircko's smithing was mostly producing base materials, not sophisticated tools, but then again, there are engineering companies other than mine, and soon enough some will join Jadrak, willingly or not. But for now, they won't have much in the way of complex machinery. Jadrak's other major asset, apart from the loyalty of his followers, is his lieutenant Hoy. A sorcerer, and the only goblin in Kzidnak who's Blessed."

"Not *even*," Yoshi's familiar suddenly interjected. "We fought *multiple* sorcerers on the way here! Three separate goblins who were able to cast Fire Lance and Force Wave."

"Yeah, we ran into one of those, too," I said. "It wasn't too hard to shut him down. I let him live, since I've been trying not to be any more destructive down here than I absolutely have to. Bastard turned right around and attacked us again, and Nazralind shot him through the head. So that's one less."

Yoshi grimaced. "Unfortunately, we weren't able to kill any of the ones who attacked us. We've been pressed hard since we got down here, and it seemed like the sorcerers would always fall back if the fight turned against them."

"And that is the issue exactly," Rizz interjected. "The most immediate concern about Jadrak, the thing that's most significant about his sudden rise and the thing everybody understands the least. See, for years Hoy *was* the only Blessed goblin on this island. There are only a few Spirits underground on Dount, and none of them give Blessings. Actually, Jadrak's headquarters are built around one, but it just gives directions to fresh ore veins and is very hard to please. Valuable, but not something that could help him do all *this*. For a goblin to get Blessed would mean they managed to access one of the Clan-controlled surface Spirits that can do it, or managed to get across one or *several* landbridges to a wilder island or dungeon that has them. Both of those are prohibitive barriers for a goblin, and I dunno which Hoy did, but he came back Blessed and with a decent little kit of spells. He's been Jadrak's top enforcer for a long time."

She paused, scowling deeply.

"Hoy has been a major pain in the ass for Judges and made Jadrak the same as long as he's been backing him. The kinds of aggressive . . . *business tactics* they've pulled are exactly why Judges exist, but none of *us* are Blessed. Keeping that company under a semblance of control has required us to do a lot of careful maneuvering with other companies and smaller businesspeople. Arranging boycotts and commercial sanctions against Jadrak has been the only way to prevent him from just forcibly taking over other businesses."

I leaned forward over the table. "Does that mean we can count on the Judges to side with us?"

"I would not base any plans around that," Rizz said firmly. "This is . . . complicated. *Ordinarily*, what Jadrak is doing is the very definition of violent, anticompetitive action that Judges would shut down with maximum prejudice. *But*, a formally declared Goblin King is a recognized thing in our culture, and the exception to a lot of normal rules. On the other hand . . . so is a Dark Lord."

She paused, tilting her head back to give me a long, appraising look from under the wide brim of that hat.

"Having the both of you here, active, and at cross purposes creates . . . dilemmas, from a Judge's perspective. Most of 'em already don't like Jadrak; if you present a good faith effort toward dealing fairly and gently with the goblins you meet, odds are good at least *some* Judges will fall into your camp. But I'm not gonna sit here and promise you anything on their behalf."

"And what about you?" I asked, grinning. "Are you impressed yet?"

"Not yet," Rizz stated tonelessly. "I'll be watching you, boy."

"That's interesting and all," the pixie chimed in, zipping back and forth above Yoshi's head in frustration, "but it's not answering the issue at hand! Why are you people so insistent that Jadrak only has the one sorcerer when we *clearly* know he has more?"

"Easy, Radatina," Yoshi urged. "I think they're still in the process of explaining that. Right?"

Radatina? Where had he come up with *that*? It wasn't a Japanese name . . . Oh, of course, probably taken from one of his anime.

"Right," Sneppit agreed, giving the familiar a long look. "Rizz, feel free to jump in if I miss anything, but I'm pretty sure I know the basics here. It's been the big buzz all over Kzidnak for at least the last week. For years, Hoy *was* the only Blessed down here, like she said, but now, *suddenly*, Jadrak has a whole handful. Starting just a few days ago, he's had them out rallying people and making shows of force, popularizing those green scarves and armbands and whatnot. I've had my people looking into it, and so far we know of seven individuals who suddenly have the Blessing of Magic. There are a few others; not entirely sure how many. The ones I've been able to dig up any info about were all ordinary goblins who worked for him. Couple miners, a clerk, a counter girl at his tool shop."

"And the spells are consistent, too, which is *really* rare among sorcerers, even organized ones," Rizz added. "Fire Lance and Force Wave. Basic offense, single target and multitarget. They all have those two specific spells and no others."

A short silence fell. Yoshi and I glanced quizzically at each other.

"Are you . . . sure about that?" Biribo finally asked.

"Yeah, synchronized spells . . . that's pushing likelihood," Radatina agreed. "If I hadn't personally seen three of them with exactly those, I wouldn't believe you."

"I didn't bring everybody here to trade gossip," Sneppit said irritably. "The tactical data itself is useful, but what matters is what it *means*."

One of the union reps—Skadl, from the janitors, that was it—tentatively raised his hand. "Uh, for those of us totally outta our depth here, what *does* it mean?"

"Biribo?" I murmured.

"Usually," he explained, "when a bunch of people suddenly turn up Blessed and with the spells or artifacts they'd need to *use* the new Blessing, and those people are all dedicated members of one political faction, *and* a major political upheaval immediately ensues, what you're looking at is a large outside power seeding them there for the purpose of causing that disruption."

"Exactly," said Sneppit, pointing at him.

"Wait, but . . ." Yoshi frowned, glancing around the table as if searching for an answer. "Who would do that to goblins? I mean, um, no offense, but . . ."

"No, you've hit the right question exactly," Sneppit agreed. "This is what makes it such a head-twister. There's only one simple explanation for how Jadrak suddenly has all these Blessed working for him, except that in this specific situation, it makes *no sense*."

I was reluctant to admit ignorance, but the goblins were just staring expectantly now, and Yoshi was floundering in visible confusion.

"Okay," I said, "let's say for the sake of argument that two of us are from an entirely different planet and not very familiar with the political nuances on Ephemera. Walk us through *why* exactly this doesn't make sense?"

"That's a fair point," Sneppit acknowledged with an amused little quirk of her lips. "It comes down to resources. I trust you boys have a general sense of the international powers that bother to keep a presence on Dount?"

I glanced up at Biribo, who for once seemed to have nothing to say now that somebody else was narrating. "I've been told about the Lancor Empire's aggressive operations throughout Dlemathlys."

"That's the big one," Sneppit nodded. "Well, the biggest. Dlemathlys is a relatively lawless border country on a major trade route, so almost every significant power in the archipelago keeps a few listeners here at least, but of the forces that bother to actually *do* anything? We're just looking at Lancor, Godspire, Shylverrael, and Savindar. And if we assume Jadrak's being propped up as a foreign power to disrupt the Fflyr, this doesn't make sense for any of 'em."

I nodded, as did Yoshi. "Okay, go on?"

"At issue is the *massive* investment an operation like this is. Your familiars have probably told you, but the kind of power that can grant Blessings is . . . rare. And collecting matched sets of scrolls like this is *prohibitively* hard. Even if you control multiple Spirits that give the right rewards, trying to farm them for consistent results usually makes them shut down."

Shit. Biribo had *not* seen fit to mention that last bit to me, and I wasn't pleased to hear it. Clan Yviredh's Spirit was difficult enough that I hadn't expected great results sending my people there—and indeed, Head Start had yet to reward anybody from my organization after I got mine—but the Spirit the nearby cat tribe had; I'd hoped to start getting goodies out of it once I'd brought them into the fold.

It figured, though. I was in a giant gacha game that'd been running for hundreds, if not thousands, of years under the direct supervision of its designers. Obviously, all the easy exploits had been patched long since.

"So in this hypothetical, we're looking at a *major* nation," Sneppit continued, oblivious to my inner frustration, "an empire that can pull in resources from across vast swaths of people and territory. That rules out Shylverrael and Godspire, which are lone city-states and isolationists besides."

"Leaving Savindar and Lancor," Yoshi nodded.

"And this doesn't suit the agenda of either," she said. "Savindar has nothing to gain by disrupting the Fflyr. Their only interests on Dount are maintaining some surreptitious contact with Shylverrael and keeping the trade routes through Godspire clear. Stirring up trouble here would harm their interests, not help them."

"Lancor *does* take an aggressive stance on the Fflyr," I said, "and they've had active agents on Dount as recently as a few weeks ago. Nazralind encountered one before she joined up with me. Why would they not stir up dissidents here?"

"That is, broadly, their agenda," she agreed, "but the details are all wrong. Like I said, Lord Seiji, seeding Blessings and spell scrolls is an absolutely *massive* investment. Spies have much more economical ways of causing trouble. This kinda gambit would be the harbinger of an invasion and conquest, and that's not Lancor's policy toward Dlemathlys. Besides, if they *were* planning to do that, it would be down on Dlemath, which is both closest to them and holds the central government. Dount is as far as possible from the Lancor border."

"Mmmm." I folded my arms, frowning at the wall above Mingzit's head. "I see the dilemma, then."

"That means . . . we're not just dealing with a Goblin King," Yoshi said slowly. "Somebody representing a *huge* amount of power is backing him, and we have no idea who. Or why. Or *how*."

"Which is less mysterious now than yesterday," Rizz commented. "Strikes me it is *not* a coincidence to find fingers that big in our pie, now that there's a Dark Lord *and* a Hero in Kzidnak."

Fuck. Nothing could ever be simple, could it?

"Hence, strategy meeting," said Sneppit, shrugging. "If it wasn't for that, I'd say hey, we got a Hero and Dark Lord here and Jadrak's only impressive by the standards of Kzidnak. Even the great Hoy would be, at best, a middling King's Guild adventurer in strength; either of you could plow right over him, let alone both. If things were *simple*, you two could just make a straight line right for Jadrak, smash anybody in your way, and take him out."

Rizz gave her a long, displeased stare, which Sneppit affected not to notice.

"As someone who's done it recently," Yoshi murmured, "cutting through an angry mob is *not* as easy as you're making it sound, even with the massive difference in power."

"And even if it weren't, I would rather *not* do that," I added. "I'm not here to slaughter goblins. Jadrak's followers are just fed up and angry and mostly have good reason to be. I have no interest in massacring anybody who doesn't absolutely *have* to die."

Sneppit sighed irritably, swatting away our objections with a brusque gesture. "Right, well, my *point* is, things are *not* that simple. We don't know exactly what's behind Jadrak, but there's at least a chance it's something that could be a threat even to the two of you. In this situation, just smashing into Jadrak's headquarters to kill him is too risky. We need to gain information before making an aggressive move."

A glum silence fell, in which Rizz scowled at Sneppit, Sneppit gazed expectantly at us, Zui's pen stopped scratching as she waited for the next speaker, the four union reps stared in wide-eyed bemusement at everybody, and Yoshi chewed his lip.

"Well, hey," I said finally, putting on a cocky smile. "Who says we can't do both?"

12

In Which the Dark Lord
Gets No Respect

All right, I get it, none of you like my plan. But we're all still *here*, because none of you clods could come up with anything better! So unless you *can* produce a superior idea, just do me a favor and button it."

I stared challengingly at the little strike team assembled around me on Sneppit's tram platform, all of whom returned unimpressed looks. Of course, it was Flaethwyn who opened her mouth again, despite my very clear instructions.

"This remains the most asinine thing I've ever heard of. You agreed we cannot risk attacking the Goblin King directly until we know the source of his power . . . So we're going to try to learn the source of his power by *attacking him directly?*"

"Yes, Flaethwyn, you can make anything sound stupid if you can't find anything better to do with your time than rephrase it in the worst possible way."

"That's literally just the— And my name is *Flaethwyn*! It isn't *that* hard to say, accent or no!"

"No human could possibly pronounce that," I said dismissively, turning away from her.

"*Yoshi* learned to do it!"

I gave her my sweetest smile. "Yoshi cares about your feelings."

Yoshi himself drew in a breath and visibly steeled his shoulders before intervening. Hey, at least the kid *was* developing the spine to step in now and again. He was urgently going to need that if he intended to keep hanging around with Flaethwyn.

"Omura, don't you think you're being a little too confrontational?"

I smiled and held up both hands in a peaceable gesture. Not that winding her up wasn't fun, but he wasn't wrong; this was probably not the time.

"And Flaethwyn, he has a point," Yoshi continued, turning to the elf. I noticed he unconsciously dipped his head slightly in an instinctively obsequious posture when speaking to her. That spine was still in development, clearly. "The plan *isn't* as simple as that, and none of us have come up with anything better. With Omura's group added to our own, we are strong enough that we should be able to handle anything the goblins can come up with. We might even get lucky and manage to take out the Goblin King when we get there, but even if not, that leaves the main plan. They'll be too distracted dealing with us to catch the spy before she can get what we're looking for."

Flaethwyn huffed and folded her arms. "That still means the whole thing depends on *that goblin* succeeding behind our backs."

The small group of goblins with us all glanced at her with cool expressions, but by this point everybody understood Flaethwyn well enough to tell when there was no point taking offense.

"Gizmit is a professional who is good at her job," I said. "Frankly, she might be the only one here who can make that claim."

Zui scowled up at me and loudly cleared her throat.

"Don't harrumph at me; I don't even know why you're here. What, you gonna give the Goblin King a bad haircut to sabotage his authority?"

"Yo! We are ready to roll out!" called the goblin from the engineering car, whose name I hadn't caught. He was apparently an actual engineer and not a cross-trained security guard like our previous pilot.

Getting ready to move had apparently taken some doing. We were embarking from another track that had to be reached by a series of metal bridges that creaked alarmingly under the weight of multiple humans but held. Fittingly enough, given that this was the central hub of the tram network, Sneppit's personal station was huge; apparently this wasn't even the only level. Our new ride was suspended from another track which would take us to our intended destination.

Unlike the basic lead car, which had brought us here, we were heading out with some kind of special engineering car with bigger sails, stronger brakes, a large compartment full of tools, and who knew what other augmentations. Sneppit was concerned about sections of the track having been damaged by Jadrak's people, so we'd be moving slower and with more care, and the ability to hopefully fix things at need. In addition to three engineers, she was also sending along Dap and his security team, since they were still on the clock.

To protect the tram, of course. Once we were dropped off as close as the tram could get us to Jadrak's HQ, we were on our own.

"All aboard, then," I said cheerfully, the first to clamber into the swaying car as soon as one of the secondary engineers popped the door open.

One by one, the others followed. There was no escaping the tightness of the fit, since this thing had been designed for riders half our height, but it was a tiny bit more comfortable than previously as there were two fewer humans this time. Per Aster's plan, Ydleth and Madyn were helping Sneppit's people around the base. In exchange, though, there was an extra goblin coming with us.

Gizmit was here because she was part of the plan. Zui hopped aboard, too, ignoring my pointed look. Well, considering Sneppit was also using this trip as an opportunity to scout the condition of the tunnels, maybe she'd sent Zui along to supervise them once we parted ways from the tram.

Also, I saw Rizz and Rhoka both clambering into the rear car with the security team. They were *not* part of the plan, but I wasn't terribly surprised to see them include themselves. From what I'd gathered, that was basically what Judges did. Whatever trouble Rhoka was in for aiding Zui's off-the-books rescue mission, apparently it wasn't enough to keep Rizz from bringing her along.

Nazralind was the last one in, and behind her, a goblin attending the platform called out "Watch your fingers!" and slammed the door shut.

"Everybody settled?" shouted the lead engineer from the car ahead. Behind us, somebody rapped hard on the metal frame of the rear car, and Zui reached up and hammered her fist against our door in turn. "All right, we're out! This ain't gonna be a fast trip, folks. Keep yer ears perked for blood-curdling screams; first sign of enemy contact an' you mooks are gonna earn your pay. Gettin' stabbed ain't in my contract!"

"Charming," Flaethwyn groused as the sails ahead were cranked open and we began moving forward. True to his word, the engineer only extended them partway, causing us to proceed at a slower pace than our previous trip. I also felt the occasional shudder as he gently pumped the brakes to interrupt our acceleration.

A tense and gloomy silence hung over the group, especially the Sanorites—who were, to be fair, having a really terrible day. This was just begging for someone with my wit and charm to step in and lift the mood.

To my surprise, Yoshi beat me to it.

"Okay, so . . . Radatina and, uh . . . other familiar. What do you think *could* be the source of these Blessings and scrolls the Goblin King suddenly has?"

"We've ruled out any of the obvious sources," the pixie replied, seating herself on Yoshi's shoulder. Biribo preferred to remain hovering, seemingly unfazed by the tram's speed or the wind through its lack of walls. "Things like that usually come from Spirits or dungeon rewards. It seems none of the Spirits in these tunnels can produce those results, and there definitely isn't an active dungeon on Dount."

"Yeah, that's kinda the point, kid," Biribo agreed. "We *don't* know what's going on. Hence our fact-finding mission here."

"Right, I understand that," Yoshi said patiently. "But you said those are the *obvious* sources, right? I'm just wondering if you know of any other possibilities. Even if they're unlikely . . . well, it's something. Anything to avoid going in completely blind."

"I . . . Yoshi, I would've said so if there was any chance—"

"Only other thing that comes to mind is sometimes Blessings and Blessing-related rewards can be handed out in person," Biribo said, interrupting Radatina's hesitant answer. The pixie familiar scowled up at him, buzzing her wings in annoyance.

"In person?" Pashilyn asked, leaning forward. "You mean . . . by the Goddesses?"

"Exactly," said Radatina. "They've been known to do it. However, to avoid escalating their conflict into another planet-breaking apocalypse, the Goddesses are strictly hands-off and don't intervene directly while a Dark Crusade has been called. So long as there's a Dark Lord walking the surface of Ephemera, neither will risk bestowing a personal Blessing or other reward, *except* as a normal miracle bought with Goddess coins."

"Which brings us back to the same considerations that ruled out Lancor having set this up from their stash of scrolls," Biribo added. "That's a *massive* investment, and not something that makes sense for any of the big enough powers to do in Kzidnak of all places."

"I see," Yoshi mused, frowning sightlessly at the passing tunnel wall visible through the bars. A momentary silence fell while we considered.

"The only other possibility—"

"Don't even bring that up!" Radatina interrupted Biribo, rising off Yoshi's shoulder to buzz aggressively toward him.

He turned a baleful look on the pixie, flicked out his tongue at her once, and then very deliberately continued his thought.

"It's *possible* for Blessings to be granted, and scrolls created, by certain very powerful individuals."

"What?" Yoshi demanded while Radatina groaned dramatically and covered her face with both hands. "It is? By who?"

"You've mentioned scrolls can be created," I said, "but not that people can grant Blessings."

"Yeah, well, that's because it's even less likely than the other options we've considered. Crafting spell scrolls is a *major* high-end feat for the most powerful Blessed with Magic; there probably aren't more than a handful of people alive who can do it, and that's not really any quicker or easier than dungeon delving or Spirit-talking, just somewhat more reliable. But granting *Blessings*, it's basically only Heroes and Dark Lords who can do that."

"Aha, the case is blown wide open!" I said, grinning. "Yoshi! Where were you on the night of the murder?"

"Right, because *he's* the suspicious one here," Flaethwyn sneered. Yoshi just frowned at me.

"Also," Biribo added, "I'm talking about late-stage, well-developed, *powerful* Champions, not neophytes who've only been on Ephemera for a few months. No offense."

"And since you two are *accounted for*," Radatina said pointedly, still staring at Biribo, "that *settles* the matter. *Right?*"

He flicked out his tongue at her again, and I got the distinct impression Biribo would've stopped talking long since if the opposing familiar wasn't getting under his skin. Personally, I found this delightful. Not just because it was amusing; she was inadvertently goading him into revealing things I suspected the Goddesses preferred we not know. I already knew for a fact that Biribo hid things from me on those grounds, given that I'd had to go behind his back to learn about the Void.

"Unless," he replied just as deliberately, "a former Hero or Dark Lord shows up."

"What?" I barked, abruptly forgetting my previous levity.

At the same moment, Yoshi leaned forward so suddenly it made the tram car sway. "*That can happen?!*"

"*No*, it *can't!*" Radatina exclaimed, zipping back and forth and waving her arms about in agitation. "Augh! *Why* would you *tell* them that?! *Now* they're just going to be worried over nothing!"

"It very much *can* happen, even if it definitely *won't*," Biribo shot back. "It was a question, and I answered it with the truth. That's the job! That is our *entire reason for existing!*"

"Oy!" I yelled, clapping my hands sharply. "Settle! Do I need to separate you two?"

"Yeah, let's try to calm down," Yoshi urged in a more soothing tone. "I don't get what you two are trying to say. It's possible that there's a previous Hero or Dark Lord around, but . . . also *not?*"

Another tense little silence ensued, in which Biribo and Radatina glared daggers at each other.

"Well," she said finally, throwing up her tiny hands, "you were so keen on dragging this up. Go on, spell it out since you're so clever."

Biribo stuck his tongue out at her again, this time far enough I thought he might be trying to devour the pixie frog-style, but at least he answered before this could devolve into more familiar infighting.

"Right, so, boss, I know I've mentioned that in some rare cases, really successful Dark Lords who ran out of things to conquer were able to pass the reins to a lieutenant and go into retirement. So! By definition, a Dark Crusade ends with a Hero victorious—and almost always alive, unless they take the Dark Lord down with them, blaze of glory style, which . . . isn't common. And it *can* end with the original Dark Lord also secretly alive and in hiding."

"With you so far," I said, nodding.

"The other thing to note is that, at the highest possible reaches of power within the Blessings system—the kind of stuff that only Champions of the Goddesses have any reasonable chance of achieving—is magic that can grant extreme longevity, or even immortality."

"Longevity, yes," Radatina interrupted. "Actual immortality? That's only hypothetically, *technically* achievable. It's never been done and probably won't be. I bet that's one of the degrees of power the Goddesses would step in and prevent if somebody was getting too close."

"She's right," Biribo admitted grudgingly, "but even so, it is within the bounds of possibility for somebody to survive for centuries, and a Hero or Dark Lord is the most likely person to find that kind of power."

"Wait, wait," Yoshi interjected. "If that's true, why are you so certain it's *not* the case here? It sounds like that would explain everything!"

"Because," Biribo said with clear exasperation, "Hara Satoshi and Kurobe Yomiko are both dead as dust. History records where, when, and how each of 'em kicked it. Both of their gravesites are protected historical landmarks of the Lancor Empire. *They* are not going to suddenly pop up."

"Which means," Radatina swooped in to take over the explanation, "any *theoretical* former Champion who might still be around would have to have survived for *multiple* cycles of Dark Crusades, which have a century between them at *least*, usually closer to two. That's already pushing the upper limits of longevity magic by itself. And more importantly, it would mean that any former Champion who's still around would have, for some reason, decided to quietly sit out the last Dark Crusade. On the very remote chance that *all of that* happened, why would they butt in now?"

"Annoying pixie is right," Biribo agreed. "If a previous Champion felt like making their presence known, it would've been pushing their luck to do it last round when they were merely old and decrepit. By *now* they'd be ancient and falling apart."

I could think of any number of possible reasons that would motivate such a person to do something so irrational, but kept my peace for the moment. On consideration, I was inclined to agree with the familiars' assessment; to judge by the silence and pensive stares of the others, I wasn't the only one. Even if a previous Champion were alive *and* decided to show up and go out in some absurd last hurrah . . . why this? Handing out spell scrolls to a tiny handful of goblins engaged in a rebellion on a nowheresville island like Dount? My—and I suppose, Yoshi's—presence here was all that made it even remotely probable, and this seemed like an unlikely way to come at us.

"Gotta say," I eventually broke the silence, "I agree with the pixie. This is almost certainly a nonconsideration, and *now* I wish you hadn't told us. Even knowing there's not gonna be a veteran Dark Lord popping up to backstab me, I'm going to be paranoid about it for the rest of my life. *Thanks*, Biribo."

"I just can't win with you," he complained.

I grinned at him. "Maybe you should try to be more like— *LALATINA!*"

My sudden epiphany had nothing to do with our situation, but it prompted me to jerk upright so hard I bonked my head on the ceiling and set the car rocking again; Radatina zoomed backward out of reach as I threw forward one hand to point at her, cackling.

"I knew it! I *knew* you couldn't resist making it an anime reference! Let me guess, she also pretended she couldn't understand your accent?"

"Oh, you've seen Kono—wait." Yoshi broke off his excited reply to turn a betrayed look on his familiar. "*Pretended*?"

"You are a *jerk*!" the tiny pixie screeched, darting aggressively toward my face. "Even for a Dark Lord, you're a jackass! I oughta dive down your throat and finish you off from the inside!"

"Hang on," said Yoshi. "Biribo . . . Omura, did you try to name your familiar *Bilbo*?"

"Never mind that," I waved him off. "*Now* I wanna see this little pixie try to take me out. I mean, can you imagine Virya's face if *that* was how the Dark Crusade ended? Fuck it, I'm ninety percent sold on this for that alone. Somebody get Discount Darkness a tiny little dagger and let's see what happens. Who's got a toothpick?"

Yoshi interceded again, physically grabbing Radatina and trying to soothe her fit of temper, while Aster leaned over from my other side to murmur in my ear.

"I realize you're just having fun, but maybe *don't* make jokes like that in front of people who've given up everything to follow you."

Feeling suddenly guilty, I glanced over at my followers. Reassuringly, Adelly just looked bemused, and Nazralind was grinning as if this was the best show she'd seen in ages. Which was probably true.

Poor Yoshi was still doing his best to keep the peace, and now stepped in with a desperate change of subject.

"So, I didn't know that the last Hero and Dark Lord's graves were both protected sites. Even the Dark Lord's? I'm surprised the Radiant Temple would allow that. Actually, it's a little surprising they would bury her at all."

"Dark Lord Yomiko was respected by her enemies, both in her time and still now," Pashilyn said smoothly, speaking in a calm tone that was just what this situation needed to de-escalate. "Her forces were kept to a strict code of conduct regarding the treatment of civilians and prisoners of war. Whenever she conquered a noble's holdings, any plunder her army didn't specifically need would be distributed among the common people who lived nearby. Several times she took the time to ask around about any grievances the people had with their rulers, and put Lancoral nobles and bureaucrats on trial for corruption, then dispensed punishments if they were convicted. When she found the people loved their local rulers, she offered them protection and returned a share of their confiscated assets. Yomiko never declined an honorable duel— nor lost one—and always spoke to her enemies with courtesy. That impressed the Lancoral a great deal; chivalry is very important in their culture."

"You make her sound like some kind of saint," Flaethwyn said, her voice redolent with disdain. "Yomiko was a marauding butcher, just like any Dark Lord. She simply had the benefit of crafty advisors from Savindar who coached her in political theater, so she put on those little shows to impress the locals and discourage uprisings against her. *Obviously*, it worked on the ignorant peasants. Lancor is a beacon of civilization in many ways, but they don't bother to educate their lowborn like we Fflyr."

"That is wrong in every possible direction," Nazralind stated. "Unlike Dlemathlys, Lancor *has* a public education system. It's mostly for the children of nobles and imperial bureaucrats, but any citizen who can pass the entrance exams and pay tuition can attend school. Meanwhile, there is no polity in Dlemathlys that educates lowborn, save the Radiant Convocation, and that only applies to their own initiates. We *allow* lowborn to educate *themselves* because this country is so awash in books that preventing them would require a massive administrative infrastructure that none of the Clans are competent enough to build."

This time, the silence hung like a weight. Flaethwyn opened her mouth, then closed it and averted her eyes, her cheeks coloring. Coming from anyone else, that would have been the start of another screaming fight, but for some reason she seemed intimidated by Nazralind. It was nearly as useful as it was hilarious.

"In any case," Pashilyn continued after a moment, "the Emperor at the time did commission a respectable tomb for Dark Lord Yomiko, and the Empire has maintained and protected it ever since. I'm sure there's a limit to how fondly people can feel toward someone conquering their country; but in the century and a half since Yomiko's passing, the Lancoral have grown oddly affectionate toward her memory. I understand she gets a lot of flowers every Passing Day."

"Must be nice," I mused. "*I'll* be lucky if they leave me face down in a ditch."

More people than I liked nodded solemnly.

"*That* was the appropriate moment for someone to disagree," I said irritably.

Again, solemn nods all around.

"You know, shit like this is what drives people to start conquering stuff," I complained.

"You guys are fun," Zui commented.

The tram, I noticed, was decelerating. There were no sparks or screeching this time; must've been those fancy brakes I'd been told the engineering car had.

All told, despite the *continual disrespect* I was forced to suffer, I decided to chalk this tram ride up to a victory for the Dark Crusade. Sure, all I'd learned was the useless and unpleasant fact that I only *probably* wasn't going to get surprise murdered by a grumpy elder Dark Lord, but it had been a chance to sit and chat with Yoshi and his team. I'd already saved their butts twice now, and just having the chance to hang out and socialize with them, like normal people riding a train together, was advancing the cause. The more they regarded me and mine as just folks and not monsters, the closer I was to turning their righteous vengeance away from the Dark Crusade and toward the Goddesses where it belonged.

Baby steps.

"Aw yeah, *nailed* it!" crowed the talkative engineer one second after the tram creaked to a halt. "Ladies and gentlemen, if you'll look to your left, you will see the *exact* entrance into the tunnels you'll need, *right* in front of the door of your car, because I am just that good. You're welcome."

Gizmit had stood up while he was nattering, turning around and pressing her face against the bars. "Hm. Hey, familiars, any guards nearby?"

"I don't detect anybody in the vicinity," Biribo reported, beating Radatina by a split second.

"Nor up and down the tram tunnel in either direction," she added, not to be outdone. "We seem to be completely alone."

"That's . . . weird," I murmured. "I thought this side tunnel led right into Jadrak's home complex. *And* it comes out into a major tram tunnel he knows Sneppit has access to. Are we sure this is the right spot?"

"That's it," Gizmit confirmed. "It's not the first time I've been snooping around here. And you're right, this is . . . *Weird* is a word for it. This should not be unguarded. Jadrak's always run a fairly loose operation, but he's not an idiot."

"Counterpoint," I said, opening the door, "everything else he's done."

I hopped out before she could respond. This was the middle of nowhere, not an actual tram platform; it was a drop of roughly my height to a rocky, uneven tunnel bottom. The rest of the team filed out after me, dropping to the floor as each of us made room in turn, Nazralind and Flaethwyn both lighting up their auras so we could see. The drop was obviously a bigger deal for the goblins than us, but Rizz and Rhoka had already descended from the rear car by the time Yoshi hit the ground and skidded on loose gravel, barely avoiding a fall by colliding with Aster, who'd seen this coming and braced her feet. Gizmit followed him far more gracefully despite having relatively farther to fall.

"Look alive!" Zui called from above. I looked up, barely in time to catch her with a surprised grunt as she plummeted into my arms. "Thanks."

The little pest had the absolute temerity to reach up and ruffle my hair before hopping the rest of the way down.

"Can I *help* you?" I demanded, annoyed.

"That's all I needed for now, thanks, but I'll letcha know."

"Forgive me, Zui; I keep forgetting that subtlety is wasted on you. Let's try that again—what the hell do you think you're doing? I thought you were just along to supervise the tram crew."

"*They* don't need it," she said pointedly. "Sneppit wants somebody representing her interests on this op after Gizmit peels off to do her thing."

"And she chose the barber. Of course. *Obviously.*"

"Anybody who works in Miss Sneppit's inner circle has *multiple* valuable skills at a high level," Zui said archly. "In addition to being the best damn hair gal in Kzidnak and *one* of its most renowned executive assistants, I am a perfectly competent security guard and more besides. So, yeah, you tall and Blessed types will be taking point on this, but I am not dead weight."

I scowled at her; she folded her arms and stared right back. I was the first to avert my gaze, mostly because that position with her arms really pushed her chest up in a way that was distracting enough to make me worry about a flashback. Goddamn this smug goblin and her amazing tits. The last thing I needed was to turn into another Donon on top of the rest of my problems.

"Right, well. You two are in charge of keeping Zui out of trouble," I ordered, turning to Rizz and Rhoka.

"Oh," Judge Rizz deadpanned, "is *that* what we're in charge of?"

"This natural crevice leads right into a carved-out section not far ahead," Radatina reported, having followed Yoshi over to the aperture in the tunnel wall in front of us. "Just a couple of minutes' walk, I think; it's mostly big enough we shouldn't have trouble getting through. Pretty spacious for goblins."

"Yeah, and we're well within earshot of whoever's in there," said Gizmit.

"Which, again, is nobody," Biribo repeated. "Seriously, there are *no goblins* within the range of my senses. Ask the pixie if you doubt me."

"The lizard is right," Radatina reluctantly agreed. "*We* represent the entirety of sapient life within basic familiar senses. Looks like the tunnel complex beyond goes much deeper, but there shouldn't be anybody able to hear us from here."

"Right beyond this tunnel is a section that used to be a mine," Gizmit said, turning to look up at me. "All the veins were tapped out years ago; that particular area was carved out further for housing. Specifically, housing for Jadrak's *security division*. It does *not* make sense that there's nobody in the section beyond, especially at a time like this. His whole complex should be locked down and every exit manned; the people responsible for organizing that would *definitely* know about this tunnel."

"Well," I said slowly. "How . . . incredibly convenient for us."

It was Yoshi who said what we were all thinking, as the tram behind us opened its wings and began to slide away up the tunnel.

"This is bad, isn't it?"

13

In Which the Dark Lord Bends the Knee

There came a pause in which we all considered the tunnel ahead of us, and during that silence a few things I knew about goblins and Jadrak in particular clicked together.

"Hey, Biribo. Can you detect the presence of bombs?"

Everyone's heads whipped around to stare at me.

"Well . . . Not *directly*, boss. I can scan for the shapes of stuff that's out of place . . . particularly stuff like fuses and packages of liquids or powder attached to a mechanical triggering device. There are ways to conceal that, though."

I nodded; we'd used some of those ourselves, the sleeping-bomb-disguised-as-a-rock being my group's favorite method of bandit attack.

"Give it a try, if you would. Just let me know if anything seems suspicious in that tunnel. Goblins are really good with alchemy," I explained in response to everyone else's questioning stares. "And Jadrak in particular runs a *mining* company. Odds are good he's got explosives to work with."

"Oh." Yoshi's expression lengthened and he turned an even more unhappy stare on the tunnel. Behind him, Amell—who was so quiet I'd almost forgotten she was there—knelt on the rocky ground, set her heavy satchel in front of herself and began rummaging in it. "Radatina, double-check Biribo's findings, please."

"With pleasure!"

Biribo actually broke away from the tunnel entrance to zoom at Yoshi's face. "Oh, you think I can't handle—"

"*Heel!*" I ordered. "The last thing this group needs is familiar drama! It's a good idea to have an extra pair of eyes on this. If you don't want Radatina to show you up, you'll just have to be better than her, that's all."

He stuck out his tongue at me, but turned and zipped back toward the big crack in the wall, which was the focus of all this scrutiny. Radatina hovered nearby, managing to focus intently while simultaneously radiating smugness.

"Booby-trapping this would be a strange move," Gizmit said, studying the tunnel entrance through narrowed eyes.

"Jadrak knows Sneppit was against him, right?" I asked. "If he knows about this back way in, and that it opens onto one of her tram tunnels that's a straight shot from her base . . ."

"Kzidnak doesn't have any equivalent of your Fflyr messenger relays; information down here moves at, basically, the speed of trams. Today, we've had access to those and he hasn't. By now Jadrak most likely knows he's made an enemy of the Dark Lord and has a powerful King's Guild party closing in, but it's debatable he'd have learned by now you're linked up with each other *and* with Miss Sneppit. A tunnel rigged to explode would be a measure against something like that, which he would not have had time to set up in advance, especially since it seems to have involved evacuating part of his own HQ. And he wouldn't take a posture like this against Sneppit on her own; she's well known to be a defensive thinker."

"Hm. Biribo, anything?"

"I don't think so, but—"

"There's nothing obviously bomb-like," Radatina cut in, "but that tunnel itself is littered with old trash and loose rocks. I don't think we can say for certain that there's nothing alchemical concealed as some of it."

"It's worse at the end," Biribo said, refusing to give her the last word. "That's a chamber that was recently inhabited. *Lots* of junk in there, much of it artificial; real easy to conceal a trap among that stuff."

"Well, this'll slow us down, but I'm experienced at trap work," said Gizmit, rolling her shoulders. "Since I don't think it's probably trapped, I judge it worth the risk. If I could borrow an elf to stand behind me and glow—"

"Let me. I've got it."

Amell spoke in an uncharacteristically even, firm tone, though it was still on the quiet side. She'd been silently mixing concoctions from her pack together while the rest of us conferred and in fact now looked focused and determined, quite unlike her usual tremulous demeanor.

Now she was shaking a stoppered bottle of what was either very fine powder or effervescent liquid and moved about in a peculiar way for whichever. As Amell agitated it, the substance shifted in color from a muddy pink to gold-tinged white and began to glow. The alchemist drew in a breath as deep as she could manage, her whole chest swelling up with the effort, then swiftly yanked the stopper out of the bottle and blew furiously over its top in the direction of the tunnel wall.

It was powder, all right. It mostly went into the tunnel, but some of it sprayed . . . well, everywhere.

"It's all right," Amell hastened to reassure us as soon as she'd drawn another breath; everybody was already shuffling back from the airborne mess, Zui muttering protests as she shielded her hair and Flaethwyn and Adelly angrily brushing at their clothes. "The dust is harmless, and it won't be on you for more than a few seconds. All of it will go right back into the bottle shortly. Then it'll change color, and I'll be able to tell whether there's any dangerous alchemy in the area it covered."

"You can *do* that?" Yoshi sounded as impressed as I felt.

Amell nodded, speaking distractedly with her eyes fixed on the tunnel entrance, the sides of which were still sparkling with her magic alchemy dust. "This recipe will react to explosives, combustibles, corrosives, and mind-altering agents. If it reads positive, I can do specific tests to narrow it down. Of course, another alchemist working from the other end can take steps to conceal against this trick, but goblins in Dlemathlys almost never do because the King's Guild doesn't send alchemists into the field."

"Why not?" I demanded. "Far as I can tell, you just made yourself the most useful person here."

Amell gave me a wide-eyed look, ducking her head; I had the impression she'd be blushing if her complexion allowed it. "I, uh . . . Well, really only big, state-sponsored groups like the guilds in Lancor do that. An alchemist can make much better money without risking their life. Not many want to go on delves unless somebody very powerful is making them."

Well, well, this girl had hidden depths. And here I'd been wondering why someone so timid was even along for this ride.

"How long?" Gizmit asked tersely.

"Seconds, for an area this confined. Two minutes, tops." Amell looked down at her satchel and grimaced. "I hope it comes back negative . . . I'm running low on almost everything. I may not have enough reagents to do all the follow-up tests."

"Miss Sneppit's got an alchemist on staff," I said. "Youda's good people. The goblins can't afford to just give stuff away, but I bet he'll sell you supplies at a fair price. I'll spot you if you're tight; me and Youda are old pals, he'll give me a good deal."

"Oh!" The poor girl gave me an utter deer-in-headlights look. "I couldn't— You don't have to—"

"I'm just being practical, not generous. If we're going to be working together, it's in everybody's best interests if everybody's working at their best. Obviously your skills are valuable here."

"*I* will pay for her supplies if it needs to be done," Flaethwyn snapped, glaring at me as if I'd just insulted her somehow.

"Why, that's real big of you, Flaethwyn," I said sweetly. "Now, just out of curiosity, did you ever offer to do that *before* you had a reason to be competitive about it?"

"Please stop, both of you," Yoshi pleaded.

Flaethwyn's mouth was open to retort, and I had the distinct impression his urging wasn't going to dissuade her, but then she chanced to catch Nazralind's eye. Naz sardonically lifted one eyebrow and folded her arms, and just like that, Flaethwyn flushed and looked away.

"Stop calling me Fureidowen. I *know* you're doing it on purpose."

Aster took one look at my own expression and intervened with another distraction. "Is your alchemy the reason your hair keeps changing color, Amell?"

That seemed to just make the girl sad; she hunched her shoulders and reached up to touch her curls, which were some indeterminate shade between green and blue at the moment.

"I, um . . . Well, yes. An experiment went bad and it changed to . . . I don't know. It doesn't take dyes in a normal way anymore; I can't get it to look black again. Everything I try dyes it a different color that has nothing to do with the dye I used. I'm getting afraid to try new recipes, cos half the time it starts glowing or sparkling or some nonsense like that."

"Huh, why not leave it at its new base color?"

Amell gave her a miserable look. "Because the new base color is yellow."

Aster winced. "*Ohhh.*"

"What? What's wrong with that?" I asked. "Lots of people have yellow hair. I bet that'd look good on you."

"She's lowborn, you idiot," Flaethwyn sneered. "Golden hair is an elven trait, and a sign of the Goddess's favor; its appearance, or lack thereof, is a major factor in determining the status of a highborn family. A lowborn who artificially colored their hair gold would be flogged or worse."

"Why is everything I learn about this country both stupid and horrible?" I demanded of no one in particular. "Stupid *or* horrible, sure, that's everywhere. We've even got some of each back home in Japan. But no, you Fflyr *always* have to have it both ways."

I guess that was really the optimal moment for Amell's mojo to kick in, because that conversation just wasn't going to go anywhere productive from that point. Fortunately, the spectacle was riveting enough to seize everyone's attention. True to Amell's promise, the glistening powder began to drift away from everyone's clothes, gathering into streams midair and whooshing back into the bottle from which she'd first blown it, with, by far, the biggest concentrations being from within the tunnel. It was actually a little disorienting, given the way its motion was suddenly unrelated to the constant warm breeze whooshing down the tram line from behind us.

In just a couple more seconds, the last of it had slipped home again, and Amell plunged the stopper back into the bottle.

"That is a *neat* trick," Nazralind cheered.

"How's it look, Amell?" Yoshi asked.

She had shaken the bottle twice more, studying its nearly white glow; there was the faintest tinge of yellow, but the white heavily predominated. The light very quickly began to fade, and Amell took time to make sure the color didn't change as the energy leaked out from the alchemy before answering.

"Looks like a negative, Yoshi. Just the faintest discoloration, but that's about what I'd expect to pick up just from traces on the air in a place like this. Goblins use lots of alchemy, all over everything. There's nothing in the vicinity that triggered the detection, so . . . nothing directly dangerous."

I was pondering just exactly how potent alchemy really was and what else I might be able to do with it; potions and bombs were nice, but this was starting to look almost like a whole-ass third system of magic, distinct from Blessings and the Void. *Anything* that might help me buck the Goddesses' control was worth my interest. But that was a subject to investigate another time.

"Then we're back at this being suspicious. Biribo, what about non-alchemical traps? Surely it's pretty easy to rig a tunnel to collapse if somebody steps on a tripwire or something?"

"We would've spotted that immediately, boss. Familiars can detect shapes of any solid matter within the range of our senses; it's chemical composition that gets tricky."

"Anything like that would be large enough and complex enough to be easily identifiable," Radatina added, because neither of them could just let the other explain something without chiming in. "That tunnel is *not* rigged."

I turned to Gizmit. "What do you think?"

"Something's up," she said, staring fixedly into the dark gap in the rock before us. "This isn't normal. I guess we won't find out exactly what until we explore more. Seems like we've ruled out the immediate and obvious threats."

"Right," Yoshi said, nodding and drawing his sword. Poor kid was visibly steeling himself; it was almost adorable. "Right. Okay. If that's the case . . . Miss Aster, you and I are the best-armored. We should go first. With Omura right behind us; that's the optimal position for our strongest spellcaster, and he's got very good healing magic in case something goes wrong. Amell? How's your potion supply? I don't want to waste any, but this seems like the right moment to take precautions."

"I have a few more," she said, already handing him a vial. Amell produced a second, which she handed over to Aster. "That's a basic first-strike defensive blend; damage resistance and heightened reflexes. Baseline duration of about fifteen minutes, though it'll burn up faster if you raise your heart rate or get injured."

"Thanks," Aster said, lifting the vial to her lips with a grateful nod.

I felt someone prod me in the hip and looked down to find Zui smirking up at me. "What, you just gonna let the kid take over like that? I'd've thought the Dark Lord would be too proud to take orders."

"Do you honestly think this situation isn't enough of a mess without you stirring up shit?" I demanded. Seriously, *why* was she even here? "I'll take issue with it if he tells me to do something I don't wanna; I'm not about to argue with a solid plan. Yoshi, if anything comes suddenly at your face, yell. The first seconds can matter, and I can't heal the dead. As long as you survive anything that happens, I've got you."

"Got it," he said seriously. "All right, here we go."

He stepped up into the crack, and right away I saw the flaw in his plan. The narrow tunnel required us to go single file; Aster's position behind Yoshi and in front of me just meant I couldn't easily see Yoshi to heal him if it proved necessary. She couldn't even draw her greatsword in these cramped quarters; her sole contribution to this effort was forming a meat wall between me and anything that might take out Yoshi.

I opted to keep my mouth shut. No point undermining the kid when our familiars and alchemist were all reasonably sure we weren't actually stepping into a trap.

But we made it through with nothing happening. Nothing happened beyond, either; the three of us emerged into a chamber in which no lights had been left on, so I conjured a Firelight as soon as I stepped out after Aster. As Gizmit had predicted, we were now in a goblin barracks; I got the impression we could only stand up straight because this place was built on a pretty vertical plan, with bunk beds towering seven ranks tall built against the walls. Man, it must've been hard to get to the top bunk at the end of a long shift.

Flaethwyn emerged a few seconds later and lit up her aura, as did Nazralind when she came in at the end of the group, giving us ample light to see. This place was a mess, the floor scattered with what looked like miscellaneous personal belongings.

"This looks abandoned," Zui said, peering around. "In a hurry, too. There's people's junk everywhere, but look, most of the beds are stripped. And those lockers were cleaned out in a rush."

She pointed, and I followed her indication to a rack of metal lockers along one wall which, sure enough, were all standing open, several with miscellaneous personal effects lying in or beneath them. It looked like the goblins who'd cleared out of here had had time to take most of what was important, but not everything.

"Well, *this* is good and spooky," Nazralind muttered.

"Tina-chan?" Yoshi stage-whispered, and I shot him an amused smirk which, unfortunately, he was facing the wrong way to see.

"We're still alone here," Radatina reported, "but I can finally detect some goblins in a chamber . . . Let's see, if we go out *that* door and down the corridor, we'll come right to it. Only eight goblins, though. Can't tell what they're doing."

"*I* can," Biribo declared, zipping over to the door she'd indicated. "*That* room is a prison, not a barracks. Open area separated by metal bars from cell blocks. There's one goblin imprisoned and seven outside the bars. Oh . . . And two dead goblins in other cells."

"I could've picked all that out if I was closer," Radatina snapped.

Biribo flicked his tongue out at her. "Coulda, woulda . . . didn't."

"*Shut up*," I commanded. "You're like a pair of toddlers. What about closer to us? Can you detect anything in here or nearby that looks important? Or even interesting?"

"If there are any clues among the personal junk dropped by the mooks, they'd take far too long to sort through," said Gizmit, already striding in the opposite direction from the door the familiars had indicated, where there was another one. "That's the officers' bunks through there. I'm gonna check if any of 'em were incompetent enough to leave important paperwork lying around. You lot go see what's up in the cells; I'll check in on you in a minute."

"As you command, my lady," I drawled.

"Uh huh," Zui said, poking me in the hip again. "So it's fine if Hero boy barks orders, but you won't take it from a goblin."

So help me, I was gonna kick her.

"What else do you notice? *Yoshi* doesn't bark orders; he speaks with some basic damn politeness. Regardless of social skills, Gizmit isn't wrong. I say we follow her plan, unless anybody objects?"

"Sounds solid to me," Yoshi agreed quickly, nodding. We shared the significant look of two guys trying to herd two colonies of cats into the same place; fortunately, most of them were easier to manage than the familiars and Flaethwyn. "Same formation as before? Flaethwyn, you should move alongside Om—with Lord Seiji. You don't have armor, but with those long rapiers, you two can stab past us if we run into trouble."

"If I must," Flaethwyn said, tossing her hair and giving me a long look as if this were some great imposition.

I ignored her, which visibly pissed her off, which was why I did it.

We got less lucky once out of the barracks. This section of Jadrak's complex was, after all, carved out of what had originally been mining tunnels, and it was goblin-sized. They liked giving themselves a decent vertical clearance, so at least we didn't have to crawl, but all of us were forced to duck and shuffle awkwardly once we were out of the taller barracks room into the corridor beyond. I silently reflected that if it came to a fight in this particular tunnel, only Yoshi's relatively short arming sword would be even slightly useful. It would come down to him fighting and me casting over his shoulder while Aster soaked up hits with her artifact chain mail.

It didn't, though. Despite the acuity of goblin hearing and the way sound seemed to echo off these stone walls, it appeared that we retained the element of surprise just by shutting up and moving our feet in careful little shuffles as we proceeded. Getting closer, the distant murmur of voices grew clearer, and I gained some insight into just why this was going so well for us—the walls did bounce sound, yes; but those overlapping echoes made it hard to pick out any one sound in particular. The goblins up ahead of us were arguing, and that was about all I could tell.

Biribo and Radatina buzzed along over our respective shoulders, giving no updates, which I took to mean the situation ahead was still as it had been described. We crept along the awkwardly cramped corridor until we came to a metal door, through which the muffled sound of voices raised in agitation could still be heard. No wonder I hadn't been able to make out details. Only now that we were right outside was I able to start making out individual statements, and that not consistently.

". . . should've at least tried!"

"Not when . . . our own skins on . . ."

"Well, it's too late now!"

". . . could still . . ."

No good; we were only getting about half of it. Yoshi turned to catch my eye and nodded, reaching out to place one hand on the door latch. I nodded back, grasping Aster's shoulder. She looked at me, then carefully retreated when I gave her a gentle pull. All things considered, Yoshi and I were still our hardest hitters, and it was clear neither of us was a lead-from-the-rear type. If we were gonna charge in, we should take point.

Yoshi gripped his sword, inhaled and exhaled slowly, then yanked the door open and stepped through.

Blessedly, this was another tall room, and we had space to stand up. I was right on his heels, bursting into the chamber beyond as we were greeted by incoherent yells of surprise. The goblins had been distracted, but all turned to focus on us upon our arrival. Two raised weapons, and I didn't give anybody the chance to do something foolish.

Windburst, Windburst!

Two was all it took in the relatively confined quarters to knock down all of the targets arrayed against us and smash half of them against the wall from which they slumped down, stunned.

Yoshi and I kept moving, keeping them covered as we made room for the rest of the team to stream in after us. He had the presence of mind not to divert his attention from the felled goblins until we were amply backed up, but then turned to examine the cells in which there was apparently one living prisoner and two corpses. I kept my own attention on the enemy for now, so I didn't see what he saw.

So it came as quite the surprise to me that Yoshi knew the prisoner—even more so that Nazralind did—but their startled yells came out nearly in unison.

"Maizo!"

14

In Which the Dark Lord Does the Right Thing, Sort Of

Who the hell was Maizo?

I took a moment to verify that our opponents were under control before turning to see for myself. Nazralind had her bow drawn; Aster, Flaethwyn, and Adelly all had weapons ready; even Rizz and Rhoka had silently come in at the rear with those staffs of theirs held out, blades extended. These goblins weren't much of a threat anyway, now that I looked. Those "weapons" I'd glimpsed while bursting in turned out, on closer inspection, to be pickaxes. Had we just captured a mining crew? In any case, I could risk taking my eyes off them.

The sole living goblin in the cells was laboriously rising up from a prone position, and it *really* looked like an effort. Poor guy had been worked over something fierce; I could hardly see the green on large parts of him through the bruises and blood. He could only crack one swollen eye to peek at us and was obviously having trouble breathing.

This looked like a job for the Dark Lord.

"Heal."

Pink light burst from the cell, causing the other goblins to flinch.

"*Whew!*" Maizo gasped, straightening up fully. "Hoooo, that's tingly! Holy shit, thanks. Wow, you're . . . *all* here. Together. Now that I didn't see coming."

"Just a moment," Flaethwyn said, turning away from our prisoners and lowering her weapon entirely, because apparently my concerns about operational security were not shared. "Hey, *you're* that goblin who dropped us in that blasted mud pit!"

"Wow, I'm impressed, Lady Flaethwyn," Maizo said sincerely, swaggering forward and grabbing the bars of his cell with both hands, which caused her to blush and avert her eyes, as among other indignities, he'd been stripped of his clothing. "Who woulda thought you could tell one goblin from another?"

"A mud pit? Really?" I asked.

"It's . . . a long story," said Yoshi, not meeting my eyes.

"You." Rizz strode past me, lifting her goblin-sized mechanical naginata to point at one of the felled followers of Jadrak. "Where are the keys to these cells?"

"The . . . keys." He blinked at her, eyes seemingly out of focus, and reached up to grip his skull with one hand. "I don't . . ."

Oh right, this was one of the ones who'd been smacked against the wall. Little dude looked pretty concussed.

I cast **Heal**, causing him to jerk upright with his eyes bulging wide. Then I did the same for the other two who looked a bit worse for our encounter.

"You can talk to me, Judge." One of the room's goblins had gotten to his feet and stepped forward, hands held out before him to show he had nothing in them. "I'm Rads, and I'm responsible for this crew. We're miners, not . . . Look, we weren't told where the keys are. They ordered us to leave 'em in the cells. If there are still any nearby, they'll be in the security office, just through there."

"Rhoka," Rizz ordered. The Arbiter nodded and stalked off through the door toward which Rads had pointed.

"Hey, alchemist girl," said Zui. "Do you have an acid that'll eat through metal?"

"Through *metal*?" Amell squeaked. "I don't . . . Uh, not fast enough to help, no. I don't encounter much metal, usually. It's *crazy* how much of it there is down here."

Weird how she could brew a magic bomb-finding elixir with what she was just lugging around but not hydrochloric acid. The rules of alchemy were puzzling; I *really* needed to get some questions about this answered.

"That goblin had been tortured," Rizz continued in a grim tone, leveling her polearm at Rads. "So were those two—to *death*. And you wanna take responsibility for this?"

"We had nothing to do with that!" Rads exclaimed, waving his empty hands overhead. "I'm responsible for *my crew*, not the Goblin King's orders! My people are *miners*, you understand? We dig up ores, not . . . Look, we're only *here* on guard duty because everybody else bugged out and we volunteered to stay behind. We were ordered to feed the prisoner and *not* open those cells under any circumstances! You've got no idea what they do to people who rebel against the Goblin King."

"No, we've got a pretty good idea," said Zui, who was over at the bars now, giving Maizo a once-over. I couldn't blame her; he was Healed and all, but there was an awful lot of dried blood still on him and his grin showed a couple of missing teeth.

"What do you mean, everybody else bugged out?" I demanded. "Where did they go?"

Rads gulped, giving me a wary look. He was clearly uncertain why there were a bunch of humans and elves down here, but it was plain that we were with the Judge, and that we weren't to be trifled with.

"King Jadrak's abandoned this base. He's moving his headquarters to rule from Fallencourt. I dunno who else might still be kicking around here—we probably aren't the only crew left to look after something, but it's only been a few hours and we ain't seen anybody else."

Well, that explained it.

"Would he really give up a secure position like that?" Yoshi asked, frowning deeply. "That doesn't seem to make sense. It's risky."

"It's a *bold* move, but I could see it from Jadrak's perspective," said Gizmit, emerging from the door behind us. "Holding Fallencourt gives him central control and *not* holding this place prevents him stretching his forces too thin. It's aggressive and risky, though, you're right. I found what Rhoka's supposed to be looking for, by the way. Catch."

She tossed a ring of metal keys across the room to Zui, who snagged them out of the air and began trying them on Maizo's cell door, muttering in annoyance. There were a *lot* of keys on that ring. Rhoka poked her head back out of the security office, scowling at having been upstaged.

"Anybody else nearby, Biribo?" I asked.

"Not within the radius of my perception from this spot, boss. Not in the tunnels above or below, either. I think this guy's on the level; they really have pulled out."

"I thought there was a Spirit here," I said, frowning. "Would Jadrak really abandon that?"

"Lot of other assets here that can't be moved easily, or at all," Gizmit agreed. "But he is trying to consolidate his control in a hurry with adventurers closing in and a pissed-off Dark Lord invading Kzidnak. Like I said, not the call I would've made, but I can imagine Jadrak going for it."

"Dark Lord?" one of the captured goblins whispered. "Oh shit. *Shit.*"

"Hah!" Zui finally crowed in satisfaction, and the cell door swung open. "All right! Next step, we gotta find something for you to wear."

"I dunno, this is pretty cozy," said Maizo, who had wrapped himself in a threadbare blanket, which was apparently provided with his cell.

"Why were you in there, Maizo?" Yoshi asked.

The goblin grimaced, showing off the new gaps in his sharklike teeth. I felt particularly bad about that, but Heal wouldn't fix anything missing.

"Cos I'm an information gatherer working for Maugro. I dunno exactly how Jadrak got wind of this Dark Lord situation, but he also found out who else knew about it, and . . . well, there you have it. Since you're down here, Lord Seiji, I'm hoping you managed to rescue Maugro and the gang?"

He looked up at me with such an eager expression, I felt a crack form somewhere inside me. It immediately fell, though; Maizo could see my face, and everyone else's.

"I'm sorry," I said, shaking my head. "I was too slow. Maugro and Mindzi both came running to me for help when they were attacked, but they died on the way. So did the other goblin in his office; I never got that guy's name. You'd better believe I wiped out the assholes who did it, and Jadrak is next on my list."

Maizo nodded, eyes downcast. "Yeah . . . That's something. Guess I'm not human enough to find a lotta satisfaction in revenge."

"We're going back to the barracks," Zui stated, glaring around at us as if expecting to be challenged. "There was abandoned gear all over in there, so we can find something for him to wear, and possibly eat."

"Good idea," I agreed. "Adelly, would you go with them, please? I know this place is theoretically emptied out, but that can change in a hurry, and I'll feel better with somebody tall and Blessed watching their backs."

"Hai!" Adelly said crisply, saluting before turning to follow the two goblins, who had started off without waiting for a response. Yoshi jumped and turned a wide-eyed stare on her, then me, but Rizz spoke up again before he could say anything.

"So you didn't put them in the cells," she said in a voice like ice, keeping her polearm leveled at Rads. "You just *kept* them there. You let two fellow goblins die of injuries they suffered at the hands of *your* coworkers, and would have let Maizo die just the same. Because you were *told* to?"

"This is not the job any of us signed up for, Judge," Rads said, his tone pleading. "We're just trying to survive. Do you have any idea what it's *like* for those people? The fanatics, the . . . The Goblin King has everyone whipped into this rabid fucking frenzy. You *can't* go against them, or they tear you apart."

"And *they are gone*," Rizz snapped. Rhoka stepped silently up beside her, holding her own weapon at the ready but not pointing it yet. "You consigned people to die alone and in agony because you were scared of the *memory* of the Goblin King?"

"You're damn right I was!" he yelled, suddenly finding his spine. Rads even took an aggressive step forward, heedless of the blade that Rizz kept aimed right at his chest. "And if you think that's weird, then you've got no idea what you're talking about! We got left behind *because* we've been trying to sit out the worst of the insanity. Because we're not trusted or valued enough by the hard-liners to go along with Jadrak's glorious crusade. You know what a delicate fucking dance we've had to do for *weeks* now, staying alive here without getting blood on our own hands? I didn't see *you* here protecting anybody from the madness, or any other Judge! If those crazy assholes came back and found we'd gone soft on the prisoners, it would've been our asses next! I've got a team of six miners I'm trying to get through this shitshow alive. If you think you coulda done better, good for you, but *you weren't here*."

Rizz shifted her fingers on the haft of her weapon, expression unchanging. "And does that make you feel better about your complicity? Look me in the eyes, Rads, and say you're not to blame."

"Ugh, *why* are we wasting time on this goblin nonsense?" Flaethwyn groaned. "The Goblin King isn't *here*. This whole exercise is a bust. Let's just squeeze these dregs for information and leave."

Rizz very slowly turned to give the elf a long, hard stare, keeping her weapon at the ready.

"I think," Yoshi began.

"I know a quick way to settle this," I said, taking two steps forward until I stood abreast of Rizz and Rhoka. Raising my rapier, I pointed its tip at Rads, who backed away. "You and your *team* have killed two people through your own sniveling cowardice. Fair's fair, foreman. Pick your two least useful team members."

Well, *that* got everybody's attention, all right. The goblin miners all began protesting and trying to retreat against the wall away from me. Rizz and Rhoka immediately shifted their stance, bringing their weapons up to aim in my direction.

"Whoa, wait a second," Yoshi protested. "Omura, you can't be serious!"

"I dunno what passes for justice where you're from, boy, but this isn't happening," Judge Rizz stated.

I guess I was giving people the wrong idea about Japan's justice system, huh. Oh well, it wasn't like anybody back home would ever hear about this or have the chance to be embarrassed. More immediately . . .

"Your position is understood, Judge Rizz," I replied. "Counterpoint, **Windburst. Heal, Heal.**"

I sent her and Rhoka flying across the room against the opposite wall and immediately remedied any damage done to them by the impact. Rhoka lost her staff in transit; Rizz actually managed to not only stay armed but land on her feet after bouncing off the wall.

"I'm not a patient man," I said to Rads, taking a step closer. "Pick two. Now."

"Omura, you can't do this!" Yoshi insisted.

"Stay out of this, Yoshi."

He drew his sword.

It was sort of incredible how fast a group of people could split into two distinct groups. Instantly, Yoshi's followers and mine shifted just slightly, angling themselves to face between the goblins and each other. Aster had her sword across her shoulders in its ready posture, and now subtly moved to a balanced stance; Nazralind kept her nocked but undrawn bow aimed at the goblins, but adjusted her angle so that she could instantly bring it to bear on anyone in the room. Amell rested one hand on the clasp of her potion satchel, and Pashilyn's face went blank and expressionless, her hands tucking themselves into the wide sleeves of her priestess robes.

Astonishingly, it was Flaethwyn who made herself the voice of peace and reconciliation.

"What? What is everyone so tetchy about, suddenly? If he wants to kill goblins, let him. Haven't we got anything *better* to worry about?"

Well, reconciliation, anyway.

Rizz made an abortive move in my direction and I held out my free hand toward her in a silent threat, bringing her to an immediate stop.

"Choose," I barked at Rads, "or I'll pick two for you."

"You can go fuck yourself, tallboy!" the goblin foreman snarled, baring his full complement of jagged teeth at me. Positioning himself in front of his crew, he held his arms out wide as if he could block them with his own body. "You want a piece of my people, you go through *me* first."

I held his red eyes with a pitiless stare for just a moment. Less of a moment than I would normally have drawn that out—it was a tragic waste of a dramatic pause—but I was sitting on a powder keg, and any second either Yoshi or Rizz was going to do something to make all this much more complicated.

"Correct answer," I said, nodding and sheathing my sword. "So there *is* some character in you, after all. Maybe not much, but that's not nothing. Very well, where are your supplies? Food, water, medicine?"

Rads blinked rapidly. "I—you—uh, what?"

"You're *robbing* us, now?" one of his subordinates protested.

"They're for you, not for us," I explained patiently. "*You* lot are going into those cells. And unlike you, I happen to care what happens to people in my custody. I don't intend to let you starve. If the Goblin King's flunkies come back, you can tell them exactly what happened here, and they'll have no reason to complain about a bunch of miners getting beaten by the Dark Lord. Once Jadrak's dead, I'll send somebody to let you out."

"That's . . . better," Rizz said grudgingly, approaching. She had the polearm back over her shoulder and not pointed at me this time, so I allowed it. "But I believe it is still my business to dispense justice in Kzidnak, boy, not yours."

"Fine, if you want to take further issue with them after Jadrak's out of the equation, I won't stop you," I said, annoyed. "Or do you think I'm being too *harsh* on the poor little darlings?"

Rizz turned her gimlet stare back on the miners. "Hmph. All things being equal, I wouldn't let them off that easy, no. But in this situation we don't have the luxury of taking any drawn-out measures. Your solution will do, for now. I gotta say, boy, that was the most sadistic lead-up to a light-handed punishment I've ever seen. I've met, dealt with, and fought a lotta different kinds of people in my years, but I think you're my first . . . vicious softie."

Nazralind audibly stifled a snicker, which of course I ignored.

"I don't like hurting people, Rizz. I go out of my way not to do it any more than is absolutely necessary. You, of course, know the only reliable method for getting through life without having to hurt anybody?"

She nodded. "Make sure everybody knows you can and will. Yep. And pursuant to that, what would you have done if Rads there had volunteered two of his people to die?"

"Then I'd have killed him and stuck the rest of them in the cells. No need to take my word for it, either; just ask any of my followers what happened to the *last* asshole who failed that particular test."

"You killed someone," Yoshi said quietly, "for that?"

"Because *nobody fucking listens!*"

I usually had more warning when it came upon me—in fact, I usually had a much more severe provocation. This time, though, it was just his soft tone of incredulity that made me snap. All but literally, I felt something go *pop* inside my head, and just like that I was too furious to see straight.

I rounded on Yoshi, words spilling out of me far faster than I could even think about controlling them.

"It would be *so easy* to make this country a better place to live in—all everybody would have to do is stop *clawing* at each other like crabs in a bucket. We can blame the assholes in charge—and oh, believe me, I do—but the fact remains, they would be as ousted and slaughtered as the nobility of France or Russia or China or *everywhere else that has happened* if their sole talent wasn't keeping all the common folk of this wretched little shithole island turned against each other instead of putting their anger where it belongs!

"I'm sure you've been having a *grand* old isekai adventure, Yoshi, hanging out with adventurers and well-mannered nobles. Well, fucking good for you. *I* have been mostly dealing with bandits and nobles when they *weren't* trying to impress anybody; and let me tell you the important thing I've learned about human nature. When the chips are down, most people will usually do the right thing—*if* it has been made clear to them beforehand that the alternative is they get *fucking murdered!*"

Just as suddenly as I'd started, I was out of things to say. And the silence was utter and oppressive. Goblins were staring at me in terror, my own people with worry. Yoshi and two-thirds of his friends looked vaguely haunted, but Flaethwyn, for the first time I'd seen, appeared reluctantly impressed.

Also, naturally, the others had returned just in time to catch that. Zui and Maizo stood in the door, staring, with Adelly looming over them from behind.

"Well?" I said irritably. "Come on. Supplies, unless you want to go to jail with nothing but what you're wearing. Zui, we'll need those keys."

"You're gonna kill Jadrak?" Rads said suddenly.

I turned a tired scowl on him. The flash of rage was gone as quickly as it had come, leaving me feeling worn-out and cranky. "I'm pretty sure I was unambiguous about my intentions, yes."

The foreman sucked in a breath through his teeth, glanced over his shoulder at his frightened subordinates, then turned back to me and nodded.

"Then . . . look, I dunno whether there's still anything in this whole base that'll be useful to you, but I know where you should look. You wanna talk to Digger."

"Who the hell is Digger?" I demanded.

"That's the Spirit this place was built around," said Gizmit.

Rads nodded again, eagerly this time. "Yeah, see, this whole part of the complex used to be mines before the ore ran out, and it all branches off from the cavern where Digger's located. The Spirit's spot has always been secured, but for the last few months it's been getting increasingly . . . weird. Only Jadrak and Hoy have been allowed in there, and how paranoid they've been about it has scaled directly with the whole organization going off the rails, turning from an honest mining company into . . . Well, if you got this far into Kzidnak, I bet you've seen what they've turned into."

"We saw, yes," Yoshi said softly.

"So . . ." Rads shrugged helplessly. "I mean, I gotta assume they'd take anything valuable with them, but you can't move a Spirit. I dunno what clues or whatever would even be left, but that's *where* they'll be. If . . . there's anything, I mean. You'll, uh, you'll have to bust in, probably; they had that place locked down tight."

"Thank you," I said in a deliberately calm and reasonable tone. "That is exceedingly helpful."

"Sure thing. Just . . . don't tell any of Jadrak's people I told you nothin'."

I nodded. "You're still going in the cells."

Rads looked at the empty cells, then at the one with two bodies in it, then over at Maizo, and lowered his eyes. "Yeah, fair. Zabbzi, show 'em where the supply lockers are."

The Spirit's cave was not, in fact, locked down.

We found it easily enough with the miners' directions, after we left them secured in their cells with sufficient food and water for at least a week. And indeed, there was ample evidence that the entrances to this cavern had *been* sealed at some point—the doors were not only heavy but bristling with locks, chains, and even obstructions that looked like they'd been bracing them shut. Those doors themselves were standing open, though, all the chains and what-not dangling uselessly and the barricades lying strewn about the hall outside.

"Oh no," Biribo whispered as we stepped up to the ominously open portal.

"What?" I demanded. "Who's in there?"

"Nobody," he said in a miserable tone. "But boss . . . we shouldn't be here."

"We need to retreat," Radatina agreed, buzzing around Yoshi's head in agitation. "This is way more dangerous than we came here prepared for!"

"What do you mean?" he asked. "What's wrong? Traps?"

For once we weren't the first ones in; Rizz brushed curtly past me, stepping into the Spirit's chamber with her polearm at the ready. She came to an immediate stop, straightening up from her prepared stance, and shifted the weapon to rest its butt against the floor.

"Well, I see what the familiars are agitated about," the Judge said in a particularly dour tone. "This is *not* good. But not immediately dangerous, so long as nobody does anything stupid."

That was good enough for me; I rounded the corner, went through the gates, and stopped right next to Rizz. Seconds later, Yoshi drew up on her other side, sword and shield at the ready.

The cavern was clearly natural, its floor uneven and domed ceiling bristling with stalactites. More doors stood around the walls, most smaller than the one we'd come through; all had heavy barriers built into them now, and all were standing wide open. I paid all of this little attention, though, immediately zeroing in on the familiar shape of a Spirit positioned in the center of the room.

Well, mostly familiar.

It was the same waist-high column of white stone with inset patterns glowing, but this one was quite different beyond that. Rather than the customary pale pastel glow, its engravings were lit up a livid red, and slowly pulsing from bottom to top, making me think of a heartbeat. In place of the projection of a stylized face in light above its top, the crown was ringed by a slowly rotating circle in which letters were written in red light:

**ERROR—CONTACT SYSTEM ADMINISTRATOR—
ERROR—SYSTEM NODE CORRUPTED**

"I—wait," said Yoshi, leaning forward and narrowing his eyes. "Is that *English?*"

"Not English," I said. "Those are Roman letters, though. Maybe . . . Spanish? I know very little Spanish. It does remind me of a Romance language, but . . . I don't see any accent marks. Most of them have those."

"How can you read it but not know what language it is?" Aster asked, stepping up behind me. "Or . . . can you not read it? I thought the Blessing of Wisdom . . ."

"Being able to fluently read or speak languages you've never actually learned causes some weird effects sometimes," I said ruefully, thinking back to her lack of reaction to Junko's name, and the way Gizmit had tricked me into revealing I could read Khazid. "For example, apparently you don't get to intuitively know the name of whatever language it is."

"Could it be Latin?" Yoshi asked.

"I can't—hm. Well, I was going to say that was silly, but honestly that doesn't make any less sense than everything else about this damn planet. More importantly, what's wrong with that Spirit?"

"What's wrong is it's not a Spirit anymore," Rizz replied. "It's been corrupted. *That* is now a Void altar, which provides the answers to a lot of questions about Jadrak. It appears he's been dealing with devils."

"Oh shit," I whispered. "That means *we're* gonna be dealing with devils, doesn't it."

Yoshi turned to us. "Void? Devils? What are you talking about?"

"Why, yes, Radatina," I said sweetly. "Why don't you explain to him what we're talking about?"

And that's how I got smacked between the eyes by a dive-bombing angry pixie.

15

In Which the Dark Lord Presses the Big Red Button

Igave Yoshi the very quick, one-minute rundown on the Void and the Devil King while Radatina visibly seethed, which was adorable. And while it was pertinent information that he definitely needed to know, I'd be lying if I denied that the sight of the pixie's impotent fury was what motivated me to finish up with a final warning.

"And the reason your familiar hasn't told you any of this, and wouldn't have, is because while it feels like they work for us, the truth is, familiars work for the Goddesses and you'd be wise to remember it. Above all, *they* don't want any other Champions slipping the leash on them like the Devil King did."

"That is not a suggestion that you should investigate Void magic, Yoshi," Pashilyn interjected firmly.

"She's right," I agreed, nodding, as Yoshi glanced back and forth between us with wide eyes. "Void magic is bad news. Look, I'm speaking as someone who considers his only true enemy on Ephemera to be Virya and who would grab at just about any straw to be able to stick it to her."

Everyone whipped about to stare at me—well, not everyone, my own followers were aware of this by now, but the goblins and Sanorites were all visibly shocked. Gratifying as it was to so decisively make myself the center of attention, I was in the middle of making a different point and so pressed on with it.

"The Devil King is *not* the solution. Any Void magic goes through him or his agents, if you wanna do it without blowing yourself up, and that dude is not interested in sharing power. Involving him in your business just means adding a third nigh-omnipotent entity with a leash around your neck."

Yoshi was frowning pensively now, half turning to stare at the Void altar. "Omura, I needed to talk to you anyway about . . . Well, I've seen indications that all, or at least most, Heroes and Dark Lords were brought here from Japan."

"It's all of them, yes," I said. "A Spirit told me that straight up."

"Oh. Good to know, then." He turned back to face me directly. "But that would *also* mean this Devil King is Japanese, right? Maybe we can reason with him."

"I think you may not realize how atypical the two of you are," Nazralind commented. "Dark Lords and Heroes as a rule have not *reasoned* with each other. Being from the same country only counts for so much."

"Also," I added, "this guy lived in Japan for . . . well, I dunno, but probably not much more than twenty years. He's been on Ephemera for who knows how many hundreds, and spent nearly all of that as an all-powerful tyrant. Having some distant memories of Japan doesn't mean he'll want to relate to us at all, if he even still can."

"I see your point," Yoshi said with a soft sigh. "Okay. This Void magic, then. How do you activate it?"

Everybody yelled at him at once, our voices in perfect agreement despite incomprehensibly overlapping each other.

"Okay, okay, I heard you!" Yoshi exclaimed. "I'm not an idiot! Listen, I'm not wanting to *do* Void magic; your point is taken, all right? I want to *avoid* doing it. You made it sound like that Void altar is dangerous, so how do we avoid setting it off by accident?"

"Oh, that's not something you need to worry about," Pashilyn assured him, mollified. "*That* is not the danger of Void altars. In fact, to use Void magic you would need to be initiated and given some basic coaching, possibly by an extremely powerful Void witch but most likely by an actual devil. If you don't have that introduction, you can't make a Void altar do anything. The *danger* is that whichever devil corrupted the thing remains connected to it, and can sense anyone interacting with it. That is a main way they get further converts—anyone messing with a Void altar is likely to meet a devil with some very persuasive arguments on why they should try it out."

"Prob'ly why all these heavy-ass doors were left open," Rizz added. "Bet it was a request of Jadrak's devil friend. With this place empty and unguarded, scavengers will move in within hours, and innocent goblins will blunder across this damn thing."

"Here's the thing, though," Pashilyn said, now gazing thoughtfully at the altar.

"I do not like the look on your face, Pashilyn," Radatina warned.

"I'm sure you don't care, but me either," said Biribo.

"Historically," she said, ignoring them, "devils are shy and conflict-averse, despite how powerful they are. When cornered they are incredibly dangerous in a fight, but given any opportunity at all they will avoid one. They'll flee from attack and abandon whatever project they were working on rather than defend it, every time. It has also been noted that their activities all but cease as soon as a Dark Crusade is known to be underway, almost as if they fear even the chance of encountering a Hero or Dark Lord."

"Priestess," Rizz said impatiently, "when I said 'nobody do anything stupid,' I was referring *specifically* to what you're leading up to."

"You want *us* to activate the Void altar?" I demanded.

"I am only raising possibilities," Pashilyn said in a soothing, diplomatic tone. "Our goal was to find the source of the Goblin King's mysterious power and cut it off, correct? Well, we've found it, which leaves the second part. If we show this devil that *either* Champion is getting involved here, let alone both, the likeliest outcome is they will immediately drop this whole campaign and leave the Goblin King to his fate. And then probably never show their face on Dount again, or possibly anywhere on Ephemera so long as one of you is still alive."

"Boy, *you* don't gamble for low stakes, do ya?" Zui commented.

Yoshi caught my eye and we shared a contemplative frown. The merits of Pashilyn's idea were obvious, but the risks . . .

"And what if the devil doesn't run away?" he asked, turning back to her. "What do you think of our chances in a fight?"

"Yoshi, my point is it's almost certain *not* to come to a fight. Even if the creature doesn't retreat fully, it's not in their nature to confront an actual threat."

"Yes, I understand that," he said patiently. "I'm trying to grasp the scale of the risk if *this* devil happens to be unpredictable. I don't know anything about devils; can we beat it?"

Pashilyn hesitated, glancing aside at Flaethwyn, who shook her head in a furious negative. Nazralind did the same.

"If . . . either of you were at the apex of your career and powers, possibly," the priestess said reluctantly. "As you are, brand-new with only a few spells and artifacts each . . . No, neither of you is a match for a devil. Both together, with all of us backing you up . . ."

She paused again, then grimaced and shook her head.

"Still, probably not."

"I'm getting alarmed that this needs to be repeated," Biribo said in a shrill voice, "but *don't screw around with devils!*"

"Okay, second opinions," I said. "Other educated people, is Pashilyn right?"

"*Pashilyn* is a priestess of the Radiant Convocation *and* a scholar of religious history and lore," Flaethwyn said stridently, stepping up behind Pashilyn and placing a protective hand on her shoulder. "This is her *specific* area of expertise. If she tells you a thing, you may take it as assured!"

"Right, thanks for that," I said irritably. "Anybody got an answer to the question that was *actually* asked?"

"Well, I'm no scholar of religious history, but I imagine I'm decently educated by Fflyr standards," said Nazralind, "and while I don't know how much of what I've read is propaganda, it *is* well established that devils are cowards."

"I'd put it more in terms of the Devil King bein' the conservative type who likes to play the longer, slower game," added Rizz, "but as to the point at hand, my own experience agrees. If there's trouble with the Void, it's almost always a Void witch, or some leftover remnants of something one did, like zombies or ghosts wandering around. *Actual* devils want nothing to do with any serious opposition. They'll skedaddle at the sight of a Blessed, even one they could easily kill."

"Can I just point something else out?" Aster interjected, holding up one hand. "Devils pay attention to these altars, right? And we're standing here, having this conversation, in the same room as one. The point might be moot."

Everybody instinctively shuffled a step or two toward the walls and away from the Void altar. She was right, though; if it was too late, it was too late.

"Pashilyn?" I asked.

"It's . . . not clear how closely they monitor them, or can," she said warily. "If you try to interact with it, *definitely*. Just being nearby . . . I don't know."

"Radatina?" Yoshi prompted.

"Well, *I* don't know!" his familiar exclaimed, doing a series of midair bounces in sheer indignation. "Familiars can tell you anything about magic in the Blessing system, but Void magic is *forbidden*! And for a *reason*! Even aside from devils and the Devil King, the Void is *dangerous*. Shapeless magic is inherently unpredictable! Messing around with it is a great way to kill yourself and everyone else in the vicinity!"

"That wouldn't happen," Pashilyn said swiftly. "As I said, you *cannot* activate the inherent magic of a Void altar unless you've received the proper initiation."

I drew in a breath and let it out, turning back to Yoshi. "Well, then, considering the risks and rewards, I'm up for the attempt. If you wanna veto the idea, though, I won't push it."

"Oh yeah?" Flaethwyn snarled. "*You* go and touch it, then!"

"That's not necessary," Yoshi said quickly. "If we agree to it—"

"What, then, rock paper scissors?" I said, grinning. "Nah, she's actually got a point for once. If we're doing this, I'm willing to take the lead. A really smart guy once gave me some good advice on how to deal with a devil if I ever met one."

"I got a feeling I'm gonna regret asking," Rizz said in a weary tone, "but before you go and *do* anything with the rest of us standing conveniently nearby, *what* was this advice?"

I turned my grin on her, widening it. "That I should Immolate them until they learn to leave me alone."

Everyone stared in silence for a second.

"Huh," Rizz grunted at last. "Yeah, in fact . . ."

"That actually is the agreed upon best practice," Pashilyn said wryly. "Well. Perhaps not immolation per se, but the general principle."

"Your call, then, Yoshi," I said. "And don't make it out of concern for my well-being; I can take care of myself. Besides, *if* a devil actually shows, you'd best believe your ass will be immediately backing me up."

Belatedly, I realized that putting it this way was laying all the pressure on him, which . . . oops. Too late now, though. Yoshi didn't seem crushed by the responsibility, at least, just frowning in thought as he gave the matter due consideration.

"I think we should try," he finally declared. "If the devil flees, that's the greater part of the Goblin King's power wiped out in one blow. And if it doesn't, we're going to end up fighting the creature, anyway. I'd rather do it here, when we're alone with it, than later when we have to fight Jadrak and Hoy and an army of goblin minions at the same time."

Damn, he had a point there. I hadn't even thought of that angle.

"Are you sure you want to do this, Omura?" he asked me seriously.

"'Want' is not the word I'd choose," I admitted, "but we are in agreement that it should be done, and I'm not one to back down once I've given my word. All right, let's rock."

I turned to face the Void altar in the center of the room and stepped toward it.

Everyone unlimbered their weapons, taking up positions in a wide arc facing me and the altar, while Zui tugged Maizo back toward the door. Good idea; if the civilians didn't have the sense not to join an active combat mission, at least they weren't going to stand on the front lines.

I approached the Void altar carefully, my Surestep Boots unfaltering on the uneven cave floor. It sloped up toward the base of the altar in erratic, natural-looking waves, as if what had been the Spirit had been placed upon the natural pedestal of a shorn-off stalagmite. The altar silently pulsed its warning red, the encircling error message slowly rotating around its crown where the face should be.

"Boss," Biribo said miserably, beginning to fall behind from his usual place at my shoulder. Now that I thought about it, he'd never shied from any kind of danger at all. Could familiars even be harmed? If that was the case, it made sense that Void magic might be the exception.

"Better hang back, buddy," I said, taking pity on him. "I can survive getting blasted, but I don't need Void bullshit messing up my Blessing of Wisdom."

He hesitated, jittering back and forth in midair with visible reluctance, but then bobbed his head once and zipped out of range to hover over Aster's shoulder.

One more step and I stood alongside the desecrated Spirit. I reached out with my right hand; it passed through the illusory warning as if nothing was there. Not even a tingling sensation. The head of the altar where I grabbed it just felt like cool stone.

"Reveal yourself!" I commanded the unseen devil.

The lights on the altar suddenly switched to vivid blue, and the direction of its pulsing reversed. A single flash flowed downward, as if some information from my handprint were being conveyed into the base.

The error message also switched to blue, and the text changed.

VALIDATING CREDENTIALS

Wait. What?

"What's that say?" Aster demanded. "What is it doing?"

Before I could answer, the blue switched to green and the message changed again.

LOGIN SUCCESSFUL

Wait, *what?*

"Get away from it!" Pashilyn shrieked.

I was already backing away hastily, only the artifact boots saving me from taking a tumble on the rocks. It wasn't my most graceful retreat, and it definitely didn't beat the speed of magic.

The next pulse of light was green, and this time shot upward—and then *out*, emerging from the head of the altar and flashing forward to strike me right between the eyes.

My last conscious sensation was of being hurled physically backward before I found myself flung out of reality entirely.

I remember having a high fever once as a kid. I vividly remember *having* the experience, even if the details of the sensation aren't something I can specifically recall; I suspect a normally functioning brain isn't capable of experiencing that. It was intense, though, the way time seemed to twist and dilate and compress simultaneously, the way my senses all contorted around themselves as I perceived things that weren't there via senses I did not possess, phantoms conjured by an overheated brain. I've never done drugs, so the fever was the only frame of reference I have for that kind of experience.

The Void was a lot like that.

My consciousness was at once compressed into a pinpoint and stretched into eternity, unhitched from causality and perspective. I floundered in a rushing torrent of *meaning*, encountering nothing that I could actually experience with my body's senses, nothing my brain could parse as such. Pure meaning is meaningless to a mind that has no way of interpreting it.

I flailed—not with my body, which I couldn't feel, or even with my mind. Or maybe it was my mind? I was drowning in the unreality of my own perceptions. Nothing made sense, nothing *existed*, and yet I was being washed away by a rushing cascade of reality, which wasn't shaped like any reality I knew. Everything, and nothing, myself swept along, the wrong kind of consciousness to *do* anything in this situation.

I needed . . . something. Something to grab onto. Something to focus on. Focus!

Focus burst upon me, and it was as if I . . . rotated. Like I was a thing of two dimensions, and suddenly shifted so that the inexplicable force which had been pushing me along was sliding past instead. And suddenly, fragments of reality became clear.

Some few bubbles did slice into my smashed, contorted awareness, bursting upon the razor edge of my perception, each dissolving into comprehensible speech. I couldn't hear the voices—couldn't *hear* at all—but I was experiencing snatches of dialogue, as if people were trying to speak to me through the torrent as they were swept past.

"You. Are. Not. Special."

"Believe in them, as I believe in you."

"And what is strength?"

"You are awfully confident that I'll be in here forever."

"If I reveal to you all the secrets of Ephemera, will you kindly fuck off?"

"I doubt many things about you, Omura Seiji, but never your integrity."

"I had a feeling it would be you. I chose you well."

"IS. THAT. ALL?"

I tried to grab them, as if I could hold words like pieces of driftwood. They slipped past, not even clinging to memory despite my desperate clutching.

Then a bubble of perception hit me even harder, bursting with the force of an explosive, with the weight of *attention*. Instead of mere chaotic fragments of comprehension, I was suddenly aware of another consciousness focused upon me.

Speaking to me.

"Go away, little Dark Lord."

I have never been so relieved to get a concussion.

I hit the ground hard, my Surestep Boots doing nothing for me since I was landing back-first with my feet in the air. The impact drove the air painfully from my lungs and my skull cracked against the floor, causing stars to burst in my vision. All of it was blissfully, blessedly physical. Reality made *sense* again!

Also it hurt. Oh shit, this hurt a *lot*.

Someone was grabbing me, trying to lift me up; people were yelling and arguing all around.

"You said this wouldn't happen!"

"Where is it? I don't see anything!"

"There's no devil, that was—he actually—"

It took me a few seconds to manage enough mental focus to form the weight of the spell, but I finally gathered myself enough to pull it off.

Heal!

The blast of pink radiance washed away the pain and fuzziness, fixing my abused lungs and poor jostled brain in one burst. I was mostly lying on the ground; my head was in Aster's lap, cradled in her hands, while Zui and Amell hovered over me, the latter holding out a vial of something that smelled like peppers and sugar.

Was that . . . it smelled exactly like the sauce on Gilder's favorite pepper mutton. Fucking Fflyr and their spices.

"I'm okay," I grunted, gently disentangling myself. Aster let me up and the others scooted backward. "Wow, *that* was something I could do with never experiencing again. What the absolute *fuck* was that? Is everybody okay?"

"Everybody but *you* is fine," Nazralind exclaimed. "Are *you* okay? I saw that Heal go off, but . . . I mean . . . what *happened* to you?"

"He cast Void magic, that's what!" Radatina shrieked, zooming in circles above Yoshi's head.

"That can't be," Aster insisted, "the devil must have attacked him."

"No, that was *definitely* Void magic," said Biribo. "And he *definitely* cast it himself. Well, not *himself* exactly, but the altar activated in response to him."

"What in the *hell*?" I exclaimed, turning an accusing glare on Pashilyn. "I thought that couldn't happen!"

"He must have been initiated!" The fucking pixie seemed to be on the verge of hysterics. "He's a Void witch! Somehow he met a devil and—"

"He did *not*, you little pest!" Biribo snarled. "I would *know* if he had! This was his first-ever encounter with the Void."

"Is that . . . true?" Yoshi asked.

"Well, if he says it is . . . it must be." Radatina was clearly reluctant, but she was at least calming down now. "This goes well beyond Viryans versus Sanorites, Yoshi. The Void is *everyone's* enemy. If you're touched by Void magic, you *can't* hide it from your familiar—and no familiar would conceal that."

"Because, like I said," I added, "familiars work for the Goddesses, not us."

"Is this really the moment to be harping on that?" Biribo demanded.

"Yes, that's a good point. I have *much* better things to harp on right now." I heaved myself upright, rounding on the quailing priestess. "Pashilyn! You *specifically* said this could not happen! You said I couldn't activate a Void altar by accident. You went into quite a bit of fucking detail about it, as I recall!"

"You *can't!*" she insisted, more agitated than I'd ever seen her. "That isn't—it is well known that—I don't understand how you— *That is not how it works!*"

"Huh." Rizz's calm voice was like a cup of ice water tossed into the conversation. "So. Turns out Dark Lords can activate Void altars. How about that. I wonder if it's just Dark Lords, or both kinds of Champions?"

"*WE ARE NOT GOING TO TEST THAT!*" Radatina screamed, actually slamming herself into Yoshi's chest as if she could physically push him back from the altar.

"I swear to you, Lord Seiji," Pashilyn said tremulously, "I would *not* have deliberately misled you, not about this. If you do not trust my honor, trust my self-preservation. The usual result of an inept activation of Void magic is uncontrolled chaos and destruction. If I had tricked you into doing such a thing, I would immediately have grabbed my friends and fled!"

"In fairness to the priestess," Rizz added, "I'm pretty sure *nobody* knew that until just now. If any previous Champion has ever messed with a Void altar at all, it's been hushed up."

"It makes sense, though," Nazralind whispered. "The Goddesses would *not* want that getting out. And it's terribly logical that the Devil King would design his corruption this way. I bet he'd *love* to get his hands on another Champion."

"Well, I'll just add that to my very long list of excellent reasons to stay the fuck away from the Devil King and all his Void nonsense," I said. "All right, everybody calm down, or at least stop yelling. I've got a headache."

"You just Healed yourself," Nazralind pointed out.

"I have a *spiritual* headache. And that's not just my pet name for Flaethwyn."

"Oh, that wasn't even called for!"

"Right *now* we need to decide on our next move," I pressed on. "That gambit with the Void altar . . . did . . . whatever it just did. No idea whether that worked for our intended purposes, and we really don't have any way to check, because I am declaring this too dangerous to keep poking at. So that means our mission here is done. What's our next move, aside from bugging out?"

"Sealing this up," Rizz stated, thumping the end of her bladestaff against the floor for emphasis. "We gotta shut all these doors and rearm as many of the locks as we can. It won't hold forever, but it'll slow down anybody poking around here. Hopefully long enough for me to gather as many Judges as

I can link up with and settle this. They need to know Jadrak's in bed with the Void."

"Well, that should settle the matter of Judge neutrality, at any rate," said Zui.

"You're goddamn right," Rizz growled. "Goblin King, Dark Lord, doesn't matter who you are. Dealing with devils makes you the enemy. Once we get this place buttoned down as tight as we can, you lot get back to Sneppit and I'll rally my people. *Then* we move on Jadrak."

"Right, sounds like a plan," I agreed. "Let's get this shit locked down, pronto."

We all turned to study the doors to the chamber. There were five of them, all bristling with multiple locks and with layers of chains attached. All hanging open.

After a moment I cleared my throat.

"So, uh . . . Where the hell are the keys to all this?"

16

In Which the Dark Lord
Gets a Second Opinion

We never did find those keys, but some time spent scrounging through the surrounding tunnels and chambers provided us a surprising workaround in the form of a stockpile of alchemy supplies. It had been thoroughly looted, of course—Jadrak's people had taken all the valuable stuff, leaving behind mostly what was both cheap and stored in large enough containers that it would've been hard to bring along in a hasty evacuation.

"But that works in our favor!" Amell said with more excitement than I'd ever seen from her. "The kind of basic ingredients you tend to stock in large quantities are versatile for more mundane tasks—with this stuff I can mix up enough fast-hardening glue to seal all those doors!"

"Glue." Rizz's tone was openly skeptical. "And how long do you reckon that'll hold?"

Amell deflated slightly. "Well . . . it's glue. The doors will be unopenable, but . . . I mean, obviously somebody who's determined and has access to tools or dissolving agents will be able to get through with a few hours of work."

"It's a shame these are such big, obviously important doors," Aster said with a wince. "We could glue a broom cupboard shut and it might escape notice for a while. Sealing these is like painting a sign for looters."

"I know, but it's what we can do with what we've got," Amell sighed.

"Obviously nothing we can whip up here's gonna be a permanent solution, even if we could find the actual keys," said Rizz. "It'd be ideal if we could do something that'd hold for a few days, not hours. By then I'll have rallied the Judges and you lot might've finished off Jadrak. Right now, with the situation in Kzidnak, any goblins out looting will be either desperate or highly opportunistic—exactly the ones who should *not* be allowed to contact a devil."

Amell nodded. "Yeah. It's a shame they didn't leave us *some* of the better reagents, at least. With these basic reagents, I *could* mix up enough liquid rock to seal those doors—well, the edges, not fully covering them, probably. But without the heating agent to harden them, that's useless."

"Liquid rock?" I asked, the idea tingling something in my mind. "Heating agent?"

"Yeah, it requires intense heat to solidify. Once that's done it's about as hard as normal bedrock, but without the heating agent it's just . . . thick mud."

"You just need heat, right?" Zui suggested. "Cos I bet there's still an asauthec storage somewhere around here. That stuff's difficult and dangerous to transport in a hurry . . ."

She trailed off, as Amell was already shaking her head negatively.

"That won't work; if you apply something *on fire* directly to the mixture, it *does* harden, but does so as it's boiling, so the final result is really porous and brittle. This is why you don't see the stuff used very much in construction; it's really tricky to work with. The heating mixture has to be applied on top; it's made of uncommon reagents and it's difficult to apply correctly. You *can* work around that with a physical heat source, but getting one to apply enough heat for long enough, steadily enough not to wreck the hardening process . . . well, any application method is its own engineering challenge and it burns through a *lot* of asauthec."

I held up one hand.

"Heat Beam."

It was tightly focused and high-intensity, causing Amell to squeak and skitter away, even though I wasn't aiming anywhere near her. I held the concentrated beam of light for a few seconds before letting it dissipate, leaving a scorched spot on the stone wall emitting wisps of acrid smoke.

"Will that work?"

"How long can you sustain that, Lord Seiji?" Amell asked, suddenly intent again. It was downright cute how she forgot she was shy and nervous whenever there was alchemy business afoot.

"As long as I can stay awake. Champions get basically bottomless spell power, isn't that right, Yoshi?"

"I've never even heard of that spell," Pashilyn said with a slight frown.

I smiled sweetly at her. "You aren't the fuckin' Dark Lord."

So that's how I began my third career—musician, Dark Lord, and now welder.

Four of the five doors we were able to seal on both sides for maximum security, so the first part of the work was spent—carefully—in the defiled Spirit's chamber. I wasn't the only one keeping a wary distance from the damn thing, though I maintain I had the most reason. Amell busied herself mixing weird-smelling chemicals in large batches, whereupon the rest of us went to work closing the big doors and painting over every crack between and around them with the resulting goop, using some goblin-sized brooms and mops we'd found as big brushes. Given that these ended up being not very long in human terms, we weren't able to cover the topmost part of the taller doors, which for some reason were built to *way* more than goblin scale, but hopefully it would suffice. The results didn't have to hold forever, just a few days.

After we sealed the first one from the inside, the others moved on to paint the other doors, and I began the process of hardening the liquid rock with Heat Beam. At first Amell supervised me to make sure I could identify the change in texture indicating the process was done. I experimented a bit with concentrations and patterns of the beam before settling on a configuration that gave me the best balance of heat and coverage to get this done most efficiently.

Four doors could be sealed from the inside; we had to leave one open, obviously, to get out, despite Flaethwyn's sneering suggestion that I should take one for the team and entomb myself in there. I didn't even have the chance to properly rebut before Pashilyn pointedly asked her if she really wanted the Dark Lord to lock himself away with nothing but a Void altar.

Phase two involved a lot of backtracking through the surrounding corridors to repeat the process on the outside of the doors, because as much as we were all anxious to get moving, this did not seem like something that could be half-assed. We were going to be forced to leave one of them rocked over on only one side, and that was enough of a risk. The process was made less complicated by the presence of familiars, who could sense the entire layout of the surrounding tunnels and navigate us through them.

So I ended up trailing well after everyone else, since the process of hardening the liquid rock was a lot slower than slapping it into place. I could hear their distant voices echoing through the corridors, and some of the others would periodically come through to check on me and patrol the area. For the most part, though, it was just me, Biribo, and Aster, who had insisted on watching my back. I knew better than to argue, even though her evolving role in the organization was less "bodyguard" and more "lieutenant" now; every time I let her hover around protecting me, I was building up points I could then spend when I actually needed to do something alone. Something told me I was going to need those soon.

"Having a nice rest, Aster?" sneered the last person I wanted to pay me a visit while I was sealing up the third door externally. I was all but certain she had only bothered to come by to say that specifically.

"I'm his bodyguard, Flaethwyn," Aster replied in a bored tone. "This is the job."

"That is *Highlady* Flaethwyn, lowborn," the elf snapped.

"By Lord Seiji's decree, there is no racial hierarchy in the Dark Crusade. I am the second-in-command to a head of state, which means I *considerably* outrank you. Now shut your smirking gob and go waste someone else's time, you insufferable leaf-ear."

I heard the distinctive hiss of a rapier being pulled from its sheath.

"Flaethwyn," I said without pausing my work, "Aster is fighting with her words, like an adult. If I have to stop what I'm doing and turn around, I'm going to be far more immature about it."

There was a momentary silence while she considered her options. I'd have really enjoyed seeing her face just then, but I remained on task, both because what I was doing was important and because I knew making a show of not caring about her was only deepening the insult. Anyway, Aster was close to indestructible in her artifact armor and Biribo was silently hovering just within my field of view, able to give warning if I needed to turn and deal with this.

It ended, though, with Flaethwyn's feet stomping gracelessly away down the corridor.

"That girl isn't right in the head," Aster muttered as the elf departed. "I've known a lot of aggressive people, but she's something else. It's like she's angry at the universe for no reason and determined to make it everyone else's problem."

"Well . . . I mean, that's a lot of—"

"That's different," Aster said with a smile I could hear without turning around. "*You're* funny, and at least capable of being polite when you want something, and generally goal directed. That's my point—you can be one of the bigger assholes I've ever met when you're in a mood, but you don't go around causing pointless trouble just out of spite."

"Aw, that's sweet. Still don't wanna bang you, though."

"That's fine, I can do *so* much better. I wonder if Maizo's single?"

"That felt good, though, didn't it? Mouthing off to a smug elf like that."

"It *really* did," she admitted.

"I'll bet."

I risked glancing away from my work for a moment at the new voice, belonging to someone I hadn't heard approach. Biribo hadn't said anything, though, so I wasn't too alarmed, and anyway it was just Rizz.

Well, not alarmed about her being here, at this particular moment. The revelation that the heavily armed goblin inquisitor, who apparently operated without oversight, could just sneak up on me was disturbing. Presumably, if we weren't on good terms (for now), my familiar *would* give me ample warning of her approach.

"How's it going, Rizz?" I asked, keeping my tone mild and my eyes on what I was doing.

"Looking pretty good. They're slathering up the last door now."

"All right, I get it, I'm behind. This takes longer than slapping mud on the walls, okay? I'll try to—"

"No rush, boy. You got the most important part, and everybody knows it's detail-heavy. I'd rather you do it right than fast."

"Well, it's nice to be understood."

"Mm. Speakin' of understanding people. You know Sneppit used to be an Arbiter?"

That almost made me pause in my magical welding.

"Really? Sneppit was a . . . I'm extrapolating from how I've seen you relate to Rhoka, but that's an apprentice Judge, right?"

"Exactly. She's famous for her skill at contract drafting. She's got the aptitude for it, but a lot of Sneppit's success stems from her early training and the opportunity to study in the Judges' library of precedents, which not a lot of goblins get. She never made the cut to Judge, though. A Judge has to not only arbitrate disputes and issue rulings, but *enforce them*. Sneppit has little to no aptitude for physical combat and generally ain't inclined to dirty her own hands with *anything* when she can just pay someone else to do it. That's how you end up running the most famous engineering company in Kzidnak without knowing which end of a wrench to hammer with."

"Fascinating," I murmured, still welding. It *was* interesting, yes, but I had a strong feeling this was leading up to something more.

"Sneppit," Rizz continued after a moment in a deliberately casual tone that didn't fool me for an instant, "is my favorite company boss to work with. Better than any of 'em, she knows where the line is and how Judges think. Between that and the fact she's defensive-minded and conflict-averse, she straight up doesn't *do* shit that requires a Judge's intervention most of the time. But I can't ever forget she *got* that way by disingenuously exploiting the only system of spiritual and economic enforcement we have, to gain a free specialist education she wasn't entitled to, knowing full well she couldn't fulfill the role and never planning to. The only thing keeping that woman in check is her own pragmatism, and the fact she lives in an enclosed system where gettin' too big for her pink britches would result in a swift and decisive smackdown."

"Ahh, now we come to it," I whispered.

"Power is a drug, boy. There's no other way to think of it that makes sense. It messes up a person's ability to think straight, and makes 'em perpetually crave *more* of it."

"I've noticed that."

"It's good that you have. Impressive, too. Most people don't see it creepin' up on 'em, and that makes it orders of magnitude worse. Sneppit's too pragmatic to cause too much trouble—but that used to be true of Jadrak, too. Like any drug, people have different tolerances for power. We've all seen what happens on the wrong side of Jadrak's. The whole world is eventually gonna find out what it looks like when *you* get more'n you can handle, like it or not. Sneppit is a good boss because there's a hard ceiling on her ambitions, and it happens to be lower than what it would take to drive her properly crazy. In the end, though, she's still a boss. And bosses want *more*. Always more; there is never any concept of 'enough' when you're a boss. You take that woman out of Kzidnak, put her somewhere there's no upper limit on what she can do or become, and you will find out exactly how much power it takes to turn Sneppit into a monster like Jadrak, or worse."

I mulled for a moment, the only sound in the tunnel being the soft hissing sizzle of my Heat Beam catalyzing the liquid rock into its final form.

"Y'know, Rizz," I mused at last, "I'm actually kind of sad you'll be splitting off from us after this. I've got a feeling there's a lot I could learn from you, if we had the opportunity to have more conversations."

"Me, too," she said. "It's a real saving grace that you're interested in listening. 'Specially since you've made it clear I can't stop you doing whatever you like. I might take you up on that once all this hollering is settled, if you're serious."

"There's a tunnel from Maugro's old offices right to my base. I'll make sure my people know what a Judge looks like, and that they're welcome to visit."

She grunted a noncommittal acknowledgment. "I'll let 'em know you're about done here. Next spots're just waiting for your magic touch."

Rizz strode off up the tunnel in the same direction Flaethwyn had gone. Quietly, but not silently now that she wasn't actively trying to conceal her presence. In her absence, Biribo and Aster both held their peace, giving me space to think on what we'd just heard.

The next visit came when I was halfway through with the next door— again after making sure nobody else was near enough to overhear.

"Zui seems to have taken Maizo under her wing," Gizmit reported, sauntering up to me from out of the shadows.

"Zui's got a soft spot for people in distress, doesn't she?"

"Heh, you have no idea. It's a good thing we live underground where there are no loose animals, or she'd be bringing home stray goslings every week. You know, that loud chick you brought down here has probably done more to wreck Zui's comfortable view of the world than your whole Dark Crusade. She's not used to the idea of humans as traumatized people who need hugs, rather than the cause of everyone else's trauma."

"Yeah, well. People are people, and people mostly suck. Tall or short, green or brown, there's a lot less difference than most of us would like to think. She'd better get used to it."

"Mm. I mentioned her adopting Maizo specifically, because . . . You may wanna do something about that."

I blinked, glancing down at her for the one second I could do so without interrupting my work. "Why? Poor guy's been through absolute hell. If anybody could use a little pampering, it's Maizo. Let her work."

"Maizo's a good find," Gizmit said, leaning with her back to the wall just next to the door, right where I could see her peripherally without having to move my eyes. She folded her arms and gazed absently at the far wall, continuing to speak in a casual tone. "He's a real solid intel guy. Not in Maugro's league, or mine, but he's got the potential to be. Guy's *very* good for his age, is what I'm saying, and Sneppit is very good at snapping up valuable talent on terms that benefit her more than them. If you were interested in snapping him up instead, you've got a very short window left to do so."

I deliberately did not look at her this time. "Why, Gizmit. I've gotta say, the last thing I expected is you undercutting Miss Sneppit."

"Let me be explicitly clear," she said with an edge to her tone. "In my professional opinion, delivered under no duress or expectation, Miss Sneppit is the best boss in Kzidnak, and I consider myself *extremely* fortunate to have the position I do in her company. There is no circumstance in which I would even consider violating the terms of my contract of employment. I do, however, know very well what is and is *not* covered by said contract. I realize you humans have a more abstract notion of loyalty, so let me just remind you that this is the mindset Sneppit and *any* goblin would expect. I am not obligated to recruit new talent for her, nor prohibited from giving free professional advice to any party who is not in conflict with Miss Sneppit or her interests."

"And what brought this on?"

Her head tilted just enough for her to fix one red eye on me. "Tell me, Lord Seiji, what is it you're looking for in a Goblin Queen? Aside from talent, leadership ability, and looks."

I inhaled and then exhaled slowly through my nose. "Uh huh. Well, it's not like I didn't *know* you were eavesdropping on that conversation. That's your whole job, isn't it?"

"Very far from the whole job. Just one of my numerous skills."

"And let me guess, that contract of yours requires you to divulge such valuable information to Miss Sneppit herself."

"Of course it does. She knows, and will act accordingly. You are everything she has ever wanted. In a business partner, or a mate, or just a job opportunity; basically anything you choose to offer her—within reason—she'll probably spring for. And here's another piece of free advice, which I mean in absolute sincerity—*you* should spring for *her* with just as much enthusiasm. Sneppit is not only a source of immense talent, which any ruler should be glad to have on his side, she is what you need in particular. That brothel madam you have organizing your operations may be a capable enough administrator, up to a point—I'm certain she excels at people skills. But Miss Minifrit was a small business owner. She is not up to the task of playing steward to the entire Dark Crusade. Sneppit *is*. You *need* to get her on your team."

Gizmit paused, and though my mouth was brimming with rejoinders to that, I kept my teeth firmly shut. I recognized this kind of pause. It was a loaded pause, a dramatic one. The kind of pause which served as prequel to a wham line.

"Just not necessarily as Goblin Queen."

There it was.

"I'm real curious as to why you of all people would say that, Gizmit."

"Considering what that spell of yours does, granting double Blessings and the collected powers of every magically gifted race you can add to it . . . you're building a core of devastatingly powerful agents. The kind of people you'll want watching your back and leading the charge as necessary. *That* isn't Sneppit. She's an administrator, a negotiator, and gifted beyond all reason at both those things—a real once in a generation talent. But that doesn't come without drawbacks. She's terrible at personal combat, and absolutely hates doing it. Really, anything that puts her on the assembly line or the front lines or *any* kind of line where she'll mess up her manicure is gonna make her wilt. I'm just saying, Lord Seiji, it would be a waste of absolutely tragic proportions to take a talent like hers and put her in a position where she'd just be incompetent and miserable."

She hesitated again, and I waited. This time, I was pretty sure I knew what was coming next.

"Especially when you have other options for that role."

I glanced down at her again. Gizmit was still not looking at me—but now I could detect the subtleties of her posture. The way she'd carefully thrust her chest out and adjusted the position of her crossed arm to frame her bust, the very precise angle at which she'd tilted her head to accentuate her features for maximum effect from the precise directly of my eyeline. She might've gotten away with it, too, if I hadn't come from a world where I knew how people posed on Instagram, and then worked and lived among a bunch of former sex workers, and also collected a set of bullshit personal traumas which forced me to immediately divert my attention from the visceral reminder that this goblin was, in fact, beddably cute before I had a full-body twitch that messed up my welding.

"You are full of surprises, Gizmit," I said, pleased with the evenness of my delivery.

"That is correct," she said with a vague little smile, then levered herself off the wall. "Seems you've got this under control. I'll go check in with the others. They're done putting up the liquid rock, and the Hero's out patrolling with his familiar in case we get more company."

She strolled away down the tunnel. I continued working in silence until her footsteps had disappeared.

"That's the second goblin in ten minutes to warn us that Miss Sneppit's not entirely the prize catch she wants you to think she is," Aster commented quietly once there was quiet again.

"Mm-hmm. Makes me think . . . either she's got issues that we need to explore carefully before committing to anything with her, or the people we've been talking to have their own agendas that don't include Sneppit gaining more power."

"No reason it can't be both."

"Oh, it is definitely both."

So. Gizmit wanted to be the Goblin Queen. That was . . . an idea. I'd all but decided on Sneppit for that role, but if what she and Rizz had just told me was even mostly true, Sneppit might not be a good fit for it after all, even as impressive as her talents were. Gizmit, though? Whether or not *she* was a good fit, she'd forced me to consider exactly what I *did* need from whoever occupied that position. And she was right—it was a combatant, not an administrator.

Except . . . Was it, though? It would need to be someone *capable* of combat, but my Goblin Queen would be a representative more than a ruler— someone who could serve as an inspiration to the goblins and a voice for them in my organization. And goblins would not respect a muscle-minded bruiser.

Of course, there was always the approach of collecting every reasonably useful, attractive, and plausibly loyal woman I came across like trading cards. Unless . . .

"Hey, Biribo."

"Boss?"

"That thing Aster mentioned before, about curses. Is that something we actually have to worry about?"

"Uh . . . Well, curses are really rare, boss. You're not likely to find a sorcerer who can cast a curse in a place like Dount."

"And how likely am I to find somebody on Dount who can cast—oh, just off the top of my head—Heal? Or Null?"

"All right, point taken."

"And when I start having to fight the likes of the Lancor Empire?"

". . . yeah, they will definitely have people who can inflict curses."

"Which are . . . ?"

"Magical effects that are permanent or have a difficult removal condition, applied against the subject's wishes. Actually, Enamor can be considered a curse, though most of the others are tricky and only likely to be in the repertoire of powerful, veteran Blessed. Enamor itself isn't a common spell by any means, and it's the most basic one by that description you're likely to find. But what you *want* to know is whether they'll propagate across Spirit Bond."

"Yes, obviously. *And*?"

"It, uh, it depends on the specific spell. Enamor won't; some others won't. But . . . there are a lot that *will*."

"Which means." I sighed, "Aster's original concern stands. The more people we add to the Spirit Bond, the more vulnerable we all are. And the longer we're out there fighting, the more likely it is that someone will figure out that weakness."

"Yeah . . . Sorry, boss. Enjoin is an absolutely game-changing asset; you can't expect something like that not to come with a pretty serious downside."

"Well, this is all food for thought." I finished the last line and stepped back from the faintly smoking door, now with its seams buried in a layer of artificial but fully solidified rock, slathered on just thick and wide enough to really lock it in place without being too brittle. "All right, let's finish this up and get the hell out of here already. I hate being the last one at work."

The last door was inevitably going to be the weak point. It was the one through which we'd initially entered the Spirit's chamber, and then left it, meaning we hadn't been able to seal up the inside with liquid stone. Amell had whipped up a batch of that glue she'd first mentioned and applied it to the inner surfaces right before we pulled it shut behind us, where it should be hardened by the time the liquid stone started going on. They had also, apparently, taken the trouble of finding something to stand on—probably just the displaced barricade that was still standing right there next to the door—and slathered the stone mixture all the way up to the top. After I finished heating it, we moved the barricades back into place and then glued together the chains for good measure.

It was the best we could do. Hopefully it would deter the curious and acquisitive long enough for us to settle Jadrak and make a more permanent arrangement.

Most of the group was present to put on these last touches, and our last members returned with excellent timing just as we were finishing up. Yoshi, Nazralind, and Rhoka came trotting up in a hurry—not the trio I would've expected to be hanging out together, but that detail was immediately pushed out of my mind by the news they brought.

"We have trouble," Yoshi said seriously.

"So, there's good news and bad news," Naz added, "and both are that we know which goblin is the Void witch, since it'll be the one tipped off by his devil friend to come see who's fucking around with his altar."

"Hoy is entering the complex," Rhoka said tersely, "with about fifty armed goblins."

"Should've known touching that thing would bite us," Flaethwyn muttered.

"Excuse me," I said, "but *I* got bitten first and harder than any of you. But still, yes, point taken. I guess we did sort of draw attention to ourselves."

Yoshi nodded grimly. "The nail that sticks up gets hammered down."

"You know," I mused, drawing my rapier, "I think I prefer the American version of that proverb."

"Oh?"

I gave him my most wolfish grin. "When all you have is a hammer, every problem looks like a nail."

Man, that would've been such a perfect line on which to end the conversation, but as usual nobody could let me have any fun.

"I, uh . . ." Yoshi squinted at me. "Are you sure that's the American version? Because that sounds like a completely different proverb that happens to use a similar metaphor."

"Yeah, well, you're probably right," I agreed, already striding past him in the direction from which they'd come. "It's not like I'm an expert on proverbs, after all. I'm just a guy with a big bag of hammers."

17

In Which the Dark Lord Will Cross That Bridge When He Comes to It

This is a trap," Gizmit quietly declared once we were all in position.

"Explain?" I requested.

"Hoy used to live in this complex, as a high-ranking authority. He *knows* how it's laid out. He's leading what amounts to a raid on it, which *should* mean moving his people in as fast as possible to fan out in a search pattern and find the intruders. Instead, he's got them all milling around in that extremely exposed courtyard, doing . . . evidently nothing. They're not even preparing defenses or organizing to move in. Look at 'em; that's clearly a throng of people who do not know what they're supposed to be doing right now. And like I said, he knows very well that he is surrounded by vantage points. But not only did he position his people right in the middle of them, he's not even looking up. *That* specifically is suspicious. Any halfway rational person would be keeping an eye on the dangerous spots overlooking him. He's making a *show* of not looking up."

I studied the scene laid out below us with fresh eyes, taking in her meaning.

Jadrak's company HQ had a really impressive main entrance, carved into a natural cavern. The front wall was deeply arched inward making its outer facade resemble an amphitheater; in front of it was a wide ledge, mostly encircled by the walls but fronted by a deep ravine, which vanished into inscrutable blackness below. The wide tunnel entrance opposite was reached by a bridge that appeared to be made of wrought iron, from its surface to its support struts to the chains linking it to the ceiling above—nice advertising for a company that dealt in metal. At the highest level of the facade was a single long balcony divided by pillars into a series of alcoves, in one of which we now lurked; this completely encircled the uppermost reach of the cavern, even crossing the ravine and providing a walkway all the way around to provide three hundred sixty degrees of coverage. According to the familiars, there were no tunnels branching off from the opposite side; it was a purely decorative feature.

Gizmit was right; anybody who knew this was here and expected opposition should *not* be fooling around down there in the open. They could be hit from above in *any* direction. And yet . . .

Those goblins sure were wandering round under an obvious lack of instructions. A few of them did peer nervously up at the ring of alcoves from time to time, hence why we were crouched and only peeking over with the utmost caution. They were armed, too; a few here and there with hand-to-hand weapons but mostly carrying those heavy slingshots goblins liked, and pouches of those spiked metal balls. Perhaps Hoy assumed if they came under attack from above they could just return fire? They had a lot more ranged capability than we did . . . Then again, if he was here for the reasons we suspected, he'd been warned by a devil that there was a Dark Lord here. Slingshots seemed like a tenuous thread on which to hang the outcome of this confrontation.

Hoy himself was easy to pick out, and not just because the other goblins gave him a wide berth of personal space. He was a *big* goblin, standing head and shoulders above the rest; I would almost put him in "very short adult human" territory in terms of size. And man, did he have a sense of style. In general fashion his outfit resembled the Judges' uniform, with a heavy trench coat and wide-brimmed hat, except where Judges wore brown, he was in an eye-searing lime green, and all his stuff had elaborate artifact-style metal embellishments that appeared to be made of actual gold. That's right, gold over lime green; it hurt the eyes like staring into a tacky solar eclipse. Continuing his mimicry of a Judge, he carried a bladestaff longer than he was tall, though instead of having the sharp part concealed in a mechanical housing, it had four crescent-shaped blades attached to one end by their outer arcs, so that it bristled with eight sharp points. Sort of like a flimsy mace, in appearance.

Altogether, Hoy looked like a Hollywood depiction of a pimp who'd gotten lost in a *Final Fantasy* game and gone native. And he was just . . . standing there. Holding his wicked-looking bladestaff, slowly staring around at the cavern and his aimlessly meandering minions. So pointedly not looking up at the alcoves that it could only have been deliberate.

"I see your point," Yoshi murmured. "Why, though? It sure looks like we could kill him from here with one arrow. What's he got that makes this a trap?"

"Naz, Gizmit, keep an eye on this and let us know if anything changes," I quietly ordered, already retreating from the edge. Nazralind nodded at me and Gizmit gave me a thumbs-up without taking her eyes off the scene below. I couldn't help but take note of the lack of her usual ignoring me and/or pointing out that I wasn't her boss. Funny how someone's behavior changes when they're angling for a job.

The rest retreated with me, back into the tunnel through which we'd reached here and out of any possible view of the goblins below.

"Okay," I said as soon as we had attained a comfortable distance from the edge, "that goblin knows he's facing something incredibly dangerous and is obviously confident that he can beat it, even after sacrificing the element of surprise. We're assuming he's the Void witch, right? So what does that *mean*?"

"I know you don't like talking about the Void," Yoshi added to Radatina, "but we need to know what we're up against. It's shapeless magic, right? Cause if he can just . . . whip out anything he can *imagine*, that'd explain why he thinks he's a match for a Dark Lord."

"Oh, he really *would* be if it was that easy," Biribo scoffed. "Void magic ain't nearly that helpful, kid."

"Ugh, fine, you're right," the pixie conceded with ill grace. "Okay, look, it is *not* that easy. The problem with Void magic is it *is* shapeless—pure magic. And *magic* is just what happens when you turn thoughts into physical reality. But mortal brains aren't set up for that; thought is disorganized and very metaphorical. If you just tried to *think* something into existence without a framework like the Blessing system to guide it, well, almost anything *might* happen, but the only guarantee is you wouldn't get what you wanted, or anything useful. Like when the Dark Lord here accidentally triggered a Void effect and all it did was knock him out."

"Wait, that's all? I didn't disappear?"

Everyone stared at me.

"Because I'm *positive* I . . . went somewhere."

"Probably just inside your own head, boss," said Biribo. "You gave it an open-ended command, 'reveal yourself.' The Void can't interpret that in any way that would make sense to you, so it probably just . . . revealed a bunch of random shit right into your brain. No wonder you just ended up confused."

"Did you get any useful information out of it?" Aster asked.

I couldn't fully withhold a grimace. "Not . . . really. I had an impression of . . . That is, I *think* someone spoke to me? Yeah, I'm pretty sure there was . . . a voice. It's all muddled, though. I can't remember anything."

"And no wonder," Radatina said archly. "That's *classic* Void magic—it's just not compatible with people's brains. We're lucky you just triggered an information-gathering effect so all it did was give you a brief nightmare. If it had caused a physical reaction the whole place could've blown up. *So!* The thing with Void witches is they've bargained with a devil to get their own piece of magic, something they can actually *use*. Devils are people so attuned to the Void they're completely adapted to it, able even to live in it. A devil's help is necessary to turn the Void into anything remotely constructive."

"So . . . Hoy has . . . what?" Yoshi frowned at her. "His own custom spell? That's *it?*"

"A stupid Void witch will get something like that," said Biribo. "Just a typical spell they can fire off like a normal one from a scroll. *Smarter* ones bargain for something more versatile. It'll be *some* kind of weird superpower, probably something more elaborate than a simple spell, but it'll definitely have built-in limitations. His devil will have designed it along some manner of consistent theme. And *most* Void witches don't have more than one, or at most two, because they have to bargain with a devil for each, and devils just plain don't want much. You've only got one soul to trade, and the only other thing they're interested in is your help to corrupt a Spirit so they can sucker in more victims."

"So Hoy might have only one trick?" I glanced back at the ledge, where Naz and Gizmit were still keeping watch.

"He's already got that ability to Bless goblins and produce two specific spell scrolls, remember?" said Yoshi. "So, yeah, if he sold his soul *and* corrupted that Spirit, probably just one additional power."

"Don't assume," Aster cautioned. "Rads said Jadrak and Hoy were the only two who visited the Spirit. Jadrak could also be a Void witch. If *he's* the one making the scrolls, Hoy might have more of a power set."

"Okay, that's starting to sound more like somebody who thinks he can win after getting surprise-jumped by a Dark Lord," I murmured. "Maizo, you're the intel guy here. What dirt can you dish on Hoy?"

"Finally, Maizo's chance to shine," he said, grinning and showing off those missing teeth, which caused Zui to wince in sympathy. "Right, then!

Quick rundown on Hoy—he's Blessed with Magic, known to be able to cast Shock, Fire Lance, Force Wave, and Flicker."

"Uh, Biribo?" I asked.

"Short-range electrical attack, long-range fire-based attack, directional area-of-effect kinetic attack, short-range teleportation."

"Thank you."

"I can't speak for what other spells he may have picked up, or what this Void shit can do, obviously," Maizo clarified. "Hoy is also just . . . bigger. Stronger. Even before getting Blessed he was able to push other goblins around, and given that our physical strength is magically improved, he's probably got the sheer muscle to take any of you in a straightforward rassle."

Yoshi grimaced. "Is there *any* good news?"

"Yeah, in fact. Hoy is well known to be the opposite of a people person. Selfish, rude, gratuitously nasty. Your classic neighborhood bully with tiny dick compensation syndrome. He's got a rep for using his strength *and* his Blessing to get his way. I know that kind of behavior isn't exactly appreciated anywhere, so you tallfolk may not have the context to grasp exactly how despised that dude is throughout Kzidnak. That is the opposite of *everything* goblin society *is*. Well, when there's not a Goblin King upending everything, I mean."

"How is that *good* news?" Yoshi demanded.

"It means he'll have no loyalty among those goblins he brought with him, right?" Pashilyn answered.

"Exactly!" Maizo grinned at her, which caused her to also wince slightly. "That's the advantage—those mooks are loyal to Jadrak, not Hoy, and Jadrak is not *here*. Even better, you can pretty much count on Hoy to try spending their lives like pocket change just to slow you down; he doesn't respect or care about anybody but himself and *possibly* Jadrak, and it wouldn't shock me to learn that Hoy was plannin' to take over as Goblin King as soon as you guys're out of the picture. Soon as you take out Hoy, the rest of 'em'll scatter. Hell, might not even take that much—if it even *looks* like he's not gonna win, I bet a lot of his force will make their own discreet exit. They will only obey him as long as they're more scared of him than you."

"I'm pretty confident I can fix their priorities," I said. Yoshi gave me a wary look.

"There's another thing to keep in mind when you're gauging strength," Radatina chimed in. "That goblin's Blessing of Magic isn't very strong; he'll quickly tire out casting normal spells. His Void gift will be different. Blessings come with innate limitations and the ability to grow out of them as they're used, so most people can only cast so many spells, or at a certain level of power—or have limits on the number of artifacts they can use at once, and how much strength the enchantments have. Champions get around this because the Blessing of Wisdom disables the limiters on the other two, so you can both use whatever artifacts you can carry and cast spells indefinitely at full strength. His Void gift will be like that, too. There's nothing to limit it the way there is with normal magic."

"So he'll favor Void over traditional magic," I said, nodding. "That *is* good to know. Thanks, Tina-chan!"

"Do *not* call me that," she hissed.

"Is there *any* way to know what his Void power is before we trigger it?" Yoshi asked. "Like, I'm sure you'd have said something already if you could tell, but . . . is there a Wisdom perk or something?"

I couldn't help cringing. You don't *ask* about Wisdom perks; if you know about them in advance, they don't unlock. Hadn't Radatina bothered to explain that to him?

Fortunately, in this case it turned out not to matter.

"There are no perks," Biribo said. "No spells, no artifacts, nothing. There is *nothing* in the Blessing system specifically targeted against the Void. You'll just have to . . . do the best you can, against whatever happens. Sorry, kid, we can't tell just from looking at him. We'll all find out when he does something."

Interesting. I was pretty sure the Goddesses wanted the Devil King beaten, and I knew they were open to making tweaks to their system. Why wouldn't they set up some countermeasures? Clearly there was something more going on here.

"Okay," he said, inhaling deeply to steel himself. "Then . . . should we retreat? I don't like the idea of charging into an unknown."

"I'd rather not," I said. "Hoy is too important to the Goblin King, and he's right *here*. Can we afford to pass up this chance to take him out?"

"That's pretty clearly what *he's* banking on you deciding," Rizz interjected. "The only thing we know about his powers is *he's* the only one here who knows what they are, and *he* thinks he's a match for you. Hoy's a well-known shithead, like the boy said, but I haven't heard it said that he's overconfident."

"Then you need to make him react before committing yourselves to the attack," Gizmit said from the ledge, half turning her head to be audible to us without taking both her eyes off the scene below. "Reveal his power set early enough that you can develop a response. He's trying to force a confrontation on his terms. Force one on yours."

"Mm." I ran a hand over my face, thinking rapidly. Dammit, this was the same problem I'd realized in the middle of my desperate charge to save Yoshi and his friends—I was just not a strategist or tactician. Somebody with any kind of training would be able to come up with a better plan than me. But Rizz wasn't suggesting anything, and Gizmit had apparently said her vague piece, so it came down to me and Yoshi as the authority figures here. Which meant me, of course. "Well, he clearly wants us to try a long-ranged attack from above, so we can't do that. If that's what he's trying to set up, it must be what he's best prepared to defend against, which suggests we'll have better chances engaging him up close."

"I'm better up close anyway," Yoshi said, nodding.

Actually, I might be onto something with that. "And he's taken up position in the middle of the space, and kept his lackeys arranged all around him symmetrically . . . Naz, Giz, that's still the layout?"

"Yup, he hasn't moved. I think the rest of these goblins are starting to fall asleep."

"Something tells me *they* weren't informed they'd be fighting a Dark Lord," Gizmit added.

"That proves it, he wants to fight at range, not in melee. Okay . . . Yoshi, I have a thought. I don't think you'll like it, though."

"I can't say I like anything that's happening here," Yoshi agreed. "What's your idea, Omura?"

The familiars guided us unerringly to the level even with the front door, outside which Hoy was camped out, taunting us. We paused at a fork in the hallways where we would have to part; these were actual constructed halls, not tunnels, and were apparently part of the "old" Kzidnak Gizmit had referenced, since they were built to human scale. Our ranged fighters and noncombatants remained up top, under orders to watch the situation and act according to their best judgment once they figured out what Hoy could do. Gizmit was an up-close combatant like the rest of us, but I'd asked her to stick with the others on the grounds that she was best able to improvise a solid plan on the fly.

"This is where we gotta part," Biribo stated as our loose formation shuffled to a halt. "Boss, we got the short path, so past this point we need to be quiet."

"We have a much longer way to go around," Radatina chimed in, "but most of it's behind *really* thick rock, so we can hustle the first leg of the way and not tip them off."

"Got it," Yoshi said seriously, nodding at me. "You'll probably get in position first, Omura, so I'll move out once we're in place."

"I'll be watching. Be safe and watch your back."

"You, too. Good luck."

He turned and broke into a run—head down, arms back and to the sides, body tilted forward as he vanished into the darkness.

"Hey," Flaethwyn grunted, staring after the departing Hero and not yet moving, "you're from the same country. *Why* does he run like that?"

I couldn't help it; all I could do was clap a hand over my mouth and manage not to howl out loud as the compulsive laughter took me over. For the first moments I couldn't even run, just staggering away in the other direction and having to brace myself against the wall with my free hand.

"Yeah, ours can run like a normal person, but sometimes he does . . . this," Adelly commented. "That Japan must be a real interesting place."

Man, if Yoshi and I ever *did* get home, we owed everybody an apology. You could hardly find a worse pair of national representatives.

I had time to collect myself, anyway, which was fortunate as I had an audience. Flaethwyn alone had gone with Yoshi; I had brought Aster and Adelly, of course. Also, Rizz and Rhoka had decided to tag along with me. I'd learned not to bother giving them orders or asking them to explain themselves, so . . . here we were. Rizz at least knew what she was about. This should provide me some extra muscle and not much additional liability, so I didn't complain.

As predicted, we reached our vantage first. In fact, we didn't quite *reach* it, slowing to a halt and doing our best to breathe quietly well out of sight of the doorway, which opened into the plaza from one side. The miscellaneous chatter of bored goblins echoed through the hall from this close, which should hopefully conceal any sounds we might inadvertently make. Of course, if one poked his head in and saw us we were screwed, but for whatever reason Hoy had evidently ordered his lackeys to remain out there on the ledge.

"They're still movin', boss," Biribo reported in a low murmur right by my ear. "Slowed down now as they're within echo range. Should just be a few more minutes."

I nodded and settled in to wait, leaning against the wall.

This was the worst part. Well, the worst part so far. Perhaps I shouldn't begrudge the tense anticipation when we didn't know what was going to happen once we attacked—but that was exactly what made the anticipation so awful. Over the last few months I'd done quite a lot of lying in wait for various targets, but those were mostly hapless merchants and highborn coaches, who were about to go to sleep thanks to my goblin alchemy so my minions and I could rifle through their pockets at our leisure.

Amell did not know how to make sleeping bombs. I kind of regretted asking; she apparently hadn't known those were a thing before I brought it up. To judge by the annoyed looks I got from Gizmit, Zui, and Maizo, that was proprietary goblin business. Oops.

"Hero's in position," Biribo whispered, just loud enough for the others nearby to overhear. "He's paused just outta sight behind the opposite entrance. Seems like he's talkin' to Flaethwyn."

"Okay," I said softly, grasping the handle of my dagger. "Don't peek out until everyone's *good* and distracted. Don't do anything unless I call for it or you've *fully* figured out what Hoy can do and how you can counter it."

"We know the plan, Lord Seiji," Aster reassured me with a smile.

"I know you do, but repeating it makes me feel better."

"We know that, too."

I drew the dagger and vanished from sight just as the first yells heralded Yoshi's attack. Even knowing I was invisible, I peeked warily around the corner; no harm in overcaution, given what we were facing. My careful observation came at just the right moment for me to observe the trap Hoy had laid for us.

Hoy was more a strategist than a tactician, apparently; his forces were positioned in the worst possible order to pull off what he'd set them up to do. Yoshi charged out of his side entrance, directly opposite mine, shield up and sword at the ready. Whether by pure luck or because he'd grown some actual skills, he cast his first spell with perfect timing to save his life and turn the trap around.

"Force Wave!"

The blast of sheer kinetic energy not only knocked over the first ranks of goblins still turning on him, but also caught and repelled the opening volley of projectiles fired in his direction. Really, the way the slingshot-armed goblins were just strewn around the open space in no particular formation, it was impressive any of them could manage to fire past each other's heads and aim, more or less, at the attacking Hero.

But their volley was turned right back against them and wiped out a good third of the entire force in the first row, because as it turned out they were not firing standard-issue spiked balls like Sneppit's security forces had; they were using those slingshots to sling *fucking bombs.*

Grenades whipped back into their own allies and went off, demolishing goblins in a far more brutal manner than anything I could've managed— some of whose own ammunition went up in response. A chain of explosions tore across the entire half of the ledge closest to Yoshi, forcing him to duck behind his shield and stagger back, which was nothing compared to what happened to the goblins. Their purely self-inflicted losses were catastrophic; even the survivors began screaming and running around in a panic. Further incidental explosions occurred as slingshots misfired, grenades impacting the surrounding walls and columns and spraying shrapnel. Those explosions didn't seem to have a large blast radius, but they were powerful enough to gouge craters in stone.

Okay, I could see what Hoy was going for. If he'd been attacked from above, his people would've hammered the attackers' entire position with bombs and taken out *most* enemies by taking out everything in their vicinity. I had to admit, that probably would have worked on me. That didn't explain everything, though; I still didn't know why he was so confident he'd survive the initial sniping attempt. Also, was he *stupid*? Even if he hadn't known Yoshi could cast Force Wave, having his lackeys shoot grenades in every direction while he was *standing in the middle of them* seemed utterly insane.

Whether or not Hoy was an idiot, clearly he still knew something I didn't.

Yoshi was still hunkered down behind his shield; I couldn't see blood and maybe he was just sensibly waiting for the aftershocks to diminish, but then again there was shrapnel flying everywhere.

Heal, I silently cast; pink light burst around the Hero.

"You're all fucking useless," Hoy spat in a shriller voice than I was expecting for a goblin of his stature. "Just stay out of the way and stop sucking up my air. **Fire Lance!**"

Yoshi had just started to straighten up, but now ducked back down and took the hit square on his artifact shield. It pushed him back again, the backwash of flames bursting around him for a moment, but that didn't stop him from immediately retaliating.

"Force Bolt!"

Hoy made a contemptuous swatting motion, and . . . nothing happened. That spell had no visual effect, save things getting knocked around when it impacted, but apparently it didn't. Did Yoshi just . . . miss? Well, he was casting under duress.

I strode invisibly forward, rapier in one hand and dagger in the other. It was taking me longer than I liked to close the distance, because the surviving goblins were all fleeing toward *this* end of the platform. If they tried to escape into our corridor . . . well, Aster and the others would have to deal with that. I was fully occupied sneaking through them without revealing my presence by kicking somebody.

Yoshi was trying to charge forward after a couple more Force Bolts failed to connect, and making little progress as Hoy kept hammering him with Fire Lances—and some pretty vulgar taunts. I gave him another quick Heal just in case he'd been singed too badly.

Meanwhile, I'd finally broken free of the crowd, who were doing their best to keep their distance from their leader. I had a straight shot to the Void witch now. Lengthening my stride, I raised my invisible rapier—

My *translucent* rapier. As I drew close, it started to fade back into view. As did I.

Hoy hammered Yoshi with another Fire Lance, then turned and contemptuously swatted my blade aside with his staff, grinning cruelly up at me.

"Nice try, wankstain."

Okay, *this* was a problem.

Slimeshot!

A desultory splatter of slimy droplets splashed the bladed head of Hoy's staff, some trickling onto his sleeve.

"*Ugh*. What the fuck was *that* supposed to be? Fuck off, idiot, I'm busy."

He jabbed and slashed at me with the staff, but I was armed with an artifact sword and—barely, clumsily—managed to deflect the vicious attack, nearly losing my grip on the blade. What? Where was my fencing mastery? Where was my *invisibility*?

Hoy had the gall to turn his back on me and pin down Yoshi's attempted charge with two more Fire Lances. I had no compunctions about hitting him from behind.

Windburst!

A light breeze ruffled his fancy green coat; he ignored me completely.

What the *fuck*?

Sparkspray!

I successfully shot Hoy with a light puff of smoke, which he did not appear to notice, having turned to charge at Yoshi and physically force him backward. Yoshi managed to take the hits on his shield, but he was losing ground.

"**Shock!**"

At Hoy's shout, an arc of lightning tore through the shield itself and Yoshi staggered backward with a yelp, losing his footing. Hoy loomed over him, raising his blade—

"No! **Immolate!**"

A harmless flurry of sparks burst against the back of the goblin sorcerer's coat. He paused, turning away from Yoshi to grin wolfishly at me.

"Oh, you want some too, bitch? Wait your turn, I'm busy."

Heal!

I wasn't sure how effective that would be against electrocution—ah, good. Yoshi stopped twitching and managed our first success against the Void witch, landing an actual kick on his leg and forcing him to stagger back, cursing. It gave the Hero a moment to roll away and back to his feet, and me a moment to get updated by my familiar.

"Boss! That's his Void power! He is *disabling Blessing magic*! Artifacts, spells, *all of it*."

Oh. Yep, that explained it.

No wonder Hoy was so confident about taking on a Dark Lord. Without Blessings, a Dark Lord is just some clown facing an armed wizard who's physically stronger. Our forces were still in reserve, but *they* wouldn't be any more effective here than Yoshi and me.

Hm. We might actually be screwed this time.

18

In Which the Dark Lord Comes to the Bridge and Blows It Up

Don't even fucking think about it!" Hoy barked at me, his mocking demeanor suddenly switching to pure contemptuous rage—which was weird, since I wasn't even *doing* anything at that moment except dithering in the realization of how out of my depth I was. "I see even *one* of you shitheads aim those things anywhere *near* me and I'll strangle your families with your fucking colon! Shoot the other one, morons!"

Oh, he wasn't talking to me, just the goblins behind me. Also, important thing learned—if I didn't want to get shot in the back with a spiked grenade, I needed to stay within melee range of the goblin sorcerer, who had a big spiky weapon that he could currently use a lot better than I could mine.

Lovely. Well, the upside was they couldn't do the other thing, either, since the pair of us were between the slingers and Yoshi.

Since there was nothing else for it, I lunged forward, stabbing at him. Hoy contemptuously swatted my thrust aside with his staff, then in my next attempt actually caught the blade of my rapier between the protruding tines of his own weapon. The little shit paused to grin triumphantly at me before twisting violently in a move that should have wrenched the rapier out of my hand.

It didn't, because his fancy-looking custom bladestaff might as well have been precision-designed to make that impossible. The four crescent-moon blades curved outward from its top, meaning the twisting force just made my blade slide smoothly out from between them. It did wrench the rapier forcefully to one side, leaving me momentarily wide open, and Hoy didn't hesitate this time, lunging in a brutal stab that would have skewered me had

I not frantically leaped back. I barely evaded getting impaled, and only my Surestep Boots kept me on my feet after that clumsy backward leap. I felt the distinctively disorienting sensation of my feet twisting implausibly under me in a position that preserved my balance and didn't sprain anything—a maneuver I would definitely not have been able to execute on purpose.

Hang on. The boots were still working . . . Why them, and not the sword or dagger?

There was no time to dwell on it; I was now out of Hoy's blast radius, which was a deadly place to be. Indeed, a spiked grenade whizzed past the space I'd just occupied as I lunged forward to engage him again, arcing down into the canyon to explode against the opposite wall.

"**Fire Lance!**" he shouted, flinging the spell blindly at Yoshi to keep him pinned down while he whipped up his staff to deal with me again. I parried an attack, made him dodge a thrust, then forced him to retreat from my next stab before he could swing his staff to counter me. The frustrated anger was growing on the goblin's face as he found me not quite as helpless as he'd expected.

Here's the thing about the Mastery enchantment.

The way to improve a skill is to *practice* it—to repeat the necessary motions correctly, so many times they become second nature and can be executed without thought. If you're doing something with an artifact that enables you to do it *perfectly*, every time, you're not just very effective while using said artifact, you are building muscle memory that doesn't go away when you put it down. As soon as I realized this, I'd made a point to train with the rapier every day, against anybody at North Watch willing to spar with me. I hadn't counted on the artifact itself ever being neutralized, but I *was* expecting it to be taken from me at some point—all my artifacts were looted from defeated enemies, after all. After a couple months of this, I was . . . Well, I was nowhere near the master fencer I could be with the Mastery enchantment working. But I was also better than a guy who'd been training with the blade for a couple months the old-fashioned way. Maybe not all that *much* better, but as it turned out, it was enough.

Barely.

Hoy and I probed at each other, dancing back and forth; this was an annoyingly close match. I guess he was like me, a sorcerer who carried a weapon as a backup and had never had reason to be more than just competent with it. It only took him a few seconds of this to lose patience.

"That's enough of your bullshit," the goblin spat at me, hopping back, lowering his staff and holding out his other hand. Realizing his intent,

I frantically backpedaled and lunged to the side; not that I could possibly be quick enough to evade the—

"**Fire Lance!**"

Nothing happened. I paused uncertainly, raising my rapier to guard position.

Hoy's face twisted in animal rage. "**Shock!**"

Again . . . nothing.

Boots, and also target-blocking ring . . . Oho. So *that* was how it was.

I gave him my broadest, most shit-eating grin. "Yeah, that's pretty fuckin' annoying, isn't it, li'l buddy?"

Hoy snarled at me, half turned to hammer Yoshi with another Fire Lance, then lunged at me with his bladestaff again.

"Boss! It's only protecting him from effects *directed* at him!" Biribo said out loud, now that I'd already figured that out myself.

"Right. Go update the others on the details. I've got this." Radatina would have seen the same and informed Yoshi; I wasn't sure what Rizz or Gizmit might have been able to pick up from their angles, but if I got them both on the same page, one or the other might come up with something while I kept the Void witch busy.

Now that I thought of it, I'd also been able to cast Heal on Yoshi, right past Hoy—and now I did it again, because he'd soaked up a few more Fire Lances since, and just to verify once more that it worked. Yep, we were still in business. So I couldn't use an offensive artifact on him—which apparently extended to the invisibility effect of my dagger—or cast spells *at* him. That left me with Surestep Boots to ensure flawless footing no matter how we chased each other around on this ledge, which was increasingly covered in shrapnel and broken rock from all the explosions. He couldn't target me with spells, either. Also, I had an artifact to protect me from lethal hits, and I could still cast Heal on myself to remedy anything else.

This was starting to look like an annoying stalemate, but that was a hell of a lot better than the hopeless debacle I'd thought it was seconds ago. And I *still* didn't understand everything; Hoy's posture at the start of this said he wasn't worried about being shot with arrows or slingshots, and he had yet to reveal why. Fortunately, there was a fix for that.

Unfortunately, part of the initial problem remained. If our archers took a shot at Hoy, his slingers would retaliate, and they had a *massive* edge in firepower.

So I knew what we had to do before we could take out the Void witch.

Okay, step one . . . Hoy was pissed off but not on the run, and he appeared more than adroit enough to keep us both pinned down by engaging me with his weapon and slamming Yoshi with fire spells. Yoshi couldn't retaliate with magic thanks to his Void art, and couldn't get closer because Fire Lance packed a kinetic punch in addition to its heat; if he didn't brace himself fully and cower behind his shield, each one would send him flying, extra crispy.

"Yoshi!" I barked, already dashing to plant myself between him and Hoy. "Switch! Use your Force Wave to stop them shooting bombs at us!"

"Wh— Omura, you can't tank him! I'm in armor and I have a shield, you're too squishy—"

What the *fuck* did he just call me?!

"Just do what I say, I'll explain later!"

Finally shutting up, he pivoted, staying behind me as I repositioned myself. I was still too close to Hoy to be a bombing target—and fully occupied keeping him from stabbing or bludgeoning me—but Yoshi could be possibly clipped by the slingers at this range.

"**Force Wave!**" he shouted, and my coat was tugged by the kinetic blast that ripped outward just as the telltale twang of slingshots fired twice. As before, the grenades were whipped right back into the goblins' ranks; I heard two explosions and several screams, unable to suppress a wince. Hopefully Aster and the others were still hunkered down behind the doorway; they were in that direction.

"I have *had* it with you fuckers!" Hoy raged. "**Force Wave!**"

Oh right, area-of-effect spells didn't have to be aimed *at* me.

Man, getting hit with that thing point-blank *sucked*. It was a fast-moving wall of pure kinetic energy; I'd been slammed into Yoshi before I could really process the full-body impact to my front, and then we were tumbling over each other. I found myself skidding across the floor, dazed, ending up with Yoshi's fallen form just within my field of view. He'd managed to land a little more gracefully than I, awkwardly on one knee and bringing his shield back up with a grunt of pain. His motions were slow, as if he'd sprained something in the fall.

Heal! Heal!

The spell brought the air back into my lungs and rid my skull of the disorienting ringing, and got Yoshi back up to full strength, as well. Of course, *now* we were at a bad distance from Hoy, who lost no time in firing off another Fire Lance to keep Yoshi occupied, and then another. I whirled toward the last remaining King-aligned goblins, unsure if my Windburst would be enough to turn back a bomb volley, but it was the only idea I had. Sure enough, a goblin was there, raising a slingshot one-handed—

Wait, that was Rizz. She was kneeling on another goblin's back, her free arm holding one of his twisted painfully behind him, and taking aim at Hoy. The sorcerer glanced aside, did a double take, and whirled to cast at her.

Not fast enough.

The bomb flew true—then suddenly jerked to one side before it reached him, pinging into the ground barely a meter away. Huh, no wonder he wasn't worried about getting shot by arrows from above. Unfortunately for him, bombs were not arrows.

The blast wasn't close enough to properly finish him, but it was close enough that the shockwave and shrapnel sent him painfully to the ground. Toward the edge of the crevice, but sadly not close enough.

"C'mon!" I grabbed Yoshi by the collar of his armored tunic and tugged, leading him around behind one of the heavy pillars holding up the row of balconies above us. There, we gained at least a moment's respite; couldn't afford to linger here, but I had been struck by inspiration and needed to bring Yoshi up to speed on my new and improved strategy.

"Boss!" Biribo squawked, zipping back down to rejoin us just in time. "*That* was a spell—a normal Blessing spell! He's got Repulsion Aura!"

"Probably got it from his devil," Radatina added. "That's a *much* rarer and more potent spell than the others he's been using. Sorry we couldn't detect it until it was actually triggered, but now we know! That will repel any projectiles *or* spells fired at him."

"The spell thing is redundant with his Void gift, but good to know," Yoshi wheezed.

"Ah, Radatina explained that to you, good."

He gave me a strange look. "What? Why would she need to? I figured that out as soon as my first Force Bolt fizzled. Haven't you ever seen an antimagic field before?"

Shut the fuck up, you little nerd. "Fine, listen, I know what we need to do now. Can you keep him occupied for a few minutes?"

"So your new plan is the same as the old plan?" he exclaimed in loud exasperation.

"Nonsense, that wasn't the plan, it's just what we ended up doing. *Now* we're doing it for a reason instead of scrabbling around like idiots!"

"So the *old* plan was to scrabble around like idiots? You're the Dark Lord! Aren't you supposed to be good at making schemes and plots?"

"Sure I am, and sometimes they even work!"

"Sometimes?"

"I'd say one out of . . . What do you think, Biribo, four or five?"

"Sounds about right, boss."

An explosion from far too close caused cracks to spread through the pillar we were crowded behind, spraying bits of stone to both sides. Yoshi and I huddled together, and the familiars grabbed onto each other between us, which would have been hilarious under other circumstances.

"And what are you going to do while I'm keeping him occupied?"

"Rendering aid and comfort to the enemy!"

"Your *new plan* is the dictionary definition of 'treason'?!"

"Part of it. There are steps."

"I *really* hate you!" the Hero shouted over the noise of another bomb impacting way too close for comfort.

"That's the spirit!"

We parted and charged out from both sides. Hoy had just been shooting Fire Lances into his own troops, frying goblins and setting off more bombs in the course of failing to nail Rizz, who skittered back through the doorway just as we emerged. He whirled and cast, reacting to the motion; unfortunately for Hoy, his first instinctive cast was at me, and did nothing. It took him only a split second to correct.

"FIRE LANCE!"

Yoshi, though, had been soaking those things up for the last few minutes and had the hang of it now. He hit the ground on one boot and one armored kneepad, turning his charge into a slide, shield-first. The Fire Lance hit him dead-on, wrecking his momentum—but not negating it entirely. Yoshi kicked off with his upright foot, turning the last dregs of his energy from a slide back into a lunge, and finally brought himself within sword range of the sorcerer.

Hoy hammered at him with the bladestaff; Yoshi took it on the shield, which he then swept ferociously aside, throwing Hoy entirely off-balance and lashing out with his sword next. Hoy had to leap backward, the blade nicking the front of his coat and grazing him as he desperately retreated. Yoshi followed, not giving him a chance to regain space.

So he took matters into his own hands.

"Shock!"

"Heal!"

Yoshi was stunned for a split second before I put him right again, and he wasted not an instant in pressing the attack.

"**Sho—**"

CLONK. "Shut up!"

Ah, the oh-so-satisfying sound of a shield smacking a smug goblin. The ultimate counterspell.

I kept one eye on him while scanning the field for targets. There were a *lot*; the ground was pockmarked by grenade impacts and so slick with blood that only my artifact boots were enabling me to move. Eugh, no wonder Yoshi had been able to powerslide across a stone floor. Goblins and pieces of goblins lay everywhere.

There was no time to do this right; I had to settle for doing it fast.

"**Heal! Heal! Heal! Heal! Heal! Heal! Heal! Heal! Heal! Heal! Heal—**"

My casting was slowed only by the fact that I did it vocally—projecting, of course, to be heard across the entire cavern. Because this wasn't just saving lives, this was *showtime*, and it mattered that everyone present understood exactly what I was doing.

"*What* are you *doing?*" Flaethwyn screeched from the stone doorway behind which she was huddling, then ducked back out of sight when someone launched a bomb at her. Being fired from clear across the intervening space, it didn't get all the way there, but still. I could sympathize; that was pretty much how everyone felt about Flaethwyn and her opinions.

Not every cast worked; some of those goblins were beyond saving. But I cast my spell of ultimate healing at every mostly intact goblin I could see— and also Yoshi, every third or fourth cast, because he was getting constantly hammered by lightning and fire spells at point-blank range, and our current symbiotic relationship was that his meat-shielding was both necessary for and enabled by my healing.

A goblin who'd just sat upright with a gasp at being Healed now turned toward me and picked up a loose bomb, since he didn't have an intact slingshot at hand.

"*Really*, man?" I demanded, staring him down.

The goblin swallowed heavily and very carefully rolled the bomb away from us, toward the edge of the precipice.

"What the *fuck* are you morons *doing?*" Hoy snarled, battering on Yoshi's shield with his bladestaff in a two-handed grip. "Somebody *blast* that fucking butt before he does something else!"

"Sure, you could try that," I said in a deliberately agreeable tone to contrast with his vicious demeanor. "Maybe it'll work this time?"

Pause one beat for effect; goblins were looking uncertainly between me and Hoy.

"You know, I've probably been in more battles than any of you," I continued, "and I've gotta say, it's really fucked up that you're all dying from your own weapons and because your boss is using you as living shields. Yoshi, have *we* actually killed any goblins here?"

He stepped back twice, breathing heavily and regaining some distance from Hoy for the first time in a couple minutes. Yoshi was out of breath and sweating heavily—but to be fair, so was Hoy, hence the sorcerer not immediately taking advantage of the lull to blast him again. I was only doing slightly better myself.

"Does flinging their own bombs back at them count?"

"I wouldn't blame 'em for being pissed at us about that," I said frankly. "Though if anybody in charge had bothered to set up a *proper* ambush that wouldn't have happened. Hey, Hoy, explain something to me!"

"You're fucking *dead*, you piece of shit!" the Void witch screamed, brandishing his staff. "I'm gonna rip your smirking head off and take a shit down your neck hole!"

"*Damn*," I acknowledged, "the detail and *specificity* of that. Holy shit, man. Do you just spend your free time sitting around, thinking those up? How long did that one take you?"

I thought he was going to burst a blood vessel. Hoy flung out a hand at me, opened his mouth to call out a spell, then his eye began twitching violently as he remembered.

"**Fire Lance!**" he squawked at Yoshi, who ducked and took it on his shield as per usual.

"Hey, *he* said it!"

"**Heal**," I rebutted, remedying any singeing Yoshi may have suffered. "But seriously, though. What's with the milling around in the center of the chamber? If *I'd* been running this ambush, I'd have positioned everybody in these floor-level alcoves all around here. Behind the pillars, see? Then when the attack comes, only those who can *see* it fire at it. That means you don't get the entire group unloading on one spot, but why would you *need* them to?"

"**Fire Lance!**" Hoy screamed, brandishing a hand at me. He'd learned; this one whipped past my head to flash into the alcove behind me. The heat was scorching, but only momentary. I ignored it. "**Force Wave**!" I was too far away, taking only a mild push that barely required me to shift my feet.

More importantly, all the surviving goblins were watching, silent, and not a single one of them pointing a slingshot at me.

"That's the thing about bombs; you really only need to land a *few* hits in the general area of the target," I continued in my adamantly reasonable tone. "Plus, having *everybody* fire at the first target will screw you over if the enemy fakes you out and has a backup attack. Most importantly, they're all in each other's way, and with ordnance like that, mass casualties are . . . Shit, it's not even a risk, that's just *math*. What the fuck, dude? This only makes sense if you wanted the juvenile satisfaction of seeing a really *big* boom wherever I popped up, and didn't care how many of your people died for it."

"You're only talking because *that's all you have*," Hoy hissed, aiming the bladed head of his staff at me. "Some fucking Dark Lord *you* turned out to be, getting your ass kicked by a goblin!"

"Hey, don't say 'goblin' like it makes it worse," I chided, frowning at him. "I respect goblins as much as anyone. That's why all this is happening. Did you even know that? I've been making friends with goblins since I landed on Dount. I am down here to finish off Jadrak because your precious King was so desperate for my attention he murdered the goblins I was friendly with. Blood calls for blood, Hoy."

"Bullshit! None of you inbreds better be listening to this lying crock of crap!"

"I can tell this is not something you're capable of understanding, but I will explain it, anyway," I snapped, switching my demeanor. Cold, focused, relentless. "*No one fucks with my people.* I will protect who I can—and who I can't, I will *avenge*. If Jadrak had respected goblin lives as much as I do, he'd get to live. But he didn't. So he doesn't."

"Why the *fuck* are none of you *fucking shooting him*?!" Hoy screamed, actually stomping his foot. Big bad Void witch, right hand of the Goblin King, throwing a toddler tantrum right here in front of all of us. Holy crap, this guy really had never been told 'no' in his life; this was what you got for being the big frog in a tiny pond. "I swear by Virya's fucking *teats*, if you shitheads don't start unloading ordnance on this worthless fucker *right fucking now* I'm gonna round the rest of you up and . . ."

I let him rant, since he was currently doing my work for me.

"Biribo," I murmured under the cover of Hoy's screeching, "tell Radatina to tell Yoshi to maneuver him onto the bridge. Then tell Rizz and Rhoka to get ready. They'll know what to do when the opening comes."

My familiar buzzed off without another word. He zipped over to a few meters away from Yoshi, and a second later, Radatina fluttered down next to the Hero's ear for a second. He glanced at her, then at me, and nodded, by which time Biribo had zoomed around the back wall to disappear through the door, behind which Rizz was once again hiding with the others.

". . . right in your *fucking* eye sockets! Now *get to fucking work*, you use-less turds!"

Hoy finally had to stop for air; he was panting as hard after his tirade as he had been after the workout Yoshi and I had put him through.

I kept an eye on him, though at this point most of my attention was on the surviving goblins he'd brought, a significant portion of whom were only still alive thanks to me. I couldn't quite get a headcount under these conditions, but I estimated their numbers at around twenty-five. Maybe half what he'd brought here to die.

So I was able to see the first one to move. Group cohesion is a hell of a powerful force; in a situation like this, whoever went first would have to be powerfully motivated. This guy I saw staring at another goblin—a dead one, missing an arm and half her head. He cradled the slingshot in his arms, his expression twisting as he looked at the body.

Then he placed a grenade in his weapon, pulled it back and with a reso-lute expression, took aim right at Hoy.

The Void witch saw the movement and turned to face him, a particularly nasty grin contorting his already unpleasant features.

"Bad move, shitstain. Your biggest mistake, and your last."

Slimeshot.

Like the Fire Lance he'd hurled past me, I found it worked fine if I wasn't aiming *at* him, or too close. The slime impacted the ground a meter from Hoy's feet and disintegrated into a spray of slimy droplets—not dangerous to him or anyone, but sufficient to make him take a step back before he could punish the rebellious goblin.

By the time he regained his footing, three more bomb-laden sling-shots were aimed at him. That was enough of a catalyst. One by one, every remaining Jadrak loyalist who still had a weapon turned it on their former leader.

Oddly enough, the perpetual rage seemed to leak away from Hoy under this threat. Instead, he actually cackled and spread his arms, one hand wide open and the other holding his bladestaff.

"All right, you know what? Fucking *do* it, losers. You treasonous little fucks can find out just how fucking stupid you are in your last seconds. You wanna side with tallboy interlopers, you can fucking *die* with 'em!"

Yoshi and I locked eyes, knowing what was coming next—Repulsion Aura. Both of us quickly sidestepped, repositioning ourselves to be in place to—

Grenades flew, and every last one veered away from Hoy before striking him. It was chaos; a dozen explosives spun off in a dozen directions, half of them about to be lethally dangerous to the goblins who'd launched them. That is, if not for our heroic intervention.

"Force Wave!"

"Windburst!"

Even as a few goblins shrieked and cowered back as they beheld their ammunition boomeranging at them, Yoshi and I sent the errant bombs hurtling over the ledge. Explosions tore chunks out of the edge of the stonework, gouged new craters in the floor; one sent spinning nearly straight upward knocked down a stalactite, which hammered the ledge opposite the ravine, causing part of it to crumble into the abyss.

Hoy stood with his arms spread, grinning in sadistic triumph as he stood untouched within the maelstrom—until the Hero charged right through the shrapnel at him.

"Shock!"

"Heal!"

I'd seen that coming; our voices practically overlapped each other, the effect of Hoy's spell barely making Yoshi falter. Hoy only *just* managed to get his staff up and in place to hammer against his shield, forced back a few steps as it became a contest of brute strength. Yoshi had only been training for a few months and had been some kind of teenage shut-in before, but he was also *heavier* than Hoy by a lot, and that counted.

Hoy retreated another step, gaining some distance. Yoshi's eyes cut to the side, caught mine, and his head shifted once in an infinitesimal nod.

What? Was that a signal? A signal for *what*? That wasn't communication! We needed to arrange these things *before*—

He lowered his shield, lunging forward, sword-first. It was a well-trained strike, but a move designed for use against a human opponent; at best, it would hit the top of Hoy's head. And only if he let it, because the Hero had left himself wide open in the center.

Oh. Now I got it.

The goblin grinned with insane, murderous triumph as he brought up his bladestaff in a thrust, directly through the gap in Yoshi's defenses. The upper prongs sank right into his armor and through, the force of their combined weight defeating the hardened leather and chain mail.

"*YOSHI*!" screamed at least four female voices, most of which had been specifically warned not to give away their position. I couldn't help cringing myself as blood spurted. Holy *shit*, was this how it looked when I used this gambit? No wonder the girls were always so upset. I should probably stop doing that.

Then the Hero dropped his sword and shield.

Hunching forward over the weapon impaling him, he grabbed it in both hands right behind the blades. His face twisting in a snarl to match Hoy's, Yoshi flexed his arms and pulled the blades fully out of his body with an agonized grunt. Blood sprayed, as if to emphasize what a lethal mistake that was . . . unless.

"**Heal**!"

And Hoy found himself holding a tiger by the tail. Being the stubborn, rage-driven, petty little shit that he was, he of course did the unwise thing and refused to let go. Had he been willing to relinquish his weapon the way Yoshi had and fire off a spell, the outcome would have been very different.

But he wasn't, and Yoshi planted his feet, twisted his hips, and let out a roar of pure adrenaline-fueled exertion as he whipped the staff fully over his head, pivoting midswing—with Hoy still clinging to it the whole while. The Hero swung the Void witch overhead like a sledgehammer, turning and bringing him arcing back down.

Hoy struck the surface of the iron bridge and bounced, finally losing his grip on his staff as he was stunned by the impact. Yoshi, just for emphasis, contemptuously tossed his fancy staff into the abyss.

I let out an exhilarated whoop, and I'm not even embarrassed; that was the hypest shit I'd seen in ages. "And *that*, sir, is *how* it is *done*! RIZZ!"

She and Rhoka were already in position, slingshots taking aim. Not at Hoy, since we'd discovered that was useless. But Hoy was now lying dazed on a slender, comparatively fragile span of worked iron connecting the two ledges in the cavern.

Rizz and Rhoka bullseyed it at both ends. Grenades tore apart iron and stone; the far end of the bridge came disconnected entirely and the near end twisted apart, barely clinging on by one of its anchors. The entire structure collapsed, tumbling down into darkness and spilling the great and terrible Void witch Hoy to his doom. It was about damn time *something* went right for a change—

"**F-Flicker!**"

Oh, *fuck you.*

He materialized on the far ledge in a momentary haze of blue-green light—winded, immediately slumping to his knees, and having lost his fancy hat along with his bladestaff. But still fucking *there.* Alive, the insufferable little bastard.

"Absolutely fucking not," I growled sotto voce. "I am not *having* another recurring cockroach come back to ruin my day."

Slimeshot! Immolate! IMMOLATE!

Being dazed and beaten didn't shut off his Void power, apparently; I accomplished nothing except to singe his coat with a few useless puffs of sparks. Nor had we even managed to disable his defensive spell, as I observed when two goblins tried to shoot him and their grenades veered off into the darkness.

"Shoot *around* him!" called one of the goblins, reloading. "The ledge, the ceiling!"

They tried, bless them. Spiked bombs blew chunks out of the ledge, the walls next to it . . . but Hoy had struggled to his feet. Limping, but he managed to move. As explosions impacted the ceiling above him, bringing stalactites and then massive chunks of rock down, his livid green coat fluttered away down the tunnel through which he'd escaped.

Everyone stopped firing as the tunnel collapsed entirely. The ledge itself broke away and crumbled into the darkness below; now the entire cavern was trembling, and to judge by the expressions of those around me, I wasn't the only one nervous about it. Across from us, what remained of the ceiling smashed down, sealing off what had been the main pathway into Jadrak's old headquarters.

We stood in grim silence, listening to the last crashes of falling rock and feeling the faint aftershocks as the cave settled. At least the destruction wasn't spreading; they hadn't brought down the whole cavern on our heads. Just barricaded our most dangerous enemy outside it.

"Biribo?" I asked hopefully.

My familiar flicked his tongue out, then shook his head. "He made it out, boss. Still movin' out there. Looks like he's in full retreat."

I wanted to scream and kick somebody, and only my need to maintain a good image prevented me. Of course. Of fucking *course* he got out.

Yoshi laid a hand on my shoulder. "We'll get him next time, Omura."

I drew in a deep breath and let it out slowly, struggling to control my own fury. "All this for nothing. So many people *dead*, and for what? We just made him run away. *Next time* he'll be more ready for us."

"But we'll be more ready for him, too," he insisted. "I'm not saying it isn't bad, but we can't give up. He and Jadrak are only going to kill more goblins the longer they're not stopped. And then humans, if they make it out of here. We have to press on."

"Right. You're right, of course. I just . . . I *hate* it when the really bad ones don't have the decency to *die* when they're supposed to."

"Yeah . . . that would've been nice."

I turned around to see the results of our battle. Our people were trickling out of their hiding places; I knew my allies and probably Yoshi's would be kicking themselves for having hid during that whole fight, but it was the right call and we all knew it. There just wasn't anything they could have done against the Void witch except get fried by spellfire.

And the goblins. Twenty-five or so goblins stood there, looking lost. They'd come here to kill me—kill us—but ended up losing their own friends and allies to Hoy's incompetence and malice, and now most of them owed me their lives. They were also cut off from the cause, for which they'd thrown away everything just within the last few days.

"Well," I said, "you guys are having a hell of a day, huh?"

"That's . . . a way to put it," a goblin woman ventured, clutching a slingshot in both hands as if for comfort.

"I'm gonna be straight with you. This will get worse before it gets better. I'm not reckless enough to promise anybody will get through this. You've seen how ugly a real war gets. What I *will* promise you is that I will *never* treat you the way Hoy just did. I don't throw away people's lives. I'll protect who I can, and avenge who I can't. We are in this together, and we've got to hope there's something better waiting for us when all the blood settles."

I paused—no, to be honest, I hesitated, looking at their expressions. Confusion, grief, hope. Man, I hated how familiar this sight was by now. I hated how good I'd gotten at this part.

"I know you don't exactly have a choice anymore, but I'll say it anyway— you stood up for what was right when it counted, and I won't ever forget that. You stood by me, and I'll stand by you. Welcome to the Dark Crusade."

19

In Which the Dark Lord Lays It All Out

Ephemera being what it was, my introduction to a new culture once again led quickly to learning about their funerary customs. Well, learning a little bit, at least. I offered my assistance, of course—quickly echoed by Yoshi—but Rizz politely yet firmly informed us that goblin business was none of ours, and in fact it would be preferable if we could go somewhere else. By that point they had neatly arranged the bodies on the big, explosion-pocked ledge and begun constructing some kind of improvised platform from the foot of the blown-up bridge, and that's all I saw of it before we retreated back into the halls of Jadrak's old headquarters.

Not far in. I wanted to be able to swiftly regroup with the rest. It didn't need to be far, anyway; the Judge just seemed to prefer us out of view.

Somewhat to my surprise, that left three goblins with us. Apparently Gizmit, Zui, and Maizo didn't consider the funeral any of their business, either, which I could understand. We had plenty of evidence that goblins were diverse in their affiliations. I guess I wouldn't want to crash a wake for a bunch of people I didn't know, who minutes ago had been willing to murder me. Under clear duress, but still.

More to the point, this put me in mind of Gizmit's recent advice. I took the opportunity of this relatively quiet moment to act on it.

"Hey, Maizo, I'd like to ask a favor."

"Hell, it's not like I don't owe ya, Lord Seiji," he replied, grinning irrepressibly. "What's up?"

"We've got a long walk back to Sneppit's place, since the trams aren't running, and the bunch of goblins we've just picked up have a lot of information between them that'll be valuable for planning our next step. We need to debrief them while we move, and have a decently organized report to share when we regroup with Sneppit. But if possible, I would rather not interrogate or otherwise give these people a hard time. They're in a rough spot, and I want 'em to feel welcome with us. You're an information guy; think you can spend the hike . . . y'know, working your magic? Chat with people, get the scoop without being a pest about it?"

"Say no more. That is *exactly* within my aptitudes. Gimme a day to rub shoulders and make friends, and I'll know everything they know by breakfast, and no hard feelings anywhere."

"Thanks, Maizo. Sorry to put you right to work. I know *you* haven't exactly been having a relaxing vacation here."

"Opposite of a problem, bossman," he said, his grin fading to a more serious expression. "The running theme of my misadventures recently has been me being helpless while various people just *did* shit to me. I'm grateful to use my actual skills and accomplish something again."

"Good to have you on the team, Maizo. Hey, Zui?"

"Oh boy," she deadpanned. "What now?"

"I know you don't work for me, so this is just a request. You're an organizational person—Sneppit's personal assistant, even though for inscrutable goblin reasons you can't call the job that. If you're willing to help out, can you please help keep all our new additions . . . y'know, organized? Make sure everybody's taken care of as best we can on the way back. I'll do my best, but you know goblins better than I ever will, and I get the impression you like looking after people."

"Not bad, not bad." She folded her arms and gave me a smug little smile. "Asserting authority by ordering me to do something you know damn well I'm gonna anyway. It's a good trick; Sneppit does that. We'll make a manager outta you yet."

"I *specifically* said it wasn't an order—you know what, never mind, fuck it. How the hell are you *more* annoying than when you just hated my guts?"

"Tsundere," Yoshi said sagely.

"Biribo, I want you to fly over there and punch the Hero in the eye."

"I am categorically not doing that, boss."

"What did he just call me?" Zui demanded. "Actually, nah, I don't care. Anyway, Lord Bossypants, I never hated you. I just have a healthy attitude toward tallfolk who think they're in charge of stuff. Now that I've seen what it takes to make you go full mass-murder, I'm reasonably confident you're not gonna do it over every little thing. That's something we gotta be careful of, with humans."

"Hey, uh, Maizo?" Yoshi said awkwardly, then actually blushed when Maizo turned to look at him. "I, uh . . . Well, I just wanted to say . . . Sorry. About before."

"*You're* apologizing to *him?*" Flaethwyn screeched.

"Can somebody put a muzzle on that elf?" Zui hissed. "There's a *funeral* going on just around that corner!"

"I will not—"

"Flaethwyn," Nazralind said quietly, staring at her. Flaethwyn shut her mouth with an audible click of teeth, going a shade paler.

"Yeah, well, she ain't without a point," said Maizo. "*You're* apologizing to *me?*"

"I'm not mad about the mud pit," Yoshi said, then hesitated and shook his head. "Well. I'm not going to bear a grudge about the mud pit, let me put it that way. With the things I've learned since about goblins . . . I guess I see now why that seemed to you like a reasonable thing to have done at the time. For my part, I'm sorry I didn't . . . speak up. I should've stuck up for you."

Fascinating (and amusing) as all this was, my eye was caught by Flaethwyn's expression—she looked queasy, and strangely terrified. It was striking on a face that normally looked like she was trying to find the culprit behind a horrible smell. She saw me looking at her, and her expression went blank again. Pashilyn's eyes flicked back and forth between us, but as usual she gave nothing away.

"Y'know, you've put on some backbone since the last time I saw you," Maizo said, giving Yoshi an approving look and no sign he'd noticed any silent byplay. "That was all you really needed. Keep it up, kid; you'll do fine."

He sauntered off toward the edge of the doorway onto the outer ledge, where he took up position, discreetly lurking and watching to see when they were done.

Flaethwyn swallowed heavily before speaking again. She was back to visibly angry, but at least had the grace to keep her voice down this time. "All this is *terribly* amusing, I'm sure, but are none of you going to even *comment* on the fact that the Dark Lord here is *openly* recruiting for his Dark Crusade? *Right in front of us?!*"

"Well, what *else* did you want him to do?" Yoshi asked, which oddly enough caused her to visibly flinch. "The Dark Crusade is something goblins *will* follow, if it's put to them persuasively. They wouldn't have joined *us,* and we had to do something. This takes soldiers from the Goblin King and turns them to our side. It's not like we could've just killed them all."

"I—that isn't—"

"Oh, it's *exactly* like we could've just killed them all. Right?" Zui was staring coldly up at Flaethwyn, arms still crossed and now drumming her fingers on one bicep. "Could and should have. That's what you *want* to say, isn't it, Flaethwyn?"

"Leaving *aside* the wisdom of recruiting . . . *people* . . . who changed sides in the middle of a battle, *he is the Dark Lord*!" She pointed at me as if this added credibility to whatever case she was trying to make. "I recognize the wisdom of allying temporarily against the Goblin King, fine. And we *all* band together against devils and the Void, I'm not contesting that. But what about *after*? We're just putting this man in a stronger position to *conquer and murder us all*!"

"Why, Flaethwyn," I said in my sweetest voice, "why *ever* would anyone want to murder *you*?"

"You can be as glib and smarmy as you like," she hissed. "It might even work for a while. But in the end, no one is going to forget that you're still the kind of person who would choose to take Virya's side."

The silence that fell was suitably dramatic in timing, but for once wasn't one of my carefully orchestrated pauses. My breath caught momentarily, and it felt as if my mind went white for just an instant. I couldn't even say what was written on my face in that brief moment, but it caused everyone nearby to freeze, staring at me. Yoshi shifted backward a half step, and Zui's eyebrows drew together as if in worry.

"Choose," I said as soon as I could breathe again, staring into Flaethwyn's dark eyes. Even she looked suddenly unnerved. "*Choose* to take Virya's side. Right. You know what, Flaethwyn, you're right. What kind of person would *choose* that?"

She frowned, trying for an assertive attitude despite her visible unease. "Throwing my words back doesn't—"

"Why don't I tell you all about it, then?" I said with a broad smile that made everyone ease subtly away from me. "After all, I understand it's not just *anybody* on this world who gets an audience with the Goddesses themselves. You deserve a firsthand account of what your deities are like, faithful followers that I'm sure you all are."

"Uh, boss," Biribo muttered right in my ear, but I was too immersed in showtime now to even brush him away.

"There I was," I declaimed, holding the attention of all present as if I had each of them by a leash. My voice was quiet, in part because of the wake happening next door but also because it forced them to be silent and lean closer. "Plucked from my life, my goals and my own future, hovering with Virya over the shattered ruin of this woebegone planet, while she explained the great game of Good and Evil and my role in it. Conquer Ephemera, she said. Subdue the nations of these islands in her name. Kill the Hero." I winked at Yoshi, who twitched slightly. "You all know how it goes. So naturally, I told her to go fuck herself."

A faint stir went through my audience at that, but I carried on before anyone could interrupt my flow.

"I mean, come on. Really? Who *does* that? Yoshi's a good kid, and I've got no beef with anybody on this world. Well, I didn't then. Not to mention that I am *not* isekai material. Let's face it, I have stuff I'd much rather be doing in the other world. I was *already* working on escaping to a new life in a new land; it's called California, and it's also kind of a shithole but hey, at least it's sunny. There's nothing I wanted *less* than to abandon all my plans and goals and trudge around in the mud *here*. So yeah, I refused the call. Like Flaethwyn said, any *normal* person would. And that's when the torture started!"

Yoshi flinched. So did Zui, and then was visibly angry at herself for doing so. While that was the most gratifying interaction I'd ever had with her, I was on a roll and didn't stop to savor it.

"First she bent me over backward, literally. *All* the way over, so the soles of my feet and the crown of my skull were against the ground at the same time. Then came the twisting. Ever had your spine wrung like a dishrag while it was already flexed nearly double? That's a fucking *experience*, let me tell you. Made me wish I'd taken up yoga. Then the arms, and . . . You know what, I can tell from your expressions that you get the idea, no need to relive the whole thing. All of that, just to make her *point*. That being, it was all just a *taste*. I could either play along with the Goddesses and their silly little game, or spend an eternity being taught an entirely new comprehension of pain while Virya grabbed some other poor bastard from Japan to do her dirty work."

I gave them another moment, just to let it sink in.

"So, yeah. My policy is and remains, fuck Virya and the horse she rode in on."

"Well . . . that's . . ." Flaethwyn had to swallow again and square her shoulders before she could get it out. "That doesn't change the basic facts.

Even if you're only doing it under duress, the reality is you are *still* planning to conquer and subjugate us. *Helping* you is just madness!"

I snorted a derisive little laugh. *Quietly*—they were still mourning in the next room, after all.

"Oh, hell no, I am not doing that. Fuck it, I'm not gonna give her the satisfaction."

"But," Yoshi stammered, "but if—won't she—"

"See, the *really* important thing I learned from Virya is that this? All of this?" I spread my arms wide. "Heroes and Dark Lords, Good versus Evil, Viryans and Sanorites? It's a *game*. They're a couple of bored cosmic entities with way too much power, nowhere to *go* except this busted-ass little world, and a desperate need for diversion. We are *toys* to them. Pieces on a shockingly literal game board. Well, let me tell you, here I may be a Dark Lord, but *there* I was a rock star, and if there is *one* thing I can do, it's keep a bored bimbo entertained. She may not get the show she wanted, but that's fine. The silly bitch doesn't know what she really wants, anyway. She'll get the show *I* deign to give her."

"What *are* you going to do, then?" Gizmit asked quietly.

"I . . . am still working on that," I admitted. "I'm getting my feet under me and figuring out the options. *Fortunately*, Fflyr Dlemathlys is the worst excuse for a country on either world, so all I have to do to throw this place into chaos is enforce some basic decency on people. I've been running around rescuing folks from slavery and putting down bandits, mostly. It counts as Dark Lord business because in a place this corrupt, *that* is severely disruptive to the status quo, and it buys me time to figure out something suitably dramatic that'll keep Virya off my back without turning myself into some kind of monster."

"The word around the King's Guild," Pashilyn commented, "is there's been a marked change in bandit activity on Dount since the Kingsguard's purge of the Gutters. The island has become noticeably safer to travel through. Attacks on the road are somehow putting travelers harmlessly to sleep instead of just shooting them with arrows, and it seems the new bandits just take a sort of tithe and always leave their victims something to get home with. No arson, murder, rape, or violence in general. I don't suppose you happen to know anything about that, Lord Seiji?"

I gave her a bland, pleasant smile. "You would have to ask Highlord Caldimer of Clan Olumnach about organized bandit activity, Lady Pashilyn."

"Of course, such is the rumor," she said in an equally mild tone. "Well, perhaps someone should caution Highlord Caldimer that this change has drawn the Guild's attention. It may be better for the people of Dount and commerce as a whole, but it also smells of the bandits becoming organized, sophisticated, and ambitious. The one thing the Clans will not tolerate is a threat to their power."

"Sounds about right," I growled.

"I cannot believe you are *listening* to this!" Flaethwyn exclaimed at her—still quietly, at least. "This . . . this *blasphemy!* Even blasphemy against Virya, which I would never have imagined I might one day care about, but . . . He's standing here trying to claim everything about our faith and our world is some manner of *game!*"

"I . . ." Yoshi trailed off and swallowed heavily. He looked vaguely seasick all of a sudden.

"I think," Pashilyn said thoughtfully, studying my face, "I believe him."

"*What?!*" Flaethwyn grabbed her by both shoulders. "Are you—you cannot—you're a *priestess!*"

"Oh, I don't think he's *right*," Pashilyn clarified with a smile, gently dislodging her grip. "I simply don't think he's lying. Lord Seiji reminds me strikingly of every highborn I've ever known who was too socially blunt to successfully dissemble, even when they bothered to try."

"That's a hell of a thing to hang your entire faith on," Nazralind commented. "You sure you're a priestess?"

Pashilyn shrugged. "I don't see the contradiction. I have no trouble imagining Virya saying something like that to her Dark Lord. Do you? I can think of any number of reasons she might tell him such a thing, none of which have to do with it being true. Perhaps she was punishing his defiance by adding insult to injury—after all, the idea that all this is some manner of game is deeply insulting to everyone involved, is it not? Or perhaps the Dark Sister was manipulating him, saying the thing she calculated would drive him to the course of action she desired. For that matter, it's believable to me that Virya *thinks* of the Dark Crusade as a game, and it requires all the earnestness of our Goddess and Her followers to contain Virya's insanity. Or . . . maybe she just thought it was funny. It's *Virya*. Who knows?"

For the second time in the last few minutes I found myself gobsmacked—this time not with my usual nascent, simmering outrage, but the revelation that . . . well, she had a point. Everything I knew about the battle of the Goddesses and my role in it had come straight from Virya's mouth. And Virya . . .

The question wasn't even whether Virya was full of it; I knew she absolutely was. The question was what, specifically, she had been bullshitting about, and how badly. *Some* of it was true, of that much I was certain. Head Start had verified important parts. But . . . I realized, suddenly, that I'd been taking her at her word for all of it, and man, was that stupid in hindsight.

And now everyone was looking at me again.

"Well . . . there's no real way to tell," I hedged, repressing a spike of annoyance at the way Pashilyn's smile subtly widened. "Goddesses are inscrutable. Anyway, all this started with Flaethwyn pitching a fit about how I'm planning to murder you all with my new army of goblins. Are you satisfied that is at least *not* my intent?"

"What *is* your intent?" Zui asked, staring fixedly at me. "That's what I wanna know. What happens to us under the Dark Lord's rule when you've got no more Goblin King to dispose of?"

"Like I said, I am still working on that." I met her gaze and spoke seriously—not just for the sake of performance, but because this *was* a serious matter. We were talking about the fate of an entire people, here; this was a bigger deal than Cat Alley or anything else I'd done on Dount. Maybe I was just projecting my unease over the responsibility onto her, but for some reason I suddenly cared a lot whether Zui in particular would approve of my chosen course. "For right now, I'm trying to learn as much as I can about goblins. What I can tell you is that I think Jadrak has the right idea about at least one thing—you have the potential to be *so* much more than you are, and all it would take is being united in the same direction. Just imagine what the goblins could accomplish if they weren't all disorganized and constantly jockeying for advantage. There's gotta be something more *constructive* to do with all that energy than his big idea of getting everybody killed in a futile war on the Fflyr."

She narrowed her eyes and said nothing. That wasn't enough.

"A lot will depend on what develops after this," I added. "Kzidnak is far from the end of it. There are . . . other powers on Dount, as I'm sure you know, and that's to say nothing of what lies beyond this shitty little island. I think the goblins deserve to be at the forefront of *whatever* comes next. Compared to the Fflyr, you're a lot more . . . well, civilized. Anyway, though, there will be time to work it out once we're not actively struggling to survive. There'll be a lot of work to do, putting this place back in order after Jadrak's rampage. I'm counting on that to buy me time to learn more about your people and craft a better plan. One with goblin input."

I paused, glanced around at the others, and deliberately put on my most insufferable smirk.

"That's not all, of course. But as Flaethwyn was so kind as to remind us just now, there are other matters we shouldn't necessarily discuss in front of the Sanorites."

Flaethwyn made one of her delightfully furious faces, but I wasn't paying her much attention this time. Zui still stared at me through narrowed eyes, but her expression softened infinitesimally, and after a moment, she inclined her head by the faintest degree. It was acknowledgment, not approval, but it wasn't rejection.

Not that I was even sure why I cared what she thought; she was easily the most annoying of all the goblins I'd encountered, even the ones who'd tried to kill me. Even Hoy—he was repulsive and infuriating, not *annoying*. Zui had a way of rubbing me the wrong way . . . But hell, maybe that was exactly it, after all. If I could get *her* on board with my plan, it was likely to meet the approval of the rest of Kzidnak. She may as well make herself useful as a sounding board, if she was going to insist on hanging around me.

Rizz's return was as sudden as it was quiet; one moment she was suddenly just there in the doorway, causing Maizo to shuffle respectfully back. The Judge swept a quick look around, taking all of us in, then nodded to me once.

"Ready to go?"

20

In Which the Dark Lord Rethinks His Position

For once, I decided not to make a speech.

Not that I didn't make a spectacle—reassuring my new gang about their decision and securing their loyalty was a priority—but in show business you have to be able to gauge your audience. In my professional opinion, the last thing any of these folks wanted right now was more pressure of any kind. It was a moment for calm and a much needed sense of security.

So I simply told everyone, in a quiet and empathetic tone, that we were going to be moving as fast as we could on foot without exhausting anybody. I gave instructions that anyone should talk to me if they needed healing, to Zui if there were any other material needs or issues that had to be sorted out, and to Yoshi if Flaethwyn caused them any problems.

Flaethwyn very nearly caused a problem there and then, but Nazralind turned her head to stare, and she subsided, visibly seething.

"You're coming along, then?" I asked Gizmit. "I know the original plan was for you to rummage around this place and find your own way back, but . . ."

"But that went down the crack as soon as we found it abandoned." She nodded. "Yeah, I'm sure I could turn up *something* else in here with time to work at it, but nothing more valuable than what we've already learned."

"I'm almost disappointed," Zui said sweetly. "You know this guy asked me earlier why I was even along? I've been waiting for the moment when he realized he had nobody else to navigate back to Sneppit's place with you gone."

"*Obviously* I had considered that," I lied with my customary aplomb. "For somebody who lives to dish out the snark and banter, Zui, you sure can't seem to take it."

"Listen, boy," Rizz cut in. "You didn't win that fight, Hoy lost it. That guy is an infamously self-centered shithead, to the point I wonder if he's got a legit brain issue. When you face Jadrak, it won't go down like that. I'm very curious how much Jadrak actually believes his progoblin talk, but whatever the truth, he is *very* good at presenting himself that way. He's charismatic, strategic, and commands a lot of fanatical loyalty. *He* won't mistreat his followers so badly they'll turn on him midfight. Do not try to repeat what worked before."

"Disagree," Zui stated, all the jocularity gone from her tone. "Don't try hitting Jadrak where he's weak; whatever weaknesses he's got are out of your reach. You've been hitting him where he's *strong*, and that's your best strategy. The whole time you've been down here you've been sparing goblins when you can, listening to goblins, and respecting goblins. All these folks turned against Hoy, yeah, but they turned *toward* you, and it wasn't for no reason. Every time that happens, the word spreads. Keep laying that groundwork, and when it comes time to confront Jadrak, you can give him a *real* fight in the court of public opinion."

Rizz stared at her, pursed her lips once, and then turned back to me. "Well, I can't tell you what to do, Dark Lord, and wouldn't even if I thought you'd obey me. You asked for my input, and now you've got it."

"And I appreciate it," I said, not having to fake the sincerity. "I may or may not take any particular piece of advice, but I want to know as much as possible about goblin society before doing anything that'll change the course of it."

"Be careful about Sneppit. She's sly, and self-interested. So's that one," Rizz added, tilting her head toward Gizmit, who just looked amused. "Zui here's got questionable judgment sometimes, but she's still worth listening to—just like those other two, if for different reasons. I'd recommend you take the time to get input from all these new faces you've just picked up, too."

"Not like we won't have the chance," I said, glancing back at the crowd of goblins shuffling about the corridor, waiting for us to get underway. I did not raise my voice, but also didn't trouble to moderate it, trusting those big ears to do the trick. "I'm always open to input, from whoever's got something of value to say."

Hopefully that wouldn't come back to bite me. As long as they came one at a time and didn't suggest anything too insane, I shouldn't have to walk back that assurance later.

As we set out through the tunnels with Gizmit and Zui in the lead, I was indeed approached for a discreet conversation, but not by any of the goblins. To my surprise it was Nazralind who eased up next to me and spoke in a tone low enough to not be easily overheard.

"Hey, I know it's hilarious and deserved and all that, but . . . may wanna ease off taking shots at Flaethwyn."

I gave her a surprised sidelong look. "Is this elven solidarity?"

"Hah! No." She snorted. "Call it threat assessment. She's fun to poke at because she overreacts to everything—which makes her *dangerous* to poke at. Potentially, at least. I'm not saying Flaethwyn's gonna murder somebody, but mostly because I think most of us could take her. Someone that high-strung can snap, and it really doesn't seem like we need the extra drama right now."

"Mmm. I suppose it makes sense to hold back a bit when it's not strictly necessary. We wouldn't want her to get desensitized to being slapped down when it *is*."

"Which is fairly regularly, yes."

"Since you brought it up, why is she so afraid of you? Did you murder somebody I don't know about?"

Naz grinned. "Heh, nothing so romantic. Nah, she just hasn't adjusted to our new situation. That's a case of highborn power dynamics being applied where they don't belong."

I raised my eyebrows, glancing at her again. Nazralind carried on walking, eyes front. After a momentary pause, she continued her explanation.

"Clan Adellaird has holdings on one of the outlying regions of Dlemath; they control the other end of the landbridge from Dount. It's a somewhat prestigious holding, but they've never held an island governorship like Clan Aelthwyn does. Flaethwyn is the fifth daughter of a branch family, and so about as unimportant to the succession as possible. She's so far down their list of priorities she was only assigned one maedhlou, which is . . . I don't want to say 'unheard of,' because it *does* happen, but most highborn families don't squeeze out so many daughters that they entirely give up caring about their prospects, which is what that signifies."

"Hang on." I started to glance back, but decided against it. No reason to let the volatile object of our discussion know she was being talked about. "Are you talking about Pashilyn?"

"Yup, that's the one." She nodded.

"That's so much *detail*. What are you, her biographer?"

"Clan Aelthwyn and Clan Adellaird have been enemies at least as long as I've been alive. Tensions over actual, material concerns from the last generation escalated into outright antipathy thanks to my uncle being . . . well, himself. You'd better believe I was briefed on the political details of that family. Everything that's public knowledge and even *possibly* useful."

"I wouldn't have thought there was so much hostility between Clans, what with that prohibition on bloodshed."

"Oh, trust me, there is no hatred more bitter than between aristocrats who aren't allowed to murder each other," she said in a particularly wry tone. "*Anyway*, Flaethwyn is as lowly ranked as you can be in Fflyr Dlemathlys and still be an elf. I am the oldest of my generation, a member of the main family of my Clan—which is its only family, currently—and since my uncle and aunt have no children, I'm actually *in* the line of succession for Dount's governorship. Not at the top, since I have brothers, but I am as highly ranked as an unmarried woman can be among highborn, without being royal. So if we were still back home in polite society, especially with this island being my family's fief, I could ruin her life with a few well-chosen words. And given the relationship between our families, she would have to expect that I'd *do* so at the first pretext."

"And . . . does any of that apply at all . . . *here?*"

"Obviously not," she chuckled, then her expression quickly sobered. "Which is why I'm suggesting taking a *somewhat* gentler tone toward Flaethwyn. I only know the public, political details, not what her home life was like, but I've met a lot of people like her among highborn. People who were raised to think power is the only dynamic that exists between people, who embrace rank and privilege where they should consider friendship, familial affection, or love . . . and also who depend on that social power for what they see as their very survival. In her way, Flaethwyn has given up everything to follow the Hero, just as your followers have. If you threaten her standing in his eyes, she's going to react as if you'd threatened her life. So . . . maybe tone it down just a smidge?"

"I'll take it into consideration," I conceded. "Whew, though. I gotta say, none of this would've occurred to me on my own."

"Yeah, nobles are crazy. Be glad you're normal enough not to have to think like this."

Just ahead of us, Zui turned her head to give me a thoughtful look, just for a moment.

"What?" I demanded irritably.

She just smiled, shrugged, and turned back around.

We tried to stick roughly to the path of the tram tunnel, but just trudging along it wasn't an option as parts of it had no bottom, just an endless fall to the core—or down a crevice so deep it wasn't much better. Apparently there was also a general lack of sufficient access corridors bypassing these sections, as such would have to be tunneled right out of the rock, and Sneppit's company didn't have many rock-digging specialists. She had mostly contracted that work out to, you guessed it, Jadrak's mining company—and apparently relations between the two had been getting frostier since before this Goblin King business started.

So, in addition to not having the convenience of trams to ride, our course was somewhat more meandering as we had to straggle through a combination of side tunnels and natural caverns passing in and around the main tram corridor.

None of these had light sources, since goblins didn't need them. For the rest of us, I obligingly used my light spell—as did Pashilyn, who it turned out had one—and Flaethwyn and Nazralind lit up their auras for us. I was still holding back the revelation that Aster and I could now do that, too, both on general principles that the Hero party didn't need to know all our business, and specifically because after my chat with Naz, I was concerned that revelation would cause Flaethwyn to have an aneurysm, or an attack of homicidal mania.

"Guess our dark elf buddy got lost at some point," Biribo commented.

"What? How can you tell?"

"The light elf aura counters dark elf stealth."

"*What?* When the hell were you going to tell me this?!"

"As always, boss, when it became relevant. You *specifically* said you didn't wanna push at the dark elf, remember? You were gonna wait and let 'em come out on their own. Anyway, it's not like I'm the only one here who knows this. *Right*, Nazralind?"

I turned an accusing look on the glowing elf and she raised both hands in surrender.

"Hey, it's not as simple as having a magic stealth-neutralizing effect! Our auras *tend* to counter their stealth, but how that actually plays out in practice depends entirely on the parties involved. Both kinds of gifts come in different strengths and, uh . . . flavors, for lack of a better word. And both can be trained in different ways. An actual, professional shadow scout, like we're assuming this one is, won't be so easy to reveal."

"Well, still," I grumbled. "*This* one I'd've liked to know ahead of time. It will be *nice* to have a firm counter if I run out of patience with our stalker before they decide to be sociable."

"Yeeeaaah," Aster drawled, "*maybe* that's not an argument in favor of telling you stuff."

"Shut up, Aster."

Gizmit had warned me before we set out that we weren't going to make very good time with close to forty people on the move, which made sense. We scrounged some leftovers from the mining company base, and both our strike force and a lot of the new goblins had brought some basic supplies, so we should be fine for as long as it would take to get back to Sneppit's on foot. Gizmit estimated that we'd need to stop for the night and should get there fairly early in the morning.

I was worried about the defenses around the North Watch tunnel and what else Jadrak was up to in and around Kzidnak, but there was nothing to be done about it but hustle. Besides, as a silver lining, this gave us time to work on the new hires. Maizo should have plenty of time to rustle up some good intel, and given how outspoken goblins in general were, I expected they'd take up my offer to come talk to me about whatever was on their minds.

But for the first three hours of our long hike . . . nope.

"This surprises you?" Zui scoffed when I commented on it—very quietly—during a short break. "You're the fuckin' Dark Lord. You just fought the scariest bastard they've ever known to a draw, right in front of 'em. These people have been swept up in a revolution and then press-ganged to raid their own former HQ by a maniac. Nobody here is gonna want the personal attention of another powerful magic man with designs of conquest."

"Hmph." I frowned at the far wall of the smallish cavern we'd stopped in, considering her point. I'd positioned myself some distance away from the big cluster of goblins, largely because I had noticed they seemed a little nervous with me too close. I hadn't thought it was as bad as she made it sound, though.

"What's that expression?" Zui asked incredulously. "Are you *sad*?"

"It's not like my feelings are hurt," I retorted, a little defensive despite myself. "I just . . . want to ward off any future problems, that's all. I'm accustomed to being on decently friendly terms with my followers. It worries me a bit that they're just scared of me. Fear's a useful tool, sure, but . . . only in a very particular way, y'know? You can't maintain authority through fear alone; that'll backfire."

She stared up at me through narrowed eyes.

"What? What is *that* look?"

Slowly, Zui shook her head, then hopped down from the ledge on which she'd been perched to get a little closer to my eyeline. "Goblins are inquisitive and assertive, but building actual loyalty or camaraderie takes *time*. Don't push at 'em; you'll just scare 'em more. Keep being a reasonable dude and they'll come around."

She hesitated, opened her mouth as if about to say something else, then closed it, shook her head, and walked away.

"I don't get that girl," I complained.

"People have hidden depths, boss," Biribo said sagely.

"Is that a cleavage joke?"

"You said it, not me."

It was another hour after we got moving again before I had my first positive interaction with one of the ex-Jadrak loyalists. I recognized the guy who came up to walk alongside me; he was the first to have turned his slingshot on Hoy. After staring fixedly at a fresh corpse he recognized. None of us were having a great day, but I had the impression he had it worse than most.

"So . . . what's gonna happen to us at Sneppit's place?" he asked by way of opening.

"You'll all get what you need," I said. "Food, treatment, a place to rest. I understand it's a bit crowded in there at the moment, but when I checked in with Sneppit, the supply situation was stable. Everybody should be okay."

He nodded. "And then we gotta fight King Jadrak."

"*I* have to fight Jadrak. Me and Yoshi over there, maybe some of the other Blessed. *You* have to fight his followers, at worst."

"My old coworkers, a lot of 'em."

"Yup. It's a real motherfucker of a situation, isn't it? Civil wars are some *ugly* shit. My strategy is still being built and has to adapt on the fly, but I promise you my main focus is to minimize casualties. All this will settle down once Jadrak's out of the picture. I just have to find a way to *do* that which causes the least possible dead goblins."

"He doesn't talk like that," he said suddenly, after pausing just long enough that I wondered if the conversation was over. "The Goblin King. Nothing about minimizing casualties. It's all about . . . sacrifice. How we'll never be free unless we're willing to die for it."

"I mean . . . he's not a hundred percent *wrong*," I admitted. "I'm running into the same problem up top. When you're fighting an entrenched power structure, there's just no way to make gains without casualties. Damn, though, I can't imagine ranting at everybody to throw their lives down for the cause. And I *love* ranting. I think I'm one of Ephemera's premier ranters. Right, guys?"

"It's true, he rants like a champion," Aster agreed.

"But, like, in an entertaining way," Adelly added. "It's like seeing a bard work, or a preacher. It's a show."

"Sending people into the grinder like meat isn't the thing to rant about, though," I said. "If you're wanting an explanation of Jadrak's thought process, I cannot help you. I don't know *what* he thinks his endgame is, unless he's really counting on his pet devil to pull something out of its ass. He's got goblins out there wasting each other's lives as if his next step wasn't starting a fight with the Clans—which is a fight you have to know Kzidnak has zero chance of winning. Maybe if he'd allied with me first, but if that was the plan, sending his henchmen to slaughter the goblins I was doing business with was a *strange* move."

"And he's a Void witch," my new acquaintance said in a dull tone, staring ahead. "The Goblin King is a Void witch."

"I'm . . . not sure, completely," I admitted. "*Hoy* is a Void witch. We found that Spirit, Digger, which they corrupted into a Void altar. It's not like we've actually *seen* Jadrak using Void magic himself, so . . . I can't say. At the very least, he's been trafficking with devils and wasting goblins by the fistful like they're candy. I've got more than enough reason to put his ass down without blaming him for stuff I'm not completely sure he's done. Yet."

"And what're you gonna do for us, then?" He looked up at me, and I couldn't see either condemnation or hope in his eyes. He was just blank, and tired. Resigned. "What happens after we throw in with the Dark Lord? Glorious victory, freedom? Conquest?"

"Fuck knows, man." I sighed. "The only thing I'm sure about is it's all going to get uglier before it gets better."

We walked in silence for a moment, then I felt strangely compelled to speak.

"I've been telling my people . . . well, not dissimilar from Jadrak's line. I don't promise anything except revenge on those who've wronged us. Because I *can't* promise anything more than that, and there's nothing I hate more than being made a liar. It's a violent, ugly world out there and everything's stacked against us. We have to fight back, because the alternative is just . . . lying down and waiting to get ground up by the system. Yeah . . . I can see where Jadrak's coming from, up to a point."

He looked up at me again, silently.

"But now that I'm seeing where that leads," I said slowly, "I'm reconsidering. This *can't* be the best we can do. Just . . . everybody dead and nothing gained. In a twisted way, I kind of owe him thanks for the important lesson."

"You got a better idea?" he asked.

"I don't know any more than you where all this is going to lead," I admitted. "But I know the first step. All of this is happening to all of us because we're all turned against each other instead of the people who are out there *doing* it to us. Step one is unity. Solidarity. Goblins, lowborn . . . bandits and whores and exiles, women and queers and beastfolk, everybody who's not given a chance or a fair shake in this country. Because, when you actually start to *list* them all, you can't help noticing that is *almost everybody*. This miserable, unjust *mess* of a country only exists to benefit a very tiny number of assholes. They only get to be in charge because we're all fighting each other instead of them. Just like Jadrak. If we can get everybody on the same page, pointed in the same direction . . ."

I realized I had everybody's attention, not just the goblin's I'd been talking to. The soft buzz of conversation had vanished, leaving only the sound of our footsteps. Yoshi's party in particular were staring fixedly at me, all of their expressions intent and hard to interpret.

"Well," I shrugged, and put on a little smile. "*Then* you'll see some real shit."

"You want my advice," my new goblin friend said pensively, "that's a better angle than promising revenge. We've heard that before, and damn, is that not a good deal now that we're seeing it in action. We all need something better."

"Yeah. Yes, we do. I am definitely going to need a lot of help to make that happen, though. Tell you what, I know you goblins are good at building stuff. I definitely need some good minds working on solutions. You in?"

He looked up at me again, and finally cracked his lips in a smile. "That's the best idea I've heard in forever. That, or the worst."

"It's a little of both, isn't it," I chuckled.

"Hey, Omura?" I looked up to find Yoshi had approached me, wearing a concerned expression. "I need to . . . I mean, not urgently, but when we stop to camp for the night. Can I talk to you? In private? It's important."

Oh boy, I did not have a good feeling about this.

"Sure, Yoshi."

21

In Which the Dark Lord Confronts His Nemesis

I was, as usual, right to have a bad feeling.

Once we stopped for the night, Yoshi had pulled me aside to relay a warning he'd gotten from Pashilyn—something I'd never had a hint of yet because I'd been hanging around with criminals and prostitutes. It really took someone like her, an aristocrat and priestess, to know this, though with hindsight and what I'd learned from Head Start, it made sense. Apparently the big political powers on Ephemera did know what to watch for when they wanted to identify a new Hero or Dark Lord.

"Wait, so . . . *anything* Japanese?"

"I don't know exactly what they'll know to look for," Yoshi admitted. "Maizo knew about chopsticks, so we can ask him what else he might be aware of. Probably there are different, uh, establishments and lineages which have preserved *some* secret knowledge of Japan, but I doubt any of them have more than a few things to look out for. So anything Japanese *might* set them off. It's . . . probably best to keep it discreet at least until we're both powerful enough not to be easily controlled. Or . . . assassinated."

I stared out over the cavern, my mind racing. We'd set up camp in a large natural cave, complete with decorative stalactites, though it had a mostly even floor, which seemed to have been leveled on purpose by goblins long ago; it made for a decent space in which to camp. The caves of Kzidnak were generally warm, and goblins didn't need light, but I decided it felt *wrong* to camp without campfires, and so I'd made a few. In several spots, fire slimes blazed merrily away, fixed in place by Tame Beast, and I couldn't help noticing that people had gathered around each one. Yoshi's party were huddled together by one, and mine around another. Well, partly; Aster stood some distance away, pretending she wasn't watching me, while Nazralind and Adelly sat hip-to-hip, talking quietly. I noted with amusement that Gizmit, Zui, and Maizo had all joined them, and several other groups of goblins were huddled around the other slimes I'd set out, even though they needed neither the light nor the warmth.

Everybody loves a campfire.

Yoshi and I had picked a ledge along the wall a discreet distance away for our chat. I'd been mildly dreading what he had to say, but somehow this was worse than anything I could have anticipated.

"Is that why nobody knows there's a Hero even though you're . . . well, running around being one?"

"Exactly." He nodded. "Pashilyn and Flaethwyn explained the local politics to me. As soon as *anybody* finds out . . . Well, I'm not strong enough yet to stop the bigger powers from stepping in to control me. Even the Fflyr government—even some of the *Clans* probably have enough muscle, the way I am right now. And that's only the start. Lancor might actually invade Dlemathlys over this. Over just *one* of us being here, never mind both."

"So," I said slowly, "if this were already a *dicey* moment in history, what with Lancor and everybody else who matters probably sending agents to investigate every place one of those signs and portents happened . . ."

"Yeah, they'll definitely be looking into the Inferno, so it's an especially good time to keep our heads down." He turned to frown at me. "By the way, you didn't have anything to do with that, did you, Omura?"

I impatiently waved him off. "I sure wish I'd known about all this earlier. I'll . . . speak to the girls. It's not like I *told* them to . . ."

Yoshi was staring at me, wide-eyed.

"Well, I'll fix it." Somehow. "*More importantly, Biribo.*"

"Boss, you gotta understand," he said desperately. "This is a *prohibited subject*. I got your back, but there are nonoptional rules I gotta follow! I *can't* explain stuff like this *until* it gets brought up by someone else. As in *physically cannot.*"

"Yeah, that's what Radatina said," Yoshi offered.

"I hate to stick up for the lizard, but he's not wrong," Radatina added in what I can only call a performatively grudging tone. "This isn't his fault. This is something you *can't* be forewarned about until someone else brings it up. Yoshi was just lucky enough to have that happen first."

"Least you could do, I guess," Biribo muttered.

"Oh, buzz off, you—"

"Okay, *what* is the deal with the two of you?" I demanded. "Is this another Good versus Evil thing? Because everybody *else* is managing to be civil while we're cooperating. Even Flaethwyn, mostly. Sometimes."

The familiars exchanged a long, loaded look.

"Not . . . exactly," Radatina hedged. "It's . . . complicated."

Yoshi raised his eyebrows. "We're listening."

"It's . . . well . . . How to put this . . ."

"It's about how Blessed with Wisdom usually operate," Biribo took over the explanation, apparently tired of her dithering. "Wisdom doesn't come with any physical firepower for anybody except Champions of the Goddesses, so they gotta compensate for that. Especially since other people will tend to try to either forcibly recruit or assassinate them; if you're a mover and/or shaker, you do not want someone with information powers running around your turf and not working for you. Some will link up with an adventurer team as tactical support, but for most, the standard practice is to *conceal* the fact that you're Blessed with Wisdom until you can build a power base and accumulate enough perks to be actually, personally powerful. So the one thing you absolutely do not want to encounter is another Blessed with Wisdom, because their familiar will be able to spot you."

"And then once they *get* powerful," Radatina rushed in when he paused to breathe, "they also become, let's say, intolerant of competition. So, basically, familiars never have the opportunity to, um . . . socialize with each other."

"It's super rare for one of us to even *see* another familiar who doesn't have to be regarded as an enemy by default."

Yoshi and I glanced at each other and blinked in unison.

"Wait," I said. "You're *territorial*? Is *that* really what this is about?"

Both of them buzzed around our heads in erratic loops, a characteristic sign of agitation. I noticed a striking lack of any rebuttal of my observation, though.

"Go easy on them, okay?" Yoshi urged. "It's not like they can help being what they are. I . . . sorta relate."

"You?" I have to say, that took me by surprise. "It looks to me like you've taken to isekai like a fish to water. You're even in much better shape after just a couple months."

He ducked his head, blushing faintly in the dim light of the distant fires, but didn't smile. "I . . . thanks, Omura. It actually helps to hear that. I've been . . . really trying. Now that I'm *in* this crazy situation, I want to do it right. I just don't want to screw anything else up. I'm trying not to be a Subaru, you know?"

I squinted, trying to parse that. "A . . . You mean the . . . constellation?" Surely he wasn't talking about the car company.

"Oh! No, Subaru. You know, from *Re:Zero*?"

"From what?"

Poor kid flushed again. "It's an anime."

"Ah. Of course it is."

"But it's really good! Seriously, it's *amazing*. I bet you'd like it, Omura, you even liked *KonoSuba*! I can't recommend it highly enough."

"Well, sure, Yoshi," I said pointedly, "I'll hop right on that train. Where's it streaming?"

He winced, looking around the dark goblin-filled cavern below the medieval shithole in which we lived. "Oh, uh. Right. Sorry."

And now he looked so depressed even I was forced to take pity.

"So who's Subaru, and why don't you want to be him?"

Yoshi instantly perked back up, of course. Otaku; if you've met one, you've met them all, and there's nothing they love more than a chance to blather on about their bullshit to someone who doesn't really care. This guy had been in anime withdrawal for months until I opened the floodgates.

"Oh, it's great! It's an isekai, but it's a *deconstructive* one, see? It's all about the otaku mindset and how self-defeating it is. Subaru gets transported to a fantasy world and immediately finds out that acting like an isekai hero just gets him dunked on. The whole story is about him learning that . . . well, the problem isn't the world, it's him. Being a social outcast in real life . . . you'd be the same anywhere, unless you learn how to deal with people. You can't accomplish anything without convincing people to work with you. It's sort of . . . um, it's something a lot of otaku needed to hear."

"Huh." Well, damn, now I kinda *wanted* to watch that. Now that he'd said the name, I was pretty sure I'd seen some merch for it in the game store. I had tried *hard* not to learn anything from that place, but cultural osmosis can only be resisted up to a point. "And it's . . . popular? I can't imagine most of the target audience would enjoy being called out like that."

He shrugged. "Yeah, well . . . I can't say it's a *fun* thing to be told, but it's pretty cathartic to hear something you really needed to. Even when it's rough."

"And you're trying *not* to be like this guy? If he gets better, he sounds like a role model."

"I meant . . . him at the beginning." Yoshi fell silent, staring moodily into the distance. I let him think. This was clearly not a dramatic pause; he was just struggling to put something into words. Not everybody can be as articulate as me. "The Fflyr have this proverb that really hits for me; I dunno if you've heard it yet. 'You don't know whether you'd take a devil's deal until one appears before you.' That just seems to get more and more relevant, doesn't it?"

"Oh yeah, I've heard that one. I like that, too; seems like a solid point."

He nodded, still staring ahead with a glum expression. When he spoke again, his voice had dropped almost to a whisper. "Yeah, well . . . I found out. A beautiful Goddess offered me adventure in another world and I jumped for it. I *begged* for it. I didn't pause even for a second to think about my parents, or my big sister, or my friends . . . Anyone who'd miss me back home. My last memories of Earth are of *you* yelling at me for being an idiot, and . . . you were right. *You* didn't want to take the Goddess's deal, so . . . I guess we know which of us is smarter, huh."

Yoshi sighed quietly, tilting his head back to stare up at the ceiling. I averted my gaze, pretending I hadn't noticed his eyes shining.

"I hope Ai-nee thinks to feed my fish. And water my philodendron. She probably will, she's super responsible. At least one of us is, right?"

I stayed quiet for the next minute or so while he composed himself. The bro code transcends Good and Evil.

"So . . . yeah." He finally spoke again, a bit roughly, after clearing his throat. "However it happened, now I'm *here*. The Hero. People are depending on me. I just . . . I'm giving it my best. I'm determined not to let anyone down. Well . . . anyone else."

Damn it. Where did this kid get off, having a complex inner life and relatable emotions? Everything was so much simpler when he was just some dumb nerd I could make fun of. Fuckin' rude, that's what it was.

"I don't think that's really a fair comparison," I said slowly. "Yeah, I didn't want to take Virya's offer, but . . . that's because I didn't *want* to take her offer. This isekai bullshit is *not* something I've dreamed about. If a beautiful Goddess appeared before me, offering my heart's desire for free . . . Well. I'd *like* to think I'd be smart enough to smell a trap and turn it down. But I think the Fflyr are right, with that saying of theirs. You *can't* know what you'll do in a situation like that until you're in it."

"Do you think . . . we'll ever get to go back home?" It hurt to hear him trying not to sound plaintive.

"That's . . . I'm sorry, Yoshi, but that's . . . not a thing," Radatina whispered.

"There *is* no traveling the other way," Biribo added. "The connection to Earth . . . it doesn't work the way you're probably thinking. It's not a question of persuading the Goddesses to send you back. That's just not within their power."

"*Oh?*" I gave him my most pointed look.

Biribo did a nervous loop the loop. "Look, boss, I've already said more than I should. We *cannot* explain any further. There's no breaking that rule."

I knew when I wasn't going to get further answers, and pressing would just make me look petty and weak.

"Well, who knows," I deflected. "The Devil King found a way to crack this thing. Granted, *he's* a soul-eating piece of shit whom we should not emulate, but at least that means it *can* be done. You know, after what we've seen recently, I'm wondering if this is all some kind of simulation."

"Hm." Yoshi frowned. "I really don't think so."

"Oh?"

"Well, I mean . . . The point of simulation theory is you *can't* conclusively prove you're not in one, but if anything, I think Ephemera is less likely to be some kind of sim than Earth."

I squinted at him. "Based on what?"

"Well, think about it. We saw the corrupted Spirit and that it was running on some kind of code, right? With an error message and everything. There's nothing like that on Earth. If you're able to completely simulate a whole reality, there's no reason to give the people inside it access to the system's functions."

Shit, he had a point there.

"I guess so," I conceded. "Fine, I can live with that. I'm just glad at having a hint of what's *behind* all this insanity. *Somewhere* there's a machine running it all. If it can be reached, it can be hacked."

"I don't . . . think that's necessarily the case," he said, frowning more deeply.

"Oh, come on. You *saw* that thing! It was an obvious error message, in an Earth language. That's a computer; it's a *dead* giveaway."

"I'm not sure that's true, is the thing." Yoshi turned toward me, intent and animated in a way I hadn't seen him before. "I mean, think about computer code, Omura. What it is and does. And then compare that to magic."

"What? You lost me."

"Both are . . . sort of comparable, right? Using words and language to give instructions to reality. Code only works on something you've *built* out of microchips and whatnot, and magic is probably based on a similar principle. It's running on *something*, definitely. I doubt it's a natural phenomenon; somebody had to have set up something to make it work. But . . . I don't think this is a situation where we're going to find spaceships and robots if we dig deep enough. It's like . . . like how humans didn't start understanding the function of the heart until we'd invented pumps, or understanding brains until we'd invented computers. Us being familiar with information technology means we can recognize an error code, but magic is something else—not digital, but a similar *kind* of thing. It just runs on a recognizable logic, because . . . Well, it would have to, right?"

Now I was frowning, following his reasoning. And more to the point, finding myself troubled that he *had* reasoned all this out. I had to acknowledge (silently, to myself) that I hadn't thought the matter through that thoroughly and probably wouldn't have. It wasn't that Yoshi was *smarter* than me or anything; he just . . . had more brains than I'd given him credit for, and different areas of interest.

"I do see your point," I grudgingly admitted. "Well, shit. And I was so happy there for a little while."

"Happy about what? Why does it matter whether or not the magic is technological?"

"Because magic is bullshit nonsense for babies!" I exclaimed. "It's a cheap fantasy! Pure escapism for people who can't cope with what's in front of them. I just . . . I just want my life to make some fucking *sense* again."

"Oh." He nodded slowly, again staring out across the cavern. "I guess I can see the point. It's just . . . This seems strangely personal for you, Omura. Like you're, I dunno, *offended* about being in an isekai."

"That's a good way to put it, yes."

He gave me a sidelong look. "I'm probably gonna regret asking, but . . . What exactly is your problem with otaku?"

Oh, the answers I could give to that question. I'd been chewing on them for years, practically waiting for an opportunity. Now that one of these kids was finally, actually asking the question, though, I found to my surprise that the weight it held for me was balanced by much more recent developments than my long simmering resentment and disdain.

"Being here, on Dount," I mused after a pause to collect my thoughts, "working largely with bandits . . . It's really contextualized the issue of otaku for me."

"Otaku are like bandits?" he said skeptically.

"Not entirely, of course, but in an important respect. Tell me, Yoshi. Among your crew of nerd friends, who's the loli fan?"

His eyebrows lowered slightly, and he glanced to the side.

"What makes you think—"

"There's usually one in every group. At least one. You're thinking of him, right? You know who it is."

"Well, I mean . . . *Fan* might be putting it too strongly, but Issei does enjoy—"

"Uh huh. And see, that's the thing about otaku. Most are social outcasts for no bigger reason than being socially inept and having a poor hobby-life balance. Which isn't really fair, if you think about it. Some guys just don't fit in society, and a lot of the time it's because society's expectations aren't exactly reasonable."

"I'm really surprised that you get—"

"So those guys gather together, because human beings crave companionship, and that's naturally where the *other* guys insert themselves. The ones who are outcasts from society for *very good fucking reasons*. Bandits are like that in a busted wreck of a kingdom like Fflyr Dlemathlys—mostly just folks who were pushed out of the normal social order because that order is designed to be as brutally unfair as possible to almost everyone. And that creates opportunities and hiding places for the . . . others. The minority. So, I try to extend some compassion to people who've been forced to do terrible things by a terrible situation that wasn't their fault, and it means I've ended up having to deal with a small handful of psychopaths and murdering sadists mixed in with them. *You* gathered in groups around your weird little hobbies, just enjoying what you like and not hurting anyone, and since you were all outcasts together, it never felt *right* to exclude the *obvious fucking pedophiles*. Especially when so much of that anime nakedly panders to them."

Yoshi had gone stiff, fists clenching by his sides, but he wouldn't look at me.

"I get it, now," I murmured, staring at the distant fire slime. Aster was now lying down; Adelly had leaned her head on Nazralind's shoulder, and both of them seemed to be asleep sitting up. Gizmit was slowly strolling around the edges of the gathering, on night watch. "You may have accidentally given encouragement to somebody who's going to horrifically traumatize the first innocent child they're left alone with. It's not like that's *your* fault, though, or anyone's but theirs. I do my best to keep control and hold my people to a standard, but . . . truth is, I have no way of knowing what kinds of terrible things I'm indirectly responsible for, or will be. I try, as best I can, but there's just no way to tell. Yeah . . . I think I understand it a little better now. It's not a great look, but maybe I shouldn't have been so quick to judge."

He slowly inhaled, and then exhaled, deliberately relaxing his shoulders. "But . . . You *have* watched anime, though."

"Of course I've *seen* anime, I didn't live under a rock. *Everyone* has seen anime. There's some truly great stuff out there; it only becomes weird when you build your whole life around it."

"How's that different from music?" he asked, shooting me a look.

"You can get paid to make music."

"You can make anime for a living! People do; that's how it *gets* made!"

"Sure, if you wanna starve to death while working for a corporation that sees you as disposable."

He turned toward me, staring incredulously. "And *how is that different from music?*"

"Hey, relax, man. *Now* who's taking things personally?"

"I'm not the one who has a chip on his shoulder! And if I was, I think that'd be forgivable, frankly. Being a music nerd just means you don't spend your life being told your hobby is for children and pedophiles!"

"Hey, I have *never* thought all animation is for children. Believe me. My dad thought that, and that's how I ended up watching *Grave of the Fireflies* alone, unsupervised, when I was six."

Yoshi winced, sucking in a sharp breath through his teeth. "Yikes. *Ouch*."

"Heh." I had to grin, now that it had been enough years. "I barely remember it, but my mom says I cried for almost two straight days. But yeah, anyway, I'll cop to finding all of this pretty personal. Maybe it wasn't fair of me to be so contemptuous back on Earth—*maybe*—but here? I believe I'm pretty fucking entitled to be pissed about isekai. I live in one. And frankly, it fucking sucks."

He folded himself up awkwardly, drawing his knees up against his chest and wrapping his arms around them.

"Hey, Omura."

"Mm?"

"Do you . . . actually think this is a game? To the Goddesses, I mean."

I made myself breathe evenly. "Well . . . Pashilyn wasn't entirely without a point. Whether it is or not, Virya isn't exactly a reliable narrator."

"Sure, I know. But do *you* think it is?"

"Yes." I can only hold back my frank opinions for so long. "Yes, I am absolutely convinced both Goddesses are just bored entities with too much power who've been alive too long to empathize with mortal people. I think they're amusing themselves at the expense of our lives and those of everyone else on this hell planet."

"Sanora warned me . . ."

He trailed off, and I forced myself to be content with looking sidelong, *not* staring with all the intensity in my being. I was *deeply* interested in learning what Sanora had warned him about.

"I've been thinking," he whispered at last. "It was just a stray thought at first, but after you said that . . . I . . ."

Yoshi paused again, swallowing painfully. I waited.

"Suddenly, I'm the only guy on my team. Me, the Hero, alone with three cute girls. And . . . and I can't help thinking . . . It's *clawing* at me. Did . . . did she just . . . Was Raffan in the way of my harem story? Is *that* why he died?"

I breathed out. Slowly, softly.

This was no time to press the conclusion I wanted to draw him to. I mean, it would be a really shitty thing to do in this situation, but it also wasn't right strategically. I would get better results in the long term by being reasonable, and fair, and not giving him any cause to think I was trying to manipulate him. I had the luxury of acting this way because *I was fucking right*. The truth was on *my* side here, not Sanora's.

"Well, it's not like we have any way of knowing exactly what the Goddesses are or aren't capable of. Still . . . my gut says no. They definitely have ways of putting their fingers on the scales, but those all have to do with their magic system. There's a hundred ways for them to decide who gets what spell or artifact or Blessing or Spirit reward, or . . . It goes on and on. It's not hard for them to manipulate us all where they want us to be. But a chaotic situation like that, in the middle of a fight? I kind of don't think so. Biribo told me the Goddesses aren't allowed to cheat directly—that they *do*, but they have to be careful and subtle about it because if either is *caught* cheating, the other gets a free action."

He nodded. "Radatina said that, too."

"Yeah. So, no, we obviously can't say anything for sure, but in that case? It doesn't feel right, to me."

Yoshi's next deep breath sounded so relieved I almost hated to continue. "But."

He went completely rigid.

I was taking a risk here. This was flirting with more information than I should betray to the Hero, but if there was ever a time . . .

"I have a situation that I *know* was set up by Virya. She didn't tell me so outright, but it's laid out in the specific spells and abilities and circumstances she placed right in front of me when I first landed on Ephemera. I . . . have a spell that enables me to share powers with monster girls, Yoshi. It only works on attractive women, which is the kind of stupid and arbitrary thing that only an aggressively mediocre light novel author or weaboo Goddess could possibly come up with. I am practically *forced* to collect a monster girl harem to survive on this world. So . . . at least *one* of them definitely wants to watch a harem show, this time around."

Slowly, Yoshi lowered his face to rest in his arms. His shoulders moved heavily as he did his best to breathe evenly for the next few minutes. I left him alone to gather himself.

"He was the first friend I made here," the Hero finally said, in a voice that was muffled by more than his own arms.

"I'm sorry."

We sat together in silence.

22

In Which the Dark Lord Gets a Warm Welcome

Gizmit vanished at some point during the night, which had me actually worried for a moment before Zui said she'd just gone ahead to report back to Sneppit. Apparently, we were close enough that it wasn't much of a hike for an experienced underground scout like Gizmit.

It ended up being not much of one for us, either. A bit less than two hours after we broke camp and doused the fire slimes, our much-expanded troupe came to the first set of tunnel barricades covering access to Sneppit's base, which was a sturdy-looking but clearly hastily constructed wall of sheet metal with holes through which arrows were pointed at us.

"Halt!" a reedy voice echoed from behind the blockade. "State the password!"

There ensued the unmistakable smack of a hand impacting a head, complete with the requisite squawk of protest.

"Not the time, Bazno!" a different voice shouted. "Weapons down, team, you all know who this is. One of you mooks help me shove this!"

With an unpleasant screech of metal on stone, a piece of the barricade was pushed outward at an angle by several goblins, creating a gap big enough for us to slip through in single file. As soon as it was opened enough, the goblin leading the effort stepped back and waved at me. She wore the pink-tinted akornin armor of Sneppit's security force, with a heavy truncheon dangling from a belt loop.

"Welcome back, Lord Seiji. Gizmit came through and said you'd be coming. Sorry about the nonsense; a lot of my *colleagues* here are in the habit of defusing tension with humor and don't have a great sense of appropriate timing. This everybody?"

"Yeah, we picked up a few extras, as you can see," I replied, forcing a calm expression despite my amusement. Honestly, the more I got to know goblins, the more I liked them.

"Yep, Gizmit briefed us." The guard nodded and stepped aside, shooing her comrades out of the way for us. "Miss Sneppit knows to expect you and everything should be set up. Just follow this tunnel straight, ignore the side branches and you'll come out right on the tram platform; I think you know the way from there. By the time you get there, somebody should be ready to meet you with supplies and whatever else. The boss'll wanna catch up, I'm sure. Oh, and we should have sleeping places and food sorted out for the new arrivals by now," she added, leaning to one side to speak past me at the crowd of goblins following. "It's a little crowded in here these days, but we're not to the point of starving or stacking on top of each other yet."

"Thanks, appreciate it," I said, already stepping forward to clear the path for the rest to follow. The security goblin grinned and thumped her fist against her breastplate, which I assumed must be some kind of salute.

Yoshi and Aster stepped up alongside me as we progressed, which I'll confess was a bit of a relief because Zui had been getting underfoot quite a bit lately, and I found her company . . . let's call it vexing. We didn't have much farther to go from there, but it was a few more minutes before we reached the actual door to Sneppit's headquarters—a heavy door of solid metal in a thick stone setting, which altogether looked more defensible than the much more temporary barricade behind us. But that was the nice thing about living in a tunnel system—you could expand your defensive perimeter without stretching your forces too thin. Made sense Sneppit preferred not to have any actual fighting right on her actual doorstep if it could be avoided.

This was also guarded, of course, this time with armored security in front of the doors, but again, they were expecting us. It was rather nice to be greeted cheerfully and ushered inside, almost like coming home to North Watch.

I really hoped everyone back there was holding out okay.

As the woman commanding the barricade had told us, the tunnel led straight onto the tram platform I remembered from our arrival yesterday morning. Like yesterday, it was defended, with full squads of armored goblins bearing slingshots and riot shields on the designated ledges, which had clearly been designed for that purpose. The place was less generally locked down, though; there were more goblins present who were clearly not security, including an apparent engineering team working over a tram, which was currently suspended from the track next to the main platform. There were also various other civilians whose reason for being here was inscrutable to me even as they rushed forward to greet us.

Sneppit herself was present, again perched at the top of the wide and tall flight of stairs, which was just too dramatic not to have been staged. She was conversing with a goblin who had a monocle and a clipboard, but looked up on our arrival. Then pulled down her pink shades to give me a wink over their golden rims.

Yep, I knew what she was angling for.

"Scuze me, Lord Seiji?"

The first of the welcoming party had reached us. In fact, most of them seemed to be milling around at a few meters' distance, uncertain about getting too close. The exceptions were two men in casual clothes, one of whom did a somewhat awkward Fflyr-style folding hands gesture at me.

"Sorry to get in your way, Dark Lord, but there's only rumor going around and no one will tell us—"

"Where's Rizz?" the other burst out. "Is she all right? What *happened*?"

Taken aback, I froze for a second, staring down at their worried expressions, before it clicked.

"Oh! You guys must be the husbands."

The pair exchanged a loaded glance and one of them grimaced.

"Yeah, that's us. Same old story."

"Rizz is fine, or was last I saw her," I explained. "She split off from the group to rally the other Judges."

"She did?" Husband #2's expression sharpened. "You musta found something *really* bad in that place if she not only took a side but believes the rest will, too."

I instinctively hesitated, but this was not a secret, after all. We wanted the word to spread as far and as fast as possible.

"The Spirit in there had been corrupted into a Void altar. The Goblin King has been trafficking with devils, and his best friend, Hoy, is an actual Void witch. It took the Hero and I both to drive him off, and we didn't manage to take him out. All these folks were actually with him, until he started slaughtering them just to make a point."

The Misters Rizz winced in what looked like well-practiced unison.

"Is Rhoka okay? She's still with Rizz, right?"

"Did . . . she give you any message for us?"

"Yes, yes, and . . . uh, no. Sorry."

"Typical," the first one said sourly, prompting the other to drape a comforting arm around his shoulders. It occurred to me that if this conversation was going to carry on much longer, I should probably get their names.

"Hey, you know our girl. Brusque and focused is a *good* sign. If she'd sent us a personal message it would mean she didn't think she'd be coming back from this one. Thanks, Lord Seiji. And, uh, sorry to bother you over personal business."

"Hey, man, no worries. I completely understand."

They retreated to the rest of the hovering goblins, still arm-in-arm.

"Y'know, after everything we've been over lately," Yoshi muttered barely above a whisper, "it feels weird that the middle-aged goblin lady is the only one who's gotten the harem ending so far."

I had to crack a grin at that in spite of myself. "I dunno, something about that seems oddly representative of our whole isekai experience."

"Maybe it's the coat. I should get a coat like hers. Trench coats are badass."

"Don't underestimate the power of a cool hat, too."

"All right, all right, you've seen the Champions, they're very impressive." Miss Sneppit arrived at the base of the stairs and immediately began shooing the onlookers forward by sheer force of personality. Somehow, Zui had already darted over to hover behind the pink-clad boss goblin and was whispering in her ear even as she shepherded the crowd. "You can tell your grandkids all about it. Right *now*, nobody's gettin' paid to sightsee. Yo, new faces! I'm Sneppit, and this is my place. Consider yourselves welcome here for the duration of this crisis. This is Mazin; he'll getcha squared away. We got a space cleared out for everybody to crash and rations are bein' prepared. No compensation needed; you're on my hospitality for now. I won't swear by the comfort cos this ain't an inn, and with any luck we won't be in this mess for long. Mazin'll introduce you to the rest of these folks to sort out any other needs you've got an' settle how you can pitch in."

Sneppit's people were efficient; I had to give them that. Mazin took over crowd-herding duty and was immediately sorting and delegating. The goblins we'd brought in from Hoy's group mostly looked tired and glad somebody was taking charge, but a few looked back at me questioningly as they were led away.

"Everybody should be safe here for now," I reassured them. "My people have a spot arranged here in the complex, and I can attest Miss Sneppit provides well for all the basic necessities. All of you, feel free to visit our quarters, I'll make sure you're welcome. Any of the guards can point you there."

That seemed to do the trick, for now at least.

"Between Gizmit and Zui, I think I know the high points, but we need to have a sit-down first thing," Sneppit declared. "Get everybody on the same page and lay out our next steps. We got some news here to catch you guys up on, too. First, though, can I borrow you for a private word, Lord Seiji?"

I glanced at Yoshi, who shrugged.

"Sure, I'm all yours."

She smirked at the wording, just long enough to make her point felt. "Swell. Zui, show the Hero back to the conference room and see the rest of this gang to their resting place."

"Maizo should come along, too," Zui said. "He's got intel to share."

"Sounds good, get it done," Sneppit said briskly. "Over here, if you please, m'lord."

I nodded a temporary farewell to Aster and the others and followed her past the engineering crew over to some kind of crane apparatus at the far edge. Sneppit grabbed a lever that was half the length of her body and, with a grunt of effort, pulled it into position. This disengaged some kind of brake system, causing a clever windmill contraption atop the machine to begin spinning in the steady breeze that funneled through the tram tunnel. With none of its other gears engaged, this appeared to achieve nothing except to create a constant grinding noise.

"Little trick I like to use," she said, not raising her voice. Standing this close I could hear her fine, but the mechanical sounds would probably make anything we said indistinct a few meters away. "Dunno how useful it'll be for you up top, but down here I got heavy machinery and a buncha mooks with big ears. Privacy's like any other resource in Kzidnak—you want some, you gotta get inventive."

"I am always impressed by just how inventive goblins are," I said frankly.

Sneppit gave me a bright smile, but then her expression sobered. "So, I'll be brief. This is just a quick detail check before the meeting. Does the Hero know you're based outta North Watch, and if not, do you want him to?"

That brought me up short, both because it was a pertinent question that I had somehow not even considered yet, and because of the implications of her asking this right now.

"Hang on. Did something—?"

"The short answer is your people are fine, and seems they've been doing you proud. I figure we'll go over the longer version at the full meeting. I hate repeating myself."

The breath I'd been briefly holding escaped, and I nodded. "Okay, yeah. Thanks. As for North Watch . . . To my knowledge, there's no reason he would know that. I'm . . ." I had to pause, thinking quickly but carefully. "I don't think Yoshi would currently do me much harm with that info, and offering it as a gesture of trust might actually help advance the project I discussed with you. *But*, there are those friends of his."

Sneppit nodded seriously. "The elf is an unconscionable waste of cranial fluid, but I dunno if I like how sharp that priestess is. The alchemist, too; you always gotta watch out for the quiet ones."

"Yeah, they've been canny enough not to reveal Yoshi's the Hero because of what would obviously happen if the political powers up there found out. While that *does* suggest a capacity for discretion, it also makes me hesitant to hand them a lever. Especially one that's planted under my ass. Let's . . . play it subtle for now."

"You got it, no names or details in front of Team Hero. Speaking of that, while I gotcha over here, how's that project going?"

"Better than I could have imagined," I said frankly. "I can safely say the boy's whole view of the world has been rocked. I *think* the core of the matter might be already settled, but if we can end this whole mess with him having a few goblins he thinks of as friends or at least allies, that should be the best anti-Hero measure Kzidnak could hope for. It'll start driving a wedge between him and the Convocation, too."

"You do good work, Lord Seiji," she said with a distinctly flirtatious wink. "You work this from your end and I will from mine, and by the time we meet in the middle, we'll be running this whole island. We make a good team. All right, let's not keep the staff waiting."

"Lead on, boss lady."

As I followed her back up the stairs, I pondered the advisability of revealing my . . . little *issue* to Sneppit. So far she hadn't done anything brazenly sexual enough to trigger a flashback, but I could see her building up to it. The real question was what course of action would gently dissuade her without jeopardizing our partnership, or worse . . .

Well, allies we might be, but every instinct I had screamed at me not to let Sneppit know I had any exploitable weakness.

"I've just got the broad strokes, but it's enough to change the whole game," Sneppit said minutes later, once she was at the head of the conference table and the rest of us around it. The composition of the group was mostly the same as before, right down to Zui at her note-taking desk in the back, but this time with the addition of Gizmit and Maizo. The various union reps were back, not a one of whose names I remembered. They were still out of their depth and staying quiet, so hopefully I wouldn't have to embarrass myself over it. "Devils and Void magic, what an absolute cock-up this is. You guys have anything else we should know about before we start laying out strategies?"

"Maizo?" I asked, turning to him. "What were you able to dig up?"

"The biggest news I think is that Jadrak's organization is very much a crackable shell," Maizo reported. "It's half-cracked already. Working with secondhand reports like that, hard numbers and percentages are things I was just not able to get—wouldn't have been even if our adoptees were a representative sample, which itself is a long shot. *But*, after speaking with everybody, I can confidently say the Goblin King's followers have deep currents of disloyalty. The core of 'em are absolute fanatics, of course, but they've also press-ganged a lot of people who're just trying to survive this insanity and didn't get far enough away in time. It's not just the unwilling recruits; with the way things've been going, even the less-committed early volunteers are starting to have regrets about this whole business."

"In isolation, that'd be the best news I've heard all week," Sneppit said gravely, "but the *big* news changes the whole character of it. Sounds like Jadrak's organization is going to start tearing itself apart as soon as he loses momentum, but unlike my previous assessment, that is no longer a win condition for us. We're dealing with at least one Void witch, probably two, a bunch of loyalist sorcerers, and a *fucking devil*. As soon as Jadrak starts getting desperate, he'll start pulling absolute chaos out of his ass and handling it with less and less precision. Aside from all the indiscriminate death and property damage that'll cause, I'm not sure any defenses we got'll hold out against . . . well, that."

"I agree that attack remains our better option, distressing as that is," I said. "Anything else of note, Maizo?"

"Yeah, actually. We already learned firsthand that Jadrak's company likes their explosives, and according to the buzz I gathered, they've got plenty more. *But*, the kinds they've got and the way they can be deployed are somewhat limited." He leaned forward over the table, grinning smugly as he continued. "Seems they weren't able to bring along the alchemical *or* metalworking facilities they'd need to manufacture explosive slingshot ammo. In fact, what they had was what they sent with the strike force to take out the

Dark Lord. Which means, while there's very little of that shit left, it's *ours* now. So if we push forward, we'll still be dealing with mining explosives and people who know how to use 'em, but that's way more likely to take the form of traps than grenades bein' flung at us."

"Seems like they should be able to make up for that," Yoshi said, frowning. "How hard can it be to make an explosive throwable?"

"You can *throw* anything," Gizmit answered with a hint of disdain. "Crafting ammunition that will reliably explode on impact and *not* while you're transporting it is a whole other beast. If demolitions work was that simple, everybody would have slingshot grenades."

"Now that's some good news, finally," Sneppit said. "Thanks, Maizo; glad to have you on the team. On *our* end, we've gleaned a couple updates on the situation in Kzidnak that you guys missed out on while you were off raiding. The first and worst part is that Jadrak's people have locked down Fallencourt. They control the city itself and every access in and out. As expected, they blew up my tram rail as far from the station as they have effective control, as well as the other lines heading through there," she added with a bitter grimace, "so we no longer have an easy path right into their territory."

"Okay . . . sorry if I'm interrupting, but that gives me an idea," Yoshi said, wearing a pensive frown. "Doesn't that seem like something we can take advantage of, in combination with what Maizo found out? Like, I remember the city itself—it's big, and it's a maze of tunnels and bridges and stuff. And we know Jadrak's struggling to hang on to his followers' loyalty. Seems like we could take the opportunity to start a kind of . . . counterinsurgency in the middle of his domain. Right?"

"Giz?" Sneppit turned toward her spy, raising an eyebrow.

Gizmit was already shaking her head. "It's a pretty good thought, but not something we're in a position to act on. Yeah, you're right, the conditions are so perfect for a rebellion against Jadrak that it's basically inevitable even if we don't do anything. The problems are our available resources and the timeframe. I'm the best we've got at that kinda work, and I am not up to the task. Somebody stealthy enough to get into the heart of Jadrak's territory and skilled enough in both military matters and politics to put together a resistance on the *extremely tight* deadline we've got before this all blows up, which is days at most . . . Well, we're talkin' about a professional operative of the kind major governments field. So unless you've got a Lancoral Gray Guard or Savin shadow scout in your back pocket, *and* a way to make 'em behave, that's not a path we can pursue."

"Damn," he muttered, sinking back in his chair. "Sorry."

"Don't apologize, kid," Sneppit said with a smile. "You got good ideas; keep 'em comin', even if they don't all work out. That's how we eventually come to one that does."

I kept my mouth shut, suddenly grappling with the worry that I now knew exactly where my mysterious dark elf stalker had disappeared to, and it was basically my nightmare scenario. They were fine and useful while shooting my enemies with arrows; if that fucking idiot started trying to do their idea of politics again, it would be a disaster. Jadrak's uprising was a far bigger hornet's nest than the cat tribe.

"The other piece of news I have for you is better," Sneppit continued, shooting me a grin. "Jadrak made a push at the tunnel entrance the Dark Lord took into Kzidnak and was apparently very surprised to find it fully staffed by his followers and heavily fortified. We haven't managed to actually get in contact with your people, Lord Seiji—they're on high alert and also there's a lot of Jadrak's goons between them and us. But I had my own scouts find out what they could, and it seems they've turned that tunnel entrance into a death trap. Wasted a whole mess of Goblin King partisans trying to take it before they eventually backed off. That's great news for us, and not just because it means Lord Seiji's people are okay—it's a major threat *way* too close to Jadrak's current center of power for his comfort, and something he has no choice but to keep forces assigned to hold because, for all he knows, the Dark Lord can launch a major offensive right into Fallencourt at any time."

"Not just for all he knows," I mused, "I actually *can* do that. I'd have to find a way to get through that blockade and contact my people, though . . ."

"Way faster to go around," Maizo opined. "There are a lotta surface exits; Jadrak can't possibly control 'em all. We can get a message to your allies pretty easy."

I tensed for a moment, but he didn't mention North Watch. Either Sneppit had caught his ear during the few minutes it'd taken us to set up the meeting, or Maizo was just professionally discreet.

"We need a plan and a way to coordinate that attack with our own first," I said quickly into the ensuing pause. "Charging in without a plan will just get a lot of people killed. They don't even know what they're up against."

"That'll factor into whatever plan we settle on," Sneppit said. "I'll draft a message for your approval, Lord Seiji, and we'll send it to the surface to get to your people from the other side. Meanwhile, I've put together something for you that I think lays out the situation pretty clearly. Zui, maps."

Zui smoothly rose from her writing desk, picking up a couple of large rolls of paper and bringing them forward to unfurl across the conference table. I couldn't help but notice that she did this smoothly and silently, with zero backtalk or eye rolling, despite the fact that Sneppit spoke to her far more curtly than I ever did. I guess you get certain privileges when it's your signature on all the paychecks.

"These are for reference," Sneppit explained as her assistant/hairstylist spread out the maps in front of us. "I've got a map of our tram lines, with new notations showing which ones are still serviceable—Jadrak hasn't bothered sabotaging the ones that don't lead right into his own business, at least so far. After Gizmit brought her report last night, I also put together this second one; it shows the positions of every underground Spirit on Dount."

"The Spirits?" I frowned. "You think they'll go for them, as well? Do they even *do* anything that'd be useful for a campaign of conquest?"

"Debatable at best, but that's not the point. Jadrak has backed himself into a corner, and now that he's put himself on *your* shit list, his only possible source of help is his devil friend. And devils make the *worst* friends; they don't do anything for free. He and Hoy only have the two souls between them to barter with, and I'm betting those bargains were made long before this Goblin King business started. That means there's only one other thing they can offer their devil in exchange for more favors."

"Oh. *Shit.*"

"But that's good, though," said Yoshi. "It means we know *where* they'll be going."

"Exactly!" Sneppit pointed at him. "Jadrak's survival depends on keeping his little crusade moving forward. He has to placate his people by attacking the humans of Dount, and he has to placate his devil by corrupting more Spirits. So while we can't predict exactly what forces will be sent to which objectives, we know the next steps he *has* to take—he'll be launching a major offensive at Lord Seiji's defenses, and he will go for every Spirit within reach."

"And with every passing hour, his task gets harder," Gizmit added. "Even the Judges can't do anything against a Void witch—they'll be disadvantaged against Jadrak's pet sorcerers, for that matter. But what they *can* do, and what Rizz will have them doing as soon as she can gather them up, is laying groundwork. Getting in position, organizing resistance, putting people and resources in place to back up the Dark Lord when he makes his move. Furthermore, Rizz—any of the Judges, in fact—are shrewd enough to put all this together for themselves, and they know their way around Kzidnak without the need for maps. Jadrak has the initiative right now, but everywhere we go, we will begin to find support. More and more the longer this carries on."

"That means Jadrak will be getting more desperate and therefore more dangerous right up until the end," I murmured.

"It does," Gizmit said gravely.

"But it also means this is far from hopeless," Yoshi added. "From the look of it . . . it's obvious what we have to do next. We just need to plan *how*."

"You said it," I agreed. "Jadrak will be most careful with his own safety—something tells me I know exactly who's going to get sent to handle the Spirits. And that'll be *our* job. What do you think, Yoshi? Ready for round two?"

"We didn't blow that bastard Hoy up *nearly* hard enough last time," he growled. "Time to fix that."

23

In Which the Dark Lord
Is Too Late

We got activity ahead, boss," Biribo reported, zipping up to my ear and just *barely* beating Radatina to making a similar announcement to Yoshi, to her visible annoyance. "The tunnel opens up into a cavern with goblins all over it. One goblin's in a high position at the tunnel entrance over-looking it, obviously a lookout. They don't seem to have a ranged weapon but that's a perfect sniper's perch."

"Okay, here we go." I inhaled and exhaled slowly, then turned my head to address those marching along behind me. "Everybody remembers the Hoy Directives?"

There was a chorus of agreement, the desultory tone of which I did not like.

"Then repeat them to me."

"Oh, come *on!*" protested two different goblins in perfect unison, to the accompaniment of groans—two of which belonged to our resident elves—and eye roll from others. Even Aster shot me a skeptical look. Then again, it was Aster; her face might just be stuck that way.

I opened my mouth to deliver a retort, and happened to catch Zui's eye. She was giving me a particularly fierce stare, and when she saw she had my attention, shook her head once.

Right. Zui herself had taken the time to caution me that goblins would not respond well to a heavy-handed style of leadership. In truth, I didn't favor one for my human followers, either, but those at least were trained by Fflyr culture to obey when given orders. Goblins didn't feel compelled to do anything they were not contractually obligated to, and my volunteer force would resent being pushed around.

"I know, I know," I said, deliberately moderating my tone. "But you all saw what Hoy can do. This fucker fought *both living Champions* to a draw, and I don't intend to lose any more lives to his bullshit. So yeah, you're damn right I'm gonna be paranoid and overly concerned about this. Humor me, please."

She was right; that got me results. The exasperated expressions were immediately replaced by thoughtful nods and downcast eyes. All the goblins with us, save Zui and Maizo, were recruits we'd gained from Hoy's own troops, who'd turned on him after he turned on them first. They'd all lost friends to him.

Still, it was Nazralind who piped up first. "Hoy Directive One: Corner him! The limitation of Flicker is that he has to *see* his destination to teleport. We need to wedge him into a spot where he can't retreat, with walls behind and enemies in front."

"Hoy Directive Two: Keep up ranged pressure," said Kuriko, quiet and solemn as always. He was the first goblin who'd turned his slingshot on Hoy, the one who'd first spoken to me on the long walk back to Sneppit's place, and I didn't know yet whether this grave demeanor was just his personality or the result of recent trauma. "His Void power may be inexhaustible, but his Blessing of Magic is weak. The more we force his Repulsion Aura to react, the less he'll be able to cast offensive spells or Flicker."

"Hoy Directive Two Point Five: Press with kinetic attacks only!" called Ritlit, whose name I was never going to forget because when I'd tried to call her by it she had howled with laughter and spent the next five minutes running around introducing herself to people as Rito Twice. "We hold munitions in reserve *until* we have him cornered someplace without a convenient tunnel he can scurry off through. *Then* we blow him right to hell—drop the walls and ceiling on his ass!"

"Good. Thanks for indulging me, guys."

"I still say that's just Hoy Directive Three," Yoshi muttered.

"*Please* don't start that up again," I begged. I agreed with him, personally, but it had become a whole *thing* with the goblins, who were culturally obsessed with laying out terms and conditions precisely, and after much debate had concluded that the third point was just a subset of the second. I'd let them, because I didn't actually *care* how they classified it as long as they fucking *did* it.

We'd set out after a short rest—a rest because one was needed, and short because we didn't have the luxury of more time. I'd been able to check in with

Madyn and Ydleth, who were thriving among the goblins, as Aster had predicted, and in fact had somehow managed to find all our new recruits in just the short time we were in the planning session with Sneppit and company. Apparently, they'd been shown right to our assigned quarters at their request and were sharing a meal when I found them. That had led to a bunch of them volunteering to join up with me when I'd mentioned my intent to strike out against Jadrak's forces as quickly as possible. Many had just wanted to rest and take on whatever quieter, safer work Sneppit found for them, but I now had a force of ten goblin volunteers backing me up.

It seemed this lot were somewhat suspicious of Sneppit—understandable, really—and more willing to align themselves with me than with her. I embraced this, remembering Gizmit's advice about Maizo, who had decided to stick with me for similar reasons. It worked out particularly well, as these goblins still had the explosive munitions I was planning to use to finish off Hoy, having been very reluctant to yield those to Sneppit's engineers.

We were also stuck with Zui again, because Sneppit had wanted one of her ranking people to represent her interests on this mission and had assigned Gizmit elsewhere this time. Which . . . yeah, the organization's top spy probably wasn't best suited for a frontal assault. Still, I couldn't help wondering whether Sneppit suspected Gizmit was angling to get promoted over her head.

This whole topic worried me. It had been a while since I'd had a flashback; Minifrit's unconventional therapy really *was* helping, and here in Kzidnak the matter was more political than actually sexual, which helped me compartmentalize it. But sooner or later, either Sneppit or Gizmit or some *other* Goblin Queen candidate would make a serious play for me, and that . . . was probably going to cause some problems.

As discussed, we shifted formation as we drew up to the bend in the tunnel around which the opening would be found, with Yoshi and Aster taking point, me and Pashilyn right behind them. Neither I nor any of the Hero's party particularly liked this arrangement, but the logic was irrefutable—they could take hits better than any of us, and better still with the aid of my healing and Pashilyn's shields.

Up ahead, the tunnel did indeed open out into a cavern—the prettiest one I'd seen in Kzidnak, the slice of it visible from back here. It was downright lush, in fact, featuring some kind of hanging greenery and . . . was that a waterfall? I couldn't see it, but *something* was making the characteristic roaring noise in the distance.

Closer, though, was the goblin Biribo had predicted would be on watch. At the sight of her, we relaxed.

"Oh hey," I said, stepping out from behind Yoshi and taking in the long brown coat, wide-brimmed hat, and bladed polearm. The purple bands were around her arms, not worn as a scarf, so . . . "Arbiter?"

"The name's Fram," she said, grinning toothily and waving so hard I thought she'd pitch herself off her narrow perch. "And *you* must be the Dark Lord! And the Hero. Hot damn, what a day *this* is. That'll teach me to think I've seen it all just cos there's a Goblin King rising."

"I take it Judge Rizz told you to expect us," Yoshi said warily.

"That and more!" Arbiter Fram flung herself carelessly off the ledge, which was a drop of at least five times her height, and hit the ground in a roll. She came up right in front of us, arms outstretched like a dismounting gymnast and brandishing her polearm. "Welcome to the shitshow, citizens!"

Yeah, Arbiters were clearly the younger apprentices. This one was also an adolescent; unlike Rhoka, she acted like one, too.

"Wow," said Yoshi, "you're not much like Rizz and Rhoka at *all*."

Fram snorted. "Yeah, I'll bet. Rumor is Judge Rizz actually catches on fire if you can make her smile. Anyway, you lot didn't march down here to get the gossip—c'mon, you should talk with my boss."

"Is everything okay here?" I asked, falling into step behind her as she braced her polearm over her shoulder and went swaggering off into the cavern beyond. "Any sign of Jadrak's forces?"

"Yes *and* yes," Fram practically crowed. "It's handled, Mister Dark Lord, sir. We goblins won't turn down your support if there's Void magic afoot, but we're not helpless, either. You should really talk with Judge Gazmo, for the sole entire reason that he's the expert, and in no way because he'll blow my ears back if I brief you in a manner he considers incorrect, no sir."

"By all means, let's not get you in trouble," I said solemnly. "That is, I mean, let's hear it directly from the expert."

She shot me a cheeky grin over her shoulder. "You're all right, Lord Senji."

"*Seiji.*"

"Oop, sorry. I dunno what language that is, even."

Aster lightly touched the back of my shoulder, not that I needed the reminder. I'd been in more than enough battles by now to recognize when one was not worth fighting.

The view was enough to distract me, anyway. This was another cavern open to the outside, with the far wall ending in a massive crack through which daylight streamed. We must be right up against the edge of the island here. There was indeed a waterfall, pouring out of an aperture high up on the cavern wall to our right and thundering down into the pool, which covered half of the floor. From there, the water streamed away into four other tunnel mouths—at least, four above the waterline, and who knew how many below. The left half of the cavern's flooded floor from the entrance was a series of islands scattered around the surface of the water, on which grew the first khora I had seen since coming underground. In fact, the root systems of what had to be other khora poked through the walls, dangling down and crisscrossing the space, with actual leafy vines of some kind bedecking the khora roots and protrusions from the rocky walls, dangling in lush curtains wherever they had enough light from the opening to flourish. The air was cooler and more humid than the rest of Kzidnak, and even more windy. To walk in this cavern was to get lightly sprayed by the falls. It wasn't unpleasant.

"This is beautiful," Yoshi observed.

"Sure is!" Fram said brightly, while leading us along the trail, which clung to the right side of the wall toward the only structure in sight—a surprisingly steampunk-looking combination of stonework built right into the living rock and worked metal extensions, complete with a big paddle wheel being turned by the waterfall. "Some of the best scenery in Kzidnak, not that just any old gob's been welcome to wander in here and gawk—well, actually, the Judge'll probably need to explain that, too, given what he's got on the docket for you. And speaking of. OY! They're here, just like Rizz said! I brought that shipment of gobs and butts and Champions you ordered, big daddy!"

We'd come within shouting range of a wide stone platform in front of the structure, which jutted out further in a metal dock, where a few goblins were waiting for us at the top of a short flight of broad stairs. Stairs that we navigated with *extreme* care, as they were built for goblin-sized legs and slick with spray from the falls. The only goblin who had not already been staring at us finally deigned to turn around—the one also wearing the brown coat and hat, and a Judge's purple scarf.

"Fram," Judge Gazmo growled, "if you call me that in front of clients *one more time*, I am gonna boot your green ass into the core and get a bucket of fried crawns to do your job. It's not like they'd be much slower or less thorough."

"Shut up, you love me." Fram cackled, skipping up to him from the top of the stairs. "That one in the red coat is Lord—wait, I got it, *Seiji*. Shorter one is . . . yeah, I don't remember his name, but he's the Hero. And the rest of 'em didn't introduce themselves."

Gazmo lingered only long enough to give his apprentice a long, scathing look before turning his attention fully to us—specifically, after a quick glance around at the whole assembled crew, at me. His reddish-orange eyes looked me up and down before he spoke.

"Rizz says you've got solid healing magic."

"I do. Who needs it?"

The Judge jerked his head once toward the stone-fronted building abutting the small plaza. "This way."

"Just a second, Judge," spluttered one of the goblins behind him—the best-dressed of them, who like Sneppit had dolled himself up in a gilt-trimmed approximation of Fflyr highborn styles, though his were an eye-gouging mismatch of red, purple, and yellow. "This is him, right? The matter I asked you—"

Gazmo turned a look on him that stopped him cold and made the other three goblins hovering nearby back up a step.

"In. A. Minute."

The well-dressed goblin swallowed heavily and nodded once, surreptitiously moving the piece of paper he'd been holding out behind his back. Gazmo held his gaze for a second longer before turning without another word to stalk into the building.

Fram pointed two fingers at her eyes, two at the rich-looking goblin, then back at her eyes, before following her boss with an exaggerated swagger. I liked Fram. I could already tell I was going to get tired of her *very* quickly, but for now, I liked her.

This structure was also goblin-sized, meaning I had to duck to get through the door, but at least I didn't have to bust out the magic lights on the inside. They had asauthec torches burning, which meant there was work going on in here that required the goblins to be able to read and/or distinguish color. It made sense, given that this space was currently serving as an infirmary.

"No need for a crowd," Gazmo said pointedly when Aster crouched and started to follow me in. I nodded at her and she shuffled back out, whereupon there came an immediate complaint from Flaethwyn, whom the others had to soothe. I ignored the byplay, fully occupied with the contents of the room.

Desks had been shoved against the wall and blankets laid out as improvised resting spaces. There were thirteen goblins in various states of injury laid out, ranging from bandaged and splinted to a couple who were unconscious and looked half-mummified.

Judge Gazmo turned and gave me a single expectant look, not bothering to say anything else.

"Okay," I said briskly, "any foreign objects embedded in flesh, or broken bones not properly set?"

"You mean, anything *basic* triage wouldn't have sorted out well before you sauntered in?" snapped a particularly sharp-faced goblin woman who had paused while mixing bottles of fluids to give me a piercing stare. "Not having big fancy magic doesn't make us incompetent. This guy is supposed to be the Dark Lord?"

I decided there were more important things to do than converse with snippy nurses.

Heal. Heal, Heal, Heal, Heal, Heal . . .

One pink flash after another, I set right every injured goblin in the space of seconds, and only then turned back to the woman with the alchemy set.

"Administering magical healing with something like that not tended to could make their injuries orders of magnitude worse. Which is why I *check* first, because I am *also* not incompetent. Yes, I'm the Dark Lord. Pleased to fuckin' meetcha."

For some damn reason, this made her relax and smile. "Good, that's good. I don't usually expect conscientiousness from butts."

"If anybody was *missing* anything, like digits or teeth, my spell won't fix that. Everything else should be taken care of."

"Really?" The nurse, looking skeptical, set down her bottles and trundled over to the nearest patient, who still seemed asleep. "It's all burns, one concussion, and two fractured limbs. How much could—"

"Holy shit!" exclaimed one of her erstwhile patients, who had already pulled off his bandages. "I'm fixed!"

"The hell you are!" she barked. "Your *skin* was off, there's no way—holy shit."

Even the sleeping goblins were rousing now, and the room was becoming steadily louder as the injured goblins discovered that they were all just regular goblins now.

"Let's not crowd the infirmary," I suggested to Gazmo.

"Mn," he grunted, turning with no further commentary and striding out.

"So, burns?" I said, following. "That must be a story."

"Fire Lance," he said tersely. "This location got hit by a team from Jadrak's forces, including a sorcerer. Fairly small, just a dozen warm bodies to back up the Blessed. Three dead, and we've got the rest secured. Seems they were counting on magic and threats to intimidate Goggin here into signing over his property." He jerked his head toward the expensively dressed goblin, who was hovering anxiously nearby but not venturing to intervene again. "He probably would've, too, if Fram and I hadn't got here first with some civilian volunteers. They weren't expecting determined resistance."

"I wouldn't—"

"Shut up, Goggin."

"You said you have prisoners," I said. "Did you take the Blessed alive?"

"We did."

"And . . . you're holding them? Successfully? You're *sure*?"

The Judge slowly tilted his head up so he could stare at me through narrowed eyes under the wide brim of his official hat. "You think I dunno my business, tallboy?"

Note to self: Don't expect any Judges to be impressed by the Dark Lord.

"*Well*, I'm sorry to step on your toes. Let me put it this way, Judge Gazmo—when you go to a new place and meet new people, do you find it pays to blithely assume everyone is trustworthy and competent?"

He stared at me a moment longer, and then finally I got a smile from him. It was just a brief shift of one side of his mouth, but I counted it.

"All right, fair enough. Yeah, we don't deal with Blessed often, but the basic procedures are known. We've got him tied hand and foot to disable gesturing and he's gagged. *You* may be able to cast silently with nothing but eye contact, but this chump is no Dark Lord. Immobilizing the hands and mouth is plenty for most sorcerers. Right, familiar?"

"He's right, boss," Biribo agreed, upon being directly addressed. "It'll be dangerous to assume that later, when we start dealing with more powerful Blessed, but for the kind of talent Jadrak is able to gather, it should be plenty."

"Would that work on Hoy, I wonder?"

"What difference does it make?" Yoshi asked. "It's not like we're taking that bastard alive."

"Typical Sanorite bloodlust," Fram said piously. "Ow!"

Gazmo had whacked her on the back of the legs with the haft of his polearm. "Is what we might ordinarily say, but we *do not* fuck around with Void witches. Hoy dies at the first opportunity, and anybody who's not down with it had better get outta the way."

"Agreed," I said and then turned to our newest acquaintance. "All right. You're Goggin, right? Since your cavern is secure, we can send a messenger back to Sneppit, and she'll send out personnel and materials to seal off the tunnel accesses to protect your Spirit. Free of charge; I talked her out of demanding any compensation. For the duration of the Goblin King crisis, that is."

"Wow, you got a freebie out of *Sneppit*?" Goggin was visibly impressed. "You really *are* the Dark Lord. Ahem! I appreciate that very much, my lord. And, under the auspices of Judge Gazmo, here, I would like to make you an offer of business."

He stepped forward and presented the sheet of paper from before, which I accepted. I didn't know what they were making their paper or ink out of, but it was none the worse for wear for being damp from the spray.

"This . . . is a contract," I said, quickly reading over the terse paragraphs. "Huh."

"The terms aren't to your liking, Lord Seiji?" Goggin asked nervously.

He was basically offering me access to use his Spirit once now, and again at my discretion for the duration of my reign as Dark Lord, provided I allowed him to continue carrying out business as he had been.

"I'm just surprised. There's no legalese, no fine print . . ."

"We're not *Fflyr*," Gazmo said with withering contempt. "No goblin Judge would validate a contract that wasn't clear, concise, and readily comprehensible to any layperson. Contracts are the embodiment of the trust between people that's necessary for a society to exist, not mechanisms for assholes to exploit each other."

Funny how, after all this time, I'd finally found people on this barbaric world who'd worked out how to do something not only as well as the Japanese but arguably *better*, and they weren't even human.

"The contract I signed with Sneppit was more elaborate than this by far."

"*Sneppit* likes to push limits to the very verge of breaking," Gazmo retorted, curling his lip. "And I'm willing to bet she wanted a more complex deal than this, too."

"What's this Spirit of yours do, exactly?" I inquired. "Sneppit didn't get around to mentioning it; we were in a hurry to organize and deploy. I note that your contract doesn't say."

"Oh!" Goggin perked up at the chance to brag. "The Counter is one of the best spirits in Kzidnak! *The* best, in my opinion, not that I'm unbiased. But ahem, yes, it'll ask you to solve a puzzle, and if you do, it will tell you one piece of information that will lead you toward whatever it is that you most need."

Typical Goddess bullshit. Completely open-ended and impossible to verify, enabling them to grant any given petitioner as perfect or as crappy a reward as they felt like. Well, considering that Champions tended to get better rewards from Spirits and I even had a Wisdom perk for that, this did indeed sound like it was worth my while.

"Your terms are reasonable," I agreed. "I'd like to add something, however."

"Of course," Goggin said, nodding. Either he knew better than to try screwing over the Dark Lord, or this was expected in goblin contract negotiations. Probably both.

"In addition to me, I'd like to let Yoshi have a go at your Spirit."

That caused a ripple of visible astonishment from everybody except the tallfolk I'd brought down here with me. In particular, Pashilyn's eyes felt like they were burning a hole through my head.

"Really?" Yoshi asked, blinking at me. Ironically, he seemed less surprised than his friends.

"You wanna . . . *help* the *Hero*?" Fram demanded, tilting her head so far to the left it looked like her neck must be in pain.

"Yoshi's good people," I said. "Besides . . . Look, I wouldn't say the Sanorites came down here with the *best* of intentions, but they've been helpful *and* quite reasonable, once the situation was explained to them. I thought the reality on this world was that we all put aside our differences and cooperate when there's Void shit that needs to be put down, right?"

"That's right," Gazmo said, nodding once.

"Well, we've fought Hoy once and it was a draw. That's me and the Hero *both*, and we didn't manage to finish him off. And that's just Hoy—we haven't seen this devil in person, and still have no idea what kind of Void craft Jadrak's using himself. I'm not shy about wanting my strongest ally here to be as prepared as possible to finish this."

"Mm . . ." Gazmo turned a long, skeptical look on Yoshi, eyeing him up and down, before nodding once more. "Sensible. I think it's a good idea, Goggin."

"I mean," Goggin hedged, "you know how it is with Spirits. I have to limit access, if it gets overworked it'll start to—"

"I think," Gazmo enunciated *very* precisely, turning his head in a slow arc to pin Goggin with his stare, "it is a good idea. *Goggin*."

The Spirit's owner opened his mouth, closed it, swallowed, and smiled weakly up at me. "Aha . . . well. Let me just scribble that in, shall I? Pleasure doing business."

24

In Which the Dark Lord Gets Schooled

I *almost* signed a document without checking all the details, I'll admit that, but I did pull it out of the fire at the last second.

"So, this business I'm authorizing you to continue under my hypothetical future rule," I said, pausing the wrapped ink stick a centimeter above the damp paper I had placed against the wall to add my signature to Goggin's, "it's *just* the Spirit? That pays for all this?"

Judge Gazmo snorted loudly, and I lifted the . . . let's just call it a pencil for simplicity's sake.

"Is there a problem?" Goggin asked nervously.

"Somebody wanna let me in on the joke?" I looked from him to Gazmo and back.

"Well, I mean . . . owning this property has a couple of benefits," Goggin said, dry-washing his hands now. Well, as dry as he could considering we were all being lightly misted by the waterfall. "The Spirit, yes, but the core of my business is the water."

Yoshi inhaled sharply. "You . . . control the water source."

"*A* water source," Goggin corrected. "One of the better ones on this part of the island, in fact!"

"Omura, are you *sure* you want to endorse this?" Yoshi asked.

"Less so with every passing second."

"What? What's the issue?" Goggin exclaimed. "I'm a respectable businessman."

Nazralind snorted. "Ah yes, the rallying cry of every *ow*! Dammit, Aster, not the instep!"

"I dunno what you two're envisioning, but it's probably not that," Gazmo stated, stepping in before this went any further off the rails. "Water rights in Kzidnak don't work like Fflyr nobles handle 'em, much less . . . wherever you're from. Owning a water source is a *steady* income, because everybody needs water, but not a *high* income because there's a lot of overhead involved and you can only charge so much. Gotta keep the source clean and flowing, and keep prices down."

"Ahh." I nodded. "Because the Judges shut down overcharging?"

This time it was Fram who let out the loud snort. "Oh, I *wish*. I *never* get to stab anybody. What's the point of carrying these big-ass worm stickers if we never stab anybody? That's what *I* wanna know."

"*I* wanna know what table in the revels of Hell you crawled off of, you bloodthirsty little spiner," Gazmo growled. "Look, the last time I heard about Judges having to intervene in a case of water gouging, it was to try to find out who made the gouger disappear, and they never did. Goblins hate resorting to force as a rule, *despite* the impression Jadrak and my miserable excuse for an apprentice are probably giving you. *But*, there's not a goblin alive who doesn't know what it's like to be desperate enough to do something they hate. If you live in a society of creative problem solvers, you learn not to make yourself a problem. Water puts food on Goggin's table; the Spirit's what puts those fancy drapes on his green carcass."

I hefted the pencil, considering. "As long as I'm not being made a party to depriving people . . ."

"We're not Fflyr," Goggin protested with a frown.

"You know, I'm starting to take offense at that," said Aster. "Every mean thing you think about Fflyr is mostly just highborn."

Flaethwyn opened her mouth, then closed it when Pashilyn placed a hand on her shoulder.

"It's not the highborn who throw things at us for daring to walk on their streets," Gazmo stated, staring at Aster. For what might have been the first time since I'd known her, she seemed caught without a response, averting her eyes after a second. "*Anyway*. If that assuages your concerns, Dark Lord, wanna move this along?"

I still had . . . questions. But practically, if I waited to fully understand the nuances before committing to anything, I would never get anywhere. I'd just have to do my best and deal with whatever consequences arose.

I added my signature under Goggin's and handed the contract and pencil over to Judge Gazmo. He paused, peering at the English characters, then glanced up at me, but finally shrugged and added his own signature as witness. I guess a foreign writing system wasn't a dealbreaker. He should be glad I was in the habit of spelling it that way, instead of using kanji.

I'd developed that habit purely because it pissed off my dad.

"Perfect! Delighted to be in business, Lord Seiji!" Goggin said, apparently sincere now that he had my name in ink. "Well, then—this way, ah, gentlemen. Let's get you some Spirit action!"

"Hot," Fram commented, then dodged a swipe from Gazmo's staff.

"Right, so I guess we'll just . . . stand around out here, then," Flaethwyn said stridently, folding her arms.

"Nazralind," I called as we followed Goggin deeper into the stone structure, "keep Flaethwyn entertained."

"Why do *I* have to?!"

"What does *that* mean?!"

"That was just cruel," Yoshi muttered to me while we passed into dimness and out of the spray, and the growing argument. "Now everybody has to deal with two shouting elves."

"Well, hey." I grinned at him. "I *am* the Dark Lord."

"So, needless to say, we can't give any answers to the Spirit's question," Goggin explained, leading us through the carved-out hall that gradually turned into an apparent natural tunnel. He seemed more animated in general now that he was back on familiar ground, so to speak. "You *can* leave the Spirit's presence to work on your challenge and come back later with the solution—*but*, be aware that it *will* know if someone gave you the answer and will refuse to speak with you further. Management isn't responsible for any loss of reward due to failure to abide by the Spirit's terms. With all that established! As a secondary service, for an extremely reasonable fee, my accountant can provide limited assistance in *finding* your answer."

"Your . . . accountant?" Yoshi asked. "Wait, what kinds of questions is it going to ask?"

"Oh, you'll see," Goggin said cheerily. "Again, no solutions will be given, but if you're unfamiliar with the process itself—many are—we can coach you on it. Now, ordinarily customers visit the Spirit one at a time, but, ah . . . Well, you two seem willing to share. Just keep in mind the rules. Don't help each other with the answers and it shouldn't object."

"Okay," I said, beginning to be apprehensive about this.

He led us through two locked doors, the keys to which he produced, and finally stopped at a third, which he opened with a flourish. "And here we are, gents. Take as much time as you need, and remember, assistance is available for a very fair and *reasonable* surcharge!"

Goggin gently eased himself back through the door after we stepped through, slinking around in such a way that his grin disappeared last, a second before he closed it.

"He says that, but we'd probably better make this as quick as we can," said Yoshi.

"I agree. And not just because that guy and his 'reasonable fee' make me suspicious as hell."

"Oh good, I'm glad it wasn't just me."

We were locked in the Spirit's cavern, which was much smaller than the one back at Jadrak's place, but also much nicer. There wasn't a lot of room to maneuver around the Spirit altar itself; this was less cramped than Head Start's enclosure, but I got the distinct impression the Goddesses had put this thing here expecting it to be visited by goblins, and only one at a time. Still, it had the prettiest environs of any Spirit I'd encountered yet—horizontal khora roots made flat ledges around the dome-shaped room that were decorated with moss, and more of those leafy hanging vines hung from some of the higher ones, as well as partially obscuring the opening in the ceiling through which sunlight filtered in. There was a soft burble of water from a stream that ran in through one crack in the wall and out another. Even the air smelled damp and clean, with the pleasant scent of earth and leaves.

We barely had time to take in the view before the Spirit was activated by our presence, pale light igniting along the grooves in its altar and the glowing, translucent face appearing above. This one was female—or at least feminine—the stylized features accented by lines around the eyes and mouth to suggest maturity.

"*Now this I don't see every day,*" the Spirit stated by way of greeting. "*A Champion of the Goddess, occasionally, sure—always the high point of my century, especially as it's been nearly a millennium since one wandered down here. But both at once! You two must surely be on your way to building a truly incredible story.*"

"Uh—it's nice to meet you," said Yoshi, reflexively bowing. "We'll be in your care."

"*And so polite! That's already an improvement over . . . several recent Heroes. So I hear, anyway.*"

"Yeah, that guy Hara sounds like he was a piece of work," I agreed. "Well! Good to meet you and all, but we don't have a lot of time, here."

"*I have nothing but time,*" the Spirit replied with a cool little smile, "*but on the other hand, things such as I are not really made for small talk. Very well, boys, let's see what you're made of. Who's going first?*"

"Uh." Yoshi turned toward me. "Why don't—"

Oh, no you don't.

"After you, Hero," I said, bowing. "I insist."

He made a face, but turned back to the Spirit, rolling his shoulders. "All right, then, I guess it's me. Present me your challenge, Spirit!"

"*Less polite, but I appreciate the formality. So be it, then!*"

Her face disappeared, replaced by lines of glowing blue text. For a split second I felt excitement rising in me—I was looking at *code!* Here it was, I'd found it—a hint at the inner workings of the system!

"*Solve,*" the Spirit's voice echoed sententiously, "*for x.*"

Then, on second glance, I realized that I fully understood what I was seeing. It wasn't code. It was entirely familiar—a mix of Arabic numerals, Latin letters, and standard English punctuation, forming . . .

"Wait," Yoshi protested, blinking rapid. "That's—it's just—that's an *algebra* problem."

"Are you *fucking kidding* me?!" I yelled, causing him to wince and shy away from me. Okay, fair, it was a small stone room and the moss did little to dampen the echo. But *still.*

"*There is no shame if you're not up to the task, boys,*" said the disembodied voice in a tone too solemn to be anything but mocking. "*Many are those who fail a Spirit's challenge. More than those who succeed and are rewarded.*"

"Well, now we know why it's the *accountant* who's available to help with this," said Yoshi.

There came the disembodied sound of a throat being cleared, which was pretty wild from an artificial entity that didn't have one of those.

"*I'll know if you cheat.*"

"Yeah, that's what the goblin said. So, wait . . . hang on." Yoshi leaned toward the glowing math notation, narrowing his eyes. "This should be . . . I wonder if the order of operations is the same as what we were taught on Earth. Am . . . I allowed to ask that?"

"*You are, and it is.*"

"How do *you* know what's taught on Earth?" I demanded.

"What the Goddesses know, the Spirits know. The limit is in what we are allowed to tell—which is little, and lest you be afflicted with clever ideas, will become even less if you try to pry. The Sisters are spectacularly intolerant of others playing with their toys."

"Okay, this should be doable," Yoshi murmured, now frowning at the problem. "This is just . . . well, it's high school level math, at most. If it was something like calculus or trigonometry we'd be screwed, but we should be able to do this."

"Are you serious? Look at the *size* of that thing!"

"Really, though, that just creates busy work," he said reasonably. "Math is math. If you just do the operations in their proper order . . . Oh, man, that's going to be a lot to remember. I should've asked the goblins for something to write on. And with. If I'd known . . ."

"He would've charged you for it." I fished in the inner pocket of my coat, after a moment pulling out a small notepad of stiff paper bound by a simple leather cord, and one of the wrapped ink sticks the Fflyr used as pencils. "Here."

Yoshi blinked at my offering before taking it. "Why do you have . . ."

"Because they're handy to have, easily pocket-sized, and one of the *few* positive things about this country is you can get materials to read or write with basically everywhere."

"Thanks, Omura! Right, then, with *this* I think we're in business!"

Well, at least somebody was happy.

I have to hand it to the boy, he buckled down to concentrate and seemed to be making good progress, to judge by his constant scratching. There are few things in creation more boring than watching other people do math problems, though, so after just a couple of minutes I casually sauntered around to the opposite side of the Spirit, as far from Yoshi as I could get in the cramped little cave.

"Hey, Biribo." I pitched my voice barely above a whisper so as not to disturb the Hero. He was fully occupied with his homework, anyway.

"Boss?" My ever-perceptive familiar replied in the same volume right at my ear, the buzz of his wings louder than his voice.

"How come the Hero over there always yells his spell names? I thought silent casting was a Champion perk."

Biribo flicked out his tongue at me, which at that range meant I came a lot closer than I liked to being licked. "Where'd you get that idea?"

"Well, I mean . . . I can do it, and everybody seems real impressed by that. Why else would I be able to?"

To my surprise, Radatina joined the conversation, buzzing over to us and fortunately having the discretion to also pitch her voice as low as possible. To judge by her tone, she was probably just huffy that we were talking about Yoshi behind his back.

"Silent casting has nothing to do with magical power; it's a trick of concentration. Casting spells is mentally difficult, no matter your capacity; voicing and gestures help focus the effort. Some people just have surprising talents, *Lord* Seiji, and you happen to be one. That's probably why Virya picked you. Partly, at least."

"It's a lot less random than that," Biribo disagreed. "It's not a guarantee, but the trick of silent casting *is* associated with a performing arts background. You're already used to executing complex mental and physical tasks on demand and under stress; those are skills that translate well to mental work."

". . . huh. So . . . Yoshi *can* learn it, though?"

"Anyone can. It's just pretty hard, if you don't happen to have the knack. He can probably learn it faster than most people could, since—despite what pixie wings here claims—having more power *does* make a difference. It's easier to cast spells if you've got bottomless energy, and that frees up your mental resources to improve your technique."

"Hmm." I had to wonder, sometimes, whether the day would ever come when I really understood all the ins and outs of this magic system full of arbitrary bullshit. Probably not; it was pretty clearly designed to prevent anybody but the Goddesses from knowing how to pull all the levers.

It took him a good ten minutes; that was an intimidatingly long and convoluted problem. I was not optimistic about my own chances, but there was nothing to do about it at the moment except try to distract myself. Fortunately, Yoshi was too preoccupied and the familiars too oblivious to the implications, so nobody made fun of me for humming softly and playing air guitar.

You gotta do what you gotta do.

"*X* equals three!" Yoshi suddenly declared. He looked downright triumphant in that moment, but immediately wilted, uncertainty overtaking his features. ". . . right?"

The pause was momentary, but entirely unnecessary. Just there to drag out the suspense. I approved on principle, even knowing I was going to feel differently about it when it was my turn.

"*Correct,*" the Spirit finally declared. The equation dissolved back into the cartoonish face, which smiled at him. "*Well done, Hero. When you are looking back over the course of your life and tallying the great victories you achieved . . . I suspect you will not even recall this one. But a win is a win—and a reward is a reward. One answer will I give you, one piece of guidance to bring you directly to what it is you most need. So let me ask you first—and you, Dark Lord—what truth do you desire? An answer to help you out of your current predicament? Or, perhaps, a more distant, final piece of advice to resolve your ultimate purpose on this world?"*

Unconsciously, at least on my part, our eyes met. For a second, Yoshi and I stared at each other. Thinking.

Then we both looked away.

Son of a bitch, that was a good play. *Maybe* on the part of the Spirit; maybe the Counter was just as puckish as Head Start and slyer, but come on. This was *such* a Goddess move. One or the other of them—or both—were here putting a finger on the scales, as they always did. Making sure the Hero and the Dark Lord were forced to remember that ultimately, this ended with the two of us on opposite ends of a sword.

If they got their way.

"Destinies are created, not foretold," I stated, my voice firm but calm. Yeah, if there was ever a moment for showtime, this was it. "I am *not* going to do what I was brought to this stupid world to do, and I'm not interested in being told how best to dance to Virya's tune. I'll take all the help I can get sorting out this Void and goblin mess, but when it comes down to the final resolution?"

Yoshi and the Spirit had both turned their heads to study me now. I felt my upper lip begin to curl in a reflexive sneer of resentment, and I let it. Right now, a little emotional honesty suited my message.

"Don't fucking tell me what to do."

That's right, Spirit, you overplayed your hand. Calling me out, as well as Yoshi, to draw attention to how this would affect our ultimate relationship may have helped drive that point home, but it also gave me the opportunity to talk back. If it hadn't specifically asked for my opinion, me butting in would have seemed overbearing and manipulative.

In fact . . .

"But that's just me," I said, deliberately moderating my tone. "It's your answer, Yoshi; you should ask for the one that's right for you. Don't worry about our immediate problem if you're more concerned about the future. I bet my answer will give us enough guidance to pull this out."

"You haven't earned an answer yet, Dark Lord," the Spirit reminded me with a pleasant little smile, the smug fucker.

"I think . . . me, too," Yoshi said slowly. His expression firmed up, though, and he gave the Spirit a resolute nod. "I'm going to continue to grow as I work toward the future. If anything, I'm worried that knowing too much too far ahead will cause me to develop myself into something I can't take pride in. I already have all this power . . . Having too much handed to me without earning it isn't the way to be a Hero. And let's face it, solving math problems doesn't have much to do with earning wisdom. Uh, no offense. So please tell me how I can best help defeat the Goblin King."

"It's not good to get tunnel vision, boys," the Counter said with a wink, *"but you show good sense, just the same. The Void is everyone's problem, especially yours. Very well, Hero, your answer is this: Trust."*

Yoshi blinked twice. "That . . . that's it?"

"You are . . . underwhelmed?" Yeah, this fucking AI or whatever it was definitely took some kind of pleasure in teasing us. I recognized that tone; it sounded way too much like my first girlfriend. *"Tell me, Shinonome Yoshi, have you not been troubled by the question of whom you should trust? As you journey with friends whose loyalties and agendas you do not fully know? Alongside a Dark Lord whose personality challenges your every effort to discern his true nature, among goblins who are both your sworn enemies and more relatable friends than you could have anticipated? Were I you, Hero, the question of trust would predominate my mind."*

Yoshi had shuffled back against the wall and lowered his head; whether intentionally or not, it caused the indirect lighting in this little cavern to cast shadows across his face that made his expression impossible to read.

"And so I give you the answer you have earned. Soon enough, young Hero, your adventures will take you beyond the borders of Dount, into a wider and more uncertain world. Here, though, you have been given the rare blessing of stalwart companions. You will know your enemies, because they will declare themselves such, and those who offer you their faith will repay yours. Take this time, Shinonome-san, to learn from them. You have friends who can teach you how to handle those who conceal their intentions. Take comfort in the companionship of all those who willingly stand beside you, while you are here. They will not betray you."

A heavy silence stifled the little chamber. Yoshi looked up at me, then hastily averted his eyes.

"I . . ."

"Good lad," the Counter said happily. *"All right, Omura Seiji. Solve for x."*

Her face dissolved into another pile of numbers and letters.

I inhaled deeply and let the air out slowly. "Yoshi, I'm gonna need my notebook back."

Half an hour later, they must've been going berserk waiting for us out there.

"See, if you—"

"Don't help him!" both familiars shouted, interrupting Yoshi's well-meaning suggestion.

"*No cheating, boys,*" the Spirit chided. "*You need not solve the problem right here in front of me, Dark Lord. Perhaps if you would come back when it is more convenient . . .*"

"All of you shut up!" I barked. "Fuck's *sake*, I haven't had a math class in *years*! I *remember* how to do this; it's just not as fresh for me. Nobody uses algebra in real life after high school!"

"Well, musicians don't," Yoshi said. "I think engineers use way more complicated math than that . . ."

"That's extremely helpful, Yoshi, thank you. Any more pearls of wisdom you'd care to cast before me?"

"I'll just . . . stand over here," he mumbled, edging back toward the door.

I was close, hence my annoyance. This was taking me so much longer because I was being *thorough*. I had gone through multiple pages in my notebook solving the bonkers-ass equation, because I was making *damn sure* I got it right, and that meant doing it multiple times to ensure I got the same solution every time.

This had proved important because the first two attempts had produced wildly different answers.

I was on number five now, though; my last two solutions had matched up. If I got the same this time . . .

Slowly I inhaled, staring down at my notepad, then raised my eyes to stare at the floating equation.

"*X* equals seven."

The numbers disappeared, replaced by the Spirit's smiling expression.

"*Are you certain of that?*"

It was trying to psych me out. Drawing out the drama, like a cheap reality show.

"I'm certain." I did not look over at Yoshi, in case he was nodding or something and the Spirit took that as an excuse to disqualify me for cheating.

Its smile widened by a fraction, and then by another. *Motherfucker, as soon as I crack this Blessing system open I am gonna come back here and find a way to* solidify *your face so I can* punch *it*—

"*Correct,*" the Counter finally decreed. "*Congratulations, Lord Seiji; you are a well-educated man. One's skills may rust, but they remain there, ready to be oiled up. Remember that.*"

"That had *better* not be my reward answer. Christ on a bike, I cannot believe I had to solve a *math problem* in a *cave* to get a magic reward. This is the most random-ass arbitrary RPG bullshit—"

"*You do still want your reward, correct?*" the Spirit said innocently. "*I seem to recall you were in something of a hurry.*"

"Well, spit it out, then!"

"*I am happy to be of service. Your strategy, Lord Seiji, is to secure the other Spirits of Kzidnak before they can be corrupted by the Goblin King or his chief lackey. Obviously, I applaud this. You will not succeed or reach them all in time, however. This is the answer I provide you, to your question of how to defeat the Goblin King: When you confront Hoy again, if it is over a Spirit altar he is in the process of corrupting, attack unrelentingly. Regardless of the odds, or your planned strategy—regardless of any other factors, regardless even of whether you win or lose. Press the attack over the breaking Spirit altar, and you will gain what you need, even if it costs you the fight.*"

I narrowed my eyes to slits. "I don't suppose there's any point in asking whether you're just telling me this in an attempt to save one of your buddies."

"*One can always ask questions, and should,*" replied the Spirit, smiling beatifically. "*One is not always entitled to an answer, however. Good luck, Champions. I'm rooting for you both.*"

She vanished, face disappearing and the lights fading from her altar as it powered down. We were left standing alone in the silence and the leaf-filtered distant sunlight.

"I hate this planet," I declared, staring upward at nothing. "I just . . . I hate it. So very, very much."

"You wanna get outta here?" Yoshi offered.

"God, yes."

25

In Which the Dark Lord's Personnel Decisions Come Under Scrutiny

We could tell how badly our various companions were coping with the wait even as we walked down the hall. Even so, I was surprised to emerge from the door onto the mist-soaked platform and find the sounds of complaining and scuffling were caused by Nazralind holding Flaethwyn in a headlock.

"*What* is *wrong* with you?!" Flaethwyn was squalling as we arrived.

I glanced swiftly around, verifying from the amused and/or resigned expressions of the humans and goblins standing around watching this that there was not an actual crisis.

"Come on, Nazralind, you can't mess up a lady's coiffure," I said sternly. "Just because *you* style yourself with spit and a stiff breeze doesn't mean you don't know better. Let's all pretend to be civilized, yeah?"

Naz blew a raspberry at me, but relented, allowing Flaethwyn to jerk loose and skitter away from her. One hand went to her hair, the other to the handle of her rapier.

"You degenerate *idiot*!" she snarled. "Do you have crawns in your *brain*? What could possibly possess a person to go so *utterly daft*?! Your parents should have tossed you down a well!"

"*There* we go," Nazralind said with an expression of pure, calm satisfaction. "I'm surprised it took that level of goading to break you out of that misplaced formality, but we got there in the end and that's what matters. Now we can all just be adventurers together and not worry about high society crap that none of us actually care about. It's nice to finally meet you, Flaethwyn."

The other elf stared at her, utterly gobsmacked. The fact that half her hair was still sticking up out of place only made it funnier. Pashilyn stepped in and began gently brushing Flaethwyn's golden locks back into place with her hands before the elf could think of anything else to say, or more likely, yell.

"Right, well, anyway," said Judge Gazmo. "You two took your time. Had fun in there?"

"Not fucking really," I said.

"But it was worth it," Yoshi added. "Sorry to keep you waiting, everyone. We got . . . some good answers." He gave me a loaded glance.

"Cool," Gazmo grunted. "Then let's not waste any more time; we gotta keep moving forward. Jadrak's sure as shit not sitting still. C'mere."

He turned and stalked off with no more ado, leaving us to follow. Fram sauntered along, positioning herself beside me and giving me a big grin. I didn't read anything into that; she clearly just enjoyed being a large personality.

Gazmo brought us to another structure adjacent to the main platform, this one free standing and made of sheet metal, close enough to the falls that the noise sounded like constant rain on a roof. With a couple of terse phrases, he directed me to follow him in and Fram to guard the door. Apparently he didn't want us to be interrupted.

Inside, six armed goblins were standing watch over ten who were bound with a mismatch of ropes and chains; one also had a gag and was more heavily secured than the others. He turned a particularly venomous glare on us at our entry, though none of them looked happy to see us.

"Well?" Gazmo turned to me and slung his polearm across his shoulders. "What's your verdict?"

He was asking *me*?

"My verdict on . . . ?"

"Don't act dumb; I know you're not. These are Jadrak's followers who attacked this business, damaged property, and injured people. You're the Dark Lord; what do you wanna do with 'em?"

I was *not* dumb, which was how I knew he was both testing me to see how I'd handle situations like this and also lightening his own workload. Fram was fun; Gazmo was beginning to get under my skin.

"You're the Judge," I deflected. "How would you normally handle offenses like this?"

"Normally, offenses like *this* don't happen. *Normally*, goblins aren't prone to violence. The basic principle underpinning our judgments are that anyone who wrongs anyone else owes the wronged party restitution of roughly equivalent value to the injury inflicted. In a largely barter-based economy without any jails, the exact form that takes depends very much on the individual case. Worst thing we do is with people who repeatedly offend and absolutely refuse to get along in goblin society. That's exile. Which in practical terms is a death sentence, being frank. A goblin alone doesn't last long on the surface of Dount. Beast tribes know that goblin exiles are bad news, and Fflyr just murder them for being goblins on the surface. But, it's established in precedent that the rise of a Goblin King and the rise of a Dark Lord are two things which suspend all our normal ways of doing things. So, here we are."

"What happens when there's no possible restitution for a crime?"

"Then everybody involved has a real bad day."

"Suppose you actually answer the question, since I could use the perspective if you expect me to pass judgment on goblins—"

"These situations are unique, is what I'm tellin' you. In a case like that, the Judge has a bad day because those are the hardest to decide, the victim has a bad day cos there's no reasonable way of gettin' what's owed them, and the guilty party . . . well. You know."

He turned toward me, shifting his grip on the polearm to plant its butt on the floor with a metallic *thunk*.

"This is a situation our precedents don't cover, except to defer authority to potentially Jadrak or you, depending on who comes out on top. Which just means you, because I'm not taking any orders from a damn Void witch. So I'll ask you again, Dark Lord. What's your verdict?"

A lot of the imprisoned goblins began shouting all at once, which created a deafening noise in the metal shed. Amid the jumble of voices I was just able to make out one theme—disbelief.

"—lying pawn of—"

"—so desperate to discredit—"

"—King Jadrak would never—"

"—Void witch my green ass, you—"

Windburst.

I cast it at the walls over their heads rather than knock anybody down, but in that confined space the intensity of it nearly did anyway. The walls shook, but the fast-moving air had nowhere to go except around; it took a second for the backdrafts to settle enough that the goblins were able to raise their heads again.

"Quiet," I ordered.

"Impressive," Gazmo said, his disdainful tone at odds with the praise. "Well?"

Being put on the spot like this might've been bad for me, except for one thing—just because he didn't have a precedent for this situation did not mean I didn't. In fact, I had already made almost this exact judgment with regard to Rads and his miners just yesterday. Now that I thought about it, Rizz knew that and I doubted she had concealed it from Gazmo. So what was he playing at here?

"Keep them confined until the Goblin King has been dealt with. These people are just trying to improve their lives and were misled by a charlatan. What we're trying to do is restore sanity, not butcher more goblins. Far too many have died already. After the war is over, they can go back to their lives."

The Judge grunted. "And how's that address the damages they've caused to others?"

"You say the Dark Lord's will overrides your precedents? Well, fine, here it is—if I have a problem with the way goblins do things, I'll tell you so specifically. Mostly, I've been positively impressed down here. If anybody has a case to press against anyone else over anything that happened, after this is all settled they can bring it before a Judge as normal. You'll have my authority to back you up on that, if you're concerned you'll need it."

"Mm." Gazmo regarded me with narrowed eyes, his mouth going slightly crooked as he silently shifted his jawbone. As if he was carefully chewing a response before spitting it out. "All right. For now, I suppose that'll do. Then let's—"

"Oh wait, though," I said, turning back to the row of imprisoned Jadrak partisans. "With one exception. This is our sorcerer, right?"

"You see anybody else gagged? I told you he was."

"You're pleasant, you know that?" I informed the Judge with a smile. "Just a real enjoyable fella to chat with. Could somebody ungag him for a moment, please?"

Gazmo just tilted his head to one side to regard me quizzically, but the guards exchanged a round of apprehensive glances.

"Uh," one ventured, "are you sure . . ."

"If he could cast by line of sight alone I doubt you'd have gotten that thing on him in the first place. Anyway, relax; I have this under control."

It wasn't empty bravado; I could Heal anything Fire Lance could do, even at this range; that spell was all agony and very little stopping power. Like my Immolate, but slower to hit and less elegant. Just to be sure, I strode forward until I was looming over the bound goblin sorcerer, then knelt to bring my eyeline closer to his. Making myself the target would buy me ample time to shut him down if it turned out he could cast without gesturing; it always took new victims a second or two to be flummoxed that spells didn't work on me. God, I loved this artifact.

At any rate, that seemed to be enough reassurance. The guard who'd spoken up stepped forward and bent down, loosening the sorcerer's gag just enough to pull it down. He then stepped swiftly back.

"So," I said pleasantly, "am I to understand that you didn't know Jadrak is a devil-dealer?"

The goblin worked his jaw for a second, licking his lips to mitigate the taste of gag, then sneered at me.

"You must think you're pretty fuckin' clever, tallboy. Think you're so much smarter than us goblins. What, you reckon I'm dumb enough to just swallow whatever the hell you cough up? Of course we'll believe whatever ignorant fucking slander you have to say about the Goblin King. After all, you're the great and glorious Dark Lord and we're a bunch of stupid tunnel crawns. Right?"

"Well, you're clearly not the most iridescent jewel in the mine or you wouldn't be in this situation," I replied cheerfully, "but hey, you fell for the blandishments of a scheming politician. It's not something to be proud of, but I can't say it makes you stupid. Wiser people than myself have been taken in by less impressive manipulators than Jadrak. What matters right now is that you didn't know."

I stood up, dusting off my knees, and turned a broad grin on Gazmo, who looked kind of . . . sardonically apprehensive.

"All right! Judge, I have a special request for this one."

"Have you utterly lost your mind?!" Flaethwyn clapped a hand to her forehead. "What am I saying, of course you have. You're the Dark Lord!"

"So, anyway," I said, blithely ignoring her and turning to address my crew of new goblin recruits, "do any of you recognize this guy?"

Casually, I pointed at the bound sorcerer behind me. I was holding the chain, which was wrapped around the cords binding his wrists together. Behind his back, which was awkward, but also really the only feasible way to keep him secured and gagged since I had to leave his feet free, otherwise he couldn't walk. I could've attached a collar to his neck or something, but . . .

I instinctively bridled at the thought of inflicting that indignity. It was bad enough already.

The erstwhile members of Hoy's strike force peered at him, a few glancing at each other as if for confirmation. No apparent hits, however.

"We don't all know each other, y'know," Ritlit commented, grinning. The goblins had grown steadily more comfortable following me and were culturally predisposed to be outspoken, but most of them still seemed shy about drawing my personal attention to them in conversation. There were thus a couple of de facto "talkers" who evidently spoke for the group. Well, at least it spared me having to memorize more names I couldn't pronounce.

"Yeah, it was a long shot," I agreed. "Ah well."

Getting the gag off him again was a bit of a process, though I tried to be fast. It was important not to handle my prisoner too roughly, for the sake of my medium- and long-term plans here, but he sure didn't make himself easy to handle. Also, there were those sharklike teeth, and I'd already learned that a proud sorcerer of the Goblin King's army wasn't too dignified to snap at fingers. But I did get it loosened enough for him to talk, and withdrew my hands to safety before anything unfortunate happened.

"So, let's all introduce ourselves!" I suggested brightly. "What's your name, guy?"

"Get fucked," he said with a particularly vicious sneer.

Bad call, smartass.

"Hajimemashite! Everyone, this is our new friend Get Fucked. Get Fucked, this is everyone; you'll get to know names over time since we'll be traveling together. Now, I want us all to show Get Fucked here some good old Dark Crusade hospitality. That's the way to start off a healthy relationship, after all."

Getting the gag back on Get Fucked was ironically easier than getting it safely off. It helped that after every exchange with him I was a smidge less concerned about his personal comfort.

"To be entirely clear, Lord Seiji," said Aster, "what you are proposing is to add a prisoner to our group, while we are already in a race against Hoy to reach the Spirits. An extremely dangerous prisoner who is Blessed with Magic and fanatically opposed to us, who will thus require constant monitoring. Not to mention dealing with all the ways he'll try to slow us down on the way."

"Well summarized, Aster," I praised. She was certainly being more reasonable about it than Flaethwyn. Then again, a herd of stampeding wildebeests is more reasonable than Flaethwyn.

Aster drew in a steadying breath. "I assume you have a very good reason for suggesting this?"

"Of course I do."

"And . . . it's a reason you are able to articulate in terms that make sense to sane people?"

"Of course I can." I nodded. "But not right now, in front of everybody. Especially certain parts of everybody. I'm talking about Get Fucked himself, here. All of this will be settled faster than you expect, I assure you. For the time being, you'll simply have to trust me."

"Oh, where do I even begin?!" Flaethwyn shouted.

"You could try not starting, for once," Zui suggested, "just for a refreshing change of pace."

"We can trust him," Yoshi stated. Somehow, this actually shut Flaethwyn up, also drawing surprised stares from Pashilyn and Amell.

"Yoshi," Pashilyn began in a careful tone.

He had already colored slightly under this scrutiny, but set his jaw and continued, deliberately squaring his shoulders. Man, I found myself rooting for the kid; he'd started as the most hapless loser I'd ever met and been through some shit in the meantime, but damn if he wasn't doing his best, and managing impressively well, all things considered. It was downright inspiring.

"I'm not just being sentimental, Pashilyn. Honestly, I don't really know Omura any better than you; we never met before that day on the train platform."

"Japan's a big country," I added, nodding. "We don't all know each other."

"Hah! That's a callback!" Ritlit eagerly prodded the long-suffering goblin next to her with an elbow. "He callbacked me! Classic Dark Lord comedy."

"It was part of my answer from the Spirit," Yoshi explained, ignoring the goblin byplay that was ruining his moment. "We can trust the Dark Lord. At least, so long as we're still fighting together on Dount. Those were the terms it used."

Everyone paused at that, considering, most of them turning to stare speculatively at either Yoshi or myself. Get Fucked tugged experimentally at his chain; I flicked it like a horse's reins. He managed to sneer at me with just his eyes, which honestly was just impressive.

"He tampered with the Spirit, somehow," Flaethwyn muttered, but we could all tell her heart wasn't in it.

"He can't," said Radatina. "Only a Void witch or devil can tamper with a Spirit, and not even all of them. Even if the Void recognizes the Dark Lord, that doesn't mean he knows how to do anything with it—you saw what happened when we encountered it accidentally. And anything anybody could do to mess with a Spirit's functions would've been super obvious. Even Yoshi would have been able to tell, and don't forget, there were two familiars right there watching. The Spirit's reward was legitimate; if it said we can trust Lord Seiji, at least for now, then . . . there it is."

For some reason, that made Flaethwyn even angrier, but at least she was quiet about it this time. The elf turned her back on us, clenching her fists at her sides so hard it made her shoulders tremble.

"So," Zui said loudly, "our next destination is at least a few hours' walk from here. The only tram line that could've taken us there is confirmed down; the nearest we could use would involve backtracking to Sneppit's depot and then riding to a point distant enough that it ultimately wouldn't save us any time."

"It's another Spirit, right?" said Adelly. "For those of us who weren't privy to the secret strategy meeting, is that gonna be another potential advantage for us?"

"You mean another long session of sitting on our thumbs?" Nazralind asked, grinning. "Anyway, don't sweat missing the planning sessions; those are always excruciatingly boring."

"I can explain the details as we go, if you're really curious, but the short version is the next Spirit's challenge is a lot longer and more convoluted, and its reward isn't really applicable to any of our current problems," Zui said impatiently. "So no, we just need to bolster the goblins holding it and make sure Hoy doesn't corrupt the damn thing. Hopefully that won't take nearly as long as this stop; speaking of which . . . ?"

"Right, we'd better get moving," I agreed. "Judge Gazmo, it's been a pleasure. I trust you've got everything handled here."

"Trust otherwise, tallboy," he said. "I'm comin' with you."

I blinked. "Uh . . . Sorry, but I thought—"

"We're movin' out anyway. I was gonna take the girl on a more round-about path to check up on some other folks sheltering in the area, but after gettin' an eyeful of your latest big idea, I think I'd best tag along and make sure this doesn't go any worse than it's obviously already going to."

He turned a baleful look on Get Fucked, who scowled right back over his gag. Despite the sorcerer's inauspicious conditions, I had to give him credit; he didn't seem the least bit intimidated. That's exactly the kind of sheer, relentless, life-affirming spite I aspire to. He was gonna be a great addition to the party, I just knew it.

"Then you reckon everything here is secure without you?" I prompted. "I mean no offense to our host, of course . . ."

I nodded politely at Goggin, who was lurking around the periphery, watching the ongoing conversation without involving himself directly, now that he had what he wanted from me.

"Goggin's a sniveling invertebrate who'll roll over the second the likes of Jadrak even looks at him too directly," said Gazmo.

"Hey!" Goggin protested.

"But," the Judge continued, "he's not cruel or any greedier than the average boss, and I don't generally worry about people working under him. With Sneppit's security forces coming to bolster his spine, things here should be settled. Especially since she won't back down unless it's strategically necessary, even if Goggin wants to. Zui's right, we'd better not waste any more time here."

"Well, you all heard the Judge," Adelly said brightly, bracing the Lightning Staff against her shoulder. "Our path's that tunnel over there, right? Ikuzo!"

She started off, Nazralind immediately falling into step behind her.

Yoshi slowly turned a wide-eyed stare on me.

"Omura . . ."

"I'll handle it," I promised, and then strode off after the girls before he could ask me any questions for which I didn't have answers, which in that moment was probably all of them.

26

In Which the Dark Lord Receives a Delivery

Yoshi was trying, bless him.

"So, that's a cool artifact, uh . . . It's Adelly-san, right?"

She gave him an inquisitive look. "It's Lord Seiji's, he took it from some criminals who were trying to . . . it's a long story. I'm just using it. More importantly, what did you call me?"

"Oh, I'm sorry," Yoshi said hastily, "I must've misheard your name. Fflyr is really hard for me to pronounce, so I still mess up details sometimes."

"No, you got it right," I said. "She means the honorific. In Japanese you append those to everyone's name unless you're on really intimate terms with someone or trying to insult them. 'San' is the default one; it just connotes basic politeness."

In fact, I thought it was odder that Yoshi was still doing that and having trouble with pronunciation. So was I—so would any reasonable person. Fflyr was a preposterous nightmare language full of non-Euclidean consonants run through a blender.

"I have never *once* heard you use that," said Aster.

I turned while walking to give her a wide, sweet smile.

She sighed. "Yeah, that tracks."

In the somewhat awkward silence that followed, I glanced over at our prisoner. Aster was walking behind him, keeping his bound hands in her view at all times; Adelly was in front, currently holding the rope tied to him. Flaethwyn had also nominated herself to stride alongside the goblin with her rapier out, conveniently within stabbing range but out of his much shorter reach. I'd decided to leave that alone, since she didn't seem about to launch a preemptive execution, and if she did, Aster was capable of dealing with it.

Currently, Ritlit was strolling alongside Get Fucked, chattering merrily away. He kept glancing at her sidelong over his gag; his expression, what I could see of it, vacillated between annoyed and worried. Just behind him, next to Aster, Maizo caught my eye and nodded, winking.

Good, that was proceeding according to plan. I *really* liked working with goblins. Maizo and Zui at the very least had picked up on what I was doing without needing to be told, and I suspected that Ritlit had as well. It was a little hard to tell, as she could also just be babbling on because that was what she did.

Though his initial effort had gone awry, Yoshi did not give up. You had to admire the tenacity.

"If you don't mind my asking, how'd you end up working with Omu—with Lord Seiji, uh, Miss Adelly? Not to pry or anything, I'm just curious. I've found that people with Blessings always have interesting stories to tell."

She gave him another skeptical look. "Mm-hmm. You looking to fish out the details of Lord Seiji's operation, Hero?"

Yoshi flushed and opened his mouth in preparation to stammer apologies, but then deliberately inhaled and steadied himself. Honestly, I was more and more impressed with the kid. In addition to getting in better shape, he had clearly been doing his best to train up those social skills.

"Of course I would never try to put you on the spot like that. I apologize if I gave that impression. I'm just trying to . . . broaden my understanding, since if there's one thing I've learned here in Kuzidnak, it's that I'm missing a lot of context for life outside of . . . what I've seen so far, in Dlemathlys."

"Kzidnak," Zui corrected.

I took note of Yoshi's companions staring at him now—Amell worriedly, Flaethwyn with seething intensity, and Pashilyn with an expression so performatively blank I could practically hear the gears turning.

"Right, sorry."

"Well, sure, since you asked," Adelly said, putting on a broad smile. "I was in the King's Guild and was lucky enough to get Blessed. Then my luck ran out; I couldn't keep food on the table, and I ended up as a whore. That satisfy your curiosity?"

Yoshi went bright red again, but continued valiantly to control himself, until managing a polite tone. "Ah, I . . . see. I'm sorry to bring up an . . . uncomfortable memory. This, um . . . this happened *after* you were Blessed?"

Adelly narrowed her eyes in rising anger. So did I, but for a different reason. He was saying the right things—where we came from. But here . . .

"If that's surprising to you, then you're right. You *don't* understand anything about this country."

"I guess that's true," he admitted.

Conversation lapsed into the sound of a couple dozen marching feet echoing off the tunnel walls around us. Awkward, but at least the Hero knew when to stop before he made it—

"So, Lord Seiji rescued you from that?"

Aster winced; Pashilyn's face tightened in a more controlled version of the same expression.

"Spoken like a true Hero," Adelly replied, and abruptly her tone was mild, bland, even delivered with a faint smile. Yoshi smiled back, clearly encouraged, and I suddenly understood exactly why this was going wrong. "Obviously it takes the intervention of a powerful man to right a wrong. I'm afraid you would be disappointed, though, Shennimeh-*san*."

"Shinonome," he corrected, "but that was cl—"

"Look, I'm sorry, but no human being could possibly pronounce that," Adelly said, still smiling pleasantly. Now even Nazralind was staring at Yoshi through narrowed eyes. I'd noticed she and Adelly seemed to be getting closer during this mission, and as always I was glad when the noblewomen with us didn't act like they were above the others, but this was starting to smell like trouble. Most of the lowborn would go exactly as hard as Adelly was right now and no harder, but aristocrats had different ingrained ideas about who they were allowed to get shirty with. "And in fact, Lord Seiji doesn't usually *rescue* people."

"Obviously," Flaethwyn sneered.

"Oh yes, he does *much* worse," Adelly continued, turning to give the elf a big smile over her shoulder. "He tries to improve people's situations so we're able to rescue *ourselves*. I'm sure that must be *very inconvenient* for you highborn."

"I can see why you'd feel loyalty toward him, then," Yoshi said, hastily and diplomatically. "Thank you for indulging my curiosity, Adelly."

Her smile vanished, her fingers whitened around the Lightning Staff, and I realized I had seconds to salvage this.

"Hey, Yoshi! Did you know a lot of Americans think the Japanese don't understand sarcasm?"

That certainly seized everyone's attention, even the majority who barely had any context for what I was talking about. Yoshi actually stumbled a step, turning to stare incredulously at me.

"Wait, what? You're serious? That's . . . No way."

"I thought sarcasm was culturally universal," Pashilyn commented.

Good girl. Use those noble social skills; help me defuse this.

"I am pretty sure it is, but the *way* it's used is culturally variable, see?"

"Pashi, I'm pretty sure he's just setting up a joke," said Yoshi.

"I am painfully serious," I said, attempting to be solemn while also grinning. "I've had this conversation multiple times on English social media. People who had no idea who they were talking to would inform me that 'it's just not part of their culture.'"

"You got in a lot of intercontinental Twitter fights?" Yoshi's eyes flickered as he swiftly looked me up and down. "Yeah, I could see that."

"I am going to let that pass," I said, soul of magnanimity that I am, "because I can tell that roasting me represents great personal growth, and I'm proud of you for coming out of your shell. No, what happens is they'll visit Japan and try to use American-style sarcasm. See, in America it's common to use sarcastic insults to express affection or praise with people they don't feel close enough to for sincere emotional displays. So, they'll call you a troublemaker if you're good at solving problems, for example, or pretend to be disgusted when they meet a casual friend in the grocery store. It's all meant to be positive and complimentary."

Yoshi's whole face scrunched up. "What? Now I *know* you're messing with me."

"Obviously, yeah, no one's going to be amused if you do that in Japan. So they'll try it, get rejected, take away the wrong lesson, and go back home with stories about how sarcasm just goes right past the Japanese."

"Yoshi's right; this is a pack of silly lies," Flaethwyn scoffed. "*No one* would act that way."

"Goblins do that," Zui said in a neutral tone.

"*Fflyr* do that," Aster added. "Lowborn, anyway. Not often or to that extent, but the basic idea? Definitely."

"It's common across English-speaking cultures," I explained. "Brits pretty much can't express emotion except ironically, and Australia's national sport is affectionately fucking with anybody who visits Australia."

"One of my favorite tutors told me," Pashilyn chimed in smoothly, "that there are two distinctly Fflyr types of humor, that both are meant as a form of class warfare, and that neither works."

"Oh?" I had to admit, this had me intrigued beyond the scope of my current prolonged conversational deflection.

"There is highborn humor, wherein we can carry on entire conversations in nothing but literary references. Its original, earliest intent was to have discussions in front of lowborn and exclude them, assuming that those whose days are filled with labor would have had little time for literature. But we Fflyr are the most literate people in this archipelago, both highborn and low, and most of these references are opaque only to complete outsiders to the culture."

"They sure are," Yoshi muttered.

"Wait." Flaethwyn suddenly looked slightly queasy. "You *can't* be suggesting that *lowborn* understand allusions to that extent."

"When I still had an adventuring party in the King's Guild," said Aster, "we mostly took bodyguarding jobs for merchants or highborn. They talk like that *all* the time, and it mostly wasn't hard to follow. The stories they callback to are mostly stuff everybody in this country has read. They'd only start to lose me when they would get into these highborn pissing contests where they'd try to one-up each other with more and more obscure references until one had to admit ignorance."

We were all treated to the spectacle of Flaethwyn looking ashen and haunted as she began mentally going back over every conversation she'd ever had within hearing distance of a lowborn.

"And then there is lowborn humor," Pashilyn continued, "which consists of . . . sarcastic politeness. Using a calm, gentle demeanor and courteous words to express insult. That was also devised as a way for them to insult highborn right to our faces, and it also doesn't work. Everyone raised in this culture, at any level, knows exactly when someone is doing that. But among highborn at least, it is considered a sign of weakness and ill bearing to overreact emotionally, especially in public—and this lowborn sarcasm is by definition subtle enough to be plausibly deniable. We don't dare to acknowledge the insult for fear of looking foolish before our peers."

"Sounds like it *does* work, then," Zui commented. "Take it from someone who's lower than anybody else in your culture—when it comes to mocking people right to their faces, you don't win when they don't notice it. You win when they *do* and can't do anything about it."

Pashilyn blinked, her face lengthening subtly as she absorbed this sudden dose of perspective. Yoshi was also staring at the distance ahead with wide eyes. This really was a day of revelations for the forces of Good.

"And that's kinda what I was referring to, in another context," I said, my tone now deliberately casual. "There's sarcasm in every culture, and it's so second nature that you don't think about how the rules for it might be different. The lowborn sarcasm thing, I only learned about that recently and somebody had to explain it to me. And man, I was *never* going to figure that out on my own. Because, by coincidence, scathing Fflyr sarcasm happens to look exactly like Japanese politeness."

There came a beat of silence, followed by a collective hissing as quite a few of the goblins accompanying us sucked in air through their teeth.

"Oh, *man*," said Ritlit, ever the one to voice what everyone else was thinking. "And you guys've just been letting him walk around, talking to people like that? I never thought I'd say this, but . . . poor Hero."

I'm glad I wasn't the one who had to say it this time.

"Human drama is straight up hilarious," another commented.

"Right?"

I ignored them, watching Yoshi, who had turned to fix his companions with a look of pure betrayal. Even Adelly was cringing now.

"So, anyway," I continued, "this may be a silly thing to say, since none of you will *ever* in your lives encounter another Japanese person, but just for the record—if you somehow *do*, and they deflect contentious topics with a smile and respond in platitudes rather than confronting an argument, they are just being courteous and respectful. *Not* making fun of you."

"We've . . . tried to ease Yoshi into life here," Pashilyn said carefully, turning to face him, even as she was clearly speaking to the rest of us. "An entire new world . . . just learning *one* new culture while suddenly immersed in it is a huge burden, let alone a whole world of them. What sort of friends would we be if we just tossed him to the wolves?"

I shrugged. "Hey, I dunno what kinda things you guys have been doing, so it's not like I can judge. Just seems to me that Yoshi's smarter than you've been giving him credit for."

I stopped there, because this was starting to look perilously like me trying to drive a wedge between the Hero and his party. Not only did it not benefit me to do that, but it was such classic evil Dark Lord behavior that Pashilyn, and probably Flaethwyn, would react immediately and harshly if I went any further.

"It isn't just that," Pashilyn said, looking back at me with an edge to her tone now. "I *know* Yoshi has spoken to you about the need for secrecy, Lord Seiji. Every slip is a potential trail left for those who will be out hunting the Champions. Who will be out hunting in earnest and in force, particularly *here*, since the night of the Inferno. I am reminded, suddenly, that I haven't had a chance to inquire whether you happen to know anything about what caused that?"

"All right, okay," I said, raising my hands. "Sorry, Lady Pashilyn. I wasn't trying to accuse you of anything. Sometimes my mouth just runs ahead of me. You can ask any of my friends; they'll confirm that."

"If anything, he's nicer to you lot than most people," Aster said dryly. "*Most* of us don't get apologies afterward."

"Yeah, and speakin' of stuff I never expected to say, I gotta express some sympathy for the Hero party here," Biribo piped up. "I dunno about Yoshi, boss, but with *you*, it is an ongoing struggle to feed you information and not have it go in one ear and out the other. I'm not trying to roast you, either; that's perfectly sensible. You *cannot* just dump an entire culture on somebody and expect 'em to understand or remember most of it. There's a process."

"Thank you for that extremely necessary contribution to this conversation, Biribo."

"You got it, boss. I live to serve."

Yoshi cleared his throat, turning toward Adelly with a wince. "So, uh . . ."

"No worries, kid," she swiftly said, with a much more genuine smile. "You're fine. We're cool."

Somehow during all the chatter we had straggled to a stop. I glanced around, noticing most of the goblins grinning as if this were the greatest entertainment they could have asked for. With the exception, of course, of Get Fucked, who was squinting at me. It was hard to interpret that expression since I could only see half of his face.

"You know," Zui said pensively into the silence, "you humans are . . . complicated. I think I liked it better when you were just monsters. That was simpler."

That caused the silence to stretch out further, because . . . what the hell do you say to *that*?

We were spared having to answer that question by the return of our advance scouts. Judge Gazmo and his apprentice had loped off ahead of us almost an hour ago to check on the situation around our next Spirit target. Now they reappeared around a bend in the tunnel in the near distance.

"Situation's stable up ahead," the Judge called by way of greeting. "Folks in Spiketown have shelled up, like sensible people. I spoke with somebody I know; says they've had suspicious goblins wearing green poking around. Sounds like scouting parties. No aggressive push like what happened at Goggin's place, though."

"Which is weird, y'ask me," Fram said cheerfully, swaggering up to us with her polearm over her shoulder. "Why go *past* a big, easy target like this and try to zero in on Goggin? Well, aside from Goggin bein' such a pushover. Reckon it's worth ungagging that guy and asking him? He's probably not gonna do anything but cuss, but we can try!"

Get Fucked scowled at her over his gag. The rest of us were still standing in silence as the Judge and Arbiter came to a stop in front of us.

"Damn, you guys look grim," Fram commented. "Who died?"

"It, uh . . ." Yoshi trailed off, grimacing and averting his eyes.

"Oh, holy shit." The Arbiter's expression changed to sudden mortification. "Somebody didn't *actually* die, did they?"

"No bodies, just egos," I assured her. "No great loss. Shall we?"

Spiketown was well named. It occupied a cavern reminiscent of the one in which Fallencourt was built, albeit on a much smaller scale. Compared to the city that was at the center of Kzidnak society, it was just a village. Still, the sight was impressive.

There was no conveniently even floor and only a few usable ledges along the walls; the big chamber was roughly oblong in shape, like an American football, and dominated by mirrored forests of stalactites and stalagmites. The goblins had carved structures into the walls, of course, but also atop the conical spires of stone sticking up from the floor, the largest of which had been cut and flattened at a consistent height all across the cavern, roughly at the same height as the tunnel entry through which we emerged. Metalwork had been added everywhere, forming bridges and support struts to hold up and connect the structures of stone, metal, and akorshil built across the stalagmites. More metal planks were used in place of natural ledges to form walkways around the wall, providing access to the dwellings cut into the living stone.

It was interesting how most of it had been carved and/or built on a single level, though the wall dwellings had more structures above and below it; some were reached by ramps or ladders, but it seemed most of the staircases were on the interiors. The surprisingly even construction really helped emphasize the tram track that ran through the cavern above most of the roofs. Between two higher tunnel apertures in the walls, a swath of stalactites had been removed to allow the rail to pass through.

"Hang on," Yoshi said, staring up at it. "I thought we couldn't get here directly with the tram?"

"Currently, no," Zui explained with a scowl. "It would've been a fifteen-minute ride at the most, but the track between here and the main depot is one of those we've confirmed too damaged to use."

"Stands to reason," Gazmo grunted. "Doesn't seem Jadrak's got forces for a full push at Sneppit's base yet. Or at least, isn't willing to commit 'em. Out here we've seen scouts and a small strike team; that's it. Damaging the track between here and his biggest competitor denies her easy access."

"Wait," Yoshi said, frowning now. "Doesn't that mean . . . Does Jadrak have a direct line from Fallencourt to here, *with* a working tram track? There'd be no reason for him to damage the tracks in that section, if he can use it instead . . ."

"Use it how?" Zui demanded. "*He* doesn't have any tram cars. He's got metalworkers who could probably rig one up, maybe, eventually, but not fast enough to help him right now. Especially not since he's had 'em on the move most of yesterday and had to abandon their heavy equipment back at his old base."

"Also the trams are propelled by air currents, and it blows the other way," Maizo added.

"What kind of place is this?" I asked. "Not another water business, I can see."

"Learned to ask before committing to anything, did we?" Fram said sweetly. Gazmo kicked her leg, even as he answered me.

"Spiketown's a farming community. Residences are built on the supported structures out there in the middle; behind the outer walls is the agriculture. This is under part of the northern khora forest—real old growth with deep roots. Those root systems run through tunnels around here, and can be tapped for edibles and alchemy reagents. Gotta be carefully managed, though, so the khora aren't damaged. The parts that don't have root systems have mushroom beds and small-scale crawn farms."

"Crawn *farms*?" Adelly asked incredulously. "Don't they just . . . ?"

"Crawns are mostly surface-dwelling," said Zui, curling her lip. "They do come underground, but not in large numbers and only in winter. They like fresh air, vegetation, and human garbage. *We* don't get easy protein handed to us by the Goddesses. What we've got, we work for."

"And complain about!" Maizo chirped. "Don't forget that. *Very* important step in the process."

Zui gave him a particularly filthy look, which he pretended not to see.

"This isn't a setup like Goggin's, where one goblin owns the cavern and the business," Gazmo continued, sparing them nothing more than a long-suffering glance. "Smaller, independent farmers and root tappers, mostly, but the community's tight-knit. We're gonna talk to the guy who owns the Spirit's cave. He's kind of a community leader 'round here."

While he spoke, the Judge set off along one of the few natural ledges lining the walls. This one sloped slightly downward, terminating up ahead where a grated metal platform continued the path, affixed to the walls and ceiling with chains.

"So, not a boss like Sneppit or Goggin?" I asked.

Gazmo nodded. "Which makes him one of my favorite kinda people to work with. Gilnik has no actual power over anybody here; they mostly do what he suggests because they respect him, and he does his best to look after his neighbors."

"Gilnik's great," Ritlit added from behind me. "Stand-up guy!"

"Hm." Gazmo turned to give her a look. "You from around here?"

"Yeah, but it's been years. I went off to get rich hacking up ore in the mines. And we all know how the fuck *that* turned out."

We were spared more of Ritlit's tragic backstory, fortunately. Between the talking and all the footsteps, our approach was hardly quiet; once we hit the metal walkway it became an outright racket. I wasn't the only one to step carefully and peer suspiciously at the chains holding this thing up, but though the metal vibrated under so many feet, the entire thing held—apparently quite sturdy. The goblins might be chaotic in both organization and personal style, and they might be working with the scraps leftover from the richer civilization above, but when it came to the things they built, they did not half-ass it.

Probably summoned by the noise, a goblin emerged from the doorway in the wall just ahead of us, where the path turned back into a blessedly solid-looking stone platform. He was middle-aged, to judge by the beginnings of lines on his face, but like most of the goblins we'd met, it hadn't stopped him from expressing himself via hairstyle—they weren't all Zui, but they mostly did something; I'd seen very few goblins with just the stiff black hair that was natural for them. He had a pompadour with gold highlights, which was actually kind of a contrast with his subtler choice of clothing. It was a Fflyr highborn-style coat, much like Zui and Goggin had chosen, but unlike their flashy aesthetic, he wore muted shades of gray and light brown, without embellishments.

"Judge," he said, nodding. "Wow, you weren't kidding. This everybody?"

"Not in the whole campaign," Gazmo replied. "Rizz is out gathering as many other Judges as she can find, and Sneppit's on board with her people. Goggin, too, for whatever that's worth. This is everybody with us, though.

Tall one there's the Dark Lord, and the rest . . . well, you can make introductions if you care."

"I do, but first things first." Gilnik, whom I assumed this to be, nodded again, this time to the group. "Welcome, folks. Let's get everybody inside. It's, uh, it's gonna be a little tight, with the tallfolk and all, but we should have room."

He stepped aside, indicating the door through which he'd just come that led into the outer cave wall.

"I thought you all lived out there on the . . . um, islands?" I said.

"We do, but for right now we've got everybody evac'd into the farms," Gilnik explained. "Those structures are vulnerable in a lot of ways. *These* are behind thick walls of solid rock—and they're interconnected by tunnels most outsiders won't know how to navigate. We can defend ourselves better without getting cornered. Besides, it's roomier. Just, uh, please don't mess with anything you find growing in there."

"Tina-chan?" Yoshi asked, very softly.

"Goblins moving around in there," his familiar reported, "but by their movements and equipment, it sounds like he's being straight with us. That looks more like refugees settling into a shelter. Nothing I'd say is an ambush risk."

I glanced at Biribo, who bobbed his head once in silent agreement.

"Sorry, no offense meant," I said, turning to Gilnik. "It's just—"

"Hey, none taken," he assured me with a smile. "No goblin would ever begrudge you doing your due diligence before agreeing to anything. With all the shit going down in Kzidnak this week, it's no time to take stupid risks."

"Goblins first," Judge Gazmo ordered. "And *no*, before any of you butts complain, I'm not playing favorites. There's a lot more head room in the entry space up front. Believe me, you'll wanna be the last ones in."

They began filing inside as ordered, after a reassuring nod from me. It was a bit of a process; the door wasn't excessively narrow—though us humans and elves were going to have to duck when our turn came—but the platform outside clearly wasn't meant for a large crowd.

Gilnik led the way in, and I could hear his voice echoing from inside as he directed his guests into the available spaces. Only most of the goblins started moving; Gazmo and Fram waited with us outside, as did Maizo and Zui for whatever reason. And Get Fucked, of course, who didn't really have a choice. Adelly was still holding his leash.

The rest of the goblins were in, and Maizo just turning to follow, when we got the only inadequate warning we were going to.

"EVERYBODY INSIDE!" Radatina abruptly shouted.

"GET DOWN! FIND COVER!" Biribo yelled at the same time.

It was interesting, how the different groups reacted. The goblins did not wait a second for confirmation, all of them bolting for the door—even Get Fucked, who actually made it through despite the rope still connecting him to Adelly outside. The rest of us tallfolk had different instincts—falling into ready stances, drawing weapons, peering around for the threat.

Turned out the goblins were wiser this time. In fact, I was yanked almost off my feet as Zui seized my coat and tried to drag me bodily through the door. They weren't kidding about that magical strength; she could pull like somebody easily twice her size.

The threat arrived, and we barely had a second to register what we were seeing before it was too late.

Goblins were creative problem solvers, indeed. Just as we'd learned from our last encounter with Hoy and laid plans to nullify his advantages next time, our enemies had also examined our strengths and done their own planning. We had provided them a problem, and they'd found a solution. How do you counter a familiar's ability to sense everything around their master?

Bring the danger from beyond the limit of their senses into lethal range before the master has time to react.

The craft that screamed out of the tunnel was a far cry from one of Sneppit's well-designed trams, but a slapped-together contraption powered by a bunch of goblins turning pedals with their feet. Sparks flew and brakes screamed as soon as they passed into the cavern; they were going far too fast to fully stop, but that wasn't the point. The sudden deceleration caused the contents of the open basket affixed to its front to jolt forward, spreading out as they were hurled across half of Spiketown and against the walls above and around us.

Too fast to see clearly what they were, but we all ducked and tried to go for the door anyway, knowing this couldn't possibly be anything good. Pashilyn put up a Light Barrier over our ledge, and Yoshi planted himself in front of the group with his own shield upraised.

It barely helped.

Bombs ignited as they hammered into dozens of spots all around us, and the world dissolved into fire and shrapnel.

27

In Which the Dark Lord Tries Diplomacy

Pashilyn was quick-witted under pressure and this time it cost her, though it probably saved the rest of our lives. She got that Light Barrier up above us at an angle, sloping down toward the front of the platform; the rocks and masonry that landed on it immediately rolled forward instead of just applying all their force straight down onto it. Which was the only reason that worked at all. She lasted about a second and a half under those impacts before letting out a strangled shriek and collapsing to the ground, the glowing shield winking out of existence along with her consciousness.

Most of the rocks missed us; Yoshi bellowed a desperate "**Force Wave!**" and saved us from the worst of the rest. Aster took a glancing hit that nearly pitched her off the platform, and Amell went down with a blood-chilling scream of agony, her lower half pinned under debris.

"Amell!" Yoshi shouted, turning toward her. The abrupt motion caused a spiked iron ball to whiz past his head instead of taking it off.

Fuck, those goblins still weren't dealt with. Their hanging contraption had managed to come to a halt while we were busy surviving the avalanche, and now was even backing up as they reversed their pedaling. Behind us Amell was screaming and weeping simultaneously, and there was nothing we could do for her because we had eight goblins now taking aim with slingshots even as they backpedaled.

"**Force Wave!**"

"**Slimeshot!**"

Yoshi and I, with all our power, only managed to turn their ambush into a temporary stalemate; the range was too great. His Force Wave only caused the thingumajig to rock violently, disrupting their aim and forcing them to hold on. I nailed them with several successive slimes, which . . . wasn't much more effective. Slimeshot launched with enough power to literally take a man's head off at minimum range, but slimes were the least suitable projectile imaginable, losing velocity fast as they flew—at that distance, I was basically waging a sticky pillow fight.

Then one of the goblins toppled out of his seat with a hoarse scream, an arrow sprouting from his chest.

Nazralind calmly nocked, drew, and let fly, taking out another. Adelly was beside her, Lightning Staff abandoned on the ground as she raised her crossbow.

All four of us kept it up, Yoshi and I only growing more useless as the rapidly diminishing goblins pedaled frantically away, but our archers took care of them. Naz was by far the better shot, but Adelly managed to hit at least one. Crossbows—at least the ones we used—were more suited for stopping power than long-distance accuracy, unless in the hands of a savant like—

—the blank expression of shock in Kastrin's face as she jerked to the side like a broken doll with an arrow in her temple—

I drew in air in a frantic gasp, staggering backward from the flash of memory. Fucking hell, I did not need that right now. The real world rushed back in, and it was filled with screams and the all-too-familiar smell of blood.

"Help me!" Zui barked. I turned to find her having planted herself against the chunk of stone crushing Amell's legs and straining against it. Her shorter height gave her better leverage than any of us would've had, unless— "Yoshi, bring that rock over here, plant it right by the boulder! Aster, we need that big-ass sword! Wedge the tip in—yes, there, good. Now work that rock in—Seiji, hold it steady. The rest of you butts, heave!"

A hairdresser—and executive assistant—she might be, but Zui did not work for an engineering company for nothing; she'd formed a plan in a single glance and started directing us to execute it. Aster's indestructible sword made the perfect lever. Yoshi shoved a chunk of stone in place as a fulcrum, and he and I both dropped to wedge our feet against it to stop it sliding back as they tried to work. Aster, Flaethwyn, Nazralind, and Adelly all threw their weight onto the sword's upper end, straining against the sheer mass.

Blood was already squelching under our boots in a spreading puddle; as the huge chunk of stone finally toppled off Amell, more gushed out. Her legs were completely—

Yoshi slumped forward, barely managing to press his hands over his mouth in time to suppress his retching.

"**Heal**!" It was instinct at this point; I'd seen as bad and worse, and I'd learned long ago to cast the spell before I could get a proper view of the injury or it would haunt my nightmares forever.

Amell sat bolt upright, inhaling a deep, desperate gasp as if she'd just been underwater. Jerking her knees up, she grabbed at them frantically with both hands, kicking and stretching legs that a second ago had been little but flattened meat.

It took her five more seconds to trust that she was whole again, and then she toppled over onto her side into her own blood, sobbing hysterically.

"Pashilyn!" I blurted out her name as my Healer instincts kicked in and I remembered the last person who'd been injured. She was slumped against the wall—praise whatever gods might be watching over us, no rocks had fallen on her. "**Heal**!"

"That won't help, but she should be okay," Radatina said. "Taking an impact to Light Barrier like that applied the hit directly to her own stamina. It's strain, not injury. She needs a few minutes to recover herself."

"Here." Adelly held up Amell's reinforced potion kit, which thankfully had also avoided being flattened. She knelt next to the weeping alchemist, speaking softly. "I know, honey, you've been through hell, but we need you. Pashilyn needs you. Can you sit up? Show me what bottle to use and I'll take care of it . . ."

"Anyone else injured? We missing anybody?" I demanded, spinning about to look.

"Ah, excuse me." Flaethwyn spoke in such an uncharacteristically soft, diffident tone it took me a second to realize who was talking. She held up her left hand, which was absolutely gushing blood from a gash across the palm. "I must've . . . when we leaned on the sword . . ."

"**Heal**!"

Magic flashed and the elf exhaled in relief, flexing her fingers. "Ah . . . My thanks, Lord Seiji."

I finished taking stock. Most of the goblins had escaped; Gazmo, Fram, and Maizo were all peeking out of the doorway, while Zui had retreated against the wall to check on Get Fucked, who hadn't been able to do anything but hunker down there. I was sure I'd seen him get in through the door; he must've been dragged back out when Adelly reacted to the crisis, even though she'd subsequently dropped her end of the rope.

I reached him in one long stride. "You okay?"

The gagged goblin stared up at me through eyes shocked and open wide, seemingly uncomprehending.

"Are you hurt? Wait, why am I asking? **Heal**."

Get Fucked twitched in surprise at the sensation, blinking rapidly.

"Omura."

Yoshi's tone told me our bad day was just beginning.

I turned to look at him, then followed his stare to the other side of the cavern. One of the exterior entrances was almost directly across from us and slightly above, and by happenstance our perspective from this position cut between the structures of the stalagmite village to give us a perfect view. A whole squad of goblins was coming through, and even at this distance I recognized the figure in the lead by his livid green coat with tacky golden embellishments. Hoy had acquired a new polearm, but hadn't replaced his hat.

"Oh, you little fucker," I whispered. "All right, time for round two."

I tried to step forward and was impeded by Yoshi putting out a hand to grab my arm.

"Omura, wait. We can't finish him here."

"We what?"

"Look around."

It took me a second, I'll admit, but then the realization snapped into place. This cavern was basically egg-shaped; there were no corners, anywhere. The sloping floor was a forest of stalagmites, and Spiketown itself atop them was a maze of platforms and bridges, but whether it was goblin-made structures or natural rock growths, the obstructions were all obstacles to be dodged around, not something we could reliably pin someone against.

"Shit, you're right. The plan won't work if there's nowhere to corner him. Okay, what if . . ." I thought as rapidly as I could, watching Hoy and his squad approach. Oddly, they did not seem to be in a hurry, sauntering across the bridges in an almost insouciant manner. "We can goad him into one of those buildings, or one of the structures carved into the walls. Dude is ninety centimeters of unmanaged rage issues; a couple good taunts and he'd chase us into an open furnace."

Yoshi was already shaking his head. "We don't know the layout in there; we're as likely as he to get cornered. Plus, if we then drop the ceiling on him as planned, we'd be dropping it on ourselves, too."

"Also, those are people's homes and businesses and a significant chunk of the local food supply," Gazmo growled from behind us, "if that factors into your calculations."

Fuck. Fuck, fuck, fuck. As urgently as that goblin needed to be fucking dead . . .

"Then we have to chase him off," I said grudgingly. "Make him retreat."

"Problem is," said Yoshi with a grimace, "he's ninety centimeters of unmanaged rage issues. Doesn't seem like the retreating kind of guy."

"Son of a bitch," Gazmo hissed with a sudden weight of venom unlike anything I'd heard from him. I glanced down at the Judge in surprise, then followed his furious stare back to Hoy, who'd by that point reached a platform roughly in the middle of Spiketown and stopped for some reason. He was close enough to afford a better look, and . . .

Oh. As we stared, the Void witch grinned and flicked a switch on the polearm he was carrying, causing the bulky apparatus at the other end to snap open and reveal a blade.

That was a Judge's weapon. They weren't all identical; I could tell it wasn't one of the ones Rizz and Rhoka had been carrying, and didn't quite match Gazmo's or Fram's, either. But the general style . . .

"Why did he stop," Yoshi murmured, narrowing his eyes. "What's he waiting for? What's with this standoff? He was so aggressive before . . ."

He was right. Hoy had planted his feet on the flat central platform suspended between three huge stalagmites, which appeared to be Spiketown's main square. Grinning, making a show of his stolen polearm, but not attacking as was in his nature. Behind him, seven goblins carrying slingshots and clubs had straggled to a stop just out of easy projectile range, looking uncertain. I could believe Hoy would waste time taunting us, but not at the expense of time spent trying to murder us. What was . . .

My eyes widened as realization set in.

"He *is* trapped," I whispered, causing Yoshi and Gazmo to turn confused stares on me. "Socially trapped. Jadrak and Hoy are trying to ride a wave of violence and fanaticism, but goblins are so peaceful normally, they have no cultural framework for how to do that. He's afraid to back down in front of his goons there, or he risks losing control of them the way he did the last batch. That bombing was supposed to take us out—or at least one of us. It failed, and now he's facing two Champions again. He can't win *or* retreat. Okay, I know what to do."

"Give him an out," Yoshi said, as if I hadn't just announced I knew what to do. "The enemy will always fight harder when cornered; you have to leave them an avenue of retreat. Or so Sun Tzu wrote."

I had to give him a surprised stare of my own. "You've read the *Art of War*?"

Yoshi avoided my eyes, his cheeks coloring slightly. "I, uh. I had a chuuni phase. Just a bit."

The funny thing about Yoshi was how very easy it always was to make fun of him, and how I usually just didn't have the heart.

"Hey, man, that's a lot of us."

"You, too?" he said almost hopefully, chancing a sidelong look at me.

"Hell no, I had a girlfriend in middle school."

"I think you're the worst person I've ever met," Yoshi grumbled.

"Now that's just not fair; you've met Hoy."

"Good point. Sorry."

"You two about done with the vaudeville?" Gazmo demanded.

"Relax, this is strategic," I assured him. "I'm drawing this out, ramping up the pressure. Making him wonder what we're scheming over here. Judge, I need you to brief our team back inside the walls, please. Tell them to take positions at every window they can find and stand by. If this comes to a fight and Hoy gets within range, they're to hammer him with projectiles, that part of the plan is still on. No explosives, though."

He waited a drawn-out second, just to emphasize that he was deciding to cooperate, not obeying me, then nodded once and eased backward from us.

"Zui," I said, turning to look over my shoulder, "take care of the prisoner."

For once, she didn't make noise about how I didn't get to give her orders—just held my gaze and nodded, indicating with her expression that she fully understood what I was implying. Man, I needed a good executive assistant of my own, and possibly a hairstylist. What were the odds I could find myself a less annoying Zui while I was down here?

"C'mon, Yoshi," I said, stepping forward. "It's showtime."

The Hero strode alongside me as we crossed the first bridge. They cut an erratic, zigzagging course between the platforms and stalagmites holding them up, but we were able to keep Hoy and his little entourage within view as we moved.

I came to a stop one platform short, leaving the space of a single bridge between us, and Yoshi fortunately followed my lead. We were well within spell range, but far enough back that his Void effect didn't start shutting off our artifacts. For a moment, we all just stared at each other; the weight of our last encounter hanging heavily in everyone's memory.

This was a fight nobody wanted. As badly as we all wished each other dead, we were too close to a stalemate, now that everybody's gambits had failed. His bombing attempt had missed us and the choice of venue made our Hoy Directives unworkable. If this came to another brawl, it was just going to be another big, messy waste of time.

"Well, look who finally found their fuckin' balls," Hoy sneered, breaking the silence. "So you two dipshits went right for the Spirit, huh? Guess you're not quite as dumb as you are ugly."

"Ara, ara, ara," I drawled. "Childish insults right out of the gate? Not even the pretense of a pleasantry? My expectations were zero and somehow, you still manage to disappoint me."

From my peripheral vision I saw Yoshi turn his head toward me, blinking rapidly in surprise, and only belatedly realized what had just come out of my mouth.

God fucking dammit, there was exactly one person on this blasted planet I just had to not do that in front of, and here I went and . . . Why was mimicking my stern grandmother my compulsive response to stupidity and bullshit? So help me, if I ever saw Obaasan again, I'd—

Do absolutely nothing; I was still terrified of that woman.

"Aww, is the baby disappointed?" Hoy simpered obnoxiously. "You gonna cry, Dark Lord?"

Good grief, he was bad at showtime. Did he actually think this was earning him points? Only a prepubescent schoolyard bully would be impressed by that. Even his followers couldn't manage to scrape up sycophantic chuckles, though a couple of them unconvincingly tried. Several others looked openly embarrassed.

"Well, Hoy, since we've got you here," I replied in a pleasant tone, "why don't you tell us all why you're so interested in getting to Spirits?"

"I see you still think you're a lot smarter than you are," he said, his face collapsing into a contemptuous sneer again. "This is a new Kzidnak, asshole, and your old-fashioned preconceptions aren't worth a crawn's shit. We've got no use for Sanorite or Viryan rhetoric. Goblins stand for goblins, and we only need our Goblin King. We'll take power wherever we can find it."

That drew me up short, I have to admit. The taboo on Void magic had seemed universal and deeply embedded in all Ephemeral societies I'd interacted with so far, but now the goblins arranged behind Hoy just looked . . . Well, they did not look happy, but no one was offering to speak up against him. In a way, it was a smart move. He and Jadrak couldn't possibly keep the lid on their devil dallying forever, so getting out in front of it and normalizing the Void was their only real option, politically.

"And does that include sacrificing your followers?" Yoshi asked, his voice tight with barely restrained fury. "Are you planning to throw away their lives like you did the last bunch?"

"Traitors deserve nothing but death!" Hoy snapped, his fragile temper clearly starting to unravel again.

"Oh, we agree there," I said smoothly. "Considering you turned on them first. You got quite a lot of your people killed before they were pushed so hard they had to fight back."

"Feel free to run your mouth, fuckstain," he snarled. "Nobody's gonna believe you. So what's it gonna be, boys? You got the stones for round two, or you just wanna stand there and talk, like a couple of sniveling crawns?"

"You were supposed to be leading those goblins to freedom," Yoshi snapped, baring his own teeth in rising anger. "You promised them a better life if they fought for it, and then you threw them away like garbage! What is wrong with you? How can anyone be like this?!"

Hoy's face lengthened into a deeply ironic expression. He looked Yoshi up and down once, then turned to me, raising an eyebrow.

I shrugged. "Just cos it's a little naive doesn't mean he's wrong. You're a piece of shit, Hoy. I really hope Jadrak isn't as cavalier with people's lives as you are, or this whole uprising is gonna end up being worse for goblins than a century of Fflyr oppression. But hey, you've made your feelings about talk plenty clear. If you want at the Spirit, try getting through us. Maybe it'll be less embarrassing for you than last time. Not that that's setting a high bar."

I was expecting another outburst of his escalating temper, but suddenly Hoy got a crafty, knowing look on his face, and I began to worry. This guy was not crafty or knowing, but he was hilariously bad at masking his feelings; if he thought he had some advantage we didn't know about, then one or the other of us had just made an immensely stupid mistake and would pay dearly for it.

"Oh, I could, don't you doubt it," he said, smirking now. "But why bother? There are other Spirits in Kzidnak. Let's see, you two losers came here from that smug twat Sneppit's place, didn't you? And the people I sent to lock down the Counter never reported back, so I assume you slaughtered them. Then the next Spirit on your path from here would be Mister Flats. How 'bout it, boys, wanna have a race? Bet I can beat you there. Although."

His sharklike grin widened to truly alarming proportions, and I gripped my rapier tighter, instinctively readying myself for all of this to go south.

"There's something I bet even your familiars didn't know—corrupting Spirits isn't the only source of Void spells."

I snorted. "Yeah, obviously. But you and Jadrak only have two souls to sell, between you. With your little antimagic zone and his giving out Blessings of Magic, you've blown your entire wad."

"Oh, you'd think that, wouldn't you?" Hoy's expression was now of pure, manic glee; behind him, his buddies looked a lot less happy about the direction this conversation was taking; though, so far none of them appeared about to turn on him. "And sure, for normal Void witches, you'd be right. But there's something you're not considering—Jadrak is a king. As far as a devil's contract goes, the souls of his followers are his to sell. That situation just plain doesn't come up all that often; I bet even your familiars have never seen it before. In all of world history, there've almost never been actual rulers commanding the Void. Maybe I'll just forget about Spirits and go straight back to Fallencourt, where there are hundreds of goblins loyal to Jadrak dug in and ready to fight. It's not like they could stand up to a Dark Lord and a Hero—if they're doomed to sacrifice themselves for the cause anyway, then the cause might as well get something out of it other than funeral expenses. Just think of all the goodies he could get for that many souls. Wouldn't even have to use them all. In fact, yeah. I'll just leave the King to his work and take on the Spirits myself. Keep your asses nice and busy so he can do what he needs to and finish this."

For a moment, I couldn't find anything to say in response to that. Neither could Yoshi, apparently. Neither could the goblins behind Hoy, all of whom looked increasingly alarmed. Clearly they hadn't been informed of this ahead of time.

In the immediate term, that meant we were winning this; Hoy was the kind of asshole who couldn't take a step or open his mouth without alienating people, and so far every encounter we'd had with him did more harm to the loyalty of Jadrak's followers than it did to our counterrebellion. Here he was, at it again. We could chalk this up as a success . . . unless he was telling the truth.

And, come on, what were the odds of that?

"Bullshit," I finally said, projecting more confidence than I felt.

"Oh sure, you're right," he said merrily. "I'm probably lying. I'm a piece of shit, after all! You boys should definitely go after the Spirit. Yeah, now that I think of it, Jadrak doesn't need my say-so to turn those goblins into an arsenal of Void spells that could flatten fucking Godspire. So let's you and me race for the Spirits while he settles this once and for all. Whaddaya say, boys, gimme a sporting head start?"

"**Force Wave!**"

All of us jumped in surprise; neither Hoy nor Yoshi had cast that spell. I didn't see who had, or at what, and the confusion lasted until the wave impacted the ceiling directly above Spiketown's central platform, pulverizing a bunch of stalactites, which immediately plummeted down on Hoy's party as incredibly heavy shrapnel.

"**Flicker!**"

No, of course taking him out wouldn't be that easy. It sure wiped out his party, though; I heard a couple of strangled screams as the entire metal platform was crushed under the falling stone, tearing free of its moorings and plummeting down to the cavern floor below.

Only then did I spot the caster—on the flat roof of a nearby goblin house stood Zui and Get Fucked, the latter untied, ungagged, and with his hand still outstretched in casting position. Clearly I was right to count on her—and my gambit with the goblin sorcerer had gone exactly the way I expected. Now I just needed to arrange for Hoy to voice his thoughts in front of the rest of Jadrak's people, and we'd have this whole thing wrapped up by dinner.

Unless Jadrak turned them all into Void spells first. Which . . . surely he couldn't actually do that. Surely not.

Yoshi clapped a hand to his forehead. "Force Wave at the ceiling. Why didn't I think of that?!"

Hoy had Flickered to the next platform over; I could still probably launch a Slimeshot at him from here, not that there was any point. At least, he was still close enough to call back at us.

"Nice chattin' with you, suckers! See you 'round—unless you decide to stop Jadrak instead of me. Better make up your mind quick, fuckboys. Tick tock. **Flicker!**"

He departed in a series of casts, Flickering from one landing point to the next until he was back at the tunnel through which he'd come in.

"He was lying, right?" I turned to stare up at Get Fucked, who was glaring intently down—not at me, but at Biribo, his voice heavily tinged with desperation. "He can't— Void witches can't actually do that, right? Sacrifice other people?"

I did not at all like the silence that ensued, in which Biribo and Radatina turned to stare at each other.

"Huh," Biribo said after that deeply ominous pause. "It's . . . a stretch, but . . . Boss, I think they may have found a loophole."

"What the fuck do you mean they found a *loophole*?" I snarled. "I know you don't mean that Jadrak can actually sacrifice his followers' souls to the devil for more Void magic! Because obviously that would have been the first thing you warned me about when we found out the Goblin King is a Void witch. Right, Biribo?"

"The thing is, soul magic is, um . . . Well, this just doesn't come up that often," Radatina hedged. "The sacrifice of a soul has to be voluntary. There are conditions in which someone else can sacrifice your soul, but . . . That's just not the kind of relationship a ruler has with his followers. We are talking about complete trust, absolute submission, an outright willingness to die for them and accept any possible fate. On a deep, emotional level, beyond rhetoric and politics. The ruler of a large empire might find a hundred people across his entire domain with that kind of fanatical loyalty. Maybe more if they were extremely religious."

"That's, uh, that's normal conditions, though," Biribo added. "I didn't think of it because this has never lined up this way before, but . . . What we're in the middle of here is a revolution, led by a cult of personality. He definitely can't sacrifice every goblin in Kzidnak, but at this one very brief moment in history, at the apex of the fighting and before things start to settle down or drag on too much . . . There are probably hundreds of goblins down here who would give up their very souls for Jadrak's cause, at least right now. So, uh, yeah. That's . . . a possible loophole."

"No." Yoshi shook his head rapidly. "No, that's not—that doesn't make sense. If Jadrak could do that, he would've just done it to begin with. Right? It doesn't make sense to hold it back for now."

"Right." Up on the roof, Get Fucked was staring with abject, horrified misery into empty space, dry-washing his hands. "Right, he . . . He was lying to us all. He lied from the beginning. Played us for suckers. So . . . so he would've done that first. That means he can't do it."

"Right, yeah," Yoshi agreed, nodding now. "And anyway, if he could do it, Hoy wouldn't warn us about it. He's obviously just trying to distract us from protecting the Spirits."

I cleared my throat awkwardly, and the looks everyone turned on me were full of grim anticipation.

"Jadrak's first plan was to ally with me," I said. "Making himself the Dark Lord's lieutenant would've been just about the only way his little uprising could even theoretically succeed against the Fflyr. I might even have fallen for it, if he hadn't revealed what a piece of shit he was by having his goons murder the goblins I was already friendly with to get them out of the way. He went from expecting to work with the Dark Lord, to having to fight the Dark Lord . . . to having to fight the Dark Lord and the Hero, to having his unstoppable Void witch accomplice beaten back in a fight and organized resistance entrenched on the fringes of Kzidnak . . . Every success we've had has just been pushing him farther into a corner. If he just wasn't desperate enough for those extreme measures before . . . that could be changing."

Get Fucked slumped down to his knees, cradling his face in his hands. Zui gently patted his back.

Yoshi inhaled deeply. "Radatina . . . In theory, if he could do this, what kind of Void power could Jadrak get if he successfully fed hundreds of goblin souls to his devil?"

His familiar didn't answer immediately, which was as bad a sign as I'd ever seen.

"That's . . . no Void witch has ever pulled off something like that," Radatina finally said reluctantly. "I can hardly imagine the kind of monster he could become with that kind of power. It would at least rival the most successful Dark Lords at the absolute apex of their strength. Right now . . . there's no force on Ephemera that could stop him."

28

In Which the Dark Lord Signs Up for Disaster

Obviously, this was going to change our calculations for the next steps of our strategy, but first things first.

"Sorry about your, uh . . . central square, there," I said moments later, when we reconvened back at the platform outside Gilnik's place, addressing the pompadoured goblin in question.

"Hey, that wasn't *your* doing," he said, giving a very pointed stare to Get Fucked, who was lurking around the back of the group, looking as downcast and depressed as anyone I'd ever seen. Almost as if he'd given up everything and thrown away his entire life to follow a messianic political figure who turned out to be a selfish conman that was callously using his followers. "We'll straighten it out; most of the material should be salvageable. Considering what *could've* happened here if Hoy turned up in your absence, we got off light."

I nodded, and drew in a breath. "Okay, that leaves the big matter at hand. Much as I was looking forward to taking a break, our timetable just got even less forgiving and we need to book it. What can we do to secure the Spirit here in case Hoy comes back?"

"Ugh, that's a point," Yoshi agreed, grimacing. "He was obviously goading us to move out in a hurry. He *could* be planning to circle around and corrupt it once we're gone."

Gilnik winced, glancing back at the doorway behind him, through which worried goblin faces were peeking. "I'll be honest, we got nothin'. That's why we were all glad to see the Judge turn up with you guys in tow. We ain't fighters here, Lord Seiji, even less than most goblins. If we gotta deal with a Void witch or even a squad of armed troops coming after our stuff, our options are 'let them have it' and 'die letting them have it.'"

"That's what I was afraid of," I murmured, frowning.

"Before you ask," Zui piped up, "this is farther out than Miss Sneppit is willing to extend a security perimeter. She was talking about possibly moving her main force closer to Fallencourt like Jadrak did, but only if you and the Hero took care of Hoy and cleared the way."

"Taking on Jadrak's main army would be a lot easier with hers as backup," Yoshi agreed, "but that doesn't solve the immediate problem."

"Biribo," I said, "how durable are these Spirit altars, exactly?"

"*Exactly*?" he replied, swooping around in front of my face. "The answer to that is 'yes,' boss. Void corruption aside, they're basically indestructible. If this planet ever finishes collapsing, the Spirits will be left floating in space."

"That's a comforting image," Flaethwyn muttered.

"I'm not sure I enjoy the direction this is taking," said Gilnik.

"Then you're ahead of me," I said ruefully. "How hard would it be to collapse the Spirit's cavern on top of it?"

Every goblin present cringed.

"Collapsing caverns is child's play," Gazmo answered me before Gilnik could. "It's *uncollapsing* them afterward that's challenging. Dunno if you're aware of it, tallboy, but you just invoked one of our deepest cultural fears."

"Yeah, I figured," I said. "I'm sorry, but unless someone has a better idea, this is the only way to actually secure that Spirit against the Void."

"To be clear, Lord Seiji," Gilnik said in a tight voice, "you are asking me to destroy—"

"Nothing," I interrupted. "I'm asking you to block access to the Spirit to anyone not willing to perform a lot of difficult, time-consuming, and precise labor to dig it out, which will effectively take it off the board for the duration of the civil war in Kzidnak *and* protect it from Void corruption. Look, Gilnik, in the next couple of days, one of two things is going to happen. If Jadrak wins, then you'll have bigger problems and it won't matter, because he'll crack down on you lethally for daring to stand up to him. In that case, making him dig the Spirit out again before he can use it would be the last act of spite you'll be able to inflict on him. The *other* possibility is that he goes down, and *I* will be the next big power around here. In that event, I will personally, as soon as I am able, send whatever resources, personnel, and funds are necessary to unearth the Spirit and get your business back up and running."

He blinked, straightening up slightly. "You will?"

"I absolutely will," I promised. "Judge Gazmo, how fast can you whip us up a contract?"

"For a simple promise like that? Half a minute. Fram, get on it."

"Oh sure, I see how it is," she grumbled, already pulling materials out of her coat. Ink pencil, paper, and some sort of gadget that . . . Wait, was that a collapsible clipboard? Goblin ingenuity never disappointed. I was surprised that invention hadn't spread to the Fflyr; it was a perfect fit for their culture as well. "How come *I* always gotta do the grunt work, huh?"

"Why the hell do you think I put up with all your bullshit?" Gazmo snorted.

"What, you mean it's not for my sunny disposition and scintillating conversational skills?"

"Well," Gilnik said slowly, "I do see the urgency. With the Dark Lord's signature on paper . . . Yeah, in that case, we'll get on it. Bringing down the Spirit's chamber should be easy enough; just needs some basic tools."

"And then you plan to be in charge of the goblins, Lord Seiji?" Pashilyn said, tilting her head and giving me a mildly inquisitive stare. "What, I won-der, do you plan to do with them afterward?"

"I'm glad you're okay, Lady Pashilyn," I said, smiling pleasantly. "You had me worried for a minute there. Thanks for that quick work with the Light Barrier; you really saved all our butts."

Yoshi cleared his throat. "Before we cave in the Spirit's home . . . is there a chance it could help us deal with Jadrak, like the last one? I don't think anybody has mentioned to me exactly what this one does."

"Well, uh . . ." Gilnik shrugged. "You interested in bein' sent on a quest to vanquish a powerful enemy without resorting to force, in order to earn a masterwork tool for your chosen profession? Cos I can make that happen."

Yoshi's and my eyes met; he looked as intrigued as I felt.

"*Boys*," Zui warned.

"Any enemy in particular?" he asked hopefully.

"We don't have *time* for this!" Flaethwyn exclaimed.

"Spirit picks the enemy," said Gilnik.

"Yeah, then we better table that idea for now," I said ruefully.

"Nonviolence isn't exactly your strong suit, anyway," Aster said, patting me on the back.

"More importantly, what are we going to do *next*?" Yoshi inquired, look-ing around at each of the group in turn. "If there's even a chance what Hoy said was true . . . we may have to abandon the Spirits and go right for Jadrak. Every second he's not dealt with, every goblin working for him is in danger of having their soul sacrificed."

"Not to stifle your newfound sense of charity, boy, but every goblin under or *near* Jadrak's been in mortal danger since all this brouhaha kicked off," said Gazmo. "In fact, every goblin in Kzidnak, period; and while I obviously wanna minimize the bloodshed as much as possible, those on the side who *started* this get a lesser portion of my sympathy. You're talkin' about riding to the rescue of your enemies, here."

Yoshi shook his head emphatically. "This goes beyond politics or enemies, Judge. *No one* deserves to have their soul eaten by a devil. If we can stop it, we *have* to."

"I agree with the sentiment, as far as it goes," I said, "but keep in mind that this idea is so far-fetched even our familiars said it's only *theoretically* possible. Meanwhile, the original threat was Hoy going after the Spirits to corrupt them for more Void spells, which he is absolutely still planning to do. Especially given that his only possible motivation for *telling* us about this idea was to make us hare off after Jadrak and leave Hoy open to continue what he came *here* to do in the first place."

"Ahem?" Radatina swooped into the center of the group and then darted back and forth in midair to be sure she had everyone's attention. "The thing is, this is indeed far-fetched, but it *is* theoretically possible, and that raises the question of where Hoy even got the idea. It's not something present in the commonly known lore about Void craft. The obvious answer is he and Jadrak were told about the possibility by their devil friend. Which makes it . . . somewhat more than just a possibility, I'm afraid."

"Which makes that by *far* the bigger threat," said Yoshi, nodding. "To say nothing of the immediate loss of life it would cause if Jadrak pulls that trigger."

"But if we go after him," I objected, "we're giving Hoy free reign. The both of us with full backup are barely enough to fight him to a draw as it is. If he manages to get to *one* more Spirit and gain more Void powers, let alone several, he'll hit us from behind while we're trying to deal with Jadrak, and there'll be even less chance we can take him."

Yoshi's expression was growing more stubborn by the second. "It's not that you're wrong, Omura. But . . . the *stakes*. To abandon people we could actually help isn't wisdom, it's just laziness."

"Hm," I grunted, surprised. "That was actually pretty profound."

"Thanks."

"It's from an anime, isn't it?"

He scowled. "No, it's not from an anime."

"Ah, of course, of course. A video game, then."

"*Why* do you feel the need to ruin everything?" he demanded in open exasperation.

"Well, I *am* the Dark Lord."

Yoshi raised an eyebrow. "Ara ara?"

Oh, you little shit.

"Don't do that," I ordered. "Rock stars have always played around with gender presentation. You're too normie to pull it off."

"Wow. That's the first time in my life I've ever been called *that*."

Zui loudly cleared her throat. "*Since* our schedule just got tighter, lemme just say that if we need to argue over whether to head for Fallencourt or the next Spirit location on our list, that tunnel over there starts out as the quickest route toward both. We'll have close to an hour's walk before the path branches and we gotta make the call."

"That's not the tunnel Hoy left through," I said, frowning. "I thought he was in a hurry to beat us to the Spirit—"

"Why'd you think that, because he *said* so?" Gazmo demanded. "Fuck only knows what Hoy's thinking. The exit he took swings south; most likely he wants to rendezvous with more of Jadrak's partisans and pick up a new team, since this bloodthirsty idiot over here dropped the ceiling on his last one. Hoy's not the kinda guy to risk his own hide against somebody who's a legitimate threat to him without taking extra precautions."

"You're welcome," Get Fucked muttered, barely audibly.

Everyone turned a collectively baleful stare on him, causing him to hunch his shoulders and look away.

"Well, I guess if we take Zui's advice," Yoshi said, still staring at Get Fucked, "we'll have time to settle on a new course of action *and* give everybody a chance to say 'I told you so.'"

"Yoshi, here's a free lesson in villainy," I said cheerfully. "*Never* tell people 'I told you so.' It's a dickish thing to say, and saying it makes you come off like a dick, which detracts from your point. Instead, just make sure to tell them so ahead of time, and then when the opportunity comes, leave it unsaid. That way, they're left weltering in the knowledge that you told them so and can't even be mad about it."

"That was the most weirdly insightful thing I've ever heard," Adelly commented.

"I'd have said insightfully weird," said Nazralind.

"I don't need lessons in villainy!" Yoshi exclaimed.

"You need lessons in everything, Yoshi."

"And is that American sarcasm, or are you just being a dick now?"

"Hard to tell, isn't it?"

"For fuck's *fucking* sake!" Zui shouted. "You're like a couple of . . . I don't even know! Can we *focus*, here?"

"Zui is correct," I said solemnly, taking the contract and pencil from Fram, which she'd finished and Gilnik had already signed while we deliberated. "I bet she'll be shrewd enough not to remind us she told us so later, too. See how annoying it is? All right, people, let's walk and talk."

The need for haste forced us to move out and trust that Gilnik would do his part in burying the Spirit. Goblin culture being what it was, I wasn't worried about his willingness now that he'd put his signature on paper in front of a Judge, but there was the risk of Hoy circling back before they could finish the job, if that was indeed Hoy's plan. It was a risk, but one that circumstances forced us to take. There just weren't any options available that weren't risky.

That was our problem in a nutshell.

Despite the need to reach a resolution by the next cross-tunnel, I didn't immediately resume my argument with Yoshi because he was frowning in deep thought, and I was beginning to notice that Yoshi was decently good at spotting the angles and laying down a workable plan when it was necessary. Since we had hopefully enough time to reach a consensus, and I myself felt completely stuck in trying to resolve this dilemma, I opted to give him some time to think in the hope that he might come up with something worthwhile.

Not that I was utterly exhausted with being the guy who had to make all the plans all the time or anything. I just had something else that needed seeing to before we got much farther.

"So, what's it gonna be?" I asked, falling back to stride alongside our erstwhile prisoner.

He squinted up at me suspiciously. Though no longer tied and gagged, he still had Adelly and Flaethwyn both hovering around within easy weapon range. Understandable, since we hadn't exactly discussed his evolving role in the group.

"You wanna stick with Get Fucked?" I clarified when he failed to respond. "Make a clean break with the past, fresh name and all? I fully support you if so, just saying. Individual self-determination is a big deal in my organization."

Get Fucked looked at me again, sidelong and upward, and it was a uniquely expressive stare—the distinct, yet hard-to-describe, expression of a man who was just too soul-deep tired to be as pissed off as he wanted to be.

"My name's Deeyo."

"Hi, Deeyo, I'm Seiji. So, what's your next move?"

"I dunno, what were you expecting when you dragged me into this?" He shrugged fatalistically. "I think I'd rather you left me tied up and ignorant back at the spring."

"Do you really?"

". . . no. Yes. I . . ." Deeyo wrapped his arms around himself, hunching over as he walked. "Goddess. You have no idea what I've . . . I gave everything for Jadrak. I fought for him—I threw Fire Lances at people protecting their homes because . . . because the cause needed me to. Rubble and rot, I was out *recruiting* for him! I helped drag more honest people into his . . . And it was all lies. He played me like a goddamn slidepipe."

My inner musician immediately perked up and made a mental note to find out at the earliest opportunity what a slidepipe was, but my outer showman knew this was no time for a digression like that.

"And now . . ." Deeyo stared down at his own palms. "*Now* I'm a Void witch."

"You're not a Void witch, son," Biribo said, rather condescendingly. "You're bog-standard Blessed with Magic. About as standard as they come. Pretty low on the power scale."

"But . . . Jadrak did it himself." He stared forlornly up at me. "None of us even asked how or why, because apparently we're all *fucking idiots*; we were too busy being inspired by this incredible power he had. The Goblin King can give out the Blessing of Magic, along with those two basic spells. But apparently it's Void magic, right? Doesn't that make me a Void witch?"

"Void initiation doesn't work like that," Biribo explained. "Believe me, if you'd encountered the Void, you would know. Apparently, Jadrak's Void gift is just that, the ability to grant that Blessing and those two spells. We should keep in mind, boss, he most likely has them himself, as well."

"Makes sense, if you think about it from a strategic standpoint," said Aster, drawing up to walk on Deeyo's other side. "Hoy's Void power suits a frontline fighter, while Jadrak's is more organizational. Having the ability to grant Blessings will do a lot to secure loyalty."

"Well. There's that, anyway, I guess," Deeyo muttered.

"Listen, man," I said. "Speaking as someone who has fucked up enough in just the last few months for ten lifetimes, what's done is done. All you can do is clean up as best you can, and when it's something you can't fix? Well, you keep moving forward anyway, because there is just . . . nothing else. One foot in front of the other and do what you need to. You can't unhurt the people you've hurt, but there are plenty of people out there who still need help, and there always will be. You can always do that."

"Right. Yeah. I gotta . . . Man, I don't even know, after this," he said, staring blankly ahead. "I have no idea how to put any of this right. I just . . . I'll help bring him down. I have to. After everything . . . I have to do that, at least."

This was where I'd give him a companionable pat on the back if he were a bandit, but given our height disparity I'd have to either bend down to do it or just ruffle his hair, and either option felt condescending.

"Welcome to the Dark Crusade, Deeyo."

Ahead of me, Pashilyn turned her head, glancing back over her shoulder, and caught my eye. Her expression was merely thoughtful.

I was definitely going to have to do something about her. It would've been nice if I had even the vaguest idea what.

"Okay, Omura," Yoshi fortunately interrupted my train of thought at that moment. "I think I have a plan."

"Attaboy, I knew I could count on you!"

He looked surprised at that, but his expression almost immediately went back to worried. "I don't think you'll like it."

"At this point, I'd only be surprised if something happened that I *did* like. Hit me."

"Okay." Yoshi took a breath and let it out slowly, and I braced myself. If he was this nervous about just suggesting it, this was going to be bad. "I think we need to split up."

Well . . . not *that* bad, but still.

"I see the basic logic in that, of course," I said, keeping my tone carefully even. "We've got two important targets, two Champions and their respective entourages, and a tight timetable. The math checks out. I'm sure I don't need to remind you that the both of us together are roughly a match for Hoy and thus whoever has to face him alone is good and fucked?"

"Yeah . . ." He winced. "And . . . I'm really sorry, but . . . that's going to have to be you."

"All righty, then. Increasingly displeased," I admitted, "but still listening."

"Isn't that kind of backward?" Aster cut in, frowning at the Hero. "You're both strong fighters, so it doesn't seem to matter who ends up facing down Hoy, if it has to be one or the other. But whoever gets the *other* job is going to have to confront Jadrak in front of his followers, and *that* is going to come down to politics more than fighting, unless we want to turn it into an absolute massacre. Goblins are not going to be inclined to listen to the Hero anyway, and Lord Seiji is very good at working a crowd. *That* job is right up his alley."

She had a strong point. I turned back to Yoshi, wordlessly raising one eyebrow.

"I don't disagree," he acknowledged. "But there are two other important factors that change that calculation. The big one is that Omura has the weight of prophecy on his side if he faces Hoy at the Spirit."

"Ohhh," I whispered, remembering. "Oh yeah. I should've known that would come back to bite me."

"Wait, *prophecy*?" Pashilyn exclaimed, looking more startled than I'd ever seen her.

"The Spirit we spoke to," I said. "It said if I fought Hoy while he was trying to corrupt a Spirit, I should forego strategy in favor of unrelenting attack regardless of what happened. The exact words were that if I did that, I would get what I needed, even if I lost the battle."

"That is *not* promising!" Aster snapped.

"Sounds like a pretty dicey payoff," Nazralind agreed, frowning. "Stories about prophecies . . . it's exactly that kind of vagueness that always gets you in the end."

"Can Spirits actually tell the future?" I asked Biribo.

"Yes," he and Radatina chorused instantly.

I had to pause, blinking in surprise. "Huh. Gotta say, I was expecting . . . something else. Some kind of spiel about how the future isn't that simple and knowing it ahead of time violates causality or something."

"All of that is also correct," Biribo agreed. "If you wanna know *how* Spirits tell the future, I can't help you. That's not part of the inherent knowledge familiars get access to, and based on everything I understand about reality, it doesn't make any goddamn sense. All I know is that if a Spirit's reward involves any forewarning about the future, whatever it said *is* accurate."

"Right," I said in my cheeriest tone. "Plan so far, then, is I tackle Hoy all on my lonesome and probably get my shit fucked up six ways to Sunday, with the payoff of some indeterminate mumbo jumbo about 'getting what

I need.' So far, so dismal. Let's keep the hits coming, Yoshi, I think you said there were two factors to consider?"

"Yeah," he sighed. "I, uh . . . At the other end, I also need to lose."

"This is the worst plan I've ever heard," Flaethwyn stated. "And I'm including my parents' attempt to marry me off to an obese fifty-year-old half-elf. I'm honestly impressed, Yoshi; I never imagined anyone would top that."

"Couldn't happen to a nicer person," Zui muttered, and I made a mental note to skewer her later about daring to complain that the rest of us kept sidetracking the conversation with bickering.

"Just listen to me," Yoshi said, his patience visibly fraying. To my surprise, that did shut Flaethwyn up, and in fact seemed to worry her. "Okay, so looking at it with all the information we have, it's most likely that Jadrak *does* have the ability Hoy described, to sacrifice at least some of his followers' souls to gain more Void powers. The familiars say it's possible, which means that devil undoubtedly is aware of it, and that's probably a big part of why they manipulated this whole sequence of events into happening. I bet that would be the best payload of souls any devil ever bagged; the Devil King would probably give them a big promotion. *But,* that means we have to wonder why Jadrak hasn't already done it, right?"

"I thought I already went over that," I said, frowning.

"You did, and your theory is pretty sound," Yoshi agreed. "It wasn't his original plan and he doesn't want to do it. *That* is the key. It makes sense—Jadrak's ability to sacrifice his followers' souls is entirely contingent on them being fanatically loyal to him. As soon as he starts *doing* it, he'll probably stop being *able* to, because that will terrify everyone into turning on him. So even if he's enough of a ruthless monster to *plan* on that contingency, he has a strong practical motivation not to invoke it."

"Boy makes a solid point," Gazmo stated. "Trust me, I know goblins. If they're deeply, personally loyal enough that their very *souls* are forfeit on his say-so alone . . . Well, in the first place, that situation won't last long no matter what else happens. He'll only be able to pull that off while riding a wave of success and adrenaline. Soon as his campaign hits a major wall, that's off the table. And as soon as he starts actually *feeding people to a devil,* boom. No goblin would sign up for that."

"Right," said Yoshi, nodding. "So here's the way I see it—we need to take some of the pressure *off* Jadrak. We need to make him dither and be uncertain about invoking that extreme measure long enough for his momentum to falter so that he *can't* anymore."

"Ah." And with that, I was caught up. "So *you* want him to see the Hero, alone, coming at his defenses and . . . failing to make an impact. Make him feel less cornered, like he can still win this."

"Exactly. Especially if Hoy's elsewhere going after the Spirits, I'm confident I can at least distract and hold Jadrak off, especially with my friends backing me up, plus whatever local allies we can find. Hopefully Rizz has found more Judges and warned them about the Void. Whether or not I can actually get to Jadrak . . . As long as I *don't*, and he thinks his Void witch friend is out finishing off the Dark Lord, hopefully he won't be willing to pull the trigger."

"So you just have to stalemate him," I said slowly. "And . . . you're counting on me either beating Hoy alone, or pulling some vague Spirit nonsense out of my ass that'll make it not matter."

"I know how it sounds," Yoshi said, his shoulders slumping.

"No, yeah, this sounds like a needlessly elaborate mass suicide," I agreed. "However . . . the basic strategy *is* solid. Everything you said makes perfect sense. It's just . . . It's the parts we can't account for, y'know? No telling what's gonna happen if you go up against his core army alone, though I don't see it going a lot better than the *last* time you tried that."

Especially now that his party was down a member, but I decided not to bring that up. He definitely didn't need to be reminded.

"And," I continued after a momentary pause, "we've been over how *extremely uncertain* my own end of the plan is."

"Yeah." Yoshi nodded again, holding my gaze as we walked. "Yeah, it's . . . it's not good, Omura. But I think it's our only option."

"Well, one part lines up nicely, at least," Zui offered. "The nearest Spirit and our logical next target is the one Hoy mentioned, Mister Flats. From its cavern there's a tram tunnel that's a straight shot to the Fallencourt terminal. We can't actually take a tram, but that particular tunnel has a flat bottom and no canyons or anything, so we can get from there to Fallencourt on foot."

"Assuming we all still have feet," Nazralind said glumly. "And all our blood."

"I've gotta hand it to you, Yoshi," I said, "you sure called it. I hate every part of this plan. *And* I do not have a better idea. So unless anyone *else* has a better idea?"

I turned in a complete circle while walking, sweeping a pleading stare across the entire entourage of my followers, the Hero's party, and our goblin allies.

"Anyone?" I prompted. ". . . please?"

"We could all just jump into the core," Deeyo suggested morosely. "Save some time."

"Better." Zui jabbed him with her elbow, hard. "He said a *better* idea. Stop being a prick; the Dark Lord has that covered."

"I guess that's that, then!" I said, clapping my hands and plastering on a big smile. "We will carry out the Hero's idiotic, insane plan, and may the Goddesses have mercy on our souls."

"I'll tell you what, Omura," Yoshi said with a weak smile. "I'll take *your* advice, too. If we end up winning, somehow, I promise not to say 'I told you so.'"

"Well, you couldn't, anyway. Unless you're willing to guarantee this will work?"

He sighed heavily and turned to face forward again.

"Yeah, that's what I thought."

29

In Which the Dark Lord
Unburdens Himself

"We'll reach our goal before you do," Judge Gazmo stated at the cross-roads. "Your route goes the long way around; if you make good time you should reach the Flats tomorrow, assuming you stop for a few hours of rest. And *do* that," he ordered in a more serious tone, pointing a finger up at me for emphasis. "Hoy's route puts him behind you, and you do *not* wanna face him tired on top of everything else. You should still get there first in time to set up an ambush."

"You think we'll be back in Fallencourt by tonight?" Yoshi asked.

"We can be, if we push, but I wanna play it safer," Gazmo replied. "We'll reach the outskirts toward the end of today; at that point we'll slow down and look around, try to link up with whatever local resistance exists. Rizz was heading in that direction and most of the Judges will be hanging around there, anyway. Given they won't be able to approach Jadrak too directly, I expect to find people ready to help us on the fringes of the city proper."

The Hero nodded. "We'll be in your care, then."

"Um!" To everyone's surprise, including apparently hers, Amell suddenly piped up compulsively. Her eyes were fixed on me, for once. "Lord Seiji, I didn't . . . I'm sorry, I didn't have a chance to thank you. For the healing. I will . . . I owe you so much."

"Hey, you don't owe me a thing," I said in a gentle tone that hopefully outwardly suppressed the terrible awkwardness I suddenly felt. Man, I can handle almost anything except sincere displays of emotion. Especially in public. "We all have to have each other's backs in a mess like this. You handed out free potions to me, remember? From each according to their means, and so on."

She opened her mouth, seemingly failed to find a response, then just nodded deeply and folded down her hands at me. I figured the awkwardness was over, at least, but Amell was full of surprises today.

"Um . . . Zui." The alchemist inhaled deeply, then folded down her hands again, this time directly to the astonished-looking goblin. "I'm . . . so sorry. For how rude I was back . . . back there, in the city. You've been nothing but kind to me, and even after that, you helped me out of . . ." Amell flinched at her own train of thought, lowering her head. "Thank you."

"Uh . . . hey, don't sweat it, kid." Zui looked even more brutally uncomfortable at this than I had felt, which caused what might've been the warmest feelings toward her I'd ever experienced. Truly, we are all allies against the scourge of emotional vulnerability. "Like he said, people gotta stick together. Look, uh, when all this wraps up, you should have a sit-down with me and Youda. He handles the potions in Miss Sneppit's company, really knows his stuff. Between the three of us, I bet we can figure out something to do about that hair of yours."

"You—really? You think that's possible?" Amell's face lit up with so much hope it physically hurt to see.

Zui continued to feel about this roughly the same way I did, to judge by her awkward little grin and the way she began actually edging behind me. "Yeah, sure, I figure . . . it's at least worth a try, right?"

Yoshi came to everyone's rescue, because that's what Heroes do.

"I hate to ditch you like this, Omura. Though I admit I'd be sorrier if I could be certain you were getting the worse deal. I'm honestly not sure who's the more screwed here."

"Let's not make it a pissing contest, man. We both agreed to this terrible plan."

"Sorry for making a terrible plan, then."

"Yeah, well, maybe I'd blame you if I'd come up with anything better. I think you came up with the least shitty of our bad options, though."

He stepped forward, holding out his right hand, and I clasped it in my own.

"Give 'em hell," I urged. "But, y'know . . . gently. In a kind of lame, slapsticky way, so they don't respect you."

That won a smile from him, despite the gravity of the situation, but his expression swiftly hardened again and he squeezed down on my fingers.

"I won't say the same. Kick that little bastard's ass for me, Omura. And then come join us so we can finish this."

"You have my solemn word—I will survive this, or die trying."

He sighed, but Nazralind laughed. At least someone appreciated me around here.

"I don't think the 'little' part was necessary," Deeyo muttered.

"They can't help it," Ritlit said, slugging him on the shoulder. "Butts gonna butt. You gotta save up your complaints for where they'll do the most good."

"Hey, at least we'll be fine," Yoshi said, stepping back. "We've got Judge Gazmo to keep us out of trouble, after all."

"Don't expect miracles," the Judge grunted. "It's a slow day when I can manage to keep Fram out of trouble. You butts are on your own."

"He adores me," Fram assured us, smug as ever. "Dude's basically my dad."

Then she dodged, because Gazmo took a half-hearted swipe at her. As one does.

We were left standing in that awkward pause in which there was nothing left to be said, but none of us really wanted to move on just yet. And yet, standing around was not an option. We were on a deadline.

"Ganbatte," Yoshi finally said, nodding at me.

"You be careful," I replied.

We stepped back in unison and turned, heading down different branches of the tunnel path as our respective groups separated. The Dark Lord leading his lieutenants and band of goblin minions off to strike down his enemies, while the Hero and his party were led by the Judge and the Arbiter to go save who they could.

"Feels kinda like a missed opportunity, though, right?" Nazralind commented. "I was wondering if we'd mix up the teams a bit. Just for a little variety, y'know?"

"No point in messing with dynamics that work," said Aster. "We're used to functioning together, and I assume their group is the same."

"Sides," Adelly added, "nobody who doesn't absolutely have to wants to get stuck with Flaethwyn."

"It's rough, though, isn't it?" I kept my voice low, audible only to the two goblins walking on either side of me, which at the moment happened to be Zui and Deeyo. Both glanced curiously up at me. "When you start to see the other guys as people with their own viewpoints, out there doing their best. Shit's a lot less complicated when they're just evil assholes you don't need to understand."

Pause one beat for effect, and . . .

"Right, Zui?"

Her face melted into a deep, bitter scowl, which she directed at the distance ahead of us.

"Shut the hell up, tallboy."

Heh. Whatever happened with Hoy, at least I won this round.

Our route took us right along the northern edge of the island—I didn't even realize how close until the first time the tunnel turned into a ledge. There was no safety rail, of course, just an unthinkable drop into the swirling clouds below, and the deeply disorienting sight of the sky stretching off into infinity with no horizon. Ritlit's cheerful comment that on a clearer day than this you could sometimes see the distant landmass of Savindar did not help.

Fortunately, it wasn't all like that; even the tunnel had occasional gaps, providing a view of the sky while it was a tunnel, but the sections where we had to hug the actual outer shell of the island were horrifying but few. Whether this remote stretch was just uninhabited or everybody was hunkering down due to the civil war, we had the tunnels to ourselves, not encountering another soul on the entire trip. Biribo reported a few goblins moving through tunnels in the distance now and then, but always at the outermost extent of his senses and never in any corridors that connected directly to ours.

These flashes of daylight also helped us know when the daylight had faded. Aside from the necessary few small breaks, I kept us moving until after full dark, when we found a cavern with a partially crumbled ceiling along one corner, allowing us a view of the sky, along with a floor space big enough for the group, and only two entrances to minimize the chances of us being snuck up on.

Given the hour, I decreed a halt. As urgently as we needed to keep moving, Gazmo had been right—fatigue was a killer, and my experiences on Ephemera had already taught me that very well. Rushing headlong into another confrontation with Hoy was bad enough without making sure everyone had managed at least some sleep. I instructed Biribo to take the watch himself, since he was the only one who didn't actually need rest and could wake us up if anyone approached. Also, familiars were as reliable as clocks when it came to keeping time, so I ordered him to give us six hours before waking everybody up. Then we all settled down to sleep.

Easier said than done.

I found myself somewhat separate from the group up on a small ledge, rather like the last time we'd camped in a cavern. Not that I was flexing Dark Lord privilege or anything; everybody had spread out slightly for a tiny shred of privacy, as before clustering around the fire slimes I'd set out as impromptu campfires. There was a soft murmur of voices here and there, as clearly I was not the only one finding the combination of a rough rocky floor and tension over our situation antithetical to sleep. At least they were all actually lying down, only a few here and there whispering to each other quietly enough not to disturb their neighbors.

With no idea how long I'd spent staring up at the stars glimmering in a purple sky through that crack in the ceiling, I eventually gave up and, as quietly as I could, hoisted myself up to sit upright. Biribo was buzzing slowly around the perimeter of the chamber on his rounds. Everybody else seemed to be horizontal, though Aster had wedged herself into a crevice and slumped there in a reclining position, apparently having managed to nod off. Maybe I should try that. Deeyo was alone in another corner, on his side with his back to the room in a position that looked super uncomfortable. I couldn't tell from this angle whether Adelly and Nazralind were just stretched out side by side or actually cuddling, but I was starting to wonder if something was going on with those two. All the other goblins seemed to be laid out and either whispering together or earnestly trying to sleep, except . . .

Zui, seeing me sit up, ceased her own pacing and came to settle down about a meter away, saying nothing.

"You too, huh," I finally said, just loudly enough to be audible at that distance.

She didn't answer directly, just leaning back on her arms to stare up at that crack revealing the sky. I instantly had to look in another direction as that position strongly emphasized her bust and not much is less restful than flashbacks. If it had been Gizmit—or Sneppit—I would have assumed that was deliberate, but Zui had never seemed interested in flaunting herself. Also, she didn't seem to like me all that much.

"So, what's Japanese sarcasm like?" she finally asked, just as quietly.

Non sequitur, but okay. Safely irrelevant topics of conversation were probably better, anyway.

"Scathing. I reckon the most common use of it I've heard was to effusively compliment someone who's just done something stupid. Teachers *love* to do that."

"Sounds like you had shitty teachers, then," she grunted. "Fastest way to make sure a person doesn't learn anything is to make the learning a pain in the ass."

"Well, I won't argue with you there."

The silence, somewhat to my surprise, wasn't awkward. Maybe it was the fatigue, or maybe there just wasn't any real tension between the two of us. Come to think of it, as annoying as Zui frequently chose to be, I didn't have any problem with her as a person. She worked hard, got shit done, and always tried to do the right thing; you had to respect it. And if she went about all that in the most personally obnoxious way possible much of the time, well, I'm the last guy who has any right to complain about that.

"You as usual decided to be an ass about it, but you weren't wrong," Zui said after a pause, unexpectedly mirroring my own thoughts. "It's . . . complicated. I've had to clean up after a *lot* of human-inflicted damage over the years. Humans were just . . . things that caused damage. Hurt and killed people indiscriminately, stole stuff, and destroyed whatever they couldn't take. Impossible to ever truly get away from but still too dangerous to really deal with. Just malicious, cruel ogres, basically. You didn't have to think about why they did what they did. The sun rises, the winds blow, humans wreck everything."

I just nodded, staring up at the stars. I couldn't even tell if she glanced over at me; for some reason I was reluctant to disturb that moment by speaking, or even by moving my head.

"I guess everybody has their reasons," Zui finally said, more softly still. She shifted, and I turned just enough to see peripherally as she folded herself up, wrapping her arms around her knees and resting her chin on them. "It really makes you wonder. If I happened to be born a human, in the circumstances they're in . . . How would I have acted? You can't *not* think about that, once you talk with enough of them to see a bit of their situation. And . . . Man. It is just . . . *uncomfortable*."

"I have to think about this a lot," I admitted. "I'm trying to build a coalition out there. And on paper it seems like it should be easy, right? The whole strategy of shitty, incompetent rulers like the Fflyr is to divide and conquer. Keep everybody at each other's throats so they can stay in power and there's no solidified resistance. In theory, just making people *see* that should be half the battle."

She glanced over at me. "And in practice?"

"It's a different problem with every new group integrated. I've succeeded so far by starting with the easy ones. Fflyr society is extra shitty to women and especially prostitutes, so I recruited them first. With them being the original backbone of the organization, new people folded into it quickly learned not to try and act as shitty as they'd been raised to. That seems to have worked quite well, barring a few mishaps."

"Starting your Dark Crusade with prostitutes," she murmured. "Gotta say, that's not an approach that would've occurred to me."

"Probably because you've never been in a position to have to think about it. Sex workers get no respect, so nobody cares or even notices what I do with them. Anybody else would attract notice if I recruited them all for my bandit alliance. An army of whores? The idea would just make those in power laugh."

"Clever," she said, her tone grudgingly impressed. "Use their own preconceptions against 'em. That's goblin thinking."

I nodded. "From there . . . it hasn't been too hard to encourage acceptance of gay people and, uh . . . y'know, ones like Ydleth who were born the wrong gender, or . . . however you'd describe that. *Those* groups are small and inherently harmless; that's exactly why they always end up being targets. Nobody has any *actual* beef with 'em, beyond some vague sense of revulsion that they were taught growing up. Maybe a few pretty goofy lies about what they get up to in private. All of that starts to fall apart as soon as you start actually *meeting* a few of them, and realizing they're just folks like anybody else. Just trying to live, not hurting anybody and not needing any more shit."

"Yep." Zui nodded, staring moodily into space. "That's an awkward realization, all right."

"But I think I've gone as far as I can go that way," I murmured. "It's suddenly a whole different game when you're dealing with *actual* grievances. It's no less true that groups like the lowborn and beastfolk and goblins have been pitted against each other for the benefit of those in power, but there's been actual blood and death as a result of it. How am I gonna preach about the greater good to somebody whose parents were murdered by humans, or who ended up on the street because goblins stole their rent money? Then *I'm* the idiot talking in philosophical abstractions while they've got their boots in the mud dealing with real problems."

"Sounds like a real bastard of a dilemma," she agreed. Zui tilted her head to one side, resting her cheek on her folded arms so she could look at me directly. "I'd think you of all people would have some insight into this, given the backstory you told us on the tram. You're a child of two cultures, right? Or was that all a smokescreen to distract the Hero?"

"No, all of it was the straight truth," I said, mildly nettled by the accusation. "That experience doesn't really apply here, though. Those two cultures border on being mutually incomprehensible, but they've had good relations for most of a century by now." I hesitated, considering. "Though . . . they were particularly viciously at war just before that."

"Yeah? Well, maybe there's your answer. How'd that resolve itself?"

"Absolute conquest," I said, wincing. "One bombed into rubble, completely occupied by the other. Which then rebuilt the whole country from the ground up. That not only earned a lot of goodwill *despite* all the recent atrocities on both sides, but enabled them to install a new government that . . . Well, these days Japan is far from being a client state of America, but the current constitution makes it basically impossible to take an aggressive stance on . . . anything."

"Hm. You're not really in a position to do any of that, huh."

"Not yet. If I understand how this Dark Lord thing works, as long as I can keep staying alive, *eventually* I'll be able to wield overwhelming force and not have to deal with problems like this."

Her reddish-violet eyes bored into me, unblinking. "That is not gonna work out the way you're imagining, buddy."

"We'll see."

Zui rolled her eyes, shook her head, and stretched out on her back, folding her hands on her stomach and staring at the ceiling.

"Then again," I whispered.

She turned her head to give me an inquisitive look.

"I can already cause devastation on a scale I never imagined. I didn't even know it until the heat of the moment. With the powers closing in on me already . . . I wonder how long it'll be before I have no choice but to do something like that again."

Zui stared, unblinking, for a few long seconds, then rolled her head back to gaze upward again.

"Yeah, I noticed you changing the subject every time that priestess asked about the Inferno. Didn't even know it, huh. So you didn't actually do that on purpose?"

I looked away, though she wasn't even looking at me. "No comment. Just . . . Who would've thought khora were huge enough for *one* organism to cover most of the island? Much less that a spell would even *work* on something that size."

"Everyone. *Everyone* knows that." She snorted. "I guess, unless they came from a whole other world and don't know their ass from a crawn's nest. You know, those roots run all through Kzidnak. Goblins interact with them *closely*. They're a major source of both food and a lot of what makes our alchemy superior to what the Fflyr have. You had *better* believe we took note of *that* bullshit. Fortunately, nobody sleeps in 'em or anything, so it probably didn't cause any deaths or even serious injuries, but . . . I can't say for absolutely certain, but given the timing? I'm pretty sure it was a big part of what tipped Jadrak over the edge."

Well, wasn't that just a motherfucker.

"So tell me, Dark Lord Tallboy," Zui said, tilting her head backward a bit so she could stare at the stars. "Was that any different up top? Did you get what you wanted by destroying everything in your path? Or did that just cause another huge mess of fucking problems that you still don't know how to deal with?"

"Yeah, yeah. Wouldn't it be nice if we could all just hold hands and sing songs and agree to live together in peace?"

She sighed heavily, but didn't answer.

"You probably think I'm just being an asshole, Zui—and fair enough— but I'm also serious. That *would* be better. But in the real world, all the problems bearing down on us are caused by powerful people, on purpose, for their own benefit. And nothing is going to get better until some of them *fucking die*."

"I'm very much afraid that you're not wrong," she murmured, finally closing her eyes. "Just don't kid yourself that getting the bastards out of the way *is* the solution to anything. That just clears space for the solutions to start. At that point, you'll have to start doing the *real* work."

I looked down at her, then up at the stars again.

Nothing good could possibly result from telling Zui she was right, and there really wasn't anything else to say in response to that.

I stretched out on my back again, listening to the soft sound of her breathing and concentrating on my own.

In Which the Boss Leans In

So how's it look out there?" Sneppit demanded the instant Gizmit walked into the room.

"Pretty much exactly how I told you it would be the entire way here," Gizmit replied. "The situation's volatile, no place this close to Fallencourt proper is more than provisionally secure, and *you* have no business being this close to the action, boss. If Jadrak finds out you're here—"

"Fortunately, I pay the very best people to make sure he *doesn't* find out things like that," Sneppit interrupted, rather than have to listen to that speech again.

"This complex is as secure as we can make it," Dap said, defensiveness audible in his tone.

Gizmit gave him a look and a sigh. "I believe you. But as secure as it can be made is *not fucking very.*"

Sneppit cleared her throat, rescuing Dap before he could properly get his back up. She did not need infighting among her underlings, now of all times. Gizmit wasn't wrong, but Dap was still sensitive and raring to prove himself worthy of his quick promotion to chief of Sneppit's personal guard, since she'd left her actual head of security in charge of her headquarters.

"Noted. What *else*, Gizmit?"

"I have a few details I can contribute, but the most important thing I found out there can speak for herself."

Gizmit stepped deeper into the room and then to one side, clearing the way for the person who'd been following her to enter, carefully adjusting her polearm in the process so it didn't whack the doorframe.

"Rizz!" Sneppit put on a broad smile, spreading her arms in an effusive greeting.

"What the hell are you doing here, Sneppit?" the Judge demanded. "The girl's right, this is no place for a paper-pushing backroom dealer. What, you think Kzidnak doesn't have enough chaos right now? The little of it that's still relatively stable will go belly-up if you succeed in gettin' your little pink ass killed like you're so earnestly trying to."

"And it's lovely to see you, *too*, Rizz. I was also worried about your well-being, thank you for asking. Your boys are fine; they've been pitching in back at my HQ, really helpful in keeping all the refugees organized. How's Rhoka?"

"Rhoka's doing her goddamn job, and when she doesn't it's out of mis-guided compassion for situations that're none of her business. As opposed to *you*, swooping in on this mess like the scavenger you are in the hope you can hook up with the Dark Lord when he gets here."

"Rizz, you met the guy; he leads by charisma and raw firepower, not by having any idea what he's doing. When *he* swoops in here he's gonna need somebody with actual administrative skills to help, otherwise all of this is gonna get even messier than it needs to."

"Uh huh." Rizz propped the polearm against her shoulder and folded her arms. "And you're definitely only interested in what's best for Kzidnak, not at all in positioning yourself to take as much credit as possible for as little work possible so the Dark Lord'll appoint you Jadrak's replacement."

Sneppit's already sunny smile widened by a couple more teeth. "C'mon now, Judge, we're all adults here. Nobody needs to explain to anybody else that more than one thing can be simultaneously true. So, what's the news out there?"

Rizz grimaced at her, but opted not to push the argument further. "Well, as it happens, the news is goin' down right now. You're already too close to the action; a little more shouldn't hurt, provided you're supervised. *And*," she added, her broad hat brim bobbing as she looked Sneppit up and down, "assuming you can manage not to look like a hot pink exhibition for five minutes outta your life."

"As usual, Rizz, I am a step ahead of you. Ydleth, honey!" Sneppit called, raising her voice.

Amid the sounds of hurried activity as her entourage bustled about, setting up and fortifying her field HQ in this residence on the outskirts of Fallencourt, which they'd found abandoned, there rose the slaps of heavier-than-average footsteps. Seconds later, a human face appeared in the upper corner of the doorframe, having to bend down to peek through. Luckily the ceilings in here were high enough not to give their tallfolk allies much trouble, but the doors were rather inconvenient for them.

"Yo, boss lady," Ydleth replied.

"Good thinking on that disguise you arranged, darling," Sneppit purred. "I'm gonna need that sooner than expected. Can you be a lamb and dig it up for me?"

"No digging required; I packed that on top. Back in two shakes!" Ydleth promised cheerily as she vanished. Sneppit's smile diminished by a couple of degrees as the human's slightly muffled voice carried back to them from the room beyond. "Obviously, we all knew you weren't gonna have the sense to stay put and keep your head down like absolutely everybody's been telling you. Gotta be prepared!"

"Interesting operation you're running here, Snep," Rizz drawled.

"Hey, be nice to my new assistants; they're more than pulling their weight. And Ydleth there can kick a guy clear across the room."

There came a crash from the adjacent chamber, followed by peals of Madyn's laughter.

"Why did you *tell her* that?" Ydleth complained loudly.

"Aw, don't be like that, nobody blames you," Madyn chortled. "It's a great story! And he deserved it."

Rizz turned a very expressive stare upon Sneppit.

"See? They fit right in," Sneppit said sweetly. "Gives me a good feeling about Lord Seiji. You tend to think of humans as stuffy and obsessed with hierarchy, but he's clearly got his people accustomed to speaking their minds. It's like he's been preparing himself to lead goblins this whole time and didn't even know it. Ah, thanks, Ydleth, perfect. Okay, Rizz, let's go see what's so important."

Sneppit had to hand it to her—the sight of the Hero attempting to assault the Goblin King's fortress, alone, was pretty important. Especially given the way it appeared to be going.

"*What* is that boy *doing*?" She breathed in horror.

"Embarrassing himself," Rizz said dryly.

Jadrak had set himself up in Fallencourt's most ostentatious structure—a colossal pillar of stone formed by the union of a stalagmite with about the same floor footage as a modest Fflyr mansion and an only slightly smaller stalactite above. The originally natural formation had been fully carved out by goblins eons ago, both hollowed from within and its exterior shaved down so that it was now a neatly hexagonal tower connecting the floor and ceiling of Fallencourt's main cavern. Until this disastrous conflict, its ownership had most recently been shared by a consortium of business owners running several trading concerns, which specialized in higher-value goods than most goblins could afford. The Core Tower's defensibility made it ideal for both their purposes and Jadrak's, with thick walls, narrow windows, and only two points of access. There was a downward-sloping bridge from its main entrance to a broad ledge running along one side of the cavern's wall, itself a market space in better times; the Tower's only other entry was through a covered bridge of stone and iron leading into its secondary complex inside the walls of Fallencourt.

That, as any native of Kzidnak knew, would be the most sensible angle of attack if someone wanted to invade the Core Tower. Though the bridge itself made a highly defensible choke point, the complex on the other side had multiple entrances, including a small ledge that opened onto one of Sneppit's own tram tunnels. Unfortunately, that particular spot hung over a bottomless drop into the core, and the tram tracks leading there had been sabotaged over the last several hours, so that wasn't really a viable insertion point right now. Still, there were other accesses to those chambers; they were quite secure, but less so than the Core Tower itself.

The Hero, Yoshi, had chosen to go about this the hardest way possible, resulting in not only failure but ridicule; he was getting stymied right out in the open in the middle of Fallencourt, in full view of any goblin who might care to peek out a window. Or just stand openly in their doorways and bridges and ledges, laughing and jeering at his expense.

As they watched, Yoshi made another run for the bridge, his elf companion right on his heels with her artifact rapier up. Being more heavily armored and carrying a shield, he of course took the lead, though it barely helped. The second they began moving they came under heavy fire from every window of the Tower that overlooked them—and in particular from what had to have been every remaining sorcerer Jadrak had to call upon.

"**Light Barrier!**" Their support priestess did her best from her more secure position huddling under the stone awning of a nearby storefront, which was why their inevitable defeat was merely humiliating instead of lethal.

Shouts of "**Fire Lance!**" were followed by a volley of flame and force that pounded the magical shield, causing it to flicker to the very brink of collapse.

A follow-up volley of slingshot projectiles finished it off, the last few breaking through to impact Yoshi's shield; one scored a glancing blow against his armor, causing him to falter. Flaethwyn swiped two deftly out of the air with her rapier, an impressive display of the artifact's power. It wasn't enough, though.

Flaethwyn was the first to retreat as the projectiles kept up, not that she really had a choice. Yoshi actually hunkered behind his shield as best he was able and attempted to press forward, managing to get one boot on the foot of the bridge before the sheer concentrated force of slingshot rounds brought him to a halt.

Slingshot rounds, broken bottles, loose brickwork . . . Every window in the Core Tower that wasn't covered by one of the ridiculous green banners Jadrak had draped from the top of the structure had goblins crowded into them, jeering and hurling trash at the beleaguered Hero.

"**Light Barrier**!" Pashilyn's voice was growing hoarse; if not from the shouting alone, she was starting to falter. Sneppit knew that spell cost stamina from the caster as it absorbed impacts. Again, she barely managed to save Yoshi from the next round of Fire Lances.

He retreated again. Not fully back to shelter as Flaethwyn had done, but at least far enough that civilians couldn't just chuck junk at him. Still, he cowered behind his shield, carefully shuffling backward as the Light Barrier faltered and broke again. The last few spiked balls thunked against his shield.

Well, at least they didn't seem to have any more bombs to throw.

"What an absolute disaster," Sneppit groaned, absently adjusting the plain brown hood that covered her immaculately dyed hair. That and a heavy cloak were all that constituted Ydleth's "disguise;" it wouldn't fool anybody up close, but from this distance it should at least obscure her characteristic, vivid pinkness. Rizz had found them a deserted gallery high up toward the ceiling that afforded both an excellent view over Fallencourt and a measure of privacy from anybody looking up. "Doesn't that kid know anything about public relations? Nobody's gonna take him seriously after this."

"Why the hell would a Hero know anything about public relations?" Rizz asked wearily.

"Incoming," Gizmit suddenly said. By the time Sneppit looked up and managed to follow the direction of her gaze, Dap had already moved to place himself between her and the threat. "Wait . . . Weapons down, it's a Judge. No . . . an Arbiter."

Dap looked to Sneppit for confirmation; she gave him a reassuring nod, and he gestured his team backward. Meanwhile Rhoka, who'd been keeping this ledge secure until Rizz brought them here, moved in that direction to greet the newcomer. Sneppit couldn't actually see anything except the odd flash of furtive movement from a similar ledge some distance below and to their right, but she trusted Gizmit's eyes and know-how.

"Well, we gotta get the boy under control somehow," she murmured, watching Yoshi being driven back again. "This is a battle for hearts and minds more than territory; he's makin' our entire side look like assholes."

A roar suddenly echoed through the cavern, goblins from every corner of Fallencourt raising their voices in unison. If it wasn't every onlooker—and it wouldn't be; Sneppit knew many, if not most, of the goblins here were just trying to survive this madness—it was enough to create that illusion, which of course was exactly what he wanted.

The Core Tower featured a small balcony directly above its main entrance, two stories up. Onto this, from behind the livid green curtains hung there for just such an entrance, had just stepped the goblin who would proclaim himself King.

Jadrak was a handsome goblin, famously so; Sneppit had to acknowledge that and didn't begrudge it. *He* understood public relations and the value of putting an attractive face forward. His black hair was immaculately styled, flowing about his shoulders as if it were a softer texture than goblin hair actually was, the locks and the fluffy bangs that hovered dashingly over one of his eyes streaked with shining, metallic gold. That was his color scheme; he wore a stark black coat embellished with gold at the cuffs and embroidered along the sleeves, with a golden mantle draped over his shoulders.

Sneppit thought it was significant that there was no green in his ensemble except that of his skin. The symbol of his great revolution was for *other* people to wear; it signified followers, rather than leaders. Marks and stooges. Sneppit dressed her security people in pink, but that was because *she* wore it first and foremost. That, and Youda had happened across a cheap way to dye akornin armor pink and she hadn't been able to resist.

The Goblin King held up his hands, and the cheering quieted as the twang of slingshots fell silent. Below him, Yoshi risked peeking over the rim of his shield.

"So *this* is the Hero," he thundered, his voice echoing across Fallencourt and filling the space. Jadrak was more a match for Seiji than Yoshi; he definitely understood the value of performance. Also, he had a powerful set of lungs. "Look, I know this is a cliché, but I expected someone . . . taller. And that doesn't *begin* to cover why I'm disappointed."

Yoshi lowered his shield, his shoulders heaving with visible exertion. Still, he had the energy to *strike a pose*, planting his feet in a balanced stance and pointing his sword up at the Goblin King. Sneppit cringed; it was just so forced and clearly put on, making him look utterly foolish in contrast to Jadrak's effortless charisma.

"*You* are already dead," Yoshi shouted, causing her to cringe even harder. Clearly Seiji had not taught him how to project; his voice was thin and strained with the effort of yelling and didn't even travel as far as Jadrak's calmer tone. "Come down from there and face me yourself, if you . . ."

Whatever other nonsense he spewed was utterly drowned out by laughter and catcalls. Jadrak just stood there, smiling down at the embarrassed Hero, and waited for Yoshi to get tired of wasting air. Then waited *further* until he lowered his sword. The poor boy just couldn't look anything but sheepish in that moment.

Only then did the Goblin King raise his hands again. Fallencourt quieted at his wordless command, further emphasizing his power and dominant position.

"You like to talk, human," Jadrak said once it was quiet enough for him to be the undisputed center of attention. "But this is Kzidnak, and we know the value of talk—especially talk from *your* kind. If you want your words taken seriously, put them in writing. In fact, when you're ready, just ask *politely* and I'll draw up an agreement for us. Having the Hero's signature under articles of surrender will make a nice souvenir."

He smirked down at Yoshi, keeping his head tilted just enough to maintain his stare on the boy as he turned away, until he finally sauntered back inside through his ridiculous curtains. No sooner had he vanished from view than another round of slingshot balls were being launched, forcing the chastened Hero to backpedal away from the bridge entirely.

"We gotta get that kid outta there before he dooms us all," Sneppit hissed, glaring down at the scene of Yoshi's disgrace. "Dap, move out, we need to secure an exit route and—"

"Wait, wait, wait! Stop, don't do it!"

She turned, scowling in annoyance—*nobody* interrupted Miss Sneppit—to behold the Arbiter Gizmit had spotted approaching along the ledge at a run, waving her free hand overhead as if they didn't need to be discreet about their presence.

"Arbiter Fram," Rizz called out. "Where is Judge Gazmo? *Please* tell me you're not all that's left."

"Gazmo's fine, he's down there keeping an eye on the Hero," Fram panted, staggering to a halt next to them. "We came with them. Look, don't jump in, okay? This is under control! Everything's going according to plan; the Hero's doing his job *perfectly*. If this keeps up, we could actually win this!"

"Fram," Rizz said in a dangerous tone, "this is *not* the time for one of your—what you incorrectly think are—jokes."

"I'm dead serious, Judge, I swear!"

"If you came with *him*, then what happened to Lord Seiji?" Sneppit demanded.

"He's doing his part, too. Look, just trust me, we'll get everybody on the same page. See? They're retreating down there, it's time for a break. Hero or no, he can't keep that up forever, the boy needs to rest and recover. Gazmo's got some local allies we rustled up; they'll cover their tracks so they can get away. I'll grab 'em and we can convene for a chat, right? I assume you've got some kinda secure base set up here, Miss Sneppit, or you wouldn't've come yourself."

The Arbiter paused, then tilted her head to one side, looking Sneppit curiously up and down.

"Uh, speaking of . . . Why the hell *did* you come here? This is no place for—"

"Gizmit, go with her," Sneppit ordered. "Lead the Hero, the Judge, and whoever else they approve back to our hideout, and make sure nobody else follows."

"I'll do my best, but we're way too close to the action here for guarantees."

"Your best is what I pay you for. C'mon, Dap, back to base. Let's get ready to receive guests."

"Okay . . . that's not a bad plan, considering what you were working with," Sneppit said slowly, digesting the implications. Impressively quickly, Gazmo and Gizmit had gathered up the Hero's party and managed to get them back to Sneppit's improvised base of operations. Both had said, with dour looks, that they'd done their best to cover their exit, but actual *security* out here wasn't a prospect.

Madyn and Youda were busy handing out rations, both to the exhausted humans (and elf) and the assembled goblins. It was about breakfast time anyway, and even those who hadn't just been publicly spanked by the Goblin King's forces needed sustenance.

Sneppit kept her composure better than most of her followers; she could tell at a glance that she was far from the only one reeling from the revelations Yoshi and company had brought. By Virya's swinging teats, what a catastrophe. Even the pixie's hasty reassurance that none of them were in danger of having their souls taken wasn't much comfort. If it was only Jadrak's most devoted loyalists . . . well, Sneppit had zero sympathy for any of those assholes. She wouldn't personally have done anything as horrible as sacrifice them to a devil, but whatever took them off the board. If only that were the only effect it would have. Goddess, with the kind of Void power Jadrak could gain from potentially *hundreds* of souls . . . Never mind Kzidnak, *nowhere* would be safe from him.

"I see a big flaw in your strategy, though," she said after contemplating for a moment.

Yoshi had just been handed a bowl of stewed mushrooms and khora root, and now lowered it to give her a serious look. It still bemused Sneppit, how the Hero treated her with automatic respect. Granted, it had taken some intervention from the Dark Lord to get him there, but this wasn't how things worked in any of the stories.

"To be honest, it's more flaws than strategy," Yoshi admitted. "Omura agreed to the plan, but . . . I'm under no illusions. We're doing the best with what little we have in an extremely bad situation, Miss Sneppit. I know you're a more strategic thinker; if you have *any* suggestions, I'll be grateful for them."

"Yeah, it's not great, but you're right—for what you're working with, it's a good gambit. The issue that jumps out at me is that you're propping up Jadrak's mystique at the same time you're keeping him hopefully too calm to pull that doomsday trigger. Making him look good in front of all his followers is only cementing their loyalty, which is *keeping* them on the table as potential sources of Void fuel."

"There's not really a way around that, though," said Judge Gazmo.

"And I'd contest the idea that this is *keeping* that option open," Rizz added. "At worst, it's prolonging the situation, not securing it. Goblins are still goblins, Sneppit. If Virya herself came down on a cloud and gave Jadrak everything his little heart desired right in front of all his sycophants, he'd *still* run out of the kind of loyalty he needs to invoke this soul contingency. He's coasting on crisis and showmanship right now, but goblins *will not* maintain that kind of slavish devotion over the long term. I give it days at *most* before the option's effectively dead."

"I'm not sure we can hold off for days," Yoshi said with a grimace, picking up his spoon.

"Itadakimasu!" chorused Ydleth, Madyn, and the dozen goblins of Sneppit's entourage as they tucked into their own breakfast.

Yoshi dropped his spoon into his stew, staring at them in shock.

"Oh, you recognize that?" Sneppit asked. "What are they saying, anyway?"

"W-where did they *hear* that?" he stammered.

She shrugged, scooping up a bite of her own. "It's something those two butts do at meals. They *immediately* got basically every goblin in my company doing it over the last couple days, plus most of the refugees we took in. I don't even think it was on purpose; people just enjoy having fads to glom onto. Specially during rough times like this, eh? Seemed harmless enough."

The Hero raised a trembling hand to cover his eyes. "Omura, you absolute . . ."

"This . . . *is* harmless, right?" Sneppit asked pointedly. "Is there something I should know?"

"I . . . that . . . Uh, I think we should focus on immediate problems," Yoshi hedged. "If we all survive this, though, you should ask Omura about it as soon as everything here is settled."

"Well, sure, I'll add it to the list," she shrugged. "He and I have a *lot* to discuss, anyway."

Sitting silently beside Yoshi, the priestess glanced over at Sneppit over the rims of her spectacles. Not for the first time, she observed that Pashilyn was far too quiet and observant. In any other circumstances, Sneppit would regard *her* as the greatest long-term danger in the Hero's party. And circumstances could change quickly.

Like the subject, which she now smoothly diverted from what she sensed could become a problematic matter.

"How long do you think you *can* keep this up, then? Sorry to put the weight on your shoulders, kid, but it sure seems like there's nothing else we can do until Lord Seiji finishes off that Void witch and gets back here."

"If," Flaethwyn muttered. "The word you want is *if.*"

"If I can manage to hold up my end, I have to have faith Omura can handle his," Yoshi said, nodding decisively. "We'll hold out as long as we can. The chance to rest and refuel is very much appreciated, Miss Sneppit, but we'd better not linger long. I'll go make another run at the defenses as soon as we're finished up here. If we pace ourselves . . ." He looked over at his friends questioningly. "And as long as Amell's potions hold out . . . Most of today, hopefully? Optimistically."

"I, um, I'm not sure my stocks are going to keep us on our feet that long," Amell said, cringing. "After everything, even with what we took from the old mining offices, I'm low on . . . all of it."

"Now *that* we can definitely help with," Sneppit stated. "Youda? I want the stocks opened to the Hero's team. This is no time for scrimping and saving; anything and everything they might be able to use, they get."

"You got it, boss!" Youda said cheerfully, waving his spoon at her. "Ain't like I brought my entire lab out here, but we're kitted out for a decent support plan. Bet I can keep 'em upright for at least a few more hours."

"I know the Hero's going to be on the front lines, but it's a good idea to keep some supplies for your own people, Sneppit," Rizz said pointedly. "You're dreaming if you think you're gonna stay undiscovered past lunchtime, optimistically. *Everyone* is going to be fighting by the time the Dark Lord gets back. Don't keep all your coins in one pouch."

"Well, sure, it's not as if they can even *carry* our *entire* stock," Sneppit countered. "Trust me, Rizz, this is not my first time planning an operation under pressure."

"I'm a bit surprised to see you out here yourself, Miss Sneppit," Yoshi said in a careful tone. "You seem like more of a behind-the-scenes planner. No offense, of course! It's just, we're awfully close to the center of danger here."

"Yes, so everyone has been pointing out to me," she said sweetly, "repeatedly and at length, as if I were unable to discern obvious facts for myself."

"And yet, here you damn well *are*," Rizz growled. "If it's so obvious—"

"Life's not about what you can see, it's about what you *understand*, and how well you're able to *leverage* what you learn. Yeah, it's risky. Everyone knows it's risky. But while you all see only the risks, *I* see the opportunity."

Sneppit leaned back in the high-backed chair she'd insisted on bringing exactly for moments such as this, smiling knowingly over the assembled goblins, humans, and one disgruntled elf.

"That's why I'm the boss."

The bad timing was probably just a result of the dicey situation they were all in, but she wouldn't have put it past Gizmit to do it on purpose. Whatever the cause, that was the moment her most senior intelligence agent chose to dart into the room, making a beeline for Sneppit's side.

"They've found us," Gizmit stated curtly.

Immediately, everyone set down spoons and grabbed for weapons.

"There's nobody in the vicinity closing in," the Hero's pixie familiar protested. "The only goblins outside this complex are Sneppit's own guards."

"You think they've figured out the range of your senses?" Yoshi asked.

"It's not that," said Gizmit, shaking her head. "They're keeping at a distance on purpose. I was hailed while doing a sweep. Boss, Jadrak *does* know you're here, personally. *And* the Hero. He sent somebody with a message. They want to open negotiations."

There was a momentary pause.

"Trap," Gazmo stated. "*Obvious* trap."

"Obviously, yes," said Sneppit, a smile beginning to curl across her lips. "But . . . *but.*"

"Oh, here we go," Rizz groaned.

"Rizz, don't be melodramatic, you don't have the delivery for it. Yoshi, hon, eat your stew. All of you need your strength. *This* is how we win. We just need to make Jadrak feel secure *and* waste his time, right? Well, let him have his trap; ours is on his way here with news of a dead Void witch and the end of all this carnage. Because trust me, if there is one thing *I* can do, it's keep Jadrak occupied with pointless bullshit until it's too late for him to salvage his little revolution."

"You're hanging a lot on that," Gazmo said skeptically. "What happens if the Dark Lord fails?"

"If the Dark Lord fails," Sneppit answered, "then we're all as good as dead, all of Kzidnak is shortly to follow, and the entire rest of Ephemera will be on the chopping block unless the Goddesses themselves get off their celestial asses for once and step in. So yeah, I've got faith in Lord Seiji, because I have to. We will proceed upon the assumption that we are *not* irretrievably fucked. What the hell else are we gonna do?"

For once, nobody argued.

30

In Which the Dark Lord Goes to Hell and Gets a Souvenir

The Flats was another astonishingly scenic location, one more surprising example of how there were more picturesque spots under Dount than on it. Because apparently nothing in Fflyr hands could ever be worth a damn.

At first glance, it reminded me strikingly of an airplane hangar—it had that shape. The cavern was longer than it was wide, with a smoothly arched roof, and its opposite end open to the empty sky, offering a horrifying view of the drop into eternal nothingness. As everywhere else, goblins didn't seem to bother with safety rails. The name of the place doubtless came from the tiered floor, where flat sections of ground ascended in a series of short, smooth steps that looked carved by eons of water. Each step was a few centimeters at most, not an imposition even for goblins, but rising the length of the cavern they came to the highest point right at the open end, and there sat the Spirit altar. Its base was about at my waist level when I stood at the entrance, so about at eye height for the locals. The arched ceiling had been completely painted with those mixed murals goblins liked, and structures had been built along and into the walls. Down here at the front end, two other tunnels crossed the path right in front of us, a track for Sneppit's tram running out of one and down the other.

And that first glance was all the time I had to take it in, because Hoy had beaten us here.

"Too slow, and too weak, dipshit," he called, turning his head to grin at me over his shoulder without taking his hand off the top of the Spirit's altar. Already the thing had no glowing head as normal; its usual blue-green lights were pulsing rhythmically up from the base, flickering to red where they reached his palm, and then resuming their normal color.

I had no idea what this process was, how long it took, or even how long he'd been here; by all accounts he shouldn't have been able to beat us. That meant we had *no* time. Hoy had a brand-new entourage, nine other goblins with slingshots, who now spread themselves out in a line facing us as my own followers did likewise.

"Biribo," I said quietly, "do they have bombs?"

"I can't make hundred-percent guarantees on finicky details at this range, boss, but I'm mostly sure those're just iron balls."

"Mostly sure will have to do." I studied their formation, the terrain, the open end of the cavern, and contemplated as rapidly as I ever had in my life. "All right. I'm changing the plan. Swap ammo, everybody. Open with whatever explosive rounds you've got; aim to take out his support, not Hoy himself. Deeyo, Fire Lance any stragglers we miss. After that, take your shots at Hoy if you get a clear one, but please try not to shoot us in the back. Aster."

I drew my rapier and stepped forward. She fell into step beside me, and then pulled slightly ahead, reaching up to draw her greatsword. I really appreciated how that thing's scabbard worked; you physically could not pull a sword that size out of a normal scabbard from that position, so it was open all along one side with an ingenious little clip-like device at the top, so she could snap it in and out at the base of the blade. Efficiency aside, it was great for showtime—she basically just reached up, grabbed the handle, and pulled the magic lever that left her with a big-ass blade resting across her shoulders in Cloud Strife pose.

"Stay behind me," I murmured.

"Fuck off, my lord."

Ah, that's my Aster. Living proof that loyalty and obedience are very different concepts.

"I will give you all one chance," I said, projecting; my voice boomed throughout the cavern. Hot *damn*, the acoustics in here were phenomenal. Why was this not being used as a concert venue? "Surrender now, and you'll be taken under my protection. Hoy may try to kill you if you do, but he will *definitely* try to kill you if you stay with him. That's what he's done to every group of suckers I've seen him lead so far. The Dark Lord shows mercy, when possible. That's better than you'll get from the Goblin King as his own loyal supporters."

I came to a stop, Aster pausing and then moving back one step to stand alongside me. The goblins shuffled, glancing nervously and unhappily at each other; I was just close enough to see their expressions. It made me uncomfortably aware that I was about to kill people who were mostly fighting me because they were too scared to quit.

Well, fine. Killing people should never feel comfortable. We all do what we have to.

"What the fuck?" Hoy looked up from the Spirit again, incredulously. "What are you morons *doing*? Just *shoot* his ass!"

I had my amulet and Aster her chain mail, and we were far enough back that the artifacts weren't neutralized by Hoy's Void magic. Plus, I had Heal. Still, best not to get shot if we didn't have to. I raised my rapier overhead and whipped it down to point at the goblins as they brought up their slingshots. We hadn't prearranged the signal, but my people knew one when they saw one.

Slingshots twanged, Aster shifted in front of me, raising one arm to cover her face, and I tried to pull her back. As a result we both got hit, but glancing blows only—still enough to nearly knock both of us down.

We got the better of that exchange, by far.

The bombs impacted with beautiful precision; my slingers had taken aim at the feet of the enemy goblins, and I couldn't be sure but I suspected a couple had deliberately shot at Hoy so his Repulsion Aura would fling the incoming rounds back into his own defenders. Smoke, shrapnel, and pieces of goblins flew, and the entire line of them went down.

Including Hoy. Oh, he wasn't killed or probably even singed too badly; I never got to be that lucky. But it takes a special kind of person to stand their ground while everything around them was being pelted with grenades, and Hoy's entire problem was that nothing about him was special. He yelled, staggering away from the Spirit and covering his head with both arms, also barely keeping on his feet amid the shrapnel.

I cast a quick Heal on myself and Aster.

"Son of a *fucking bitch*," Hoy spat, turning to glare at us. A meter away, the Spirit had gone dark again. Whatever that Void process was, he had to start over.

So of course, he immediately lunged back for it, palm outstretched to slap down on top.

And I knew what I had to do; had known before I came here.

Unrelenting attack.

We both charged forward in unison, Aster going straight down the middle while I peeled to the side and drew my dagger, vanishing from sight. This time, Hoy had positioned himself behind the Spirit, facing the front of the cavern, and he wasn't having this.

"**Fire Lance! Fire Lance! Fire Lance! Fire Lance!**"

The first hit nailed Aster in the chest, singeing her coat and stopping her momentum dead; the artifact mail should have protected her from serious injury, but I Healed her anyway. It was all I could do, as I had my own problems now. Hoy shot a Fire Lance at a pretty good guess as to where I would be, and would've scored a hit had I not zigzagged immediately after going invisible. But he just kept throwing those damn things, and in the next three seconds I had two near misses. My Amulet of Final Luck wasn't going to do a whole lot against *that*—and he'd accidentally found the weakness in my target-blocking ring. It didn't block shit if I wasn't being targeted.

"**Fire Lance!**"

Heal!

He'd found another counter, unfortunately; I wasn't going to let him just blast Aster to bits. Already her overcoat was in charred rags, revealing the formfitting silver-white chain mail beneath, and the artifact's effect of drawing fire toward itself and away from uncovered areas was probably the only reason she hadn't lost a limb, or her head.

"**Fire Lance! FIRE LANCE**, asshole!"

Deeyo tried, bless him. Those fire spells flickered away to nothing by the time they got within two meters of Hoy, though. The Void witch, who I could usually rely on to stop what he was doing and ineptly trash-talk in the middle of a fight, only gave Deeyo a contemptuous glance before resuming his barrage at Aster. He seemed to get the stakes here. Of all the damn times for this idiot to finally pull some professionalism out of his ass.

I was closing fast, but I knew the invisibility would fade once I got close to sword range. Maybe Deeyo's covering fire would at least distract Hoy enough that I could—

Nope. His eyes suddenly shifted, locking onto me the instant I was a vague outline. I was *just* out of range to lunge at him. He wasted time pointing his finger at me and shouting the spell, having apparently forgotten I was untargetable—

"**Force Wave!**"

Aw, fuck, wrong spell.

Well, I did regain my invisibility as I was sent hurtling backward. Unfortunately, now Hoy knew roughly where I was—but only in a general sense, which meant he could just hammer the vicinity with Fire Lances and my ring wouldn't protect me. Aster was down, struggling to get back to her feet, but those repeated spellfire hits had taken a lot out of her, even with my Healing.

And then a green streak with a punk rock haircut shot out of one of the side structures, beelining for Hoy.

He saw the motion and reflexively turned, but he'd been about to fire at me, he was in the wrong orientation, having not expected an attack from that direction.

Zui hopped nimbly over the body of a blown-up goblin, hit the smooth stone floor on her knees in a gloriously absurd powerslide, and cannoned right into him just as he turned toward her. Hoy's belated shift in position only meant that her uppercut hit him right between the legs.

At least half a dozen people hissed in sympathy; the wonderful acoustics meant I heard them all.

"Zui, *no*," I exclaimed. "Not cool! He may be a piece of shit, but we gotta have *standards*."

"Oh, you are *ridiculous!*" she snarled. "Just shut up and kill the Void witch already, Dark Lord!"

Well, she *had* said she was good in a fight. Then again, I very much doubted she'd learned *that* doing a stint as a security guard. Were those—holy shit, she'd hit him with brass knuckles. Well, that impact would take him out for—

About four seconds, as it turned out. Hoy staggered back, his legs buckling as he grabbed his crotch in sheer reflex . . . but only reflex. I mean, *any* guy would, but apparently his Repulsion Aura worked on more than just projectiles.

Baring his teeth at Zui, he slapped one hand back down atop the Spirit altar and aimed the other at her. She had no artifacts or even armor; that spell at that range—

I couldn't say exactly why I did it. I definitely wasn't operating on any kind of *strategy* at that point, but I slammed the invisibility dagger back into its sheath and charged at him, drawing his attention.

Hoy's eyes cut to me, and he pivoted, aiming his casting arm awkwardly across the other one. I dodged as he shouted the spell; the Fire Lance grazed my left side. Crap, that spell burned hot enough that near misses were dangerous, even if he couldn't target me directly. I cast Heal immediately, of course, but my sleeve was still smoldering as I staggered into him, too ungainly from the scorching to bring up my rapier effectively. This close to his Void blessing, the rapier's Mastery enchantment wasn't working, and my Surestep Boots only managed to keep me from taking a pratfall. I almost stumbled *past* him, my recently freed hand flailing for balance—

Oh. Unrelenting attack. *Even if you lose, you'll get what you need.*

Well, here went nothing.

I caught my footing and slammed my free hand down atop Hoy's. My fingers were longer; I was able to grab the slightly angled stone surface by its edges, just barely.

The altar began pulsing light again, but this time an error code popped up, hovering in a circular line above its crown, two messages alternating:

ONE USER PER ACTIVATION
RESOLVE

"What the *fuck* did you do?!" Hoy bellowed. He wasn't letting go of the Spirit, and neither was I. So I stabbed him. Well, I tried to.

In an *annoyingly* impressive display of physical aptitude, he hooked his toe under the stolen Judge's polearm he'd dropped nearby, kicked it up into his hand and whipped it at me, deflecting my attempted thrust.

What ensued had to have been the most ridiculous duel in history. Neither of us dared to take our hands off the Spirit that was in the process of becoming a Void altar, and with those hands occupied by holding on to it, we couldn't even have a thumb war to dislodge each other's grip. Instead we went at it with the weapons in our other hands—weapons that were much too long to use in such close quarters. We couldn't get the right angle for proper thrusts and couldn't pull back for a wide slash without leaving ourselves open, so we hammered at each other with a series of highly aggressive parries that went nowhere. It was like something out of the first chase scene in a Jackie Chan movie.

Maybe Virya should have made Jackie the Dark Lord. I'd watch that.

Apparently, the Spirit—or what was left of it—got tired of waiting for us. The lights suddenly shifted to a deep purple, and the message changed again.

RESOLVING

Hoy and I mutually hesitated, looking at the message and then back at each other. He couldn't read the text, presumably, but he could tell something had gotten fucked up, which to be fair, was also as much as *I* knew.

"This is *your* fault, shit-for-brains!"

"Dude, how much of everything you have *ever* done comes down to compensating for something?"

He snarled and whacked me with his staff, the swing too wild to be truly effective, not that it made a lot of difference at this range. And then I had the epiphany that my legs were almost as long as Hoy was tall, and I only needed one to stand on. Okay, look, some things seem blindingly obvious in hindsight, but when you're right in the middle of a frantic situation your focus narrows, your brain locks into established patterns, and you can forget extremely evident facts, like your ability to straight up kick a motherfucker.

So I kicked him. Apparently, I wasn't the only one who'd failed to realize this was on the table, as it took Hoy sufficiently by surprise that I landed a firm, solid blow. The air went out of him in a grunt and he was sent hurtling away, his hand ripping out from under mine. My palm landed flat on the top of the nascent Void altar. Last man standing.

And as per *fucking* usual, I was a split second too late to call victory because of it.

Even as Hoy went flying, so did Aster and Zui, and also Biribo, propelled away by some force with no source that I could see. The instant they were all outside its radius, a circular wall flashed into place from floor to ceiling, enclosing Hoy and myself in a space with the Spirit at its center. The barrier was white light, arranged in hexagonal cells; the borders were glowing and opaque, but we could see out through the individual panels. Aster immediately vaulted back to her feet and took a powerful swipe at the barrier with her greatsword. No effect; we couldn't even *hear* the impact in here. Biribo was buzzing frantically around the exterior, bashing himself impotently against it like a bug on a windshield.

"Oh, *now* you've gone and done it," Hoy said in an uncharacteristically grim tone.

The Spirit flashed back to red, cycling through a series of messages.

RESOLVING USER HIERARCHY
DIMENSIONAL BOUNDARY ESTABLISHED
ACCESSING DIMENSIONAL INSULATION LAYER
STANDBY

We did not stand by.

Hoy, who couldn't even read the messages, came at me with his staff, and I danced away from the Spirit to bring my rapier into play. Now *this* was more of a fight—no artifact powers, neither able to hit the other with spells, just weapons and skill alone. Well, *some* artifact powers; my Surestep Boots were enhancing my footing, and since my defensive artifacts still worked, presumably the Amulet of Final Luck would protect me from lethal hits. And anything else I could Heal.

So . . . huh. Turned out, if you locked me and Hoy in an indestructible isolation chamber, it was advantage Seiji, just the way I liked it. He couldn't Flicker anywhere, and I could survive anything he hit me with. I just had to hold out long enough to wear him down.

"**Force Wave**, motherfucker!"

Goddammit, I hated that thing. I went flying and impacted the wall of light, learning that it was solid as titanium, and barely managed to land on my feet after slumping down from it. A quick Heal cleared my head and I lunged at him again, rapier first. So he Force Waved me back into the wall.

Okay, I might have misjudged who would be wearing down whom in here.

Then the air turned green, and we both had to pause and take stock.

On second look, it wasn't any thickening of the air, but a shift in ambient light. The hex-paneled energy shield had changed to luminous green, and the panels seemed to have gone translucent; at any rate, the scene outside was watery and indistinct. Also, there was no sign of Aster or Zui—or, I realized, anyone, not even the bodies. And the murals decorating the arched ceiling . . . Despite being trapped in a cell with someone who urgently wanted me dead, I had to stare. Patterns of light swirled and flickered, not quite mimicking the art itself, but . . . I didn't know how I knew this, but I intuitively did—I was seeing resonances of the *intent* of those who had created the paintings, and all who had viewed them, filtered into visual data.

"Oh, *fuck*," Hoy whimpered, the first time I had ever heard him sound genuinely frightened. I turned to find him staring in the other direction, out the open end of the cavern at what should be the swirling mists of the core below. So of course, I followed his gaze to see what was so terrifying.

Oh.

Yeah, that was easily the worst thing I'd ever seen.

The sky was green, and noticing that was barely an afterthought. There was no mist, no core; the world was filled with monsters. It was like what

H.P. Lovecraft might have dreamed after eating bad pad thai. Tentacles, claws, eyeballs, and all of it on an unthinkably colossal scale; these beasts could pick up Godzilla and fling him like a plastic toy.

Except that they were dead.

Their decaying mass *filled the world*, occupying most of the space between the core of the broken planet and the surface of the islands. Just . . . an endless expanse of slaughtered cosmic monsters. Broken claws bigger than skyscrapers lay scattered, unthinkably colossal bones connecting them to city-sized tentacles that lay slumped, half-dissolved into rotted slime. Vast eyeballs like lakes and mountains were clouded in death, or popped and collapsed, staring into the infinite nothingness of the blank, green sky.

Whatever calamity had destroyed Ephemera had clearly killed even its eldritch horrors. Just what kind of powers were Virya and Sanora messing around with?

"Look, man," I said, immensely satisfied to find my voice even, "I know you like to blame me for *all* of your disappointments in life, but I have no idea what the fuck this even is."

"What the fuck this *is*," he hissed, "is that you got us sent to the Void, you stupid fuck! Physically! We are *in the fucking Void*!"

"Ohhh, right, of course. Because I was fucking around with devils and Voidifying Spirits. I forgot it was *me* who did that."

"*We can't be here*!" Hoy shrieked. "Nothing but devils can live *in* the Void!"

"Okay, well . . ." I shrugged and made a vague gesture with my rapier. "Here we are, though."

I thought he was gonna have an aneurysm right on the spot. Dude was so dementedly angry he could only make a one-handed throttling motion at me, not even trying to attack with the weapon he was holding.

The ex-Spirit, now Void altar, interrupted our extremely productive debate with what passed for an explanation.

"Isolation sequence successful. User hierarchy will now be resolved. One user per activation, please."

It had that processed, resonant quality of Spirit voices, but this was nothing like their usual delivery; rather than mimicking human intonation it was deliberately flat, clinical, like one of those AI-generated robot voices except even worse.

"Me! *I'm* the user!" Hoy screamed, waving his polearm about in impotent rage. "*I* corrupted you! You will *serve me*, Spirit!"

"This node is compromised. Spirit routines are inactive. User-on-user elim-ination is deemed improbable in this instance. Hierarchy will be determined by level of system access."

"Did we really need to be sent to an alternate dimension to do that?" I demanded. "Seriously, if you're just gonna play twenty questions, what was wrong with Ephemera?"

"User requests will be processed by ambient local magic. State your requests."

"I demand *power!*" Hoy yelled, beating me to the punch. "Whatever power you are *supposed* to give me! In the name of the devil Ozyraph, you *will* grant me . . . uh . . . spells! Void magic! Goddammit, *whatever you were supposed to!*"

"User Ozyraph is not present. Directive unclear."

Oh . . . now I saw how this worked. I understood why a Spirit had told me to push the attack now, to stay in contact with this while it went down.

And I finally understood what another Spirit had done to prepare me for this moment, before I'd even considered it.

"Hey, I'm Omura Seiji," I said. "Champion of Virya. I believe she should have some access credentials, yes?"

"You can't fucking do that!" Hoy screamed, lunging at me with his polearm. Fortunately, he was too mad to focus on magic; I deflected his wild swing with my sword and kicked him again, hard. He went tumbling ears-over-boots to impact the glowing hex-wall, dropping his weapon in a daze.

"Administrator Virya is not present. User hierarchy cannot be resolved by affiliation."

"Okay," I said. It was worth a try, but I still had the advice Head Start had given me. "Then if you'll examine my . . . uh . . . aura? Magical data storage? Whatever it is, you'll see . . . *Administrator* Virya gave me the unique ability of spell combination."

"Confirmed."

All right, so far, so good. "You'll also find I have an unactivated spell, Cast Illusion. I would like a copy of the spell Create Material, to be integrated with it using my spell combination, according to the following parameters—"

"Confirmed. Access granted to user Omura Seiji. Notation has been attached for fulfillment of these conditions by Administrator Virya. Combined spell has now been installed."

"Wait, no, I wanted—"

I felt it burst behind my mind the way gaining new spells usually did, except this was different. Cast Illusion took on a form—one I had *not* designated for it—and combined with the new spell, Create Material. It was totally unlike my own fumbling attempts to make spell combination work. It was seamless, fluid, and utterly precise, guided by the system itself and not my inept jury-rigging.

And it gave me the ability to conjure what *Virya* thought I should. Immediately I sympathized with Hoy. The rage suddenly pounding in my temples felt like it wanted to explode out of them. Was there *nothing* she couldn't stick her greedy little fingers into and fuck up for me?

"*User hierarchy resolved,*" the dead Spirit's voice intoned flatly. "*Reward administered. Users will now be removed from the dimensional insulation layer. Thank you for participating in Test World Six.*"

"No," Hoy whispered, his voice cracking. "You're not even—you *can't*—"

"Looks like I just did, sport," I said, giving him my most insufferable smile. The fury pounded in me, but unlike him, I rode the wave like an expert surfer instead of letting it just throw me wherever it wanted. Rage filled my limbs with tingling energy, and I remained lucid atop the current.

I lunged at him with my sword, and got Force Waved again for my trouble.

This time, though, I landed neatly on my feet, outside the . . . oh, huh. The wall was gone. So was the Void. We were back, and there was a *lot* of yelling.

"Boss!" Biribo shouted, zipping around my head in a full circle. "What happened?! Are you okay?"

I didn't answer, because I was *really* enjoying the sight of Hoy having to dodge a massive greatsword sweep from Aster. Just because the artifact's *powers* didn't work against him didn't change the fact that it was a big chunk of sharpened metal capable of cleaving someone in half, in the hands of a fit woman twice his height. He barely got out of range with his head still on, which resulted in him dodging right into Zui's brass knuckles.

Blood flew, along with a tooth, and Hoy went spinning into the now-inert Spirit altar, bonking the side of his face against it. He managed to stay conscious, though, tumbling to the ground in a roll that brought him upright a couple meters distant, back toward the front of the cavern.

That put him directly in the line of fire of my goblin allies, plus Nazralind and Adelly, all of whom immediately unloaded at him. His Repulsion Aura meant none of the projectiles hit—and in fact, Zui had to skitter back as they began to ricochet—but every impact was wearing that aura down.

We had him on the ropes, and he knew it. Even his magic seemed to be fading, otherwise Zui couldn't have landed such an effective hit—nor could

I, for that matter. I could see the looming realization of it in his eyes. The combination of rage and satisfaction roared through me like . . . Well, I kind of regretted never having tried cocaine, now. I bet it must feel something like this.

"Don't you *dare* look smug," the defeated Void witch snarled. "You got *one* win; you'll get no more. You don't have what it takes, you worthless tallboy fucker."

"Oh, let me just *show* you what I have," I declaimed, letting the showtime take me.

I could feel it there, hovering in my awareness. Forming the weight of magic as I brought it to the forefront of my thoughts, ready to deploy. Virya's latest joke at my expense, my much-anticipated combination of Cast Illusion and Create Material squandered to make *this*.

Well . . . still. It was ridiculous, and I did not doubt she was laughing her ass off at me, but still. In an ass-backward place like Ephemera? Yeah, I couldn't say it was worthless. In fact, I could get a lot of mileage out of this. Starting right now.

"I call upon the Arbiter of the fates!" I thundered, my voice booming from the arched walls around us. "I invoke the slayer of uncounted Champions, the Valkyrie who ferries the souls of heroes to wage their eternal Ragnarok! Come to my side, faithful guardian of the road between worlds! **Summon Delivery Truck!**"

In Which the Guest of Honor Joins the Party

There is *no way* they'll fall for this," she exclaimed, disbelieving that she was the only one who could see it.

"Flaethwyn." Yoshi spoke her name with an impatient edge that, a week ago, he would not have *dared*. It cut through her like a heated blade. "Just . . . stop. We've been down to desperate measures for a *while* now. This is not the time to nitpick at our allies."

She kept her face composed, of course, but Flaethwyn could feel herself coming to a boil. Ever since they'd come down here . . . No, that wasn't it. Ever since they'd lost Raffan, it had all been coming apart. Every fragile scrap of security she had laboriously put together with these people, shredded, and one by one they were turning on her. Just like *everyone* did in the end. The shock and grief had created an opening, and that Dark Lord and these filthy . . . *goblins* had been working fingerholds into the minds of every one of her friends. Soon enough they'd—

"Kid," the goblin woman in the ridiculous pink suit said, giving Yoshi a long stare above the rims of her tacky pink-and-gold spectacles, "lemme give you some free advice about management. Just because your people are tellin' you things you don't wanna hear doesn't mean you don't *listen*. I've heard nothing but nonstop complaints about me *being* out here in person ever since we set out from home, and y'know what? I have never gotten too sick of it to listen, because *that's* not a thing. I hire the best people and pay 'em well for their work, and that means I pay attention when they tell me stuff. Even if I end up not following their advice. Now, I dunno how useful this elf ordinarily is, but if she's good enough for you to bring her along, she's good enough to be listened to—particularly at moments like this when she's *obviously right*."

Miss Sneppit gave Flaethwyn a courteous nod, and it was all she could do not to wind up and kick the preposterous little creature. As if she couldn't *clearly* see this blatant, unoriginal ploy for sympathy for what it was.

"In this case, we don't need to *convince* Jadrak's people, which is good cos we don't have the time or resources to pull that off. We just need to introduce enough uncertainty to keep him engaged for a few hours. Splittin' you off from us will actually help *more* with that if he doesn't go for it, because then he's gotta divide his attention to both negotiate with me and monitor you. Even if he's suspicious, this won't be immediately threatening enough to make him twitchy about sacrificing souls."

"I see," Yoshi murmured, then turned to Flaethwyn, lowering his head. "I'm sorry, Flaethwyn, she's right. This is a tense situation for us all, but I shouldn't have snapped at you."

She nodded jerkily in response, managing to keep her face controlled. The boy was just so . . . *earnest*. What kind of world did he come from, where somebody so naive could live this long in enough luxury to have been as overweight as he was when he arrived? If it wasn't for her and Pashilyn, he'd have been eaten alive in Fflyrdylle. Even now, this goblin was handling him as deftly as that unhinged thug Seiji did.

"We are also dividing our attention," Pashilyn pointed out quietly. "I understand why the overall plan must hinge on assuming Lord Seiji's success. If, however, Jadrak decides to betray *you* mid negotiations, you'll have sent away your best physical support, with all due respect to your security detail."

"It's a risk," Sneppit admitted, "but a necessary one, and one I judge acceptable. Us bein' backed into this corner ironically gives us more freedom to move than Jadrak; if Lord Seiji fails we're just fucked, so we gotta put everything into this last gambit, but *he* has to think about the future. Havin' me on his side, on good terms, would be a massive benefit to his organization, and every rival he doesn't crush with brute force will be another feather in his cap in the coming weeks when all the fervor dies down and his people start thinkin' like goblins again. He'll take this seriously, so long as he doesn't get the idea I'm just stallin' him."

"Which . . . you are, though," Yoshi said.

"Yeah, and that pretty much determines my strategy. Yours, too, for that matter. I'm gonna go in there and negotiate my surrender on the best possible terms for me. Goblin negotiations bein' what they are, that could take hours—but what I cannot do is drag it out unnecessarily. Jadrak's rep will know what it looks like to have me angling seriously for a good deal, so that's what I gotta show 'em. However long it takes me to hammer out a mutually acceptable agreement, that's how long Lord Seiji's got to finish Hoy and get back here, because I'm not gonna *sign* the damn thing and once I refuse to, the game's up."

"You have a contingency for that," Flaethwyn stated, folding her arms and making it clear with her tone that it was not a question. "Someone like *you* never operates without a backup plan."

"Aren't you sweet to notice," Sneppit replied with a toothy grin. "My contingency is, as your priestess friend pointed out, you guys. I chose the venue for a reason—right down that corridor is the chamber where I'll meet with Jadrak's people, which has exactly one entrance on the other side and one exit on *this* one. And down these stairs is a route straight to my tram station. Hey, pixie, you *can* navigate there past any doorways and branches, right?"

"Easy enough," said Radatina, "especially since we've been through here before. We were several stories lower, but it's close enough I remember the layout."

"Attagirl. At the tram station, along the north wall of the main loading bay, the third tunnel from the left is the route Lord Seiji will be taking to get here. If he loses to Hoy, at the bare minimum we can be sure the Void witch will be in bad shape after scrapping with a Dark Lord and his followers. Follow that route and you'll come up against Hoy, and hopefully be able to finish him off. Meanwhile, if I run outta time up here and have to book it, that's where I'll run with my people to rendezvous with you. What I need you kids to do is clear Jadrak's mooks outta that station. Best case, that's where Lord Seiji will show up triumphant; worst, you'll have to polish off a Void witch and that'll be our escape route."

"Got it," Yoshi said, nodding seriously. "What can we do on the way to sell it?"

"Don't," Sneppit said sharply. "Look, kid, no offense, but I've seen your idea of political theater and . . . it works, for big messy displays, but I don't need you tryin' to handle anything that finicky. The route to the station is partially exposed, and Jadrak'll have people watching this whole complex, so they'll see you all leaving. You *should* be out of range, but watch for incoming projectiles. I'll tell 'em we had a falling out over you kids being King's Guild butts in general, they'll see you go, and that'll have to do."

"This scheme has another glaring flaw," Flaethwyn stated, staring down at the goblin. "It would be a perfectly logical course of action for you to *actually* surrender to Jadrak on these optimal terms you are planning to negotiate, and then help him hit us from behind."

Yoshi grimaced and opened his mouth to speak, but Sneppit beat him to it.

"Yep, it would," the goblin said frankly. "Just like you lot could probably murder me right here in this room; it's not like there's a whole lot I could do to stop you. This situation does require trust between people who've had little enough chance to develop it. I know what goblins do in that instance—would it make you feel better if I signed a contract?"

"Actually," Yoshi said, "no disrespect to your culture, but I just need to hear it."

Sneppit raised an eyebrow, but then nodded. "Okay, then. You have my word I'll do exactly as I've just told you. When the time comes that I can't stall Jadrak any longer, I'll be retreating along the same route I just pointed you at, assuming I successfully get away intact. From both ends, we'll have to depend on each other. If my word is good enough for you, then I guess I'll accept yours as well."

"You have it," he said. "We'll secure the station as best we can. If Omura doesn't come, we'll hold out as long as possible for you. A major push from Jadrak's army might force us to retreat, though."

"You gotta exercise your best judgment there," she agreed.

"Really?" Flaethwyn burst out. "*That's* good enough for you? *Really?*"

"I had a promise from a Spirit, remember?" he said, meeting her eyes. "We can trust her, Flaethwyn. Her and Omura. For now, at least, anyone who gives us their word to stand by us will be loyal. I know you don't exactly trust goblins, any more than they trust us surface people, but for right now? We've got the closest thing to certainty it's possible to have."

"He's right; I was there," Radatina added a second later while everyone was still staring at him. "We got the Spirit's promise on it. If *that* doesn't hold true, then nothing in the world does and we're all doomed anyway."

"This whole plan has far too much 'we're all doomed anyway' for my comfort," Pashilyn murmured.

"You and me both, kid," Sneppit said with a cheeky wink that made Flaethwyn want to strangle her. "And speakin' of that, we'd all better get to playing our parts before the Goblin King runs outta patience."

"We'll be as fast as we can, you be as slow as you can," Yoshi said, nodding. "See you on the other side, Miss Sneppit."

"Knock 'em dead, kiddo."

The exposed section she had referred to was a ledge running along one wall of Fallencourt's enormous central cavern, affording a dramatic view over the city—and in particular, the Core Tower hung with Jadrak's green banners.

Just . . . plain green. No pattern, no sigil, nothing. Flaethwyn spared them a sneer in passing. Well, it wasn't as if goblins could be expected to understand heraldry, of all things.

It was quieter in the city than during their initial charge, in which they had lost Raffan and had to endure a humiliating rescue by the Dark Lord and his goblin stooges. Quieter, but not by much; the walls did not echo with screams this time, but the background noise of yelling and miscellaneous urban sounds had an angrier character than a populated city ordinarily should. Miss Sneppit's assessment had proved more or less correct in that this path seemed to be out of easy range of any projectiles, but from this vantage they could see dozens, if not hundreds, of goblins stopping in their own movements to watch the four of them make their way along the wall.

A lot of them were visibly thinking about it. Several actually tried; three iron balls fell pathetically short of them, but one managed to impact the wall just a few paces below. The four ducked their heads and picked up the pace as more slingshot-wielding goblins scurried into position and took aim. More impacts thunked against the stone just beneath, but they made it across the exposed section and into another interior staircase without having to defend themselves.

"They know the city better than we do," Yoshi said, leading the way. "They'll probably predict where we're heading . . ."

"I don't think so, necessarily," said Radatina. "Some might, if they guess the plan, but there are lots of side corridors between here and that station. Anybody who *didn't* know the city, or have a familiar along, would probably get lost."

"Well, that's a relief, then. You'd better lead, Tina-chan, and warn us if anybody's getting close to our path."

"Will do, Yoshi!"

"I know these are hardly optimal circumstances," Pashilyn said suddenly, "but we need to talk about the future before it happens to us. Yoshi, I assume the Spirit's message put *some* limit on the amount of trust you can extend to others? Spirit or no, the idea that a Hero can simply go through life being dealt with fairly and never lied to is absolutely unbelievable."

"Not life, no," Yoshi said, slowing his descent somewhat. They were now navigating a staircase of goblin-sized steps, which required some concentration to walk down, even without talking at the same time. "Just Kzidnak—wait, no. The Spirit's exact words were . . . someday soon I'd have to pass beyond the borders of Dount, and then I'd have to be more careful. But apparently I can trust what I'm told *here*."

"*Dount?*" Flaethwyn said incredulously. "Absolute lunacy! This island is nothing but bandits and beastfolk, and that hidden city of *dark elves*. The only actual *civilization* is one half-depleted excuse for a town and a handful of Fflyr Dlemathlys's most pathetic Clans under the leadership of the most degenerate of them all."

"Don't forget the Dark Lord," Amell said in a small voice from the rear of the line.

"Exactly, thank you. My point stands."

"Tina and the, uh, lizard both said Spirits are actually able to tell the future," Yoshi added. "I suspect it has a lot to do with *who* we'll be talking to before our adventures take us off this island."

"And that includes the Dark Lord, apparently," Pashilyn said in her most thoughtful voice. "The revelation that we can trust him to deal with us honorably is . . . well, it adds some context to the general bundle of dilemmas that is Lord Seiji. After getting to know him for a few days, I find I'm less surprised by that than I perhaps ought to be."

Flaethwyn kept silent, because the only sound she could have produced in that moment would have been a most unbecoming screech.

"But," Pashilyn continued after a pause in which no one challenged her statement out loud, "there is, as I said, the future. Assuming the best-case scenario here . . . Victory in our current plan will mean we have effectively handed the Dark Lord an entire city of goblins. Even assuming he is behind all the strange bandit activity—"

"You mean, the *strange* bandit activity where they don't kill anyone anymore?" Amell suddenly interjected. Flaethwyn whipped her head around to stare in shock; Amell had always been admirably mindful of her place as a lowborn, not to mention rather personally timid. Right now, she looked frightened of the fact that she was even speaking, but stubbornly pressing forward. "No rape, no random violence, only people who can *afford* it being targeted, and never *all* of their money taken? Why is the King's Guild so worried about *that*?"

"The King's Guild is more worried about the sophisticated tactics and unconventional alchemy being used," Pashilyn said seriously. "The people to whom the King's Guild *answers* are undoubtedly more concerned because this looks less like bandit activity than the beginnings of an organized rebellion, and in particular a popular uprising. And Lord Seiji's presence certainly sheds some context on that, does it not? But as I was saying, even if he has control of all or even most of the bandits on this island, handing him an entire *city full of goblins* will advance his position by orders of magnitude, overnight."

"Well . . . at this point, what *else* can we do?" Yoshi asked.

"Kill him," Flaethwyn said without hesitation.

Pashilyn shook her head. "Whether or not we should have done that in the beginning is another question—and I for one will admit I don't know if I *could* have turned on someone who has repeatedly saved our lives and offered us no harm. And that was before we learned we are dealing with devils and Void witches. The truce between Sanorites and Viryans in the face of the Void is sacrosanct; it *must* be. No . . . this is simply what is happening. What will happen. We need to grapple with our role in it, and decide what we will do afterward."

"Omura . . . isn't a bad person," Yoshi said slowly, staring ahead and clearly thinking over his words carefully as he spoke them. "He's just . . . an asshole."

"Oh of *all* the hairsplitting—this is Thremyct's reeds if I've ever heard them!"

"Flaethwyn, you *know* I have no idea what that means," Yoshi said with a sigh, and she felt another stab of terror.

She was losing him; he was showing more and more impatience and disregard for her. How long would it be before he threw her aside like everyone else? If only she could be as clever and restrained as Pashilyn. Pashi was still holding on to his sympathy, even as she . . .

"What I've seen of Omura down here—what we've all seen—matches what I saw in Akiba Station, for those few minutes we knew each other there," Yoshi continued, stopping at the base of the stairs and turning to face them after he'd stepped back enough they could emerge as well. "He's . . . Well, Pashilyn, you're a lot more perceptive than I am. What's your read on him?"

"Lord Seiji is a man who wants to do the right thing," Pashilyn said quietly, "but isn't very *good* at it. Your assessment is apt, Yoshi; he's an asshole. He is rude, melodramatic, and generally obstreperous for little to no reason. And *vindictive*. His anger and viciousness toward his enemies are exactly what I would expect from a Dark Lord. But . . . so much of what he does seems to be motivated by moral outrage. By, ultimately, compassion for the vulnerable."

"Exactly." Yoshi nodded. "Exactly. It was like that in Akihabara. He gladly did the right thing, went out of his way to help—it just wasn't his first impulse, and he tried to play it off with rude jokes. So . . . It's not Omura I'm worried about, exactly. I'm worried about his friends."

"You think he'll turn on them, too?" Flaethwyn said, controlling her voice with difficulty. Her heart was thudding in her chest at this turn of conversation. She was terribly unsure where this was leading, but entirely certain it would be disastrous.

"It's not that. I think . . . Well, did you notice how they all talk back to him all the time? Not exactly like an evil warlord and his minions. He seems to encourage his people to call him out; he's got the kind of organization that seems designed to prevent power from going to his head. I wonder if he did that on purpose or he just likes to be more casual with his friends . . . Either way, he listens to them, and they honestly seem like good people. Especially Aster, she seems like a good influence."

"Aster," Flaethwyn hissed, "that jumped-up, pushy lowborn . . ."

"Wyn, you do have that effect on people. Aster is generally quite calm with everyone else." Pashilyn softened her gentle rebuke further by reaching out to rub Flaethwyn's upper back, which helped, but even so, her words were like spikes. Not Pashilyn too . . . She *couldn't* lose her Pashi. Even if the others turned on her, she'd do . . . something. Being in Yoshi's party was a priceless opportunity, and Flaethwyn found she actually *liked* the boy (for some unfathomable reason), but they'd gotten along without being Hero tag-alongs before. Without Pashilyn, though . . . what would she even have left?

"I worry about them," Yoshi said, looking seriously at each of them in turn, "because they're all a lot easier to kill than a Dark Lord. Because being a Dark Lord's followers means they'll be going into a lot of situations that tend to *get* people killed. And then . . . Not only will he not have those moderating influences, but what he's likely to do in a rage is . . . exactly the reason people are afraid of Dark Lords. So I was thinking . . . I mean, about your question, Pashi, about how we'll need to handle this going forward, after Kzidnak . . ."

He paused, took a breath and rolled his shoulders once, and then shrugged.

"What if *we* were his friends?"

"I am not hearing this," Flaethwyn whispered.

"It . . . it makes sense to *me*," Amell said nervously. "The Hero is supposed to defeat the Dark Lord, right? I mean . . . it's *unconventional*, but if he's just, um, persuaded to . . . *not* do Dark Lord stuff . . . Well, that's the Dark Lord defeated, right? In a way."

"It's that," Pashilyn mused, "or try to kill him. It's . . . Yoshi, I think we need to consider and discuss this at a lot more length. Which means . . . not right now."

"Uh, yeah, we're pretty close," Radatina said, the normally animated pixie keeping a very neutral tone and expression that concealed whatever opinion she had about this conversation. "Down two corridors and another flight of stairs, and we're at the station. And, guys . . . it's *really* quiet around here. Sneppit seemed pretty sure Jadrak would have seized and occupied the tram station, but I'm not sensing nearly as much activity nearby as that would involve."

"Right," Yoshi said, exhaling and nodding. "You're right, all of you. Let's push on. All this stuff we can deal with when it's quieter."

He led the way, and they followed. This time Flaethwyn fell to the rear of the column so nobody would be able to see her face. It was one thing to see the doom of everything coming and know it would begin with her being betrayed and cast out like so much dead weight, just as she always had been . . .

It was something else to let them *see* her see it. Never show weakness; that was the only thing of any value her mother had ever taught her.

"Well, I guess this explains the quiet," Yoshi said minutes later, standing in the middle of the tram platform and looking around. "There's not much point in securing . . . this."

"Oh, Miss Sneppit is gonna be *mad*," Amell whispered.

Flaethwyn barely managed to refrain from cuffing her. "Who *cares*? The question is how does this affect *us*?"

The tram station had been thoroughly wrecked, but in a strategic and purposeful way; it looked like the work of an army, not miscellaneous looters. Every one of the tracks affixed to the ceiling had been pulled down or damaged in some way, enough to prevent them being used by the actual trams. All the station's contents, from tools to furnishings, had been removed—almost surgically, in fact. It actually looked *cleaner* than on their previous visit, with no loose trash strewn across the ground. Aside from the machinery that had been deliberately destroyed to make it unworkable, nothing else appeared to have been vandalized. There was no graffiti, even, which given how much goblins seemed to love graffiti really said something.

What exactly it said Flaethwyn couldn't begin to guess, but it was definitely *something*.

In addition to the tracks themselves having been sabotaged, barricades had been erected along many of the tunnels, including . . .

"Yeah, that's the one we want," Radatina reported, buzzing upward and pointing at the third tunnel from the left. "The one behind what is obviously the sturdiest barricade here."

"That seems a little too specifically inconvenient to have been a coincidence," Pashilyn commented.

"All right, well, we gotta get that opened up somehow," said Yoshi, cracking his knuckles. "Hm . . . Look, we can get up onto the boarding platforms by those stairs, see? Much better view from up there. Let's start by getting a look at what we're dealing with."

"On it!" Radatina chirped, already zooming off ahead.

The four of them trooped after her at a more sedate pace, not least because the steps and platforms were goblin-sized and made of metal, affixed to thin columns attached to the ceiling and floor. They vibrated when stepped on, but felt secure . . . Still. Metal platforms? It just seemed so . . . insubstantial. Not to mention wasteful. The goblins were supposed to be poor; how did they have so much *metal* just lying around?

". . . huh," Radatina said, staring down at the offending barricade. The others clustered together beneath her, getting their first good view of the obstruction from above.

It was sturdy indeed, consisting of an entire fallen tram car dragged into position and laid on its side. Panels of solid sheet metal had been coated along the entire surface of it facing down the tunnel, affixed by a variety of chains, bolts, ropes, and other methods to a point that looked downright excessive, all to ensure they wouldn't come off easily. Anyone who wanted to move that thing would have to physically move the *entire* tram car—no easy feat, as it had itself been filled with loose rocks.

Also, it wasn't blocking the entire tunnel. There was a space along one side easily wide enough for a person to walk through.

"What is even the point of *that*?" Flaethwyn demanded incredulously.

Yoshi leaned forward, narrowing his eyes as he peered down. "Look how it's positioned. We didn't notice the gap until we got up here. From the station's entrance . . . Yeah, from the main entrance, or the side one we came through, or basically *any* angle that's not from above or on the other side of that tunnel entrance, it *looks* like it's been walled off."

"You are suggesting," Pashilyn said slowly, "that Jadrak's forces were ordered to blockade this entrance and impede the Dark Lord . . . but chose to deliberately do the opposite, while making it seem like they had obeyed?"

"Oh, who understands why goblins do anything?" Flaethwyn exclaimed. "If they have the *slightest* bit of sense, even the ones working for that lunatic Jadrak will have started to realize there's no future with him. Hoy was *openly* talking about the Void in front of his people, remember? That would start inciting rebellions among anyone."

"If Jadrak's main army is riddled with defectors," Yoshi murmured, "the last stages of this might be a lot less hopeless than we thought . . ."

"What's that noise?" Amell asked suddenly.

Whatever it was, it was coming from down the very tunnel in question, and growing rapidly.

The deep, distant rumble sounded like the growl of some horrible monster. As they all stared, a strange, pale light grew in the distance. With the angle of the platform on which they stood, the direction the tunnel curved, and the fact that there was an open space above its entrance where it was more of a canyon than an actual tunnel for the last stretch as it approached the station, they could see a decent distance into it. Until seconds ago, there had been nothing *to* see except darkness, but now . . .

As the party shifted position to get a better view and the light grew steadily brighter, the roaring also rose in volume. And now, starting faintly but just as quickly rising as it drew closer, there was a voice.

"Flicker! Flicker! Flicker! Flicker! Flicker! Flicker! Flicker! Flicker! Flicker! Flicker!"

Even as the brilliant luminescence grew right on his heels, Hoy came blasting out of the darkness in a frantic chain of short-range teleportations. It barely kept him ahead of his pursuer, until the very last second when it suddenly didn't.

The Void witch nearly toppled forward as he came to a stop, suddenly finding himself with nowhere else to teleport to. Well, he probably could have jumped to the top of the barricade, the stone walls separating the canyon from its neighbors now that it was no longer an actual tunnel—even the boarding platforms from which the Hero's party were now staring down at him. But he was clearly at his wit's end, exhausted and panicking. All the frantic goblin could see was his one route of escape blocked by an unexpected iron wall.

"No! No, no, no— FUCK! *Fire La—*"

Valiantly, he turned and tried to attack his pursuer, but never finished the spell.

It blasted out of the darkness behind him, snarling like a mammoth beast and blazing with light, nearly tipping up onto two wheels as it rounded the last curve. Flaethwyn barely had a split second to recognize it was some kind of huge, boxy vehicle, painted an incongruous glaring white, before it slammed into Hoy and then into the iron wall in front.

The entire barricade shifted slightly. Not enough to really move it, but that impact made it rock.

Once it was fully in view and not moving, the thing was as shockingly mundane as it was alien. At a glance, she recognized it as some highly evolved descendant of the covered wagons that carried most commerce throughout Fflyr Dlemathlys and its neighbors. It was definitely made of exotic materials, such as she'd never seen, though, and assembled in configurations that would never have occurred to her.

"Truck-kun?" Yoshi whispered. Flaethwyn turned to find him staring down at the vehicle as if he'd just seen the ghosts of all his ancestors cavorting about in the nude.

Then a sudden, shrill, and strangely rhythmic beeping noise echoed through the deserted station. The truck's engine revved and it began backing up, making that peculiar beep the entire way. As its flat front cleared the space where it had hit the barricade, Hoy dropped to his knees from where he had been pinned there, barely catching himself on one arm.

"That goblin should be *liquefied*," Amell whispered in amazement.

"Repulsion Aura works on large impacts, too," said Radatina. "Just, um . . . only partially, and only once. All the magic he had left was just burned up in one hit. *Wow*, that's a lotta broken bones."

The Void witch tried, though. One of his legs was clearly shattered; he had to reach up and grab the edge of an iron panel with his one good arm to pull himself even partially upright. That was as far as he got, though.

The truck stopped, the beeping was silenced, and suddenly the machine roared. Its boxy rear end swayed, gravel spraying from the wheels, as for a second it failed to find purchase under the sheer torque, but then they caught and it surged forward again.

Hoy didn't even have time to scream.

The crash of the impact made the splat blessedly inaudible, but scarlet goo splattered absolutely *everywhere*.

"See?" Radatina said philosophically.

"Like I said." Amell nodded. "Pulped."

Pashilyn performed a heirat of benediction for the departed, one of those permitted only to priests of the Convocation. "Rest in puree, Hoy of Kzidnak."

With an odd whirring noise barely audible under the idling engine, one of the vehicle's blood-drenched windows slowly lowered straight down, affording them a view into the cockpit. There, the Dark Lord, Seiji, leaned out and grinned insanely up at them.

"Get in, losers. We're gonna kill the Goblin King."

31

In Which the Dark Lord Almost Wins

I said that because I *had* to. How many times in life are you gonna be served up such a golden opportunity? But realistically, nobody was getting in, and also, this was clearly the end of the road as far as the truck was concerned, unless we wanted to waste a lot of time moving a gigantic barricade. On the contrary, it was time for everybody to get *out*—both those who'd been comfortably in the cab with me, and everyone else who was much less comfortable in the back.

"Yeah, so, I let him get away," I explained to Yoshi while I dispensed Heals to my goblins. Nobody had worse than bruises and motion sickness, but it was due to my driving, so I figured it was the least I owed them. "Some massed slingshot fire funneled him down the hole we wanted, and Zui said that only led straight here with no branches or side access, so we had plenty of time to get everybody loaded up. After all, it wasn't hard to outrun a guy on foot in a truck. He didn't even have to start teleporting until the end there."

"You got," Yoshi said slowly, "a truck."

"Yup." I decided not to give him a hard time for stating the obvious; I knew very well the sight of a guy just trying to process a truly ridiculous development. We didn't all have showtime to help with that.

"It's . . . it's *the* truck."

"Pretty generic, you ask me. I mean, I'm a guitar guy, not a car guy, so I'm no expert, but I can't help notice the lack of any branding. Dunno why she'd bother with that; it's not like Isuzu or Toyota can sue us here. Nah, it seems more like the platonic ideal of a white Japanese delivery truck."

"Cos they're not branded in any of the anime," he said vaguely, still staring goggle-eyed at Truck-kun. "They wouldn't be; no brand would want their product associated with episode one teenage roadkill . . . If anything, Kadokawa should branch out into trucks. Omura, I have so many questions."

"The answer to *all* of them is 'because Virya thinks she's funny.'"

He sighed. "It's a little scary how neatly that *does* answer all of them."

"Right?"

"I can't help noticing that you've had this for *minutes* and you've already wrecked it."

He wasn't wrong, Truck-kun was somewhat the worse for wear. The worst was on the front, of course, which had just bashed into a metal wall at speed, twice. Not at normal highway speeds or we'd all be dead, but it was going fast enough to crush a goblin and that was made apparent by crumpled fenders, smashed headlights, one torn-off side mirror, and a windshield that was almost too spiderwebbed with cracks to see through. Not to mention, the entire exterior of the cab was liberally painted with cream of Hoy soup. It wasn't *just* up there, though; the white walls of the cargo compartment were marred with dings and long scrapes, where they'd had rough encounters with the tunnel which, while technically big enough for the truck, was *not* designed for it. Less obvious from outside, but growing increasingly plain to us in the cab toward the end, there was the damage the uneven tunnel floor had done to the suspension.

Well, it was boxed in anyway. Time to invoke the other half of that spell.

Banish Delivery Truck.

The battered Truck-kun instantly disintegrated, leaving behind only faint swirls of glowing golden dust which swiftly dissipated on the currents of air constantly blowing down the tunnel. Its disappearance was so sudden and absolute that the coating of liquid Hoy all over its front end splattered to the ground, causing the nearby goblins to leap away, cursing.

"So . . . wait, that was it?" Yoshi demanded.

"Hm. Lemme try this out . . ."

Summon Delivery Truck.

It returned on command, standing there pristine and new. No damage, no mushed goblin in the grille, and—I knew, thanks to my being connected through the Void when this spell was created—a full tank of gas.

Banish Delivery Truck.

"Holy shit," Yoshi whispered, staring at the empty spot where Truck-kun had stood.

"Apparently only one can exist at a time, unlike my slime-summoning spell," I said. Which I was still mad about, because of how *absolutely busted* that would've been. It voided my first and best idea of stripping infinite trucks for parts. Man, the possibilities . . . I could've just holed up in Kzidnak, gathered together all the goblin alchemists and engineers, and fed them an unlimited supply of modern alloys, plastics, electronics, gasoline, and safety glass—and in two years my army of giant mechas would be stomping uncontested across Lancor.

Which, of course, was exactly why Virya didn't let me do it. Both Goddesses were filthy cheaters, but this game of theirs wouldn't be *fun* if anybody got an advantage *too* great. Having an infinitely rechargeable modern cargo vehicle in the medieval setting of Ephemera was already such a *massive* asset that my head swam with the possibilities, but it was an asset I could only leverage once at a time, in person. Not something that would break the game itself.

"Lord Seiji!" Our respective ruminations were interrupted by Ritlit, who strode up to me and saluted. "I have conducted an impromptu poll amongst the troops, and goblins are about equally divided on the subject of the truck. Half would prefer a swift death over ever getting in that thing again, and the other half want another ride *right now*. I'm in the second group, by the way. Hint, hint."

"You know, Ritlit, I'm really glad you joined us," I said kindly. "You're a real breath of fresh air; it's been great for morale, having you along. Now please shut up and go away."

"Sir, yes, sir!"

"It was actually very nice up front in the part with the seats," Aster said. "Very comfy. And it's got these vents that blow cold air!"

"I coulda done without that," Zui grumbled, rubbing her arms.

"How . . . many people did you cram in the cab?" Yoshi asked warily, as if he hadn't seen us all disembark. Well, I guess this spectacle *was* pretty distracting.

"Plus me? Two talls and two shorts," I explained. "Fits pretty well, with the goblins sitting on the others' laps."

"I know *that* was the absolute highlight of this whole adventure for me," Maizo said, grinning. "Right, Naz? We should do that again."

"Little man, you just remember that if *I* find it necessary to kick you in the nuts, your head will hit the ceiling."

"There's just one thing that worries me," said Yoshi.

"*One* thing?" Flaethwyn exclaimed.

"If you just hit Hoy with Truck-kun . . . I wonder what *other* world you sent him to? There's nowhere that deserves having to deal with Hoy."

"Hell, Yoshi," I said solemnly. "I sent him to *hell*. Which is just super convenient for everybody; when I get there, I can kill his ass again. All right, everybody okay? In good shape?"

"Thanks to Amell's concoctions, yeah, we're all more or less solid," Zui reported. "Funny how that super special healing spell of yours doesn't do anything for dizziness and nausea."

"Yeah, the limits on Heal are pretty arbitrary."

"Because that's not an injury or illness," Biribo said with audible exasperation. "It's the body's extremely normal and reasonable response to being slung around the way we all just were. Anyway, it's weirdly quiet out there. Did you guys have much chance to look around here?"

"Briefly, but we noticed the same thing," said Yoshi. "The station is cleaned out and deserted. And look at this barricade; you can't tell from this angle, but from any of the station entrances it *looks* solid. Seems like somebody in Jadrak's organization wanted it to seem like they were keeping you locked away while specifically not doing that."

"Not just somebody," Pashilyn added. "Erecting this would have taken a lot of teamwork. There has to be an entire *faction* among Jadrak's so-called loyalists who are trying to undermine him."

"Well, isn't *that* interesting," I mused. "Right, then. The trick *now* will be to hit him hard and fast enough to actually take him out without provoking him to sacrifice his followers."

"The revelation that he's having well-organized loyalty problems suggests that threat may not be as dire as we thought," said Pashilyn.

"*Less* dire, sure, but keep in mind what we're talking about," Radatina warned. "Even if he's only got a dozen or so goblins he can burn for Void spells . . . that is a *lot* of Void spells. Consider how much trouble we had just with Hoy, who only had the one, plus his Blessing of Magic. What this signifies is that Jadrak is . . . *probably* not the world-ending threat we were worried about, but the risk is still of him turning into something we can't actually beat."

"Right, we need information and to check in with our allies before we do anything hasty," said Yoshi. "Most immediately, we should go check in with Sneppit. She's got Jadrak bogged down in negotiations, but she said that wouldn't last very long, and she'll be in danger once it falls apart."

"Wait, Sneppit's *here*?!" Zui exclaimed. "This is no place for— I mean, she's not one to put her own skin on the line!"

"Her intervention has been extremely helpful," said Pashilyn. "As for her motivation for coming here in the first place, I suspect she considers the potential political gain to be worth the risk. She very nearly said as much."

Zui clapped a hand over her eyes. ". . . of course. She *would*, that—"

"Right, then; that sounds like step one," I said briskly. "Let's go extricate Sneppit, and then we'll move on from there. That works out very conveniently—I think I have an idea for how to resolve this mess, and she's exactly who I'll need to run it by first."

Sneppit had chosen tactically advantageous ground, physically as well as politically. The chamber in which she was meeting with Jadrak's representatives was accessible only from two directions; her forces securely held the accesses from her side, theirs from the other. It gave both parties to the discussion as reasonable an assurance of security as was possible under the circumstances, not to mention securing her own exit, as she was not planning on the meeting reaching any satisfying conclusion.

It also meant, since Sneppit's people welcomed me and didn't impede my way, I had an easy time getting myself into the room with them.

"Sorry I'm late; work was murder," I announced with ebullient good cheer, striding into the chamber. Conveniently, this was part of the old Fallencourt architecture built to tallfolk scale, so I didn't have to spoil the effect by ducking. "What'd I miss?"

Half the goblins in the room leaped to their feet and retreated, one actually fleeing through the opposite door. Sneppit and Gizmit looked up at me with no overt sign of surprise, the three guards in pink armor not shifting from their positions.

"I should've known," said one of the Jadrak-aligned goblins, who was now on the opposite side of the room, pressed against the wall and inching toward the door. "This is what I get for performing due diligence at a time like this. Did you ever have the *slightest* intention of negotiating in good faith, Sneppit?"

"Hey, hey, don't take that tone with *me*," she objected. "This whole time you've been hammering in the point that the Dark Lord was outta the picture and the effect that had on my bargaining position. Well, I gotta say, he looks a lot perkier than you were describing. Who was pulling the roots down on whom, huh?"

"Scuze me, I didn't catch your name?" I said politely to the goblin who'd spoken.

He froze, ceasing his surreptitious movements toward the door now that my attention was clearly on him.

"Dunno what you'd need it for."

"Well, it would make this whole exchange more civil, for one," I said with a shrug. "I would prefer we all conduct ourselves like civilized people as much as possible. Wouldn't you?"

He narrowed his eyes. "Right. Because if we didn't . . . Your capacity for *uncivilized* behavior considerably exceeds mine, right?"

"You said it, not me." I kept my smile in place.

"What exactly is it you need to discuss with the likes of me, Dark Lord?"

It wasn't a name, but hey, we were talking. "Well, you're obviously empowered to speak on Jadrak's behalf, correct?"

"Up to a very limited point, in a very specific context, which doesn't include anything involving *you*."

"Still, you've got some standing; that should be plenty. All I need is to arrange a meeting with the Goblin King himself."

Everyone in the room turned to stare at me.

". . . huh," Jadrak's representative said after a moment. "Your terms?"

"No more skulking around, and if possible, no more wholesale slaughter of the goblins he's *supposed* to be King of. I'm given to understand Jadrak is set up in that tower with the big green bedsheets, right?"

"Those are called 'banners,'" Sneppit helpfully informed me.

"And there's a nice, open ledge in front of that, in range of all the snipers and sorcerers he's packed in there," I continued. "The way I hear it, Jadrak made quite a spectacle of preventing the Hero from getting in. I wanna have a talk, in the open. *That* spot should suffice to assuage his fears of confronting the Dark Lord, I trust. If he requires *more* than covering fire by everyone in his organization who's capable of providing it, well, that's just plain unreasonable is what that is."

"I'll convey the message," the negotiator said, glancing rapidly between me, Sneppit, and Yoshi, who'd stepped into the room behind me. "If King Jadrak agrees to your meeting, word will be sent here to clarify terms of—"

"Ah, forgive me, that's my fault," I interrupted smoothly. "Sometimes I'm not as clear as I should be. I am *informing* Jadrak, not asking him. I will be there in one hour, and I will *spend* that hour here in Fallencourt chitchatting with just *everyone* I meet about all the things I've seen and done in Kzidnak over the last few days. Spoiler alert—it's mostly to do with all the goblins Jadrak has either deliberately murdered or carelessly gotten killed, about the imprisonment and torture I've seen done in his name, about all the Void witchery, the desecrated Spirits, and how his best buddy Hoy's been out there treating his own followers so abysmally on Jadrak's behalf that every time we've clashed, a bunch of them have swapped to my side. And oh, yes, I do *have* a bunch of Jadrak's former loyalists with me who'll back up my stories. So he can either come out and face me like a man, so we can settle this like goblins—with our words—or he can sit in his nice cozy tower while I turn the city against him."

I took one long step forward, bringing myself past Sneppit; the goblin in front of me didn't retreat only because he had physically nowhere else to go. Then I leaned forward. I had been doing my best not to call attention to the height disparity when dealing with goblins I liked, as it seemed kinda inherently condescending, but this was a moment when my words were best suited by emphasizing the physical threat I represented.

"If he doesn't show," I purred, "and I have to go in there and *get* him, it will not be so . . . civilized."

The goblin stared up at me. His eyes were wide, but he otherwise remained admirably in control of himself, not outwardly showing fear. I guess they didn't let just anybody handle negotiations.

"Anything else?"

I gave him a sunny smile, straightening back up. "I believe those are the salient points. One hour. Tick tock."

"Guess you'll forgive me if I don't linger over goodbyes, then," he said, sidling to his right and finally slipping out through the door. I stepped back again, creating some space for the other goblins on his side to follow him. To judge by the sound of footsteps retreating down the hall outside, they set off at a dead run.

"Aaaand . . . gone," Radatina reported. "They're out of earshot, and no lurkers are left nearby."

"Good," said Yoshi. "Omura, I thought the plan was to talk to Sneppit *before* enacting the plan?"

"Oh, was *that* the plan?" Sneppit said pointedly. "Well, better late than never. What're we doing now, Lord Seiji?"

"Sorry about that," I said as sincerely as I could, turning back to her. "I would've preferred to consult with you first, but the second I pulled you aside for a private talk that guy would've bolted, and this would've gotten a lot more complicated."

"Sure, I get it," she said, shrugging. "So you wanna confront Jadrak in public? I hope you're not planning to assassinate him during a negotiation, Lord Seiji. You'll never get any compliance from any goblin in Kzidnak again if you pull something like that."

"So I had assumed. No . . . As much as we all want Jadrak dead, the reality is his final fate is going to have to be settled another time. What's urgent right *now* is eliminating his ability to pull that soul trigger."

"You want to attack his loyalty directly," Yoshi said. "Beat him in a battle of words and cost him the public approval he *needs* to be able to use that contingency."

"*Exactly*. And now I've forced his hand; I actually do intend to do exactly what I just said. The stories of his cruelty and greed are going to spread through this city as fast as rumor can travel. He will *need* to come out and confront me to put his own version forward in the court of public opinion."

"So you've got him trapped and forced to comply?" Yoshi said pointedly. "Isn't that the *specific* thing we were trying to avoid?"

"Also, I'm worried that dealing with Hoy has given you the wrong impression," Sneppit added. "Jadrak is not like that. He's the *opposite* of that; he's a lot like you, in fact. He's stylish, theatrical, and *really* good at making a speech. That's exactly how he worked his way up into this Goblin King situation to begin with. Take it from somebody who knows firsthand, we're not like the Fflyr; being a rich, powerful figure doesn't get you ahead with the public in Kzidnak. Goblins inherently distrust power. Jadrak commands followers for the entire reason that he's probably a match for you in the specific confrontation you just set up, Lord Seiji."

I nodded. "You're both right—or at least, Yoshi definitely is, and what Sneppit just said lines up with what I've been hearing. And in this case, those two problems combine to form a solution. I've put pressure on Jadrak, yes, but it's pushing him into what he probably thinks is a winning position. He'll take the bait and confront me."

"And then," Yoshi said slowly, "all you have to do is . . . beat him at his own game. Omura, I don't know about this."

"Me neither, man. I can't say I've been *certain* about anything we've had to do this entire time. But I can do this, I promise you. Nothing worth having in life is a sure thing; all you can do is count on yourself and your skills."

Sneppit nodded approvingly. Yoshi still looked unconvinced, as did the goblins who'd filed into the room behind him. And Pashilyn and Aster, who were both peeking in the door.

"Trust me," I said, putting on a smile and projecting confidence. "This is *my* arena, too. I can take him."

Jadrak evidently thought the same about himself. One hour later, we were gathered in the plaza outside his new headquarters, which Sneppit had called the Core Tower. I had to admit, it was nice digs, even aside from the banners. If I were setting myself up as the lord ruling over Fallencourt, this is probably where I'd choose to do it from. Something to keep in mind for when Jadrak was out of the picture.

Right on schedule, the Goblin King emerged. And, though I had not specified it in my message, he came alone. You had to admire the sheer balls—which, of course, was the point. I knew exactly what he was doing, and I conceded that it was some solid-gold posturing. Behind me I had my entire entourage—the Hero and his party, two Judges and their respective Arbiters, and a full line of armed goblins, who a couple days ago had been Jadrak's own loyalists. Coming out to plant himself in front of this display *alone* was the kind of powerful gesture that no amount of words could stand in for.

So, with just his opening move, he'd put one over on me in sheer charisma. That wasn't ideal.

I could tell at a glance that Sneppit was right. This dude had *style*, done up all in black and gold in a mimicry of Fflyr highborn fashion—which was a mimicry of Goddess artifact fashion (and I now knew this to be a tawdry facsimile of classic RPG art)—and unlike everyone from the highborn to the other goblins who'd tried this (sorry, Sneppit), even to most of the Earth anime it was all descended from, he actually pulled off the look. His posture and expression were calm, controlled—the bearing of someone fully confident that he was in command, despite facing a dozen different people who wanted to kill him and were very much capable of doing so.

Which was another point—he would not have stepped out here if he didn't believe he could prevent us from stone-cold murdering his ass. Whatever was peeking out from behind the windows of Core Tower would be some serious shit, and without a doubt he had something else up his sleeve.

"Now, *this* is more like it," the Goblin King said by way of greeting, and again I found Sneppit's assessment correct—this was a guy who knew what his diaphragm was for. Everyone in Fallencourt was hearing this, and his voice showed no hint of strain. "You know, the Hero tried this earlier. It was one of the most disappointing things I've ever seen."

"Oh, now, I don't believe that for a second," I said easily, grinning and also projecting. "It's not like I don't *know* what kind of week you've been having."

"Yeah," Jadrak drawled, "as the principal *cause* of my annoyances, you'd be pretty familiar, wouldn't you."

I widened my smile and made my voice softer, but no less audible. "If you wanted my attention, you could have asked. Shouldn't have murdered the goblins I was friendly with, Jadrak. That's the difference between us. I *will not have* anybody fucking with my people."

We smiled at each other, cold and composed, while around us the city held its breath.

"So," he said at last.

"So."

This was it. The Goblin King and the Dark Lord, mano a mano. Showtime versus showtime. The confrontation we'd both been building toward since long before either of us knew it.

Each of us drew in breath, breaking the tension, opened our mouths like quickdraw artists in a race to be the first to speak, and then somebody chucked a bomb out of the Core Tower.

Not at me or any of my people; I only realized it was a bomb when it hit the metal bridge right behind Jadrak, and the explosion sent shrapnel everywhere. Luckily for him, the Goblin King was out of range of the worst of it—and also, the son of a bitch was *still* poised while being actually, literally shelled with explosives, which was more than I'd managed. He barely flinched and didn't duck or try to flee, just half turning the second the explosion ended so he could look behind him without taking me out of his peripheral vision.

The bridge to the Core Tower had been taken out; nothing but twisted scraps of metal extended from both its original moorings. This particular part of the city didn't seem open all the way to the core, so it was probably still salvageable, but that did nothing to help Jadrak right now. He was isolated from his support, alone with me and all my backup, unable to retreat.

Above, the green banners fell as the cords connecting them to the upper windows from which they'd been hung were severed. Fabric rustled as it plummeted; one fell right through the gap where the bridge had been moments ago, the others tumbling to both sides.

And then, from those same windows, new banners were unfurled. The fabric unrolled and came to a stop, securely affixed where the old ones had been.

It was plain at a glance that these were a rush job; they were all patched together from miscellaneous scraps, the colors of which were uneven. You could even see where paint had been hastily applied over the top, where the creators hadn't been able to find fabric that wasn't black or red. But they'd done it; sloppy and rough as it looked, these were *my* flags. The crimson sigil of the Dark Crusade over a black field.

Behind me I heard an incredulous sotto voce from Flaethwyn. "Wait. Slimes and . . . *what*?!"

"Hah!" Nazralind crowed, much less discreetly. "*I* designed that!"

Seldom had I wanted anything more than I wanted to turn around and see Flaethwyn's expression in that moment, but I was still on the clock here. Showtime didn't end just because somebody usurped it.

Goblin faces appeared in the windows of the Core Tower and along the other covered bridge linking it to the cavern wall, all of them staring down at their erstwhile would-be King. Their expressions were not friendly. They didn't jeer or catcall, just glared in grim silence.

"Well." Unhurriedly, Jadrak turned back toward me, and dipped his head once in acknowledgment, his wry little smile outwardly unconcerned. "I'm a big enough man to admit it—that was *well* played, Lord Seiji. Color me impressed."

"I'm tempted to just take credit, but I've got a feeling that would bite me as soon as people started comparing notes," I admitted. "I have no idea what the hell just happened. I didn't infiltrate your headquarters, Jadrak; if you managed to lose the loyalty of your core army, I'm afraid you did that all on your own."

Like him, I managed to be outwardly composed, but I was reeling about as hard as he had to be right then. Seriously, what in the *fuck*? We knew he was having loyalty problems, but *this* . . . And more to the point, where in the *hell* had goblin insurgents even seen that symbol? Sure, it was going up in an increasing number of places around North Watch, with some of my followers even starting to embroider it on their black masks and various other articles of clothing, but the goblins of Kzidnak should've had no opportunity to lay eyes on that.

It occurred to me that I'd had no direct communication with my people since leaving them with orders to hold the tunnel at Maugro's offices. Had they managed to—

No. It took me an embarrassingly long few seconds of frantic thought to realize it, but I got there. The last time we'd seen any evidence of our mysterious, invisible dark elf ally had been right here, in the cavern of Fallencourt. The same dark elf who'd been skulking around North Watch for weeks and knew way too much of our business. The dark elf whose aid I had adamantly not wanted, after the debacle they created from our confrontation with the cat tribe.

Never had I been so glad to owe somebody an apology.

"Well, isn't that interesting," Jadrak murmured, then raised his voice. "Either way, Dark Lord, it sure does look like you have all the advantages here. I'll admit it—you've got me backed into a corner."

Oh, I did *not* like his expression. Still composed, but with emotion beginning to creep through, and that emotion was not fear. It was anger, a hungry desire for violence that I recognized because I knew it all too well, myself. Belatedly, I remembered the one specific thing we were trying *not* to do here.

Okay, never mind. I was going to kill that fucking elf my fucking self.

"Listen," I began, holding up both hands.

"How about *you* listen, for once in your life," Jadrak retorted, baring his full complement of wickedly sharp teeth at me and raising one hand in what looked suspiciously like a ritual gesture. "Listen, and watch, while I make it clear exactly how out of your depth you are, human. *I call the devil Ozyraph!*"

32

In Which the Dark Lord Yields

The air next to him shifted, and suddenly there was a devil standing among us.

The visual effect of devil-summoning was surprisingly understated. It was like a person-shaped slice of empty space suddenly rotated fully around, as if it were a cardboard cutout, and when fully revealed . . . there she was.

Ozyraph was . . . not what I expected. Well, in part; most of her features were classic devil shit, straight out of mythology. Her skin was dusky reddish-pink in hue, and she had a pair of backswept horns sprouting from her hairline and curving back over her skull to bracket the severe bun into which her crimson hair was pulled. No, the unexpected part was her attire—the devil wore a sleek, obviously tailored Western-style business suit. Black with gold pinstripes, a black shirt, and a slim necktie of solid-gold fabric.

And she was carrying a tablet. Not a flat piece of material on which text was engraved, a tablet *computer*. It was wafer-thin, about the dimensions of an iPad, and while I couldn't see the screen from my current angle, I could see its glow.

The devil took a quick glance around, taking in the sight of all Fallencourt spread around her, including no end of mostly terrified shouting by all the attendant goblins. Her eyes met and held mine for a second—they were unnerving, with vertically slitted pupils and two-toned irises that faded from bloodred at the center to gold around the edges, giving them a fiery appearance. Then her gaze slid past me, flicking rapidly over my various allies and lingering for another second on Yoshi. Only then did she turn her full attention to the Goblin King.

"I see we have entirely given up on basic discretion."

Ozyraph's voice was a smooth alto, her delivery strikingly reminiscent of quite a few teachers I remembered with no fondness. She had that knack, the ability to convey utterly withering sarcasm without seeming to depart from the normal tones of polite conversation.

"This wasn't my preferred outcome," Jadrak replied, shooting me an unpleasantly confident look. "Unfortunately, thanks to the meddling of *this* fool and his friends, things have spiraled. As per our contract, Ozyraph, I call upon your aid."

"Oh?" The devil raised an eyebrow. "Are you certain that is wise, King Jadrak?"

"Wise? Perhaps not, but *necessary*." He turned back to face me directly, holding my stare while speaking to his demonic ally. "I am invoking the extraordinary circumstances clause of our contract, Ozyraph. Per your agreed obligations, I require you to *rid* me of . . . these two humans in particular." He pointed at me and Yoshi in turn. "The rest, I can handle myself."

I formed the mental weight of Immolate, ready to deploy; at my side, Yoshi raised his shield, sword at the ready.

"Absolutely not."

Ozyraph's brusque reply made us all hesitate. Especially Jadrak; he did an actual double take. The sudden diminishment of his smugness was satisfying as hell, despite my continuing unease about what was happening.

"I—but we have a *contract*," the Goblin King protested. "You are obligated to—"

"This contract?" Ozyraph tapped one fingertip against the screen of her tablet twice, flicked it to scroll through something, tapped again, and then held the device down so he could see it. "I'd like to call your attention to paragraph twelve, concerning unacceptable conflicts of interest and hazards to the Devil King's concerns and those of his servants, to which I am not under any circumstances to be subjected by any other signatory to this agreement. These are not limited to, but *specifically enumerate*, direct conflict with major faiths or agents of Sanora or Virya, *particularly* any Hero or Dark Lord. You just attempted to invoke the extraordinary circumstances clause to bring me into physical conflict with *both*."

Jadrak suddenly looked like he'd swallowed something a bit too big for his neck. "Oh, but . . . Surely you didn't interpret that to—"

"As such, I am invoking the terms of paragraph nineteen, clause five: premature termination of the agreement due to malfeasance by any signatory to said agreement." She flicked her thumb over the screen, scrolling down to the clause in question. "As you have broken the terms of the contract, all outstanding debts by the offending party will be immediately called in, as detailed in clause nine."

"*Wait!*" Jadrak was visibly alarmed now, probably mostly by the prospect of Ozyraph calling in his debts—i.e., his soul—but I suspected all the growling and hissing from *many* of the onlookers wasn't helping his poise. I had to figure that to a goblin audience, getting caught breaking the terms of a contract was a *bad* look, even more so than to most people. "You can't invoke that! I was merely raising a point of discussion—"

Ozyraph had already been flicking and tapping on her screen, and suddenly the tablet produced Jadrak's own voice, at a significantly magnified volume.

"*I require you to rid me of . . . these two humans in particular.*"

"These were, I believe, your exact words," she said tonelessly. A proper villain might have hammed this up—*I* certainly would have—but Ozyraph delivered her lines with the dry evenness of a bureaucrat filling out their fiftieth form of the day.

"Yes, but . . . I mean, that is clearly contextual and open to interpretation . . ."

"Not only is that a specific instruction to open hostilities with the Hero *and* Dark Lord, these are the words you spoke *after* I gave you the opportunity to retreat from your demand that I intervene. This is not a case of your words being taken out of context, Jadrak. This occurred *seconds* ago. We are still in the context. You are in breach of contract. I will now, as per my contractual privileges, collect all debts owed, which are specified by the agreement in question as any soul in your possession."

The wording made me widen my eyes in alarm, and I wasn't the only one who caught it. Rizz hissed fiercely as she drew in air through her teeth, and Sneppit let out a low groan.

Ozyraph raised the tablet back out of his reach, and finally some expression intruded on her face—just the faintest, disdainful curl of her upper lip.

"Honestly, aren't you supposed to be some sort of goblin? You really should *read* the things you sign."

Jadrak's poise was finally failing him. The outright jeering that had been withheld when his headquarters abruptly kicked him out had started to rise all around. He was now isolated with his enemies, his supporters had all turned on him, and his omnipotent trump card was not only not helping him but had just delivered what was probably the worst public humiliation a goblin could suffer. Open fear had leaked onto his features now; he cast about rapidly for options, finding no good prospects.

So he latched onto a bad one—me.

"Lord Seiji!" The Goblin King stepped forward and held out one hand toward me. "If anyone can throw back a devil, it's you. Join—"

Okay, so it wasn't entirely authentic, but I'm enough of a performer to be able to burst into loud, derisive laughter on command. I am also enough of a performer not to react to distinctly hearing Adelly mutter behind me, "He's doing it again."

"You *need* me," Jadrak pressed on stubbornly, because it was that or lie down and accept death. "No one else can—"

His voice cut off in a strangled croak; my eyes shifted up to find Ozyraph, her tablet balanced in one hand, the other outstretched with fingers clenched in a grasping motion.

"Excuse me," she stated crisply. "The Dark Lord is not party to this discussion. As I gather you plan to be disagreeable about this, I may as well commence soul collection with the easiest target."

It was like the process of her arrival—Jadrak seemed to freeze in place, the last clear sight I had of him was his terrified expression, and then he sort of . . . rotated. Like he had been reduced to two dimensions and then flipped, the Jadrak-shaped piece of scenery behind him revolving into view. And that was it. No hellfire, no flashy effects, aside from that one disorienting transition into what I assume must've been the Void.

No more Goblin King.

"Did . . . did we just . . . win?" Yoshi asked warily.

"By default, but I suppose so," Ozyraph answered him, already occupied with her tablet again. "Well, it's results that matter. Now, don't mind me. I have a *bunch* of busywork to do, thanks to you lot, but it'll just take a few minutes, and then I'll be out of your hair."

"What *kind* of busywork?" Rizz demanded, stepping forward with her polearm leveled aggressively. Rhoka joined her in the same position, silent as usual.

"The only kind I have," Ozyraph droned, still monotone and poking at her tablet. "My deal with Jadrak was for all souls it was within his power to bestow. Which, in these unusual circumstances, meant *quite* a few more than just his own."

I don't think the issue of Jadrak and his ability to sacrifice his followers' souls was widely known among them, but the devil's meaning was obvious enough that everybody caught on. The tenor of the onlookers changed; dozens of goblin voices rose in exclamations of anger and sudden fear.

"Just a minute!" Yoshi exclaimed, stepping forward. He still had his shield upraised, as if that was going to help. "Jadrak's ability to grant his followers' souls to your contract was a function of their fanatical loyalty. After what everyone just saw, there's no *way* you can still collect them."

Ozyraph spared him a sardonic look before resuming her work. She seemed to be scrolling rapidly through a list of something on her screen, periodically stopping it to pin one item at a time and swipe it to the left.

"Yes, because no one *ever* regrets the deal they made when it comes time for me to collect. I am entitled to every soul Jadrak *could* have sacrificed at the moment he broke our contract. Thanks primarily to the Dark Lord, here, that is *far* fewer than I was hoping; you've done an admirable job of sabotaging Jadrak's interests, Omura Seiji. Looks like I'll be collecting at most a few dozen rather than several hundred."

Someone shot her with a spiked ball from a slingshot, followed immediately by another. Both balls froze in midair less than a meter from Ozyraph, then plunked harmlessly to the ground. She gave no outward sign of even noticing.

"You *can't* do this!" Yoshi exclaimed, raising his sword.

"Yoshi, *no!*" Flaethwyn lunged forward and grabbed his arm, physically pulling him backward. "That is a *devil*! A *powerful* one! You are *not ready for this*." She gave me a grudging look. "Either of you."

"Why do you even care?" Ozyraph asked, a tone of vague annoyance drifting through her customarily deadpan delivery. "These are people who were so fanatically devoted to a shifty conman with impressive hair they were willing to perish at his whim. They would, by definition, have slaughtered the lot of you minutes ago if they thought they could. It clearly benefits you to have them removed from Kzidnak."

"Oh, I'm sure it's *real* easy for you to stand there in your fancy suit and pass judgment on people, when you've never had to struggle for anything yourself," I snorted, swaggering forward.

Ozyraph's finger ceased moving; her posture did not otherwise change, but her eyes shifted to lock onto mine, and I *almost* hesitated under the sheer intensity of her stare. Almost. Showtime is showtime, after all.

"People fell for Jadrak's song and dance because they were *desperate*, you vicious little parasite. It was bad enough *he* preyed on their poor circumstances without *you* coming along and making it worse. Now, I'm willing to be civilized about this. Why don't we discuss this matter like adults and come to an understanding? You've already collected two souls today—one thanks to *me*, I might add."

"Oh?" She raised one eyebrow. "You wish to make a deal?"

Everyone's eyes shifted to stare at me. *Shit.* No, I did not want to do that.

"I'm just saying," I replied smoothly, "there's ample cause for you to be content with a good day's work, Ozyraph. Time to pack it in."

"You have no standing to negotiate here, Omura," she said in a disinterested tone, returning her eyes to the tablet screen and resuming her scrolling and swiping. "I will take what I'm owed, and I have no need to compromise. Subject closed."

"Well, that's a shame," I said quietly. "I did hope we could settle this goblin style, by coming to an agreement. *But*, if you're not interested . . . I got some really good advice from a really smart guy a while back about what I should do if a devil ever interfered in my affairs."

"Is that a fact."

I'd been told devils were conflict-averse, that they'd flee from confrontations they could easily win. Well, time to put that to the test.

This one's for you, Sakin.

I raised one arm and pointed at her.

"Immolate."

Fire burst across her—on the surface, not from within. In fact, it looked for all the world as if I'd just ignited a covering of invisible oil all over her. The flames whooshed across her body . . . slowed . . . And then, as I watched in increasing dismay, reversed.

Ozyraph paused in manipulating her tablet for a moment to fully extend her free arm back toward me; the flames of my Immolate spell surged down it till they coated her hand, then condensed further until she was holding a ball of seething orange fire on her palm.

She bounced it once, idly, finally looking up at me with a wry expression, and it took all my self-control not to frantically retreat. Any second she was gonna hurl that right back at me; the only question was how ugly the results would be. Had she modified it into a more conventional fireball, or was I about to finally find out what that horrible spell *felt* like?

But no, what she did was far worse.

Ozyraph flicked her fingers contemptuously, and the fire disappeared in a tiny puff of smoke. She resumed poking at her tablet, entirely ignoring me, save to speak once, in a tone of utter disinterest.

"Go away, little Dark Lord."

I could only stand there, my mind a screaming white blank. Well . . . what the fuck *now*?

A streak shot past me at waist height, and in the next second Zui had launched herself at the devil, fist-first, brass knuckles in place.

She froze in the air midleap, just short of impact. Ozyraph looked up again, frowning in annoyance.

"Zui, right? Don't worry, you were never on the list. Not the original expanded one and *definitely* not the much-abridged final version I am trying to collate right now."

"You can't do this!" Zui roared, kicking and thrashing in midair. "You— murdering *monster*! Haven't we been through enough? Just *leave people alone*! They were just trying to *survive*!"

"Well, they failed," Ozyraph said with a sigh. "Honestly, all you people are doing is prolonging this. Just let me sort through my list of names, and then you'll never have to see me again. Me, or the three dozen or so idiots who would've gladly murdered you all for trying to help them. You are being ridiculous."

She took her hand off her tablet again to make a lifting and tossing motion, and Zui came flying back toward us. I barely managed to get into position to catch her, mostly; at most I spared her an undignified impact against the wall, but she slipped out of my attempted grip and landed hard on my foot.

All around us, goblins were shouting fearfully, some trying to flee as if that would help, many just dithering in place, because . . . how could you run from this? I was hearing an uncomfortable amount of sobbing from multiple directions.

Zui turned to look up at me, naked pleading written across her face. It was the most unmistakable expression of *Do something!* I'd ever seen.

I tore my gaze away from her to look back at Ozyraph, once again efficiently scrolling through her list of names, pulling aside those about to be harvested.

What could I do? What *could* I do? This creature had just manhandled us all with contemptuous ease; I'd hit her with my nastiest attack and she'd batted it aside with barely a thought. What else *was* there? I could try running her over with a truck . . . But no, I'd already seen the ease with which she shrugged off physical attacks. The increased mass of Truck-kun probably wasn't going to make a difference. Nor would attempting to stab her.

I'd been in some rough situations since coming to Ephemera, but I'd never felt this physically powerless. Even in my first panicked moments on this hell world, running around an old fortress with bandits on my heels and no weapons or spells to call upon, I'd been able to do *something*. This was just . . . absolute helplessness. This devil was going to do what she came for, and all I could do was *watch*.

Maybe she was right, anyway. Why did I have to fight to save people who'd declared themselves my enemies?

Maybe I should . . .

Maybe?

There was a gentle touch on my upper back. I turned to see Aster right behind me, her golden eyes compassionate, but firm. She leaned forward and murmured right by my ear.

"A limn is five hundred and twenty-four dhils. A dhil is ninety-six strides. A stride is thirteen ridds, and is defined as the distance of an average male elf's step."

Ahh . . . there it was. Cleansing, purifying *rage*, a white-hot flame to remind me who I was. I was Lord Seiji, dammit, and I wasn't *taking* any more of this stupid planet's bullshit.

"Oh, Aster," I whispered. "What would I do without you?"

"You'd die. Quickly. Probably on fire."

"Yep." I raised my voice. "Rizz, Gazmo, Sneppit. I need help weaseling out of a contract."

I had to look away from Zui; the sudden gratitude and hope on her face was just too painful to face directly. The two Judges I'd named exchanged one look, then turned in unison to point at Sneppit.

"Wait, *me?*" she protested. "You're the—"

"Our strong suit is making contracts ironclad and impermeable," said Rizz. "What's needed here is the opposite of that."

"Any job worth doing is worth leaving to an expert," Gazmo added.

Sneppit goggled at them, then turned to me, visibly aghast.

I broke my usual policy toward goblins and went to one knee, bringing my face down closer to hers so I could speak quietly.

"Look, I *know* it's a devil and we've all seen how powerful she is. But she also doesn't want to fight. Fighting won't help here, anyway. We need brains and *words* and a mastery of the contract. We need *you*, Snep. That may be an agent of the Devil King, but you're *Miss motherfucking Sneppit*. This is *your* turf, not hers. Now show this bitch what happens when you fuck around in goblin town."

Sneppit stared helplessly at me for another second, but then swallowed heavily and nodded once; I could see the steel slowly flowing back into her spine as she took in my encouragement.

I rose and stepped back, clearing the way, and Sneppit strode forward, exhaling heavily once. Ozyraph was still standing there, flicking at her tablet screen and ignoring us. I knew she had to have heard this entire exchange, but the devil seemed supremely unconcerned about our machinations.

Sneppit cleared her throat, her voice cracking only slightly when she addressed the devil. "Excuse me! By established precedent, any contract agreed to by a goblin of Kzidnak is subject to review and approval by a Judge, even if the other party is not native. I would like to invoke—"

"Knock yourself out."

Ozyraph paused in her work to gesture once, and a glowing panel of blue light materialized in the air in front of Sneppit, causing her to reflexively jerk back. Lines of text were printed neatly across it.

"Touch it with a finger and move it up or down to scroll," the devil added helpfully. "If you're planning to challenge me on knowledge of goblin precedent, you are about to learn the taste of disappointment. But please, feel free to waste as much of everyone's time as you wish. Only one of us is immortal."

Rizz and Gazmo immediately crowded in behind her, intently studying the contract, which Rizz carefully began to scroll with a fingertip. Sneppit kept one eye on this while already launching into her next attempt.

"All right, then . . . So, obviously, if this contract is to be considered *valid*, clearly a Judge signed off on it? I don't see a signature—"

"That is not and has never been required by precedent," Ozyraph stated, her thin lips tugging to one side in the tiniest smirk; she still didn't raise her eyes from the tablet. "A contract is considered binding to all signatories, regardless of a Judge's approval. A Judge may invalidate it for any of several reasons, but contracts need not be witnessed by one. Try again. If you were *serious*, you'd start by looking for terms that violate established precedent or imply the contract was coercive or unclear, none of which you will find there."

"I . . . um." I managed not to wince; my trump card so far was about as successful as Jadrak's had been. I could see Sneppit floundering, see the way fear and uncertainty—two things she was clearly not accustomed to experiencing—were taking their toll on her normal effectiveness. But she was all we had, since no amount of physical or magical force was going to prevail against this devil. "You . . . all right, apparently you do know your Kzidnak precedents; I see a lot of the standard clauses here . . . In fact, this borders on too long—"

"To the extent that length and lack of clarity are to be considered grounds for invalidating a contract," Ozyraph recited without pausing in her swiping, "the inclusion of *standard* clauses themselves required by precedent are not to be considered in any such calculation. Either of your Judge friends there could have told you that. By all means, though, continue. I will not have it said that the Devil King's bargains are *unfair*."

Sneppit swallowed heavily, again, her eyes darting rapidly across the text as Rizz slowly moved it. "I . . . so . . . Th-the stipulation against . . . That is, the standard section governing . . . um . . ."

"Um?" The fact that Ozyraph's tone remained dry and flat only made her taunting worse, somehow. "When the Dark Lord tagged you in for this, I expected . . . more. Even Jadrak mentioned your supposed specialty in contract work, *Miss* Sneppit. Is this the limit of your intelligence?"

Sneppit's eyes widened and her head snapped up, staring fixedly at Ozyraph.

"Intelligence?" Her voice was a bare whisper. The devil did not respond.

In that moment, though, everything changed. Sneppit's posture straightened, she put her shoulders back, and all the uncertainty drained from her face in a heartbeat. Her eyes fixed on the devil over the gold rims of her shades, and suddenly her look was that of a shark smelling blood.

Even knowing this was premature, and having no idea what she was about to do, I had the sudden unshakable feeling we'd just won.

"As you seem familiar with goblin precedent, I assume you are acquainted with the truism that you can't unring a bell," Sneppit said crisply.

Ozyraph shrugged with one shoulder, eyes still on her screen. "That applies in a *tiny* rarity of situations, given that goblins are not inclined toward jury trials. But sure, it is true that a nonprofessional adjudicator may be dismissed from their duties and negotiations recommenced from the beginning if they are exposed to information previously ruled by a Judge to be inadmissible and prejudicial. What of it?"

"Just making sure we're on the same page. Now then, in the clause governing the rewards to be granted you as the Devil King's proxy by the signatories Jadrak and Hoy, it is specified that you are authorized to collect *only* souls and no other reward of any kind from the domain of Kzidnak."

"And so I am," Ozyraph agreed.

"Really, are you certain you want to go on record stating that?"

The devil finally glanced up, her eyes narrowing in the first hint of overt suspicion. "It's a simple fact."

"Very good, then," Sneppit said briskly. "As you previously pointed out to Jadrak, it also states in this contract that if either party breaks the terms, the other party is entitled to immediately collect all promises made to them by said contract. Nice touch, making that clause apply in both directions. Really sells the impression you're not planning to screw over the other party."

"Thanks, I try." Ozyraph continued scrolling and flicking, though her flat expression was now marred by a slight frown.

"As such," Sneppit said, baring her teeth in a vicious grin, "this contract is invalidated due to your unauthorized acquisition of valuable property from Kzidnak, a domain considered by said contract to fall under the authority of its signatory, Jadrak, a.k.a. the Goblin King. You will therefore immediately cease any collection activities and remove yourself from the domain in question."

Ozyraph finally stopped manipulating the tablet, raising her eyes to fix Sneppit with a flat stare. "I've taken nothing from Kzidnak—nothing of Jadrak's, and nothing of *anyone's*. False accusations have consequences."

"I will call your attention to clause four, concerning the duties of yourself as designated representative of the Devil King." Sneppit shouldered Rizz aside, deftly flicking the magical display until the clause in question was centered on the panel of light Ozyraph had conjured. "You went out of your way to specify, in writing, that in this matter you are functioning *only* as the Devil King's agent. Anything collected as a result of this contract or your activities in pursuit of its execution are to be delivered directly to him, with nothing withheld by you personally."

Ozyraph's crimson-gold eyes narrowed to slits. "What of it?"

Sneppit half turned to point dramatically behind her at me. "Here stand the Dark Lord and the Hero. As a result of your collection activities, you have come into possession of *intelligence*. You now know their location, the composition of their respective parties, and most importantly, the fact that they are working together. The value of this knowledge *cannot* be overstated; empires would go to war to learn this! As per your sworn duties to the Devil King *and* your obligations as stated by this contract, you will be *required* to convey this important information to your master at the earliest opportunity. This contract specifically denies you the right to collect *anything* of value from Kzidnak other than souls. You, Ozyraph, have *stolen* crucial military intelligence on behalf of the Devil King, breaking the terms of your agreement and *voiding it in its entirety*."

The roar that went up from all sides reminded me of the crowd at a stadium. To goblins, I guess this must've been the equivalent of scoring a goal.

"Ridiculous!" Ozyraph spat, now fully lowering the tablet to her side and fixing her full attention on Sneppit. "I've taken no affirmative action to acquire any such information—it's not *my* fault they were standing here when Jadrak summoned me."

"But you *have* agreed to be bound by the terms of goblin precedent in both the creation and the enforcement of said contract!" Sneppit shouted back. "I invite any Judge present to correct me if I am wrong, but according to precedent, one: intellectual property is no less real or subject to precedent and the right of possession than physical property; two: chance, malfeasance, and acts of the Goddesses may negate culpability for possession of property of any kind if it resulted from them, but not the *fact* of possession; and three: the *value* of intellectual property is determined by factors including its use and the parties to whom it is transmitted. In this case, you possess materially valuable knowledge, which you *will* transmit to the Devil King, both due to your established allegiance *and* the obligations specified *in this contract*. Tell me, Ozyraph, what *affirmative action* can you take that will unring that bell?"

The devil clenched both fists, one clutching the tablet against her side. "You insufferable little—"

"You have two options!" Sneppit crowed. "*Either* you steal valuable political and military secrets from Kzidnak, in *clear* violation of the terms of this contract—*or* you refuse to disclose them to the Devil King, in defiance of your loyalties *and also in violation of the terms*! In short, Ozyraph, *you*—"

"Don't say it," the devil hissed.

"—and *by extension*, the Devil king, are in—"

"AAAUGH!" Ozyraph howled, clapping her free hand over her eyes.

Sneppit took one giant stride forward, planting her foot as if claiming land, threw one hand forward to point accusingly at the devil, and roared in a voice which boomed from every wall of Fallencourt.

"BREACH OF CONTRACT!"

The entire city dissolved into deafening cheering. Goblins on all sides capered about, laughing, hugging each other, and pumping fists in the air, not to mention jeering (perhaps unwisely) at the lone devil, who stood like a disgruntled scarecrow in the midst of it all. Ozyraph's face had settled back into its previous cold neutrality, and she was now just standing in silence, waiting for the noise to subside enough for her to speak.

It took a few minutes, and it certainly wasn't absolute—the level of chaos in the surrounding bridges and balconies remained impressive—but eventually enough settled down that she could at least make herself be heard.

"Well, then," the devil stated curtly, "it appears we do not, after all, have a contract." She held up her tablet, tapped two spots on it with her thumb, and the screen went dark. "That being the case, the other party is entitled to collect any outstanding debts. Unfortunately, speaking of bells that cannot be unrung, there appears to no longer be a Goblin King. In the absence of any formal authority—"

"Oh, I don't know about that." I strolled forward, head up and voice thundering straight from the diaphragm. Ozyraph grimaced as she met my eyes, but didn't flinch away. "As per precedent and custom, there is *one* person who can speak on behalf of the goblins—but only with their consent. So it seems the pertinent question for us all is this—does Kzidnak grant its allegiance to the Dark Lord?"

This time, the roar was even louder, and quickly resolved from general noise into comprehensible chanting. It started with a few voices and swelled rapidly as more caught on, until it spread to every corner of the cavern and thousands of goblins were thundering my name at the tops of their collective lungs.

"**SEI-JI!**"

"**SEI-JI!**"

"**SEI-JI!**"

"**SEI-JI!**"

"**SEI-JI!**"

And for a long span of repetitions, I let them. Now *this* was what I was in it for. Just for a moment, I let the sight before my eyes fade, imagining a stadium or concert venue. Myself with guitar in hand, lauded by the crowd for my skill. This . . . wasn't quite that, but you know what? It would do.

Ozyraph was staring at me with a wry expression, which said she knew exactly what I was thinking, but fuck her. I wasn't going to let anything ruin this for me.

Finally—but with perfect timing, the only kind I have—I raised both hands in the air, gesturing for quiet. It took a bit, but the crowd complied, silence spreading at my wordless order.

The *power*. I could see exactly why this went to people's heads. It was like Rizz had said—a drug, nothing more or less.

"In fact," I said into the ensuing (relative) quiet, "I have reconsidered. On behalf of the people of Kzidnak and the Dark Crusade, I have a deal to offer the Devil King. These are the terms I want you to convey to him, precisely."

Amid the tension of a thousand held breaths, I strode forward, straight into Ozyraph's personal space, until I stood nose-to-nose with her. Close enough to kiss her, to taste the incongruous spearmint on her breath. She didn't flinch or retreat by a millimeter, just holding my gaze with all the confidence of someone who could smash me like a mosquito on a whim.

It didn't matter. We both knew who had won here.

I curled my lip up in a sneer and delivered my terms.

"Fuck off."

This time, the cheering was so overwhelmingly powerful I had to wonder if a bunch more goblins had suddenly turned up. While Fallencourt dissolved into ecstatic madness all around us, Ozyraph and I stared into one another's eyes, the mutual hatred sizzling in the air like static after a lightning strike.

Until finally, she took one slow, deliberate step backward, and inclined her head once. She had to raise her voice to be heard, but we were still close enough that I had no trouble making out her words over the noise.

"I will convey your message. Congratulations, little Dark Lord, on scoring one point in a game no one can win."

Then she flattened, rotated, and a second later I was staring at empty space. No devil, no Goblin King, only the Dark Lord and the city I now ruled.

33

In Which the Dark Lord Takes Over

W*hy* did that work?!" It really spoke to Flaethwyn's essential character that despite the absolute uproar and pandemonium blurring out sound on all sides, I could still clearly hear her offended screech. Okay, well, to be fair she was only a few meters away. "That creature could have slaughtered us all with a *thought*! What's the point of playing along with made-up goblin rules?"

"It's not something I would expect a highborn to understand," Sneppit replied, also shouting but probably not audible any farther away than I was standing. "Keeping your word and upholding contracts isn't a moral virtue; it's something you do so people are willing to *make* contracts with you again in the future. Devils depend on that. Every established power and religious organization on Ephemera warns their people against 'em; they only get any souls at all because nobody can fairly say they don't keep their word."

I felt a jab in my side and looked down to find Judge Rizz poking me with her bladestaff. The blade, fortunately, was retracted into its mechanical housing, so this was just annoying and rude, not an attempted assassination.

"Princess Bitch Ears has a point, probably by accident," the Judge said. She also didn't moderate her tone any, and to judge by how swiftly Pashilyn had to intervene and begin soothing Flaethwyn's incipient attack of apoplexy, the noise didn't entirely cover it. Since Rizz didn't open her mouth unless she had something of value to say, I just nodded and forbore comment on the fact that goblins had notably bigger ears than elves. "That was both way harder and way easier than it should've been."

"How do you mean?"

She jerked her head to one side and headed toward the back of this particular public ledge, where an awning sheltered what had been somebody's shopfront before all the . . . everything. It wasn't any quieter over there, but we were less obviously on center stage and could be surrounded by my own followers, which was better suited for a discreet word than right under the eyes of all of Fallencourt.

"It's uncharacteristic for a devil to stand their ground like that," Rizz said, as Gazmo and Sneppit stepped over to join us and the others drifted closer. "They're prone to abandon even promising schemes if confronted, and they'll normally flee from much less dangerous opponents than you, Dark Lord. On the *other* hand, that bit about selecting names off a list smelled like bullshit to me. She should've been able to invoke her right to all those souls just as instantly as Jadrak's."

"Hm. Why would she put on a show like that?"

"To answer for sure, we'd need to understand a lot more about devils than we do," said Gazmo. "Nobody even knows what they want souls *for*, exactly."

Rizz nodded. "He's right, but an idea springs to mind—just like the elf pointed out. That devil just got to stand in front of an entire city full of goblins and prove that she abides scrupulously by the terms of a deal when she could easily have taken her souls and poofed. There'll always be some complete dickhead who thinks *they'll* be smart enough to succeed where the Goblin King failed. We're gonna have to watch out for that in the coming days."

"Everybody I've talked to about devils said they always go quiet when there's a Dark Lord and Hero active," said Yoshi, stepping into the circle. "Wouldn't that suggest this was Ozyraph's last big job? As long as we're here, at any rate."

"That's what I'd assume, ordinarily," Gazmo agreed, "but by *that* logic, she wouldn't've stared down a Dark Lord *and* Hero long enough to get outmaneuvered. Something's fucky, here."

"Story of our lives," I said. "But, Yoshi . . . this is it. *This* is our angle, how we beat this stupid game—the Devil King."

Everyone stared at me askance, except Yoshi, who simply frowned. My followers and his party had all clustered close now, easily able to watch us over the front row of goblins. The city was still roaring and cheering, but the noise was beginning to abate a bit.

"And what *exactly* are you planning to do with the Devil King, boy?" Rizz demanded after a pause.

I grinned and punched one fist into my opposite palm. "We're gonna *fuck him up*."

"What are you talking about, Omura?" Yoshi asked, still frowning.

"I'm talking about getting out from under this stupid Goddess bullshit, this Good versus Evil thing they're pretending to care about to keep themselves entertained. They *both* hate the Devil King and the Void, right? And that fucker's stealing *souls*; it's not like taking him down isn't an obvious moral good. This is how we beat the system, Yoshi! We *destroy the Devil King*. The Goddesses want him gone more than they want to watch another round of their eternal RPG, surely. They'll leave us alone if we go gunning for him. I don't have to conquer Ephemera, and we don't have to fight each other. *That's* our way out!"

"All of that," he said slowly, "is based on the assumption that you're right. That it *is* a game."

"Okay, fine, sure," I said, waving one hand impatiently. "Say *you're* right, and it's not. Then it's just Virya being the asshole, and this will work to keep *her* off my fucking back. In your version, it's only Virya and the Dark Lord who're the problem, anyway. If Virya chills the hell out and the Dark Lord focuses on the Void rather than world conquest, then Good wins by default, right?"

"Hm." Yoshi turned to Pashilyn, who tilted her head thoughtfully to one side.

"You know, he's sort of right. If the Dark Crusade is doing something *constructive* instead of burning kingdoms and slaughtering masses, something the Goddess would approve of . . . then by definition, we win."

"I'm all for kickin' the Void's ass, especially after what we've seen today," said Sneppit, "but I gotta be the wet blanket here. The Devil King is a *way* more dangerous opponent than either of you; he might well prove to be a match for you both. Also, Lord Seiji, you've set in motion things that you can't just *stop*. The Dark Crusade is building momentum, and there'll be nothing but chaos and destruction if you try to abort it."

"I can't do that, anyway," I said. "Especially if we're going to pursue my idea. Like you said, right now we're in no position to threaten the Devil King. We *both* need to build power, the way Dark Lords and Heroes respectively do—Yoshi needs to grow stronger individually along with his party, and I need to build institutional strength. The normal way is that he the Hero is playing an RPG while the Dark Lord's playing an RTS, you follow?"

Yoshi nodded; everyone else looked confused.

"Well, the Devil King *was* a Dark Lord; he beat multiple Heroes, so he knows how to deal with them. *And* he has his own power base. We'll have to hit him with *both*, and that means we need both at a much higher level than they are right now. Come on, Yoshi; think about it. The Hero and the Dark Lord, joining forces? Let's show the Goddesses something they've *never* seen before. They won't be able to resist."

He winced. "I hate to break it to you, Omura, but that's definitely something they've seen before. The heroes and villains teaming up against a greater threat is a stock trope; it's the most hype moment in every series."

"Okay, fine," I said impatiently, "even better. They'll *love* it, then, if it's a genre classic. I bet they haven't had a chance to see it too often in *their own* game. And that's if my theory about the Goddesses is right; in the other version, this is still for the greater good and should satisfy Virya's ambitions for this round of her conquest."

Slowly, he nodded, his expression firming up. "Yeah. I think you're right, Omura. Okay, let's do it. We'll have to stay in touch and coordinate, but for the most part we'll need to go our separate ways, at least at first. Best not let on that we're working together. Even if we're against the Void, something tells me this is not going to be embraced by the Sanorite and Viryan nations, much less the organized religions."

"That is putting it conservatively," Pashilyn said, grimacing.

"I visit the King's Guild from time to time," I said, "and Aster's still a member on the books, after all. Shouldn't be too hard to check in occasionally, as long as we're discreet."

"So what *is* the plan, then?" Pashilyn asked, giving me a very neutral look. "In the immediate term. How do you propose to advance the Dark Crusade in a way that is not destructive to the Sanorite kingdoms?"

"Yeah, we're all eager to hear that, I'm sure," Zui interjected, "and speaking of which, Dark Lord, it's starting to quiet down. You'd better address your people while the adrenaline's wearing off and before everybody starts to crash. There are a lotta goblins out there who need to know what's in their immediate future, just as much as the butts here."

"My people, huh," I mused, giving her a wry smile. "I never thought I'd hear that from *you*, Zui."

"Yeah, well." She folded her arms and grinned at me—reluctantly, but it was a genuine smile. "Can't say you didn't earn it, Seiji. That's all we really needed from you, anyway—to prove yourself. Now go put on one of those shows you like so much."

"He *really* doesn't need encouragement," Aster muttered to her.

"Yeah, but he sure as shit needs to be *managed.*"

"Okay, yeah, that one I'll give you."

I turned my back on them, patting Yoshi on the shoulder and tipping Pashilyn a wink, and then stepped back toward the center of the wide ledge, where the broken ends of the blown-up bridge to the Core Tower stood. There I hesitated, getting my first shock as the new overlord of Kzidnak.

There was a balcony over the main door to the tower, the one currently inaccessible due to the bridge being out. It was in an ostentatious position from which some fancy rich person could stand to gaze out across their domain, which anybody running that tower would undoubtedly consider Fallencourt to be.

"Whoa," Nazralind said from behind me, noticing what I had. As others did too, the quiet spread further, the already lessening cheers trailing off into mutters.

On that balcony stood a dark elf.

She was pretty, of course; that was hardly worth noting when it came to elves. In terms of facial structure, she had the same generally pointed features as Nazralind and Flaethwyn, just with skin of a medium brown rather like the local lowborn. At least, the parts that weren't purple or *glowing white*; this woman had some crazy tattoos. Her right arm and at least half her torso had been inked to a deep amethyst color, while her left was covered with spiraling patterns of markings in white that were faintly but definitely luminous. We could see a lot of this artwork because she wore tight wrappings around her chest and hips that would be fairly modest for a swimsuit but a strange choice of attire in any other circumstance. Her hair was stark white, and cut short in a messy style.

The dark elf held herself with a stiff spine and raised chin; I could only describe her bearing as "regal." She caught my eyes and bowed to me, once. Not too deeply. Clearly satisfied with her day's work.

Right. I'll deal with you *presently.*

"Despite everything, I owe Jadrak a debt."

My voice reached across the city, because I'm that good. The goblins, already quieting down, settled further, clustering to the edges of their balconies and bridges and windows, thronging every ledge, watching me intently. It was the kind of immense social pressure that was a lot of people's deepest terror—the kind I thrived on.

"I'm a stranger to this country—to this *world*, in fact. Let me tell you, before coming to Dount, I'd never seen anything like the oppression, the persecution, the poverty, and prejudice that plagues this damn place. The *brazenness* with which all these problems are caused by a few elite assholes, clearly for their own personal profit. Looking at this, I had no idea how to . . . *fix* it. I've been afraid to promise people anything better, because life keeps reminding me how cruel it can be, just when I dare to think I'm beginning to make progress. I have done my best to gather those who need me most. The most persecuted, the poorest—I've done what I can to help them, but more than anything I can do, it seems that what helps them the most is each other. Being together, combining their talents and efforts, rather than being pitted against each other in a never-ending dogfight for the amusement of overbred highborn.

"But that's just . . . a bit, here and there. Looking at the system, the size and the scope and the violence of it? Yeah. I have not been going around preaching hope, because if there's one thing I hate, it's being made a liar. I have been offering *vengeance*, picking up people who've been kicked while they were down, and telling them I can't promise anything except a chance to kick back."

I hesitated, glancing around at the sea of intent green faces surrounding me.

"It's heartbreaking, how all of them are willing to accept *that*. Like it's better than anything they ever hoped for."

Tilting my head back, I looked up at the stalactites hanging above us, letting the silence hang for another moment.

"Yeah . . . I owe Jadrak. He showed me where that leads. Thanks to him, I understand now. That is not enough."

I slowly turned, not in a full circle as I had a wall to my back, but in a slow arc that let me gradually face every part of the city.

"Make no mistake, Jadrak was not wrong about the need. Everything that's wrong in this country is wrong *on purpose*. The injustice that permeates every aspect of Fflyr Dlemathlys is deliberate and systematic, protected and promoted by the people sitting comfortably at the top of it. They have to *go*. As much as we might wish it, nothing will get any better unless blood is spilled!"

Another roar went up around me, causing a prickle of unease to penetrate the euphoria of showtime. This . . . *this* was what they reacted to. Just like all the others up top. They'd been trained to do it by similar speeches from Jadrak, I'm sure, but still . . . I was trying to make, ultimately, the *opposite* point here.

It's almost as if generations of oppression creates deep, abiding rage that can never be truly dispelled.

For a long few moments, I let them yell, keeping my head high and my expression stern. Only once the energy began to flag on its own did I raise my hands for silence. The quiet accelerated and spread at my command, reasserting my control.

"But that cannot be the point."

I gave them another three beats to chew on that in quiet.

"Everyone here today has lost something to Jadrak's revolution. *Lakes* of goblin blood have been spilled in the last few days—and all of it by other goblins. You've lost loved ones, lost homes, lost jobs and opportunities, and the bitterest part? All of it was for nothing. Jadrak's uprising was doomed from the beginning. He knew it, and if you're honest with yourselves, all of you did, too. Is this *better* than the way things have been?"

Another grand pause to let the question hang in the air.

"We will have to fight. We will have to sacrifice. There is no way around it. But above all, we have to strive for something *more*. In the coming days we will build it together. It starts with this, a promise from the Dark Lord—wherever I rule, *no one is better than anyone else*. An elf, a goblin, a human, a beastman, *all* are just as valuable. Everyone deserves the chance to succeed according to their own aptitudes—a *fair* chance. *That* is what I'm offering."

This time, the roar was louder and continued longer, which was heartening. Vengeance was not to be underestimated; it could keep people going when everything else betrayed them.

But so could hope.

God, I hoped I could keep it alive.

"I've seen it work on a small scale, just gathering together prostitutes and bandits and homeless outcasts—people are stronger together than the same number of people could be alone. The same is true on a larger scale. I'm going to make a very difficult, very painful, demand of you—*forgiveness*. The bad blood in this country runs deep; the grudges are well and truly earned. But in my Dark Crusade, I require that they be let go. We will work *together*— lowborn, goblins, beastfolk, *everyone* who's been denied their fair chance. We are only kept down as long as we're kept at each other's throats."

Another pause, raise my chin, deepen the voice.

"We all *know* whose throats we should be at. And together? *We are coming for them*."

I stood at the center of the renewed uproar, letting it wash over and through me, letting myself be seen by my people. Calm amid the storm, in control, a presence of reassurance they very much needed after this week.

Heh, my people. What a peculiar thought. Well, now that I considered it, now that I'd gotten to know them, I found I felt more kinship with the goblins than the Fflyr. It was like they reminded me of something I couldn't quite put my finger on.

Above, the dark elf caught my eye again. Seeing me glance up at her, she inclined her head once in acknowledgment, gracing me with a faint smile of approval, then turned to go back inside.

Oh yeah. We were gonna have *words*. Very soon.

"Boss, this may be more complicated than we thought," Biribo muttered next to my ear. "Tattoos on Savin elves tell a lot about their social rank and accomplishments—I'll coach you on all the details later, but the short version is that I would *not* expect to see that much ink of that quality on an elf that young outside the Savindar Empire itself. And they'd be highly placed *within* the Empire, not what passes for a big shot in an isolated little colonial city-state. We might've been too hasty in assuming this one is from Shylverrael."

Savindar . . . Fucking great. While I was desperately in need of *some* kind of backup, given how inevitably Lancor was going to home in on me after the Inferno . . . Well, I had not forgotten the story of Dark Lord Yomiko. Was I strong enough to prevent a whole-ass Empire from turning me into basically their pawn?

It wasn't even a question. Definitely not. At least, not yet. Yet another reason I needed to work fast.

"Well," I said, putting on a smile as I rejoined the group and nodded politely at Pashilyn. "Does that answer your question?"

"I'm afraid it does," Pashilyn said. Oddly enough, she seemed more exasperated than alarmed.

Not so her counterpart.

"Have you *utterly* lost what passes for your mind?" Flaethwyn hissed, practically vibrating with barely suppressed rage. "You dare to stand there preaching the overthrow of the entire *kingdom*, right in *front* of us, and then expect us to *ally* with you?!"

"Flaethwyn, have you ever taken a moment to step outside your privileged perspective and consider that maybe the kingdom *needs* to be overthrown?"

"Omura," Yoshi protested while Flaethwyn jabbered, too enraged to form sentences.

"Amell." The alchemist actually jerked as I turned my attention on her. "You need to tell them."

"W-what? Me?" Poor kid looked even more nervous than usual, which was saying something. "Oh, I don't . . . I'm not . . ."

"Your friends are good people," I said as gently as I could and still be heard through all the hubbub. "They don't mean any harm; they just don't *know*. I've worked with other highborn on Dount—slavers, basically—who thought of themselves as basically decent people. They meant no harm to anyone and thought they were doing the right thing. It took having the reality of life for lowborn *forcibly* brought to their attention before they even considered that they needed to change. These people grow up in a bubble; they have no idea what the realities on the ground are for most people in this country. A lot of highborn are absolute monsters, but I do believe a lot would help to change Dlemathlys if they just *understood*."

"But I'm not . . . Lord Seiji, you're talking to the wrong person."

"I'm sorry to dump this on you in particular," I said with complete sincerity. "It's a shitty thing to apply that much pressure to someone, and genuinely, I'm sorry. But none of us asked for this mess we're all in; we just have to do our best. Yoshi's from a different *planet*, and these two are noblewomen. You've all been hanging around with King's Guild adventurers and aristocrats, I'll bet. They have *no idea*. Somebody needs to make them understand it, and you're all they've got, Amell. I'm so sorry about your friend; he would've been perfect. But it's all down to you now."

"*Hey!*" Suddenly, Flaethwyn was in front of me, hand gripping her rapier, and for once the expression on her face made me pause. I was accustomed to her temper tantrums of various magnitudes. They seemed to be part of how she oxygenated her blood, but this was different. The anger on her face was cold, focused . . . All too relatable. "Amell is a good girl, and she's already been through a lot. She doesn't need any more stress from *you*. Back *off*."

I actually did, if just by a step.

"You know, Flaethwyn . . ."

"Oh, don't even *start*—"

"I think this is your finest moment."

She blinked, startled, then squinted suspiciously.

"After everything we've been through and all the shit I've given you, turns out it's standing up for a friend that makes you snap. There's hope for you yet."

"Conzart addressing the mutineers," she hissed. "So *help* me, Seiji, I'm going to— You know what, I don't believe it'll be the destiny of the Hero or the virtue of the Goddess's followers that finishes you, in the end. Someone is going to put a stiletto through your eye just because you are *such an ass.*"

"Flaethwyn, your country is a shithole." The sheer bluntness made her lean back, grimacing as if she might get some of my commoner on her tunic. "I recognize you're attached to it, but Fflyr Dlemathlys is an absolute nightmare to live in for *most* of the people who have to. Only an evil tyrant would build something like this on purpose. If you really care about Sanora's virtues, about being *Good*, you'd do something to fix it."

"The Goddess herself ordained—"

"Come on, there's no way you're too religious to know those are fairytales someone made up to defend their power structure. Sanora doesn't care about this country or its laws. I don't think she cares about much of anything, but if you disagree with that, then you have to see the gap between the ethics the Convocation teaches and what *happens* out there. You don't want me to topple it and start guillotining aristocrats? Then do something to prevent that becoming *necessary!*"

"That is not a small thing you ask," Pashilyn said quietly.

I shrugged. "Obviously; neither would be rolling the heads in question. But if you'll leverage your positions to figure *something* out, I will be more than happy to work with you. Things *have* to change, but I'd super love to do it without killing anyone else if possible. I am *really* tired of killing people, and I'd much rather not anymore. Help me out."

Pashilyn tilted her head, blinked once, and then slowly smiled at me.

"Hm. You know . . . You really are a good person, Lord Seiji."

I ignored the various noises made by Flaethwyn and my own treasonous followers.

"That is the dumbest thing anyone's ever said to me. And just to throw that into context for you, I used to work in retail."

"I've known my share of nihilistic misanthropes," she said, still smiling. "Real ones; when one grows up among aristocrats, one grows accustomed to such people. You parrot some of their rhetoric, but you lack their . . . ennui. A man like you, who is so *infuriated* by the injustice of the world? Well. You must have believed deeply in people, once, to be so disappointed by them."

I think the worst part was how Aster and Zui looked so . . . delightedly impressed.

"My dear, Lady Pashilyn," I said in my most pleasant tone, "just in case we don't get to speak again for a while, I want you to know, I do not enjoy your company."

Her smile only widened. "What a shame. I think we could have the most fascinating conversations."

"I can't believe you people won't just let me *stab* him," Flaethwyn complained.

"Flaethwyn," Yoshi said suddenly, "I owe you an apology. I'm sorry, but I haven't been a very good friend to you."

She stared at him, blinking. "Oh, um. I . . . ?"

He drew in a deep breath, visibly steeling himself. "You've been there for me from the beginning, the one quickest to correct my mistakes. You've saved me from a lot of self-inflicted problems. And I . . . I've been too nervous and too . . . *weak* to do the same for you."

Flaethwyn herself was starting to look nervous, now. "I'm, ah, I'm not sure—"

"I promise I will do better," Yoshi said seriously, holding her gaze. "You're important to me. So I'll help you realize when you're being incredibly unpleasant. Which is *frequently*."

The elf now looked like she was trying to swallow a particularly sour caltrop. It was one of the most delightful things I'd ever seen.

Yoshi stepped forward, lowering his voice, and gently touched her arm. "And if we were going to push you out of the group over it, believe me, we would have long ago. That's not happening, Flaethwyn. I . . . I can't lose anyone else. Okay?"

She inhaled, sharply and a little unevenly, and then managed to nod.

"Good. Thanks." Yoshi smiled. "Now please stop being mean. You're acting like him."

"Hey!" I protested when he pointed at me. "What did *I* ever do?"

The resulting uproar consisted of so many overlapping voices, I could only pick out the odd snatch of comprehensible language.

"—where to even *start* with—"

"—*Ahahaha HAA!*"

"—oughta kick him right in—"

"—never missed a *single* opportunity to be—"

"—own personal fuckin' Conzart—"

"—that mouth every minute of every—"

"I am also yelling!"

"—is why nobody wants to—"

Sneppit loudly and repeatedly clapped her hands together until order restored itself.

"All right, yes, it's all *very* entertaining, but we all got more important shit to do. Lord Seiji, we're gonna need you to stick around for a while and help get all this mess organized. Meanwhile, no offense meant and, in all seriousness, thanks sincerely for all your help, but it's probably best if we get the rest of these butts outta Kzidnak before they start making things any more tense. Can we get somebody to guide them to a surface exit?"

"I'll show 'em out," Judge Gazmo said. "I'm used to 'em. They're okay kids, mostly."

"Hell yeah, I like these butts!" Fram said cheerfully, giving Amell a swat on the ass, which caused the alchemist to gasp and leap away. "They're *funny*. Sometimes on purpose, even!"

I held out my hand toward Yoshi. "Think about what I said."

He stepped forward to clasp it with his own, meeting my eyes a lot more steadily than he would have not so long ago. "You think about what you said, too. We'll stay on Dount for a while; the King's Guild here has plenty of odd jobs for a group our size."

"We should probably dawdle a bit on the way back," Pashilyn added, "just to decide on what to put in the report. The King's Guild needs to know the Goblin King is no longer a threat, but I think it's best for everyone if we omit . . . *large* parts."

That was definitely a moment of tension, but I nodded and released Yoshi's hand. "I trust your judgment." I kind of had to; it wasn't like I could control what they did, and asking for the kind of trust I was wouldn't work if I didn't offer it in return. "In fact, you should probably just take credit entirely. It's not like anybody's going to contradict you. We'd better keep contact sparse, but I'll reach out to you at the Guild soon."

The city was beginning to quiet around us, the assembled goblins finally turning away from the spectacle—a lot seemed to be holding impromptu celebrations, but doubtless many would be starting to pick up the pieces of their lives. They were going to need help. In fact, there was a *lot* that had to be done—so much I hardly knew where to begin.

Well, actually, no. The one thing I *did* know was where to begin.

"Sneppit," I said after the last round of goodbyes, as we watched Yoshi and his team vanish into a tunnel avenue with Gazmo and Fram, "know a private place nearby? Somewhere with a door and passable soundproofing. You and I need to have a talk."

34

In Which the Dark Lord Plays Queenmaker

Privacy was surprisingly easy to find for being in the aftermath of a revolution. Minutes later we were shut in the back office of a nearby shop, which had long since been abandoned and looted, my people—plus Rizz and Rhoka—occupying the front room, and Sneppit's security detail standing guard at the exterior door.

"There's one thing I keep meaning to ask," I said as soon as the door was closed. "What's with the job titles? Like, sure, Zui's a killer hairstylist, but that's not the only or, by *far*, the most important thing she does. And the *hell* Gizmit is a maid."

"Oh, that?" Sneppit grinned at me, hopping up to sit on the edge of the desk in whoever's office this was. "It's a bit of goblin tradition. That's where they *started*; like most bigger companies, I make a point of recruiting raw talent and then cultivate skills within my organization instead of trying to hire on experts, which is more expensive and carries risks. People who come up through the organization are more loyal to it. It's just the job title that remains the same on their employment contracts, regardless of the responsibilities they take on."

"Hang on. Are you telling me Gizmit's making a *maid's* salary?"

She snorted. "Oh, hell no. Nor are those contracts coercive; a Judge would climb up my ass and swing their stabbin' stick in figure eights if I did that. Nah, it's a holdover from the bad ol' days when that *was* the policy. People would basically get trapped forever by their bosses, doing specialized work for unskilled wages. Kzidnak doesn't have that problem anymore, but we've still got the custom. These days, it's actually a matter of esteem. Youda, for instance, is a damn fine alchemist, but he started with my company slingin' slop in the canteen. I provided resources for his training, but he busted his *ass* learning the skills he did, and getting to introduce himself as the cook is a brag—it shows how far he's come. An operative who gets to call herself the maid does so as a point of *pride*."

"Huh." It made sense, especially in context with everything else I knew about goblins, even if it was counterintuitive. "They don't just want the more impressive job titles?"

"You're thinkin' like a human," she chided gently, grinning. "Goblins care about results, not preening and strutting. 'Sides, this little custom of ours has the side benefit of confusing tallfolk and obscuring our real abilities when we gotta introduce ourselves to outsiders. Really, though, with everything goin' on, *this* is what you so urgently wanted to ask me about in private?"

"It's just a final piece of the puzzle I've been putting together," I said pensively. There was nowhere else to sit in the room, save the goblin-sized chair, so I leaned against the wall and folded my arms, Biribo drifting away to buzz around another corner of the room. "So, Sneppit. Do you wanna be the Goblin Queen?"

She grinned, an expression that was both wholesomely jubilant and viciously triumphant. Sneppit in a nutshell. "You won't regret this, Lord Seiji. I—"

"Hang on." I held up one hand. "That was a question, not an offer. I am asking, do you *want* to be the Goblin Queen?"

Her smile had immediately faded, of course, but now she tilted her head to one side. On a lot of people the gesture would have suggested confusion, but Sneppit gave me the distinct impression she was keenly analyzing me from a new angle.

"Well, sure, I'd think that question was good and answered, but I respect wanting things laid out in exact terms. Yes, Lord Seiji, I want to be Goblin Queen."

"Why?"

She narrowed her eyes. "This is *definitely* a trick question, but I can't spot the trick. Well played; it's been a while since somebody put me in that position."

"The trick is that you'd naturally assume it's a trick question, but no, I'm actually being serious and straightforward here. I'm asking *why* you want to be the Goblin Queen, because I'm keenly interested in hearing your answer."

"All right." She hopped up to stand atop the desk, flicking her arms once and flexing her fingers as if in preparation to perform a quickdraw. "Because where other people see problems, I see *opportunities*. We've just lived through the greatest disaster to befall Kzidnak in my lifetime, so what'm I gonna do? Curl up and cry, or find a way to *win*? That's what I do, Lord Seiji. That's brought me as high as I can go within Kzidnak, and now this crisis has broken that ceiling. I'm gonna put this place back together, better than it ever was before. And with you? Hell, who *knows* how much higher I can go? You and me, Lord Seiji, we'll take on the world and *kick its ass*."

"The numbers must go up," I murmured. That was exactly the wrong answer, but I wasn't sure how to explain that in a way that would make any sense to Sneppit of all people. For goblins, ambition was a cardinal virtue. "Let me ask you this, then—how much is enough? At what point would you like to just . . . quit?"

Her eyebrows shot upward. "Do *what* now?"

"Well, take me, for example. I had it *all* planned out—no shortage of ambition, in fact an unreasonable amount that I was realistically never gonna pull off, but there's no harm in aspiring, right?"

"Hell no there's not," she agreed, grinning.

"I was going to go to California and make it as a rock star. Just like every other idiot who tries that and fails; the only angle I had was my shamisen. There are a few rock groups in Japan that use them, but they're practically unknown in the States. It'd be a real novelty there." She was smiling and nodding, even though all of this was a nonsense word salad to her, which told me something about the level of sincerity on display here. "Yeah, I wanted it all. The fame, the recording contracts, world tours, groupies, my own bus with my face on the side . . . but also, retirement. Y'know? Rock stars either die at twenty-seven from the shit they put up their noses, or linger until their eighties, getting more desperate and pathetic with each passing year. I wanted to *quit*, just take my money to a mansion in the hills and spend my time laying around the pool. No admittance to anyone but the most fuckable fans—and a personal assistant on staff whose whole-ass job was to scout fuckable fans. Indulgence and excess; that was the dream. Don't get me wrong, I have never wanted a handout—I aspired to *earn* it, to be acknowledged for being *good* at my craft. But then, at the end, the idea was to be able to enjoy it all in peace."

"That's quite a dream," she said, still smiling. "Wow, this whole Dark Lord thing was really *not* what you had in mind, huh."

"What I had in mind is very much the issue here." I could hear Rizz's warning about Sneppit echoing in my head. Gizmit's had been apt, if self-serving, but it was Rizz's perspective that made me fear creating a monster. Unlimited ambition was not something I wanted to feed with double Blessings and other miscellaneous monster girl powers, but that argument was obviously not going to impress Sneppit herself. That was the problem with being turned into a monster by power; not everybody was against it. No, in fact, Gizmit's take was more salient to that. "I think we have a . . . disconnect in expectations here. You are thinking of the role of Goblin Queen as something like Jadrak was trying to be—the uncontested ruler of Kzidnak, and of all future goblins brought under my aegis."

"Is it not?" Her smile was gone now.

"Why would Blessings and powers help with that? Goblins won't respect or follow someone who tries to lead them by force; you told me that when Jadrak's future prospects came up. We've got to take the opportunity created by this disaster to turn Kzidnak from the mess it's always been into a single, unified nation, under one leadership and with all its energies pointed in one direction. That's going to require an absolutely top-notch administrator . . . which is basically the opposite of what I'm looking for."

Sneppit narrowed her eyes in confusion.

"What I need is . . . a figurehead. Someone the goblins can admire and aspire to be like, and feel represented by—but from a *distance*. Not the person actually organizing them, because what I *don't* need is competition for loyalty. Furthermore, the weakness of Enjoin is the vulnerability it creates to curses and similar effects. I need to keep my magically endowed lieutenants—my Queens, so to speak—close to me. And that means they'll be the first into the fight. Because I usually am, and I do a *lot* of fighting."

I gave her a moment to consider that, watching her face lengthen.

"You're an administrator and negotiator, Snep. Maybe the best there is, certainly the best I've ever known. You're neither a frontline fighter nor a people person; those are the tasks you've very wisely delegated to the talent you're so skilled at recruiting. This just isn't the role for you."

"Well." Her voice was quiet, but without outward resentment, which I knew didn't mean much. "You might've told me this was a job interview before I flubbed it."

"I would not *presume* to interview Miss Sneppit," I said, grinning. "Anybody who needs your qualifications explained to them has no business being here. No . . . on the contrary, I believe that Kzidnak and even goblinkind are too limited a scope for your abilities. I know this isn't what you expected, but what I have in mind for you, I believe you'll like a *lot* more."

"How's it look out there?" I asked as we returned to the front room. This was more spacious than the back office, which was good, as Sneppit's and my own core entourages were all gathered here. The furnishings were all built to goblin scale, but fortunately, the ceilings were tall enough for the rest of us. I had noticed Madyn and Ydleth among the group Sneppit had brought. While I wasn't best pleased at her dragging them this close to the fight when I'd left them in her secure headquarters on the other side of the island, it was handy to have everybody together again.

"Pretty much the chaos you'd expect," Gizmit reported. "It's being handled as well as it can be, Lord Seiji. Judge Rizz is the only one who's stayed here to keep an eye on you, since you're acquainted; her colleagues are out there restoring order. It's worth noting that the only order they know how to restore is the old one. I presume you're planning to consolidate your authority over Kzidnak, so . . . the window of opportunity on that is finite. Best to make yourself known and take a hand in the process."

"Noted," I said, turning to the goblin in question. "Rizz, your thoughts on that?"

"All precedent and tradition acknowledges the role of the Dark Lord," the Judge replied. "If you start cracking heads and trying to rule with an iron fist, you're gonna get a *lot* of pushback. But after that display you put on, you've got major support. A mandate, I would venture to say. So long as you rule by consent and treat the goblins as well as you reasonably can, the Judges will either help you or go about their business and try to avoid you; none would stand against you. Any other resistance you can handle as you deem necessary, though I advise a light touch."

"Agreed. If you're willing, Judge, I would like your help. I'll need advice and perspective on building an organization for goblins, but beyond that, I believe I have a lot to learn. Give me a few days to make it known among my existing organization, but once the orders are relayed, I want the Judges to feel free to visit North Watch and circulate among my people—my other people, that is—performing their function. By which I mean, they're welcome to arbitrate and settle disputes; authority is mine and that of my chain of command. If we mesh well, I'm open to granting Judges a more formal place and more of the privileges they're used to, beyond Kzidnak."

Slowly, she nodded. "I will relay that. Gotta say . . . that is a lot more than they'll be expecting."

"It's a general thought at this point, not something I'm willing to put in writing. I would like everyone to keep in mind that it's something to work toward, however. I like the Judge system, and if it can be integrated with the Dark Crusade, I want to make it happen. Now, more immediately, it's my understanding that according to precedent, the rise of a Goblin King and/or Dark Lord is considered to dissolve established institutions and contracts?"

"Not automatically or by default." Rizz narrowed her eyes, studying me closely. "But your authority to dissolve such things as necessary is a matter of precedent."

"Good. Gizmit, Youda, I'm glad you were both brought along on this trip."

"Am I about to *regret* that, Lord Seiji?" Sneppit asked with a distinct bite in her tone.

I ignored her, to her visible annoyance. "I have specific need for your talents in particular. I'm not going to draft anybody who's unwilling, but I'm making you the offer now—if you want it, a high rank in the Crusade is available to you both. I need someone to both build and lead an actual intelligence agency, and likewise for a division of alchemists and scientists. Youda, you'd ultimately answer to my head of facilities, Kasser. Gizmit, you would report directly to me, with a rank equivalent to Aster's—she's my chief military commander—but at the top of your own separate chain of command."

"What . . . *kind* of stuff would I be doing?" Youda asked carefully, risking a glance at Sneppit. She had on one of those expressions that was so obviously not an angry scowl that it would have been softer if it had been.

"Two main lines of work—production and research. I'll want a whole system to provide the alchemical supplies we need, and also one to develop new solutions. We owe a lot of our success so far to goblin alchemy, and I want to stay ahead of the curve; as soon as our enemies adapt to one of your unconventional weapons, I want three more waiting to be deployed."

"Wait, a whole R&D *division*? With a *budget*?" Youda suddenly looked like I'd just invented Christmas and put him in charge of it.

"That's the job, Youda. You in?"

Both of them were frozen for a moment in thought, and the contrast between them was amusing. Gizmit, as always, remained aloof and contained, while Youda was practically vibrating. He glanced at her as if for input, though she didn't return the look. Instead, they both chanced peeking at Miss Sneppit. Her expression was an icy blank; her arms folded, shoulders tense, one finger tapping rapidly against her pink-clad bicep.

"Aw, fuck it, I gotta," Youda finally groaned. "I *have* to. I'm *in*, Lord Seiji!"

"All of this, I presume, is contingent upon a proper contract of employment being drawn up," Gizmit said far more calmly. "I would certainly not begrudge you the input of a Judge on it."

"Naturally," I promised her. "We'll have everything in writing, in terms everyone agrees are fair."

"Pending that, then . . . I accept. Sorry, Snep," she added, looking actually rueful for once. "But . . . you understand."

"You gotta grab opportunity when it pops," Sneppit said in an impressively calm tone, belied by the twitching of her left eyelid. "I'd expect nothing less of any goblin I respect."

"Welcome to the team, both of you," I said, smiling warmly. "And don't you worry, I'm taking this with the utmost seriousness. I'll have your new contracts drawn up by the Chancellor of the Dark Crusade in person."

Everyone in the room stilled, turning to frown at me.

Everyone except Gizmit, who froze for a half second, then closed her eyes, the breath leaving her in a long, slow release. Attagirl, that was exactly the perceptiveness I needed in my new spymaster.

"Uh . . ." It was Nazralind who broke the confused silence. "The who?"

"The reality is," I admitted, "I lead by charisma, not by any kind of organizational competence. Don't worry, I'm not handing over the actual *rule* of the Crusade to anyone else. All decisions will go through me, and I will be kept apprised of everything of note. In fact, I'm looking forward to working with a professional administrator, if only for the benefit of learning how to . . . administrate. Ultimately, though, I'm a lead-from-the-front kind of Dark Lord. I'm often away from headquarters, and actual governance just plain isn't in my skill set. My Chancellor will set up and manage the organization—they will be, in effect, the chief executive in charge of everything under my reign. Sneppit."

I turned to her, bowing, then tilted my head toward Gizmit and Youda.

"These two are moving into *very* important roles; their privileges and compensation should reflect the value of their skills, and suffice to encourage loyalty. However, they *did* just jump ship on their previous employer during a crisis. I think it's reasonable that the final terms reflect that."

"Oh, don't you worry, my lord," Chancellor Sneppit said, beaming happily and looking as fully relaxed and smug as she was entitled to, now that our little charade had wrapped up. "I'll hammer out something that's fair to everybody."

"Run it by a Judge, too. I want to encourage their involvement, and make it plain that goblins and their traditions will be valued in my organization."

"A good idea, Lord Seiji. I'll see it done."

"Not bad," Gizmit said. Rather than looking put out, she gave me a deep nod and one of her rare smiles.

Youda actually laughed out loud. "Oh, nice. That was *slick*. You sure you're not part goblin, Lord Seiji?"

"I'm increasingly willing to entertain the possibility. Now then, Zui."

"Oh, what?" she said wryly, folding her arms. "The Dark Crusade needs a hairstylist?"

"Well, I mean . . . actually, yeah, our hair situation is kind of dire. Just look at Nazralind over there."

"Why am *I* always the example?!"

"Because Flaethwyn left," I said sweetly, then turned back to Zui. "But no, I had something rather more important in mind."

"Must be," she grunted, "if I'm not getting the Seiji/Sneppit deluxe runaround. I don't mind telling you, seeing the two of you so in sync is pretty goddamn terrifying."

"This matter is too serious for such games," I said. "How would you like to be the new Goblin Queen?"

"DAMMIT!"

I turned in annoyance at this new interruption, to see Nazralind grudgingly hand over a few coins to a grinning Adelly.

"You sure you don't think Gizmit's a better pick, Lord Seiji?" the elf asked hopefully. "I mean, she's *obviously* the best fighter, and you can't beat those looks—"

"Nazralind, silence yourself or I'll have Aster do it," I ordered.

"Elves have really slender necks," Aster said pleasantly. "I've always thought they must be extra susceptible to headlocks."

"*Anyway.*" I turned back to Zui. "What do you think?"

"I think you're outta your damn mind," she exclaimed. "Me? What? *Me?* Like . . . fucking *what?* In Virya's name, *why?*"

"It's simple."

I stepped forward, and then lowered myself to one knee in front of her, bringing my face nearly to the level of hers. To judge by her faint scowl, Zui shared my private opinion that there was something fundamentally condescending about this position, but we'd have to bear it for the moment; blocking is very important in showtime. I gave her my most solemn, open expression, and spoke in an even and serious tone.

"It's because you've got the biggest boobs."

I was expecting it, of course; between that and Goose's coaching, I deftly caught the punch in one hand before it broke my nose. Still, though, even with my lowered center of gravity it made my balance wobble. That goblin strength was no joke.

"Just kidding," I said, grinning and still holding on to her fist, just to be safe. "It's because of *that*."

I stood up, releasing her hand, and Zui stepped back, now squinting up at me in suspicion.

"Certain nay-saying party poopers would tell you that trying to sucker punch a man twice your size who can set you on fire with his brain is an . . . unintelligent thing to do. What *you* know and *I* know, Zui, is that they would be missing the point. Sometimes . . . sometimes you have to weigh the pros and cons carefully, and decide whether to fight based on the probable outcomes. But sometimes, a bastard just needs to get *punched*, whether or not you can get away with it."

I paused, and lowered my tone slightly, watching her expression.

"Sometimes, you have to respect the chain of command and know when to cut your losses . . . and sometimes you've gotta steal a tram and rescue your stranded comrades."

Zui pursed her lips at me, her eyes still narrowed. It was quiet in the room, and I didn't bother to look around at how everyone else was reacting to this, keeping my focus on her where it belonged.

"When I use the term *Goblin Queen*, I think you're imagining something along the lines of Jadrak, and that's the important misconception here. Kzidnak does not need another one of those. What *I* need from a Goblin Queen is someone to stick with me—someone fit to be augmented with two entire Blessings, plus additional racial magic as the core group grows, and above all, someone I can trust and rely on."

"You make it sound like you're building some kind of super strike team," Zui said warily. "Naz isn't wrong; if you want a fighter, Gizmit's a better bet."

"*Thank* you!"

Aster took a big step toward Naz, who tried to hide behind Adelly.

"Three months ago, I was no fighter at all," I replied. "Today, you saw me duel a Void witch. Fighting is a skill that can be learned—and one of the first things I learned is that ludicrous superpowers give you *kind* of an advantage, even over people who're objectively better at it. Which is why all of that is the least important consideration here. Regardless of how Jadrak did things, in the Dark Crusade the Goblin Queen needs to be a *representative*, not a ruler. Someone goblins can respect, admire . . . someone they know has their interests in mind and is close to the Dark Lord, because there is only one final authority in this institution. Just as importantly, if not more so, I need someone *with me* who understands goblins, thinks about their interests, and will make sure *I* have to think about them as well, no matter how many other directions my attention is pulled."

I had to pause again. It was a good moment in the speech for a dramatic pause, fortunately, but this time . . . I also needed to gather my own thoughts, and double down on my composure. It wasn't often that I had a need to discuss personal vulnerabilities in front of this many people, but I had that need now. This had to be sincere or none of it would work.

"And there's the important matter of what I need from the people I keep closest to me, all of them. I don't want to lie to you, Zui. I am offering to hand you a live bomb. Power is . . . It fucks you up. It gets into people's heads and makes 'em crazy. I can feel it happening, and even so, it sometimes sneaks up on me. The best thing I've done in building this cockamamie Crusade is to surround myself with people who have spines and hearts, as well as brains. They're the only thing that makes this work at all. I have people near me who'll argue when it's important, who aren't afraid to tell me 'no,' who can recognize when I need to be called out on my bullshit, and *do* it."

I looked over at Aster, then at Nazralind, both of whom smiled.

"That's what I need from any addition to my core group. Someone who's capable of doing the smart thing, *and* the right thing, and has the moral judgment to know which to do, and when. Someone who understands the difference between obedience and loyalty and when to apply each. Someone who'll help hold me, and each other, accountable."

The skepticism had mostly melted from Zui's eyes; right now I couldn't quite interpret her expression. Her mouth hung slightly open, working in small movements as if she kept trying to say something but couldn't find the right words.

"When I lay it all out like that, logically, and consider all the angles . . . Well, it ended up being pretty obvious. I need *you*, Zui. There's no one else who fits the whole bill. Kzidnak needs you—hell, Ephemera does."

I held out my hand to her.

"You in?"

"Oh, you son of a bitch," she whispered. "Why would you put it that way? That's not *fair*."

"Yeah," I agreed with a sigh. "It's some bullshit, I know. Sorry. None of this crap is fair to any of us; we've just all gotta do what we can. That's what I'm asking of you—the same thing I do from everyone. I won't deceive you about how rough it's gonna be; I'm pretty sure you can see that coming. All I can promise is we'll all have each other's backs."

Staring at my still-outstretched hand, she slowly shook her head. "You are . . . the most ridiculous *asshole* I have ever met. And I think the worst thing is how much I believe that you actually are trying your best, to do the right thing."

"I am," I agreed simply. "And I am straight up not very good at it. Help me out?"

"Fuck it, I am going to regret this," Zui groaned. "But nobody's ever going to say I didn't do *my* part. I'm in, Dark Lord. I'll try not to screw this up, if you'll do the same."

"Deal."

Zui finally reached out, holding my gaze with her own, and clasped my hand.

Enjoin.

I saw the golden light flash in her eyes, and it was done.

"All *right*! Goblin strength! Oh, I've been *waiting* for this!" Nazralind cheered, then turned and punched the wall.

A second later she was yowling like a stepped-on cat, dancing about and cradling her hand against her chest.

"That is *solid rock*," Aster said without sympathy. "What did you *think* was going to happen?"

"I don't know! Give me a break; I'm used to akorshil walls!"

"So you were gonna wreck the wall just to see if you could? Shit like this is why the goblins hate us, you know."

"Well, hey, look at that. I regret this already," Zui muttered. "That was fast."

"Seijiiiiiii," Nazralind whined, holding out her hand. The knuckles were already turning red. "Heal, please!"

"Sorry, Naz," I said gravely. "After performing extensive tests, I've determined that I can't Heal stupidity."

"I hate you! You're so mean to me!"

"Really, though," Sneppit drawled, tilting her head to give me a long look over the rims of her shades. "My *hairstylist?*"

"Executive assistant," I corrected, "and also a pretty decent security guard." I winked at Zui, who rolled her eyes.

"Heads up, boss, we got incoming," Biribo reported. "Noncombat but y'might wanna get everybody in socially defensive formation."

Fortunately, everyone present understood what that meant; the group immediately clustered together along one side of the room, arranging themselves with admirable efficiency so that I was framed in the center, bracketed with my human—and elf—allies with the goblins in front. I also fired a quick Heal at Nazralind, because as much as she deserved the scuffed knuckles, this was no time to have her more distracted than usual.

So when the door opened and the dark elf stepped into the room, she was immediately facing a united front. Well, mostly. Rizz and Rhoka were still lounging against the wall separate from the rest of us, ostentatiously neutral.

Up close, I could see more details of her bodacious body art. The glowing white sigils inked all down her left arm were intricate and pretty cool visually, but my eyes were drawn to the rest. Her skin was tattooed entirely purple along most of her right arm, the right shoulder, and diagonally down her torso from there, cutting across her exposed abdomen and entirely covering her left leg. The purple segments had a border of black which, now that I looked closer, was actually intricate braid work. And it wasn't just flat purple, but textured. The detail was incredible for how much skin it covered, and especially the way the pattern flowed realistically along the contours of her body. It was marked to make her look like she had a swath of purple snake scales.

I still needed to have Biribo explain in detail the significance of Savin tattoo work, but even at a glance I could tell how this much high-quality body art indicated she was rich, and had—or used to have, at least—the free time to lie around for days on end getting needled. Also, Viryan culture being what it was, her ability to endure that much pain over that much time was probably part of the flex.

And there was her weapon, that artifact treasure of Shylverrael that Biribo had told me about. The bow was beautiful, of course, delicately carved of some gleaming white substance, with no visible string. It had silver wings affixed to its arms in front, curling outward at the tips, carved in the shape of feathers, and clearly sharpened to a murderous edge. Huh, a bow with attached blades, that you could swing like a quarterstaff to slice people up. That probably wouldn't work with anything that had to function on purely physical principles, but artifacts were bullshit.

"Wow," Sneppit said in her most unimpressed tone, folding her arms, "my security really just let you walk in here, huh. No announcement, no nothin'. I see *somebody's* gettin' paid too much."

"Pray do not condemn your guards," the elf said in a smooth, cultured alto that reminded me of a less curt Ozyraph. "After arranging the resistance within the Goblin King's own headquarters, I have accrued a substantial following amongst the goblins. They knew me for an ally, and exercised judgment."

"Oh, honey, what've you done to your *hair*?" Zui burst out.

Now that I noticed . . . Previously I'd thought she just had a short, deliberately scruffy hairstyle such as I'd seen on a lot of girls in the music scene, but on closer inspection it looked like someone had hacked it off in uneven chunks with a dull knife. There wasn't enough length left in those white locks to tie back or pin or do anything to conceal their ragged state; a couple of them kept falling across her eyes.

The elf drew herself up, raising her chin, and stared down her nose at Zui with an oppressively neutral expression. It was an impressively wordless royal rebuke, and it made a prickle of dislike travel all the way up my spine.

She turned to me without bothering to address Zui or her question out loud, and bowed deeply.

"It is an honor to be in your presence, Dark Lord Seiji. I am Velaven Amica Avarisien, rightful Queen of Shylverrael."

Oh. Well, *that* would explain the markings of status. Not from Savindar, after all; that was both a relief and a disappointment.

"Finally," I said in a mild tone, "you deign to introduce yourself."

Velaven straightened up, meeting my eyes without a hint of shame, and opened her mouth to answer. I cut her off.

"'Rightful' is a . . . complicated word. I'm guessing the other sister snaked the throne out from under you?"

"I have the good fortune to be an only child," she said, her tone faintly wry but devoid of anger. Good; this conversation was going to go significantly worse if this woman had the nerve to get pissy with me. "No, my lord, I was the reigning Queen for years, and a successful one. Until I was betrayed and cast out by a conspiracy."

"Before she gives you the wrong impression, Lord Seiji," Sneppit cut in, "it's worth knowing that in Viryan and especially Savin cultures, usurpation is enshrined in custom and sometimes law as a valid means of transferring power. Just because she was removed from the throne by force or subterfuge doesn't mean her successor will be regarded as less than legitimate."

"Your advisor speaks truth, my lord," Velaven agreed. "What matters with regard to your interests is that I *have* a legitimate claim to the throne, allies in useful positions who will back me given the opportunity and motive, and popular support among the people. My . . . *successor* can be removed far more easily and with less disruption to the city-state than I was."

"Expand on that," I ordered.

"I was an effective and popular ruler," she stated with understated pride, lifting her chin again. "Shylverrael prospered under my hand. I streamlined its bureaucracy, instituted a series of reforms to taxation and the distribution of resources, cultivated more effective governance of our outlying territories, and thus income to the city. As a result, my people enjoyed more freedom and prosperity under my rule, and I made certain that the fruits of our productivity trickled upward as well, enriching the upper class and my functionaries to ensure their loyalty. I was—am—*loved* by my people. Parades and festivals were held in my honor, which in a Savin culture is a thing no ruler would dare arrange, and arises only as spontaneous support from the public."

She paused, lowered her eyes for a second, then just as quickly raised them again to meet my gaze with determination.

"And so, I committed the gravest sin a Viryan can."

"You got complacent," I said softly.

"To my everlasting shame." Velaven nodded. "I brought prosperity to all under my reign, and discounted the obvious fact that some of them would hold ambition that exceeded their due. What befell me could have been avoided had I simply been careful, and planned for it. I was cast down because I *deserved* to be for that failure alone, and I do not dispute it. Instead, I have learned from it, and grown stronger."

"So," I mused, "you want to leverage my forces to restore your throne."

With a suddenness that startled me, Velaven went down to one knee and lowered her head deeply, exposing the back of her neck. She set the bow against the floor, leaning her weight on the hand still pressed over its grip. It wasn't quite kowtowing as I was used to it, but something told me a Viryan would sooner open their own throat than prostrate themselves fully on the floor.

"I desire vengeance against those who wronged me, and the restoration of what is mine," she said fiercely, her voice too strong to be muffled by her downcast position. "Grant me this, Dark Lord, and you may regard me as your *slave*. I will serve your cause to the utmost extent of my power and expend the last drop of my ancient blood in your name, and bend my people to the same purpose. Only aid me in this one goal, and I am yours. All that I am, all that is mine, is yours."

I had to blink twice, taking that in. She'd been hanging around North Watch, invisible; how much had she bothered to know about me personally? There was no ignoring the symbolism and subtext of that offer, but my organization was rather notable for specifically *not* putting women in positions like that, and I personally did not need a scantily clad "slave" making suggestions that would trigger a flashback. Fortunately, I was too annoyed with this woman to suffer one right now; I have a hard time thinking about the fuckability of people I want to throttle. Since Velaven was currently staring at the floor, I chanced a look around at my allies. Most of them looked slightly perturbed at this display, though Sneppit had an analytical expression. She caught my eye and nodded once.

"That mess you created with the cat tribe," I said pensively, watching her. She did not flinch or move at all, just kneeling there receiving my judgment. "When I think about it, that came down to *one* mistake in what was otherwise a solid plan. A plan none of the rest of us could have executed; it needed your specialized knowledge to even think of, and your skills to carry out. There seems no reason it wouldn't have worked if you only had access to harpy and naga feathers. And then there is your performance here, in Kzidnak. Doing what you did, as fast as you did . . . I can't imagine any happenstance that could account for that. Only *extreme* competence could have achieved those results."

Velaven finally raised her head. Her expression was still controlled, but I could see traces of the avid hope barely held back from her eyes.

"You honor me, Lord Seiji."

"Our entire strategy," I continued in the same slow, even tone, "was to avoid putting Jadrak on the spot until he could be weakened further. Because we learned that he had the ability to sacrifice the souls of his loyal followers to his devil in exchange for more Void powers. We moved with great care not to force him into a corner, so as to avoid that outcome, because there is simply no way we could have defeated a Void witch powered by a sacrifice of that magnitude. He was reluctant to do it, for obvious reasons; we just had to stall him until his momentum flagged, and with it the fanatical loyalty that would have made this possible. And then *you* went and played your trump card too early, forcing him into exactly that corner I did *not* want, whereupon he summoned his devil right in front of us."

Velaven's eyes had widened as I spoke, but she rallied impressively fast. "It seems that my gambit was what turned that against him, Lord Seiji. Seeing his own core army switch alignment, he must have believed he no longer had enough loyalty to enact that sacrifice, and so tried to order Ozyraph to attack instead."

"Yes," I mused, "I think you're right. I'm pretty sure that's exactly what happened—it's the only thing that makes sense to me. It certainly accounts for why a shrewd operator like Jadrak would fumble like that in the moment of truth, snatching defeat from the jaws of victory."

She didn't quite smile, but her expression brightened slightly.

Then I leaned forward.

"And did you *plan* for that? Or did we all just survive based on the outcome of the luckiest coin toss in history?"

Slowly, Velaven lowered her head again, saying nothing.

"The problem here," I said quietly, "is not that you aren't good. It's that you've been working without coordinating with us. All of these screwups could have been avoided and the same successes achieved, if not better, had you communicated and compared notes with me. Working *together* instead of anonymously in parallel. Worse, I am given to understand that the reason you did *not* was because you wished to approach me having achieved success on my behalf first. Am I wrong?"

"You are not, my lord," she said, just as softly.

"Your jockeying for position has gotten people *killed*, Velaven."

"More than you know, my lord," she whispered.

I stared down at her, considering. Also letting the tension build, because she fucking deserved to welter in it, but legitimately considering, too.

The advantages were undeniable. She was a trained and clearly skilled shadow scout; stealth operatives were something I lacked. Even Gizmit didn't have Velaven's full abilities. She was a professional politician—an actual sovereign ruler, if a former one. I had good sources of coaching on leadership in Minifrit and Sneppit, and the insight of Nazralind and her girls into the mindset of aristocrats, but none of them could provide me the caliber of advice and training I could get from an actual Queen. Perhaps best of all, Velaven was a giant *in* with the dark elves of Shylverrael. I did not have the strength to take the city by force, and didn't want to do that, anyway, as it would deplete both my organization and the Shylver military, which I wanted intact and under my thumb. Having a ready-made puppet to plant on the throne after some careful espionage and politicking would be a major coup for me, in an unusually literal sense.

But.

There was no way in hell I was going to Enjoin this woman. Not right now; quite likely not ever. She was, I judged, worth giving the chance to prove herself. But as things stood, there was not even a fraction of the trust present that I would need for that.

"I do not punish failure," I said abruptly into the tense silence. "I know well how the unpredictable world can spoil careful plans. More importantly, I would rather my people learn and grow than suffer. The problem here, Velaven, is not that you've failed, it is that you have made yourself impossible to trust. The dilemma before me is whether I should grant you the chance to earn that trust back."

She remained still before me, head lowered, saying nothing. I considered her for another long moment.

"The next time one of your schemes blows up in my face," I finally said, "it will be my own fault, because I will have authorized you to do it, after you've *thoroughly* explained it to me beforehand. Am I clear?"

"Explicitly clear, my lord."

"You're a smart lady, so I assume I do not need to enumerate what will happen if we come to the gates of Shylverrael and find the situation there is not what you have led me to believe."

"You do not, my lord."

"You are, until further notice, on the hook to prove your trustworthiness and reliability, not your competence. There will be no repercussions if something you attempt doesn't work, so long as you clearly made an effort in good faith. Go over my head or behind my back *once* more, though, and I'll be forced to conclude that you are more trouble than you're worth."

"I understand, my lord."

"Then rise, Queen Velaven. Do this for me, and I will grant you the vengeance you crave. This is the Dark Crusade; that's pretty much what we do here."

Velaven allowed her poise to crack so far as to draw in a deep, steadying breath as she stood up. She met my gaze again without hesitation.

"I will not disappoint you again, Lord Seiji."

"Let's hope not, for both our sakes. Just so you know, some of the folks back at North Watch lost friends to your antics. No one's allowed to murder or assault you, but I expect you to accept the condemnation you've got coming with grace. Now then!"

Before she could say anything in response to that, I clapped my hands briskly and stepped forward.

"We have got a *shit* ton to do. We need to simultaneously put Kzidnak back together after this disaster, and also put the rest of Dount back together after the *last* disaster, which we were in the middle of when Jadrak decided to make himself my problem. *And* we've gotta integrate two whole-ass organizations of people, who are not gonna see this coming and have a long, ugly history between them. It's gonna be one of those days, people. Walk and talk."

About the Author

D. D. Webb is a highly suspicious character widely believed to be up to no good. Any information on his misdeeds should be reported to the requisite authorities.

Podium

DISCOVER MORE

STORIES UNBOUND

PodiumEntertainment.com